A TIDY ARMAGEDDON

A TIDY ARMAGEDDON

A NOVEL

BH PANHUYZEN

Published by ECW Press
665 Gerrard Street East
Toronto, Ontario, Canada M4M 1Y2
416-694-3348 / info@ecwpress.com

Editor for the Press: Michael Holmes
Copyeditor: Jen Albert

LIBRARY AND ARCHIVES CANADA CATALOGUING
IN PUBLICATION

Title: A tidy armageddon / B.H. Panhuyzen.

Names: Panhuyzen, Brian, 1966- author.

Identifiers: Canadiana (print) 20220477256 | Canadiana
(ebook) 20220477272

ISBN 978-1-77041-688-8 (softcover)
ISBN 978-1-77852-108-9 (ePub)
ISBN 978-1-77852-109-6 (PDF)
ISBN 978-1-77852-110-2 (Kindle)

Classification: LCC PS8581 A638 T53 2023
| DDC C813/.54—dc23

This book is funded in part by the Government of Canada. *Ce livre est financé en partie par le gouvernement du Canada.* We acknowledge the support of the Canada Council for the Arts. *Nous remercions le Conseil des arts du Canada de son soutien.* We acknowledge the funding support of the Ontario Arts Council (OAC), an agency of the Government of Ontario. We also acknowledge the support of the Government of Ontario through the Ontario Book Publishing Tax Credit, and through Ontario Creates.

Canada Council   Conseil des arts
for the Arts   du Canada

Canada

PRINTED AND BOUND IN CANADA   PRINTING: MARQUIS   5 4 3 2 1

for
Lex

and in memory of

Spencer
2011–2019
such a good boy

and

John Panhuyzen
1934–2015
such a good dad

"What consumerism really is, at its worst, is getting people to buy things that don't actually improve their lives."

— Jeff Bezos

"They have succeeded in accumulating a greater mass of objects, but the joy in the world has grown less."

— Fyodor Dostoevsky, *The Brothers Karamazov*

"Oh Lord, won't you buy me a Mercedes-Benz?"

— Janis Joplin, Michael McClure, and Bob Neuwirth

1

A vee of Canada geese passed across the slot of sky that ran east to west between two nine-storey walls. It was late August, and they were heading south, early migrators, the machine of instinct persisting, despite the day's heat, despite enormous changes in the prairie landscape.

Sergeant Elisabeth Sharpcot had heard them, their plaintive honking, moments before they shot overhead, lit by sunlight, and she could hear them long after they vanished beyond the south wall.

For a moment she let herself pretend that everything was all right, that the world was fine, and birds flew south, and her daughter Lana was safe with her dad, and there'd be something to watch on TV tonight.

But two young privates under her command were dead, and in front of her stood a wall, 28 metres tall, over 90 feet, composed entirely of watering cans. Not just a wall, but a solid block that extended an unknown distance north. Watering cans. Millions of them.

Watering cans in every colour imaginable.

Watering cans decorated with flowers, vegetables, hearts, animals, scenery, checkerboards, stripes, polka dots, abstract designs, or words: Garden, Gardener, Flowers, Grow, Breathe, Home, Love, Friends, Happy, Mom, Nature, Peace.

Watering cans made from wood, plastic, acrylic, aluminum, glass, brass, bronze, tin, copper, clay, ceramic, stainless steel, and every other material humankind has ever used to produce containers for hydrating plants.

Watering cans with vessels smooth, ringed, embossed, rippled, dimpled, peened, distressed, galvanized, and plated.

They came in every style: art deco, Edo, mid-century modern, Minoan, Victorian, Etruscan, Jalisco, Ming, Delft Blue.

They ranged in size from miniatures for a doll's house to enormous novelty cans the size of rain barrels.

And they represented every conceivable form: cylindrical, bell-shaped, bulbous, conical, spheric, cubic, cuboid, dodecahedral, icosahedral, or made to look like frogs, cats, dogs, rabbits, pigs, sheep, mice, hedgehogs, elephants, ducks, geese, fish, whales, honeybees, snails, chameleons, dinosaurs, garden gnomes, and Mickey Mouse.

Handmade 4,000 years ago in Mesopotamia or manufactured last month in a Guangzhou factory.

Old, new, corroding, shining, cracked, smashed, crushed, or crazed.

And all of them arranged, *Tetris*-like, to fit together in the most efficient, compact manner and to form a wall that was essentially flat, aside from the protuberances of the cans themselves, handles or spouts or the curved flanks of their vessels, from ground to sky.

All of it held together without any detectable bonding agent, the formation maintained by friction and gravity and some unknown force that kept the mass of the ones above from crushing those below.

A wall of watering cans stretching away to the left and right as far as the eye could see. Millions, hundreds of millions.

The sight of them, the very idea of them, was nauseating.

And if Sharpcot turned 180 degrees, she would find herself facing another wall, of precisely equal height, and assembled with the same method and precision, and no less imposing, no less sickening, and yet producing an entirely different optical effect due to the smaller scale and colour, size, and shape of the compositional items: bottle openers.

Bottle openers with handles made from tin, zinc, aluminum, nickel, chromium, titanium, iron, copper, silver, brass, polycarbonate, glass, stone, bone, horn, and wood; in myriad colours, with a plate reading Las Vegas or Niagara Falls and accompanied by a flamboyant vista; manufactured from flat steel, engraved with Pabst Blue Ribbon, Trinkt Rathaus-Bràu, Meredith Public House, World's Best Dad, Kirsten & Ron 2015, I ♥ Beer; many fashioned as a novelty item: anchor, hand, fish, skull, dog's paw, bicycle, ninja, violin, bullet, key, Tutankhamen's sarcophagus; some shiny and new, most used, and many old, rusted, cracked, broken, or so ravaged by time and exposure or lying buried in a landfill or the ruins of a lost village or shipwreck on the sea's bottom that they were little more than an outline, a few joined fragments, strands of matter.

Like the watering cans, they numbered in the hundreds of millions, probably billions, packed together to form a wall of the same height as the watering cans and likewise representing a block. Those walls extended east and west until they each ended at an intersection with passageways that ran north and south, and beyond which stood countless monuments made from other manufactured goods, all similarly stacked nine storeys high.

Sharpcot and her section of soldiers — previously eight, but now, after an incident of sudden, horrific violence, six — found themselves in a passageway four metres wide, 14 feet, between watering cans and bottle openers.

She glanced wearily at those walls.

The chime of an entrenching tool filled the passageway. Standing knee-deep in a hole, the brawny form of Corporal Owen Tse jabbed the tool into the earth and tossed soil onto a growing mound.

A few paces away, Sharpcot's second-in-command, Master Corporal Dorian "Jack" Wakely, squatted in the grass with his back to the watering cans and smoked his last cigarette, smoked it down to the filter — the last one ever, barring an unlikely encounter with the block that held them all. The Cigarette Block. He knew it was out there, somewhere on the prairie. It would be nine storeys tall, vast, and, if they reached it soon enough, still fragrant of tobacco, the scent instilling a delight he used to feel after he'd quit, after Daisy had begged him to quit. Those times he'd suffered a lapse in resolve: emerging from a corner store (crazy now to think of shops crammed with varied goods) clutching a fresh pack. He'd strip off the cellophane and pop the lid and part the foil and bring the tips of the paper-wrapped barrels to his nose for a prolonged sniff. It was like coming up for air after weeks underwater.

He watched Sharpcot drink from her canteen before she joined Tse in the hole. He thought about getting up, sparing her the labour, but she shrugged off her jacket and went fervently at the digging. Psychotherapy for her failure. For the deaths of her recruits.

But it was his failure too. He flicked away the butt he'd been rolling between fingertips.

"Take a break, Corporal," he told Tse, who nodded and dropped the shovel, wiped his brow, and climbed from the hole. Wakely stepped down beside Sharpcot and took the tool in his grip and chopped at the hard dirt while his body cried sweat.

Wakely arrived into this nightmare also through digging, but digging from below, out of the earth. A pinhole of daylight appeared, an aperture that opened as he poked at it with the entrenching tool, soil in his eyes, his mouth, and the opening grew to an oval of pink sky, and he worked until it was big enough to cram his shoulders through. His head at ground level, noticing the world was awry but not yet allowing himself to determine how, he worked his arms out and pressed his forearms against the earth on each side of the hole and grunting and kicking

14

hauled himself up. Dusted the soil from his hands and shook it out of his hair and off his shoulders, wiped his nose. Spit a gob of muddy saliva.

He stood on prairie grass beside the hole. It was dawn and he inhaled to the peak of his lungs, the air splendidly fresh after the stale atmosphere of the bunker.

He faced an enormous wall of toilets.

He lit a cigarette and took a long drag and leaned over the hole and called down.

"Private Bronski. Go get the boss. Pronto."

Three weeks before, the eight members of Three Section of Two Platoon of Bravo Company of the Second Battalion of the Princess Patricia's Canadian Light Infantry had gone reluctantly into a defunct nuclear bunker, an abandoned complex of office space, strategy rooms, infirmary, communications centre, and dorms, recently stocked with food, water, batteries, and equipment.

The order to go below came without explanation. The group of course had theories: it was a psychological experiment; it was punishment for their lacklustre performance during infantry exercises. But Sharpcot knew by the brusque way Lieutenant Blake ordered them into the bunker that he had no idea why it was happening.

Sharpcot had heard rumours, crazy rumours, spooky rumours, none plausible.

Of one thing she was certain: selection of her group for this duty came from high up, from Base Commander Wenz himself. Because he hated her.

So on a hot August morning, they passed through the bunker's doorway with full rucks, ready for combat, rifles and ammunition stowed in the weapons locker, crates of supplies to keep them fed for weeks. They brought paperbacks and tablets and e-readers, playing cards, board games.

They dined each evening in a cafeteria with a tile floor and suspended ceiling, the walls painted institutional beige, fluorescent lighting replaced with low-power LED pot lights. The food came in cans and pouches. Afterwards, they would assemble in the lounge with its tattered 60s-era furniture, to play a game or watch on the old CRT television a movie selected from a cardboard box and its meagre collection of VHS cassettes: *The Breakfast Club*, *The Apprenticeship of Duddy Kravitz*, *A Room with a View*, *Mystic Pizza*. They watched them so many times they could recite whole scenes, Private Abigail Deeks eerily adept at imitations and accents.

At night, or when they wanted to be alone, they retired to one of the two dorms, split by sex, each with 24 iron beds.

Sharpcot remembered Blake's unreadable expression, how he wouldn't meet her eye. "See you when I see you," he grunted, before he and a skinny corporal she didn't know closed the stainless steel blast door, a foot thick, tapered to nest in its reinforced frame. She cranked the wheel at its centre, sealing them in.

After three days Sharpcot sent fireteam Charlie, Privates Kyrylo "Loko" Boyko and Abby Deeks, to check on it. They ran down a tunnel ribbed with reinforced steel, through a hard right turn to a small lobby where the door stood as shut as they'd left it. The pair lingered, wondering if their task required more than simply looking at it. Boyko put a hand on the wheel, at which Deeks uttered a *tsk*, and Boyko withdrew. She put her ear against the steel and listened, heard nothing but the flux of her own circulation. She stepped back and they looked at each other, and Deeks would report later to Sharpcot that a change of expression manifested on Loko's face, "like he'd slipped on ice and just caught himself," though they were each standing motionless. They raced back up the tube to report. Sharpcot glanced up from a Nordic crime novel.

"We'll check tomorrow. Go back to what you were doing," she told them, and they did, Deeks to re-reading Alison Bechdel's *Fun Home*; Loko to battling Leader Brawley for a Knuckle Badge in Nintendo *Pokémon Omega Ruby*.

Every day that Sharpcot sent runners to check the door increased the section's anxiety, and when they reached eight days, Loko started to go, to use Deeks's term, "wiggy."

There was no room for wiggy in here, and Sharpcot let Loko know it. He said he'd try harder.

A day later she found him kneeling in a corridor banging his head against the floor. She ran to fetch her bottle of lorazepam, which she'd brought but hadn't yet used. She tapped one into her palm and pressed his shoulder.

He sat up and glared at her with bloodshot eyes, muttered, "I don't care. I don't care." But when he spotted the pill, he seized it and swallowed it dry. After half an hour he melted on the cold linoleum into a fitful slumber.

Not long after that came the Great Divide, as Abby Deeks coined it, when the group split into factions according to sex.

On Sharpcot's side, quippy Deeks, outspoken activist Adonia Virago, and the odd Cheree Leclerc, all of them growing increasingly cranky, sarcastic, and — she hated to say it — catty.

On Wakely's side, wiggy Loko, cool Corporal Owen Tse, and perpetually aggrieved Travis Bronski.

Victims of rage to date were the Monopoly board, torn in half by Bronski when he landed for a third time on Virago's well-appointed Park Place, and a glass cabinet in the bunker's medical lab, again Bronski, who hurled a rotary-dial telephone through it. Someone had also festooned a conference room in ferromagnetic tape, but Sharpcot chose to see that as an act of artistic expression rather than vandalism.

She so invested herself with the conviction that expressions of anxiety were normal and expected that she became unnerved early in the third week, when all of it stopped, and lethargy descended on the group.

A distant chirping woke her one night, bringing relief for its novelty. While not the hoped-for arrival of their liberators, it offered a break in the routine, a problem to solve.

She set out with a flashlight and followed the sound to a storage cupboard that housed a series of 24-volt gel cells. One was sounding a low-voltage warning. She checked a few of the others, and all displayed dwindling charges. She didn't know the exact implications — days left, hours, minutes? — but she silenced the alarm and looked at her watch. It was just after 3:30 a.m. She went to the kitchen for coffee, heated the kettle on a gas ring. She was stirring in the sugar with a plastic spoon when Wakely appeared, looking his usual trim and alert self even at this hour.

"Morning," he said.

"Not quite," she replied. "But there's hot water."

He made himself a cup and leaned against the counter, blowing steam and taking short sips, and asked, "What's the problem?"

"The batteries," she replied. "We got to get out of here, Jack."

"Air's going stale too," he said, and though she hadn't noticed, his saying so made it apparent.

"Don't mention that around Private Boyko. I'm almost out of pills."

They debated briefly how and when to go about it: after breakfast, collect their things, bring the whole section down to the lobby, open the big door and return to the world of wind and sky, whatever the consequences. In the end, they let everyone sleep and carried their mugs down the long tunnel to stand before the blast door. She set a hand on the wheel, but before spinning it said, "It'll be dark out."

"Not as dark as in here," he replied, and she nodded and cranked the wheel. It spun freely, drawing the dogs through the cylinders. She pushed on the door, but it wouldn't budge.

Wakely stepped forward and they each put their weight against it, without effect.

"Something's against the door," he said with aggravating calm.

The bunker, a buried, one-storey concrete box, lay with its entrance set into a shallow hillside and sheltered within a corrugated steel vestibule, with the blast door opening outwards, to resist the force of a proximate nuke.

"Could a landslide cover the door?" Wakely wondered.

"I'd think it would be engineered to avoid that, but anything's possible."

"I guess that's what the alternate exit is for," Wakely replied, and they sprinted back up the tunnel.

Wakely clambered up the ladderway, and with Sharpcot's flashlight clenched in his teeth, rotated the crank and pushed on the circular hatch. It moved, but only a millimetre. He pushed harder, and the amount of travel, while minor, along with the soil that sifted from around the seal, managed to mitigate the dry chill of claustrophobia churning in his belly.

In the dark at the foot of the ladder, Sharpcot heard dirt hit the floor. "What about it, Jack?"

He came down with his face set calmly.

"There's some play."

He wiped the flashlight and handed it back, and she cast it on the floor to a scatter of soil.

"You think it'll open with some force?" she asked.

"I don't think it'll open outright, but it's a step," he replied.

"Let's get Corporal Tse. And not tell anyone else yet," she said.

Tse squeezed his powerful frame up the ladder tube, and Sharpcot and Wakely heard him throw his shoulder into the hatch a dozen times, each stroke accompanied by a grunt, followed by a spill of grit and gravel.

He came down rubbing his shoulder, said, "That's all I got just now."

"Might be enough," Wakely replied, and mounted the ladder, skipping every other rung, and he pushed on the hatch to find that it lifted an inch, enough to drive his fingertips into the dirt and draw more inside. He heard it crackle on the linoleum below. He ran fingers along the opening, dug until he'd excavated a small cavern. Then like Tse he rammed his shoulder repeatedly into the hatch, each blow accompanied by a cascade of soil from the opening. When he pressed it upward again he got his entire hand into the gap and swept it around and clawed out handfuls of dirt.

He worked until his fingers were raw and his arms ached, and descended the ladder filthy with soil, and he dusted his hands and told Tse, "Keep at it. We'll get help."

He and Sharpcot ran to the dorms. Sharpcot turned on the lights and winced when she considered the power they sucked from the dying batteries.

Private Leclerc swung her feet to the floor and immediately began to dress, but Sharpcot had to yank blankets and coax Virago and Deeks awake. She heard Wakely's voice from the other dorm, shouting Bronski's name. She imagined Loko emerging from his benzodiazepine funk.

When they assembled in the hallway outside the dorms, Loko stood hunched, eyes ringed in violet. But when she asked if he felt fit enough to participate in their escape, he nodded emphatically.

The top of the ladder could accommodate one worker at a time, and they switched frequently, using bare hands at first, better still with gloves, and then someone grabbed a handful of cutlery from the kitchen and they went at it with serving spoons. The others collected the dirt mounding at the foot of the ladder into buckets and carted it off to the radio room, with its charts and decrepit transmitters, and dumped it there.

The hatch's travel increased as they toiled, until it could swing fully into the cavity excavated above it. The labour accelerated, pairs of workers using entrenching tools to dig vertically into the dirt, boring towards sky. When the ceiling became unreachable they lifted a stepladder into the hole and worked at the top of that.

By day's end exhaustion shut them down, and they reluctantly abandoned the labour to rest.

Wakely rose early the next morning and as punishment for various incidents the day before recruited Travis Bronski to accompany him. Bronski was nodding off on the floor below the ladder when Wakely broke through into the dawn and hauled himself to the surface and called down for the private to summon Sergeant Sharpcot.

Dorian Wakely stood beside the hole facing a wall of toilets, nine storeys tall by his estimation, which stretched off in both directions as far as he could see. Perspective merged it with the wall that ran behind him, a wall composed of rough workstations of some sort, made from steel and painted black and red and blue, a scattered few in orange and yellow and lime green. Most had a motor mounted horizontally across a bench, with hand cranks, vices, knobs, and dials. He stepped back for a wider view. A few were clean and new, but most looked hard-used, grease-stained, scratched, dusty, rusty. Some held a plate mounted above the console or on the motor itself: "Model C9370 Brake Lathe" or "Precision Combination Brake Station" or "QUALITY BRAKE SERVICE built by RELS MANUFACTURING." He scanned the stack, taking in brand names: Ammco, John Bean, West, Ranger, National Auto Tools, Jori Machine, Hunter, Bosch, Luzhong, DBL-Smart, FMC, Auto Pro-up. He took another step backwards and bumped into toilets and spun and returned to the middle of the alley.

He took a drag on his cigarette, studying the scene, this narrow alley four metres wide, nearly 30 metres tall.

A magenta sky in the east, scrimmed with cirrus, darkened to deep blue above.

He speculated on what this could be. A practical joke? Act of terrorism? Experiment to test response to a visual non sequitur? A dream? But he could reconcile none but the latter. Except he always knew when he was dreaming, because of the Afghan boy and the wired artillery shell. The boy hadn't missed his dream cameo in seven years. Wakely squinted up and down the passageway but did not find him. Was he finally banished, to be replaced with toilets and brake lathes? And what could encountering these in a dream signify?

"What in hell?" he heard and looked to the hole to see Sharpcot stalled halfway out of it, gazing around in disbelief. "Are those toilets?"

"Yeah," Wakely replied. "And brake lathes."

She cranked around and looked.

"Used in auto shops," he added. "When you take your car in for brake service, the mechanic will use a break lathe to resurface your rotors—"

"Whoa, Jack."

"Right. Mansplaining. Right. Sorry."

She climbed up and moved to the lathes, reached out tentatively to touch a motor casing. She turned one of the cranks, flicked a switch from "Disk" to "Drum."

"Toilets are real too," Wakely said. "I'm pretty sure because I backed into them while taking in the lathes."

She sniffed, and the smell beyond Wakely's cigarette was auto garage meets public washroom.

They stood for a long minute, regarding it all, until their eyes met.

"What the hell's it about, Jack?" she asked.

"No idea, Sarge," Wakely replied. "I don't even know how this could be arranged."

"You think maybe it's a . . . maybe it's a dream?" she asked.

"Best explanation," he replied, and finished his smoke, ground the butt under his boot.

"Yours or mine?"

"No kid and no artillery shell. So definitely yours."

She squinted at him. "Or a test? The whole thing, the bunker, then this. To see how we react." She lifted her eyes, ran them along the walls, the toilets, the lathes. "You spot any surveillance? Better keep cool."

"Roger that. Keeping cool," Wakely acknowledged.

"What the fucking fuck is this shit?" a voice strained by hysteria cried out. Sharpcot and Wakely turned to see Bronski peering from the hole, head swivelling around in panic.

"Cut that right now, Bronski," Wakely ordered. "Go down and bring up the manpack."

"But what the hell is it?" he called, climbing out. "Where are we? What are these fucking walls? Are those goddamn toilets?"

Wakely moved towards Bronski, who flinched and put his hands up, retreating to the hole.

"And do not, repeat, do not mention any of this to the section. Get the radio and come right back, got it?"

"Master Corporal, sir!" he replied and took one last astonished look before disappearing down the hole.

"Screw this," Sharpcot muttered after a moment, reached into a pocket and pulled out her phone. She gave a glance to Wakely before turning away and powering it on. After a breathless minute, at the upper left of the screen, "No Signal." She waited, then took a step away from Wakely, lifting the device. Nothing. She went into the settings, opened the Wi-Fi tab. A wheel spun as the phone hunted unsuccessfully for a network.

"Anything?" Wakely asked. He had his own phone out, held it aloft like a torch. "I got zero."

"Walls must be blocking the signal."

"Sure," Wakely said, and Sharpcot shot him an irritated look. "What?"

23

"Just — stay cool." She gazed around, looking for a surveillance camera that would be recording their responses. She saw none, but that meant nothing.

Bronski came up wearing the radio backpack and Wakely and Sharpcot stowed their phones. Wakely went behind Bronski and got out the aerial and microphone and screwed them into the ports, handed Sharpcot the mic. She turned the radio on, keyed in the band, brought the handset to her ear. "Opal Journey, this is Shark Belly at location November Juliet Quebec seven-niner, over." Static answered back, and after a few seconds Sharpcot repeated: "Opal Journey, this is Shark Belly transmitting from November Juliet Quebec seven-niner, come in please."

"Toilets," Bronski said in a dazed voice as he studied the wall in front of him. He turned his head to the brake lathes, and as Sharpcot repeated the call a third time he muttered, "The fuck are those?" Then back to the toilets. "I mean look at how those fit. There's like no space between them. It's a huge fucking game of *Tetris*. And somebody got a goddamn high score."

"Bronski, shut it," Wakely said.

"Shutting it, Master Jack, sir!" Bronski yelped and stood at semi-attention, arms at his sides, head wheeling around. The rising sun struck the highest toilets and cast a glare into the passageway. A cool dawn, but Bronski was sweating. Sharpcot continued to call into the radio, tried different channels, got nothing. Bronski noted no chatter on the other frequencies, didn't know if Sharpcot or Wakely had noticed.

"How about our position?" Wakely asked.

"We've got to be exactly where we were," Sharpcot snapped. "Obviously the bunker didn't move."

"Obviously," Wakely replied.

"Fine. I'll check the Dagger." She seized a strap on Bronski's backpack and cranked him about and dug around until she came up with the DAGR in its camo case. She turned it on and the little screen lit up and she watched it intently, waiting for a GPS lock.

24

Wakely studied her as she squinted at the screen. "Nothing, right?" he asked softly. When she didn't reply, he said softly, "Elsie."

She turned and walked a dozen paces down the passage, holding the GPS above her head.

Bronski looked at Wakely with raised eyebrows. Wakely said, "Radio waves can be dodgy. Jamming or interference or malfunction." Or everything's been fried by an electromagnetic pulse, he thought. EMP, from a nuke. Though that would hardly explain walls made from toilets and lathes. "Straighten up, buddy. You slouch."

Bronski sucked in his gut and straightened.

"Permission to speak, sir."

"I keep telling you, Bronski, I'm not 'sir.' I work for a living." Wakely glanced at Sharpcot, still fiddling with the GPS. "Go ahead."

"When can we make some calls? You know, with the baby coming any day now."

"Really, Bronski," Wakely said. "Really. Your wife is pregnant? I didn't know that. I had no idea. I guess I missed it when you told us every minute of every day for the last three weeks."

Sharpcot returned, and Wakely didn't need to ask to know she'd got nothing on GPS.

"Let's get everyone out," she said. "Make our way to HQ."

He checked his watch's digital compass, shook his head. "All that steel," he said, nodding to the brake lathes.

She looked at the sky, stepped to the hole, and peered down. "The radio room is at the northeast corner of the bunker, and judging by the sun, I'd say this — alley? Passageway? Whatever you call it, runs east-west. The base is north-north-west from here, say a track of 345 degrees."

"Sounds about right," Wakely said.

"Which would be — thataway." Sharpcot pointed at the wall of toilets, her finger almost perpendicular to its orientation.

"Yeah," Wakely replied. "I'd call that route problematic."

25

"We'll go west. This stack can't go on forever, right? Let's see what's past it. Distance to HQ is less than four klicks, as the crow flies."

"I could take some people and do a recce."

Sharpcot considered this as she regarded the walls, then looked each way along the corridor.

"We won't have radio contact through all this. Makes more sense to stay together, don't you think?"

"It's a sound idea," he replied flatly.

"Looking for real advice here, Jack."

"I agree, Sarge. If we split up, we'll lose contact."

"So we evac the bunker. Pack personal effects for later pickup. Travel light, move fast."

Wakely stepped close and dropped his voice. "Protocol?"

She thought a moment, glancing at the walls, considering what would happen if this was a practical joke and they showed up armed and armoured. But whether this was a test or the real thing, they had no contact with HQ and had to assume a hostile situation.

"Full Fighting Order."

"Including ammo?"

She hated the idea of some of the section — Bronski and Loko — walking around with live rounds and grenades. It was always the dudes who gave you trouble. She sighed.

"Combat situation. FFO, like I said."

"We should post a guard."

She eyed the tops of the stacks, suddenly aware there could be combatants nearby and she hadn't secured the area. This was a bad place to be, in a hallway with no exit other than a hole in the ground. Unarmed and basically in her pyjamas.

"Private Bronski, you will stand watch while the MC and I get our things."

"Me? Alone up here? I'm unarmed!"

"Not true," Sharpcot said as she stepped into the hole and began to descend. "You have your wit."

26

Bronski walked an agitated circle and let out an anguished moan as Wakely followed her into the hole.

While Sharpcot visited the women's dorm to wake the others and collect her things, Wakely stepped into the men's and turned on the lights and called loudly, "Gentlemen, anyone who wants to see the sun today will make themselves combat-ready. Full battle rattle."

Tse was already on his feet, pulling on pants and boots, lacing up. Wakely cast a glance to Boyko, who'd needed a double dose of lorazepam to calm down after last night's digging failed to yield an exit. The kid was sitting up, clutching his blanket, eyes dark-rimmed and wide as drugs fought adrenaline. Wakely went to his own bunk and unplugged his iPad and shut it off to conserve the battery. He'd got through a bunch of novels in the last three weeks, had just started a new one, a J. G. Ballard dystopic about a flood, which he was reading to appreciate the climate crisis. He liked novels that provided practical information.

He pulled armour over his T-shirt, followed it with his TAC vest. He took the photo of Daisy he kept pinned at the head of the bed, tucked it into the vest's map pocket, stowed shaving kit, cigarettes, lighter, iPad and charger, a bag of yogurt-covered raisins, mostly empty, into his kit. He hated the idea of leaving his valuables here for someone else to pick up but knew they had to travel light and quick.

"Private Boyko," he called as he grabbed his helmet. "I need to see you on your feet."

Boyko swung his body around and planted his feet on the floor, stood up, and made a show of stretching.

"Jag on, Private. You have five minutes to pull yourself together. Tse, you're with me."

They went into the hallway, turned a couple of corners and stood before a steel door, where Wakely fished into his collar for a key on a string, unlocked the door, and went in. It was a stationery supply room, still stocked with yellowed foolscap and manila envelopes. Propped against the room's cabinets were the section's weaponry: six C7A2 rifles and two C9 light machine guns. From a clamp for a broom hung two holsters, each containing a Browning 9mm pistol, and below it on a shelf labelled "File Folders," ammunition for each. A couple of crates of C7 magazines, as well as boxes of ammo. Cartons of C9 ammunition. Boxes of frag and smoke grenades. There were also bayonets, PTTs, and NVGs, but he didn't consider those for this short expedition. Let the CO send a squad of grunts to collect it all later.

A couple of small cartons on a shelf caught his eye, and he studied one. The word "Dosimeter" in five languages, brand name "SOEKS." Considering the possibility of an EMP, he tore it open and pulled out the device, smaller than a cigarette pack. There were a couple of AAA alkalines in the box, and he popped them in, switched it on. He glanced at Tse standing in the doorway as it booted up. A bar on the left side of the screen climbed, and large digits appeared: 0.09, and below that, the word "Norm" in green.

"All good," he said and looked at Tse, who nodded. Wakely left the device powered on, tucked it in a vest pocket, stepped out of the room to admit Tse into the space to collect his C9 and ammunition. The big man donned his helmet to free his hands, secured the extra barrel to the back of his vest, collected boxes and belts, and arranged the machine gun for carrying, collected and stored grenades. Privates Abigail Deeks, Adonia Virago, and Cheree Leclerc arrived in their vests and combat jackets, toting helmets. Wakely sent them in to retrieve their rifles and ammo, helped them cram magazines and grenades into their vest pockets.

Wakely sent them up to relieve Bronski, then gathered his service pistol where it dangled in its holster, dropped the magazine and checked it, put on the holster, and seated the weapon.

He found his rifle, ran a quick check, hung it on his shoulder, and loaded his vest.

Sharpcot stepped into the doorway in armour and vest, helmet on, carrying her rucksack. "Where's Boyko?"

"Dragging his ass," Wakely said, passing pistol and holster, her rifle, then handing up mags one at a time as she filled her pockets.

Bronski and Boyko arrived together, the former looking jumpy and scared, laden with his pack and an orthopaedic pillow he had insisted on bringing below. Loko with wide, bloodshot eyes.

"You ready for sunshine and fresh air, Private Boyko?" Sharpcot asked.

"I heard it's all fucked up," Boyko replied in panic. "Sergeant."

"You couldn't keep your mouth shut for five goddamn minutes, Bronski?" Wakely demanded.

"I thought he should know, sir. Didn't want him to suffer a shock."

"So the telling didn't shock him?" Wakely spat.

Bronski laughed uncomfortably, then slapped Loko on the shoulder. "Was it a shock, buddy?" Loko's eyes bugged out and he looked queasy and fearful. Wakely snapped, "Bronski, get in here and collect your rifle and mags. Then bring your pack and that godforsaken pillow and leave it in the commissary."

Bronski complied, and Wakely handed Loko his rifle and mags, sent him on his way.

"I'm going up, Elsie. Anything you need to do here?"

"Gotta collect my things. I was too busy pressing the women to do my own kit. See you up top."

Wary of leaving the section alone even briefly, Wakely hurried to join them at ground level.

Sharpcot returned to her bunk and gathered and wrapped in a rubber band three novels, shut her daily planner — filled more with point form thoughts and feelings than plans — and packed a picture frame with three photos of Lana, 14, and who, in the girl's words during their most recent encounter, hated

Sharpcot's "guts, gizzards, entrails, and viscera." She regretted the gift of a hardcover thesaurus the girl had requested for her last birthday.

She gathered toiletries into a pouch decorated with yellow cats, got her phone charger, and slipped into a plastic bag a small spider plant she had grabbed from the CANEX when they'd stocked up on snacks, consumed long ago, to bring below. A dose of greenery which had sustained her underground. She brought her rucksack and the plant into the cafeteria, where the other kits had been scattered on the floor and tables. She spent a moment arranging them in neat rows, ready for pickup. Bronski's pillow on top of his pack.

She hadn't eaten today, unwrapped a granola bar, got a flashlight from her kit, and headed for the power room, taking bites as she walked.

Low-battery warning lights blinked as she hunted for the master switch. She found the lever, pulled it. Stood in pure darkness, recognizing that she should have turned on the flashlight first. The ventilation's cease left a deep silence. She traced a thudding sound to the beat of her own heart. This was the last moment of peace she would ever experience, of this she was certain. Something big had happened up there, and however hard she tried, she could not fathom what it was or how it had come about. Or what it meant for the world.

2

W ith the section assembled in the passageway, stunned by what they found, Sharpcot provided a matter-of-fact description of the failed attempts to contact headquarters, and their inability to get a GPS fix. She attributed both to electromagnetic interference, possibly by deliberate jamming, and suggested they were being tested: isolate a section for several weeks, let them effect their own escape, then present them with an enigma.

She knew she wouldn't have their full attention until they could assess the situation themselves, and she invited them to activate their phones, quietly hoping someone's device would work. While they each tried and failed to acquire a signal, she attempted again with the radio, running through frequencies, receiving nothing but white static.

Wakely studied a map of the area, noting their position and the location of the base, but pocketed it when he realized the obstacles around them would dictate their path.

Virago snapped photos of the blocks, the corridor, took a shot of Deeks gazing up at the toilets. "For my Instagram," she said when Bronski asked why.

"Good luck posting it," he muttered as he turned off his phone and stowed it.

When all the phones were away, Sharpcot allowed several minutes of free discussion, to see if anyone could offer a viable theory.

"Is it like, a junkyard?" Adonia Virago proposed.

"Exceptionally well-organized," Cheree Leclerc said in her unvarnished, factual tone. "Significantly anal-retentive, whoever made this."

"How thick are these walls?" Virago wondered. "And how long is this . . . corridor?"

"I think we're going to find out," Deeks said quietly.

"So how," Loko asked, his voice quavering, "Did it get here, and so fast? We were down there for three weeks. Who builds a junkyard in the middle of a prairie, on top of a military bunker?"

"Here's a point," Abigail Deeks said, her voice a quiet drawl. "It wasn't built on top of the bunker's emergency exit. Those toilets or the brake machines there could have sat right on top of the hatch, and we'd be stuck down there to die like rats."

"Now we're rats in a maze," Loko said.

"Despite all my rage," Deeks added.

Sharpcot noticed Wakely shuffling away from the group with his eyes on the ground.

"What are you looking for, Jack?" she called.

He stopped 40 metres down the corridor, propped his rifle against one of the brake lathes, and kneeled at the foot of the wall.

"Everyone stay where you are, and keep alert," Sharpcot ordered. "Watch down the western passage." She came to where Wakely kneeled and squatted beside him. "What are we looking at?"

Wakely plowed at the soil with gloved hands until he encountered a protrusion. He excavated a strip of steel that ran under the wall of lathes, and as he cleared it, she saw the corner of a grate, which was almost entirely covered by the bench against which he'd leaned his rifle.

"Bunker vent," he said. "There's a curved intake pipe under the grate, which conceals it from ground visibility. Draws fresh air into the bunker, goes through a carbon filter. There are four of these."

"Where are the others?" she asked.

Wakely nodded at the wall. "Covered. That's why the air started to go bad, but not so bad to kill us. There's enough space between the pedestals of the benches to allow airflow."

"Deliberately? You think these were set down in such a way that they knew we'd still get air?"

"They?" Wakely asked.

She paused, trying to construct an image of someone — something — arranging these objects in enormous stacks. But the picture was untenable, and she resorted to stating, "Someone did this."

"We better get moving," Wakely said as he stood and brushed off his knees. He walked back to where the rest of the section assembled. She rose and looked at the grate, trying to govern a whirlwind of thoughts, and followed.

"Pick it up, everyone," Wakely ordered, waving them into formation, moving past them. Tse fell in beside him.

"Should we cover up?" Bronski asked from where he squatted, a jar of camouflage paint in his hand.

"You got toilet porcelain white in that pot?" Deeks asked.

"Or auto garage grime grey?" Virago added.

"Yeah, why not spell out National Auto Tools on your forehead," Deeks said.

"Why don't you girls go fuck yourselves," Bronski replied.

Wakely pivoted and lifted a gloved hand with his fingers spread, and as he silently counted down one finger at a time, the rest of the section scrambled into formation.

"Right," he called. "Let's keep it tight and quiet. We are moving west until we find a way north."

"So looking forward to a hot shower," Virago muttered to Deeks before Sharpcot jabbed a finger at the ground beside her and Virago moved into position there.

With nothing resembling cover, the section advanced cautiously in fireteam pairs: Delta team, Wakely and Tse, up front, Tse toting the Minimi machine gun like a toy, and Loko and Deeks of Fireteam Bravo at the rear, Loko carrying the other C9. Alpha and Charlie teams, Sharpcot and Virago in the first and Bronski and Leclerc in the second, proceeded along, bracketed by the light machine gun teams.

The walls on each side continued along in the same fashion, with toilets of every shape and design, most white, but a few pinks, blues, greens, yellows, two-toned, painted or inlaid with designs, and there was even a gold one before which they paused for a brief debate about whether or not it was actual gold. Towering on their left, brake lathes of many brands, styles, conditions, colours. The wall height remained consistent, following the roll of the terrain, the dips and rises. The sky a blue slot above them. They went more or less quietly, attempts at conversation quashed by Wakely whirling and pointing at the person speaking. Wakely and Tse scanned ahead and above, while Sharpcot turned frequently to remind Bravo team to watch the rear.

They'd been moving cautiously for 10 minutes with no break in the monotony when Wakely spotted a change ahead: the brake lathe monument came to an abrupt end, followed by a gap. Past it stood a new block, its faces patterned with thin, multicoloured horizontal strips, each an inch wide, which created a dazzling polychromatic matrix. Toilets continued on the right. The gap appeared to be a new passageway, running south. Wakely halted the group, and Sharpcot came up beside him, murmured, "It's another goddamn block. Can you tell what it's made from?"

"Not from here. Should we look?"

"Check that passage first."

Wakely nodded and flagged Tse forward, directed him to take position at the corner. Wakely edged past and glanced rapidly around the corner, saw a vacant corridor, and stepped back. Then he raised his rifle and entered the intersection, swept the distance through the scope.

Tse took position beside him, said, "Whoa. More."

Aside from the texture of the walls, it was geometrically identical to the east-west corridor behind them, same width, same height, though the wall on the right, with its flat, vari-coloured surface, extended only 30 metres before it ended at a new passage running west, parallel to the one they'd been navigating. Beyond it towered another block, same height again, but made from a new material, hard to discern from this distance, objects in plastic or metal: black, yellow, red, orange, blue, many silver, all with labels, a brand name, and a large number — through the scope Wakely saw 30, 25, 10, 12, one that said 5M/16'. Most of these items were four or five centimetres in diameter, square, some round or rounded, stacked and packed in every orientation.

They were retractable measuring tapes, used in renovation and construction, carried on the drywaller's belt, one in every toolbox. They went on for a distance, brake lathes on the left and measuring tapes on the right, ending, far off, at another east-west corridor, with new objects forming the blocks beyond. He grappled with the recognition that this phenomenon continued as far as he could see, then realized he'd spent too long looking, needed to report.

He lifted his eye from the scope and called, though he wasn't sure he meant it, "Clear."

The section crossed the intersection, some halting to look down the passage. Sharpcot urged them on. Tse took the south-west corner and maintained watch as Wakely stepped beside Sharpcot where she was inspecting the new block.

They saw densely packed strips, each about an inch wide, from paper-thin to a millimetre thick. The colour variation created a dizzying moiré effect. Wakely pulled off a glove and ran it along the surface. It felt rough, like the edge of a poorly bound book.

A bleak feeling overcame Sharpcot. They were not supposed to find more. They were supposed to step out from between brake benches and toilets and advance across open prairie, leaving the blocks behind to be explained later. She looked at the section, these recruits in her care, pacing slowly along the passageway, gazing around in awe.

Wakely moved in close to study the wall. He'd noticed a protruding yellow tag, reached into his vest and came up with a multitool, with knives and saws and screwdrivers folded into the handles, and which he arranged to produce a pair of needlenose pliers. He closed the tip on the protrusion and pulled. The strip was lodged tight, but not as tight as one would expect with storeys of material, tons of pressure, crushing it from above. He wiggled and tugged and it came out like a worm from the earth, and he stood holding it pinched in the pliers while he examined it. The strip was of yellow plastic and printed with a multitude of green blocks, each containing text: SXSW, 2013, MARCH 12–17, MUSIC, with the words NO RESALE and a serial number, plus additional words and fine print.

"Let's see it," Sharpcot said, and he passed it from the pliers into her hand.

"It's a wristband," muttered Virago. "I mean obviously." She tapped the end with a finger. "It was used, then cut off." Holes ran down one side of the strip, with a plastic stud driven through one. Sharpcot circled it closed, holding the cut ends together to form a bracelet.

No one spoke, and then everyone was speaking. These were wristbands? All wristbands? How many wristbands?

Sharpcot borrowed the pliers from Wakely, stepped to the wall and got the tip into the spot where the yellow strap had come out and pulled, and this one came away with greater ease. It was white and made not of plastic but ripstop paper, Tyvek maybe, and on it was printed "Het Scheepvaartmuseum, Amsterdam." The date printed on it was 16 days before they'd gone into the bunker. Virago asked to see it and Sharpcot passed it over, then went back to the wall and drew another, this one easier than the last, fluorescent orange and blank. She passed it into waiting hands and went to the wall again and came away with a red band with a picture of a whirlpool on it and the name of a waterpark in Tennessee.

She continued to draw out bands, came away with medical bracelets, the kind they tag you with at the hospital, with names and statistics (Kurt Shelty, M 46; Eileen Schrader, Female 76, Dementia, Fall Risk; Apoorva Das, June 11, 1969, MR# 10109949, Rm. 209, Chittaranjan National Cancer Institute) and QR codes and barcodes and doctor's names and medication doses. Others came from rock festivals (Glastonbury; Austin City Limits; Kappa FuturFestival: Turin, Italy; Good Vibrations 2011: Australia), from resorts in Greece, Mexico, Indonesia, from museums in Portugal, South Africa, and New Zealand. She pulled more, excavated a hole in the wall with straps collapsing to fill it, and everyone had a handful to examine, comment on, compare.

They came in paper and plastic and vinyl and woven fabric, fastened by peel-off adhesive or tab or stud or metal crimp. Every colour and texture. Some appeared unused, tamper-proof fasteners intact and ready to be snapped around a wrist, while the majority had been cut or torn off. They assumed every state, from freshly manufactured to frayed beyond recognition, ripped, stretched, bleached, stained, soiled, shredded, sliced, and blemished by diverse substances: mud, blood, pop, liquor, mustard, and various unidentifiable liquids. Some emitted a rank odour.

"I got one for beer," Deeks said, showing it off, the word BEER stencilled in big letters. "Is this good here?"

"Ride free," Bronski muttered as he fingered one from an amusement park. "Ride free, it's a free ride, no such thing as a ride free."

"Got one for Stagecoach Festival in California," Virago said. "Anyone wanna trade? I loathe country music."

As Sharpcot pulled more from the wall, one made her pause. It came from Tinkertown, an amusement park in southeast Winnipeg. She'd last taken Lana there three years ago, when the girl was 11, on the threshold of being too old for the place. This band was at least that old, had been snipped off with scissors. A brownish liquid fouled it in a long, bulb-ended drip.

The day came back to Sharpcot in all its vividness and fury. Lana was well on her way to developing her teen character of fragile outrage. She had recently started grade six. It was a glorious September day, too hot, the park crowded. Sharpcot could see the strain of the new school year, the heat, the park's congestion wearing on the girl. They should probably leave, but Sharpcot desperately wanted to preserve the experience. She had to return to Shilo tomorrow for a long stint, and she and Dwayne had bickered that morning in front of the girl.

While negotiating a throng of exasperated parents and whining kids, a white dude in a baseball cap passed them and flicked Sharpcot's cup where it said "Coke" as he said with a smirk, "Rum *and*, obviously."

"What did you say?" she demanded. He stood a head taller, but that didn't scare her.

"Just drink your drink, Indian," the man said, and grinned at his buddy, a shorter guy with a goatee and sunglasses.

"I fought the Taliban, motherfucker," she was about to say, but before she could, Lana spilled her full cup of root beer all over the man's pasty legs. He jumped back as if scalded and the crowd folded into the space he left, and Sharpcot took the opportunity to escape.

"Oh baby, your drink!" she cried as she pulled the girl along.

"Worth it," Lana said, squeezing her mother's hand.

"Was that an accident?"

"Duh," the girl replied.

They made for an exit, Sharpcot overcome by a blend of pride at her daughter's response, and dread for the girl's future if she sustained that attitude.

She let the strap slip from her fingers, then called out to the soldiers, who were passing wristbands around, showing them off, trading them, "Listen up, Three Section! Pack your souvenirs, firm up, and let's get going. Move!"

38

Wristbands vanished into pockets and pouches, most were tossed on the ground, and as Sharpcot started to move, she realized Virago wasn't beside her. She turned to see the young woman collecting bands and cramming them back into the gap in the wall from where they'd come.

"Private Virago," she called sharply.

"Are we just going to litter?" Virago asked, continuing to collect bands.

Wakely opened his mouth to enforce the order, but Sharpcot held up a hand and went to help.

When they finished, Wakely and Tse led them away from the intersection, advancing along a corridor walled with wristbands left and toilets right. Sharpcot saw Private Deeks slip her phone from her vest for a furtive glance, let it go. She wanted to check her own phone for cell coverage, but resisted, concealing her anxiety. Lana would be at her summer school class and couldn't take a call anyway, not for an hour. They needed to reach the base, where there'd be access, or at least an explanation for why there wasn't.

"Hey Jack," she called. "Let's pick it up."

Wakely quickened the pace. He glanced down to watch his boots flick through the prairie grass and noted that the blades extended beneath the blocks on both sides, flattened by their weight. Grasshoppers popped out of the grass as he walked. He saw swallows dart through this canyon of toilets and wristbands, and when they cleared the walls sunlight struck their iridescent backs.

He remembered the swallow that had struck the window of their shed. Daisy cradling it in her palms where it lay panting. As he watched he thought it could go either way: the breathing could cease, or the bird could — and at that instant, as if hearing his thought, the swallow jerked its wings and was airborne and gone. And in his mind's eye he sought not the bird as it ascended away, but Daisy, kneeling in the grass, her palms yet spread, but she too vanished, and he searched for her, ran along the flagstone path, passed between the flowerbeds. He burst through the screen door and into the house where Daisy would be. Where Daisy wasn't. Cancer had dragged her away six weeks before they'd gone into the bunker. Isolation had seemed like a good idea at the time. He'd spent the weeks below irrationally hoping there'd been a mistake. They would emerge from the bunker and she'd be there, alive, waiting.

He dreaded returning to the house filled with their stuff. Mostly junk, but junk they'd owned and tolerated together. Things she had brought into the relationship, into their home. A blanket box made by her grandfather, painted lurid colours by Daisy herself. She talked about sanding it down to the original cedar, and he said he would do it, but she never let him start. Now he'd have to face that box, painted by Daisy's hand, its psychedelic swirls of yellow and blue and red. He couldn't sand it now. He would not erase her.

Tse drew him from his reverie. "Sir. Something ahead."

Wakely stopped and studied the distance through his rifle's scope. On the right, beyond the toilets, a corner formed by large objects, less featured than those they'd previously encountered, and in muted hues: dark green, grey, black. And on the left, past wristbands, what looked like foliage.

"We're going to check it out," Wakely said.

He and Tse edged forward. Wakely scanned the tops of the blocks. Sunshine gleamed on the porcelain of the toilets, extending partway down the wall, maintaining shade in the passageway itself, a mercy in the day's increasing heat, which was exacerbated by their pace, their vests and jackets and helmets, the weight of their weapons and ammunition. He fixed his eyes on the approaching intersection.

"Transformers," Tse said, and Wakely thought he meant the cartoon, the movie franchise, the toys, but when they got closer he saw that Tse was correct — they were electrical transformers, enormous blocks painted grey, blue, green, bristling with ceramic isolators, encumbered with cylindrical oil conservators, cooler tubes, control boxes, their cases finned by heatsinks. He was accustomed to encountering these in the wild, set on gravel beds in fenced compounds, where they gathered wire from high tension towers and reduced voltages for residential use. Humming menacingly. Chainlink adorned with lightning bolts and dire warnings. Now here they stood, silent, stacked to the sky, some fresh and new, most weathered, corroding, some faced with legions of cooling fans. Sunlight glinting on their isolators — those too in all varieties, from squat, cinnabar pagodas to enormous accordions of glass.

"What do you figure that to be?" Wakely asked, nodding to the tangle of green that constituted the corner opposite. Could it be a forest? Had they reached the boundary of the blocks? But he didn't know of any forest in this part of the prairie. As their approach revealed more, he was crushed to see it was another nine-storey tower. It had an irregular top, cones of green foliage against the blue sky. After he and Tse checked the passage, Wakely stepped into the intersection and looked south. On the left, wristbands for 30 metres, followed by the western face of the measuring tape block. On the right, tangled greenery, stretching into the distance like a hedge, 90 feet tall.

He crossed the intersection to study the greenery and then understood. "Merry Christmas," he muttered, reaching into the foliage to yank a plastic branch from a socket in a tree's trunk. It carried a scent, the branch, this block, a manufactured stink, repellant because his brain told him he should smell vegetation, but it was all PVC and polyethylene, and, worse still, some corporation's shoddy simulation of pine. He stepped back to take in the wall, saw a mix of types, some of slick design, realistic, needles made from textured fabrics, but also a lot of trashy, low-grade models, unabashedly phony. Some were pre-decorated with LED lights, or with permanently fixed tinsel and ornaments. A few were stark white. He spotted high up in the wall a hot pink one, another, baby blue, others in orange, violet, silver, gold. One candy-striped red and white. Some flocked with artificial snow. He shuddered at the idea of setting one of these abominations in a family room for the duration of the Christmas season.

As he backed away he found himself in the midst of the rest of the section, which had drawn up behind him and were moving in, fingering the phony branches. Deeks humming Radiohead.

"You okay, sir?" Virago asked him as he took another step back. "Look, it's just fake trees."

Two weeks before Christmas, for every year of his childhood, he and his parents and siblings would visit a tree farm north of the city. They'd trudge through deep snow to cut a tree, not the tallest or widest or best-formed, but one that called out to them, one with the right character to stand for the season beside the fireplace. They would drink hot chocolate and snack on home-made cookies, trimming it with vintage glass ornaments from their dad's family, from his own childhood. Then would come that sad day they had to undecorate its browning branches and trundle it to the curb.

An annual ritual. Until their dad left. It was a fake tree after that, with plastic ornaments, the same pathetic tree year after year. It's when his life turned fake. The day his dad left.

He spied Sharpcot in his peripheral, and he blanked his expression before facing her. She nodded to the northbound corridor.

"That'll take us to HQ, right?"

"Should," he replied as he got out the map and indicated their approximate position southeast of the base. He moved a fingertip in a northbound line to represent the new passage, which, if it continued, would place them east of the base.

"Right everyone, you got five minutes before we take this last leg. Go ahead and check your devices."

Phones came out, but disappointment immediately damped the mood. Virago snapped pictures of the Christmas trees, the transformers, photographed each of the four passageways.

Sharpcot stared down at her phone. No signal. No location. She flipped aimlessly through the screens, the icon grids, then found herself looking at the last text message to Lana. "Even when you're mad, I never stop loving you. See you in a few weeks."

3

They turned north, escaping the trees. Transformers on the left, and the toilet block on the right ran only 70 metres before it broke at an eastbound corridor, followed by a new monument, this one composed of tan paperboard tubes stacked in columns of widely varying widths, from slender piles three centimetres thick to fat pillars a metre and a half wide.

They checked the passageway, crossed it, and regarded the block.

The collection included plain brown tubes, plus many branded Sonotube, Bomix, Formatube, Newform, Tubbox, Quik-Tube, Handiforms, and Caraustar EASY-POUR. While assembled from random lengths of uniform diameter, each stacked column stood precisely the same height as the toilet and transformer blocks.

"They fill these with cement to form columns," Sharpcot said. "Something being built here?"

Wakely smacked a thick tube branded "Sakrete" with the flat of his hand, and it boomed hollowly.

"Empty," he remarked.

"Though they're not only construction tubes," Leclerc stated loudly. "Uh, sorry."

"Go ahead, Private," Sharpcot said.

"Well, some look like paperboard cores for winding paper, or textiles, or film. You know, like newsprint or carpet or twine or reams of plastic."

"Construction tubes and cores, basically the same thing," Sharpcot noted. "But also not."

They continued north along tubes and transformers for a kilometre before they reached on the right a new stack, this one formed from thousands of strata of fabric with sewn or fringed edges. Sharpcot managed to pry a couple of layers apart to see that these were rugs, the one revealed finely made, patterned in ruby red and forest green, with embedded threads of white silk. She bent forward to smell it and took in a rich and organic scent. She thought it must be wool. Musty, but in a comforting way; old, but well preserved. Another layer she opened showed something newer, also wool, but fresh, colours vivid, the scent more immediate, with a mild chemical tang, as if it had been treated. The few minutes they spent investigating disclosed rugs of every vintage and quality.

Wakely looked up the wall of them and drew from an inner pocket of his vest a notebook the size of a deck of cards, palm trees and a blue lagoon on its cover. Daisy had given it to him to record bad thoughts, the ones that careened into dark spirals. She said it would push them out of his head and onto paper. He'd written in it just once, at her urging. It was three in the morning and he'd bolted awake in terror, sweating, crying. She held him and whispered, "Now write it." He lifted the book from the bedside table and jotted it down, and ever since, the notebook's entire contents existed on page one, in the upper lefthand corner. It read, "dead boy."

Now he fanned once through its blank pages and turned to page two. He wrote:

toilets
brake lathes
wristbands
tape measures
fake xmas trees

45

electrical transformers
paperboard tubes
wool rugs

His handwriting was neat and small and he ran the list close to the margin, with minimal spacing. Conserving room in case he felt the need to record a new dark thought.

He had one now, but did not write it.

Sharpcot watched him, saw the emotional struggle he endured with the notebook. He was always closed up, but she'd known him a long time, had served with him in bad places — she thought immediately of Helmand Province and Operation Moshtarak — and she understood the way his emotions unspooled before he regained control and reeled them back in. He knew her just as well.

As he put away the notebook, he caught her looking, and she turned her attention to the wall opposite, this immense block of power transformers. Even in their idle state, they gave off a dull, electrical smell, a scent of ozone. Their condition varied enormously, from slick and new and modern to cracked and corroded and dated. One of the older transformers, set high up, appeared art deco in design, with tapered isolators and streamlined fan cowlings, and another looked antique, assembled from riveted slabs of black steel, faced with giant knife switches and rusting dials and indicators, lenses cracked or missing. Oil glazed the sides of some, and in places trickled out and along the ground, contaminating the prairie grass in puddles and rivulets of varying hues, from clear to yellow to dark brown. Leclerc commented that old transformer oil used polychlorinated biphenyls and advised everyone to minimize contact with the product. As usual when she spoke in polysyllables she was largely ignored, though Bronski asked her what that meant.

"PCBs," Leclerc replied lightly.

"Right," Bronski said without comprehending.

But Virago had heard, and she called out, "Hey everybody, PCBs are really bad shit. Keep away from that oil. Unless you want cancer."

They shifted to the right as they continued to walk north, closer to the carpets, but the warning didn't deter Loko from reaching out whenever they passed a transformer faced with a heat exchanger and running a fingertip along the fins, producing an annoying flutter. Eventually Bronski shouted at him to stop, and Sharpcot shouted at Bronski to shut up, and also, Loko, stop that.

As midday approached, the sunlight, which had been inching down the lefthand block, propagated across the passage, flooding it wall-to-wall, producing a shadeless canyon of desperate August heat. The sun hammered their backs, and they sweated in their helmets and gear, but Sharpcot would not let them strip off layers, recognizing the possibility that this was either a test or the real thing, and they had to remain equipped, protected, alert.

The carpets came as a relief from the resonance of the paperboard tubes, dampening their voices and footsteps. Sharpcot walked along watching Wakely beside the bulk of Tse, weapons at rest but ready, both vigilant, cautious, and she studied Charlie team ahead of her, Bronski fidgety, muttering under his breath, and Leclerc, short and freckled and heavier set, alert like a bird, taking it all in. Sharpcot glanced behind, Loko beside Abby Deeks, Loko's gait betraying his anxiety, Deeks looking amused, curious, casual. Sharpcot gazed at the carpets, wondering if they were composed of natural fibres only, as they'd seen, or if there were other materials: nylon, polyester, acrylic, whatever else you could use to make rugs. How were the things they'd encountered so far in these blocks categorized — by morphology, composition, or function?

"You okay, Sarge?" Virago asked, and Sharpcot realized she had slowed when these thoughts led to a deep question: Who? Who had done this? Who and how? And why?

She shook it off.

"Master Corporal Wakely," she called, and Wakely turned, eyebrows raised at the formality of her tone. "What do you estimate our position to be, in relation to the base?"

Wakely looked at his watch. "We've been walking for close to two hours, with lots of pauses, as you know. We've covered about six klicks. We're near."

"This is mental," Bronski said, pressing a sleeve to his soaked forehead.

"Shut it, Private," Sharpcot ordered. "Jack, should we break?"

The sun inched westward, sending a shadow down the transformer wall and spreading onto the ground, and they drifted into it to cool down.

"Let's keep moving," Wakely said. "For 10 minutes. Or until the next intersection."

There was a collective, reluctant grunt from the section, and they shuffled forward. Sharpcot knew she had to hold things together or this was going to slip. It might be a test, under surveillance to study responses to a bizarre situation, but she also knew it was impossible to contrive something of this scale in reality. Each time her mind closed in on the possibility that any of this was true, it reeled for a way out, an alternate explanation, and kept rolling through the same theories: vivid dream; hallucination evoked by a psychedelic that had been administered to them, the way LSD had been given to American soldiers in the 1950s; some kind of hypnosis; hyperrealistic virtual reality simulation.

What did it mean for Lana? Was she safe? What did it mean for the world?

They'd passed at least two kilometres of transformers on the left, and half that of carpets on the right, when an intersection appeared ahead, a four-way, with new items forming each corner. The group's progress slowed. The left block was made from concrete tablets, while to the right stood a mass of stark, variegated white.

48

Wakely brought them to a halt four metres short of the corner, and Sharpcot said to Virago, "You're with me," and they pushed past Wakely and Tse.

"Sarge, let us . . ." Wakely said, and she shot him a silencing glare. She lifted her rifle and stepped to the corner where an enormous transformer painted dark green stood at ground level, and without waiting for Virago to take her position, she checked the corridor east and west. It was another unrelenting passageway. To the left, transformers as far as she could see, and across from them, a block of vertically stacked concrete slabs, each a metre high, three metres long, most of varying degrees of grey, some striped black, white, yellow; many dotted with reflectors; still others embellished in varicoloured swirls, illustrations, graffiti. Their condition ranged widely, from clean and new, caked with mud and grit and soot and roadsalt, patterned with rusted grids of rebar, chipped, bashed, cracked, cratered, shattered, and smashed where vehicles had struck them, and also bulletpocked, or so she guessed, recalling the dread of hunkering behind a line of them in Kandahar Province while AK rounds crashed against the opposite side, the air thick with concrete dust and gunsmoke.

They were those modular barriers set along roadways and in constructions zones, with wide bases tapering in two stages to tops a foot thick, used to direct and funnel traffic, protect pedestrians and construction workers, and, in places she'd served, as defence against suicide bombers and assault.

The other new block, which occupied the righthand corner, was made from millions of compact white objects a couple of millimetres thick, a dozen centimetres long, and nested horizontally. These stretched out of sight to the north and east.

"Clear," she called, and continuing to survey each of the four aisleways, she made her way to the white block, Virago at her side, vigilant, scoping the block tops while the rest of the section spread into the crossroads behind them. Sharpcot pulled off a glove and ran her hand along the rippled surface. She had

49

a sense of what the objects might be, but had to be certain. She met Virago's eye, then turned her rifle and raised the butt, bashed it into the wall a few times, until objects cracked free and fell to the grass, some broken.

She bent and picked up an intact one.

"Spoons," she said. "Plastic spoons." The sight of them, the recognition, started a wheel of nausea churning in her belly. She glanced at the others, expecting them to be just as panicked by these objects, but they were gazing up at the concrete barriers.

"Looks almost normal," Deeks said. "Like a depressing, windowless building. I worked construction in Edmonton two summers ago. This is how you'd stack them. But someone went overboard."

"Jersey barriers," Leclerc said as she kicked one. "They're engineered to minimize vehicle damage if struck. In some places they call them K-rails."

"Thanks so much, Wiki," Bronski grunted.

"Up yours, shrimp," Leclerc shot back.

"Shrimp? I'm taller than you!"

"She means your brain, shrimp," Deeks said.

"Fuck you guys."

"Something you'll never do," Deeks retorted.

"Fuck you g—" Bronski started to say again, but shut his mouth and stomped away.

Sharpcot stepped into the centre of the intersection to take in all four passageways. She fingered the smooth bowl of the spoon in her hand, glanced at the block. This was a lot of spoons. Beyond millions — billions.

She didn't extend the estimate casually. Lana once told her a million seconds is almost 12 days and asked her to guess a billion. Sharpcot said a lot more, like 10 months? The girl laughed and said, "Guess again!" Sharpcot ran through a year, then two, then five, the girl shaking her head with each increment. When she got to 30 Lana's eyes widened and she said: "Not even! It's almost 32. A billion seconds is like, 32 years!"

A billion spoons? She lifted her eyes along the wall, the full height, a nine-storey building, then tried to reckon its length, but couldn't see the ends. She stepped to the carpet wall and sighted eastward through her rifle's scope, made out a vertical line where the spoons ended at another intersection, beyond which stood a new wall composed of an indiscriminate material. She made a guess at the distance: 250 metres. Reminded herself it wasn't just a wall. It was a monument that ran north, for possibly the same distance, which meant she could see only a fraction of its bulk.

She let a memory that had been dogging her come around: Lana chastising her for putting a disposable spoon and yogurt cup in her lunch. "We're supposed to bring a litterless lunch," Lana stated as she upturned her lunch bag, spilling the empty cup and spoon onto the counter. "They won't let us throw it out at school."

"Yogurt is good for you. And it's just one spoon," Sharpcot had replied, but this stack summoned a billion voices, all of them saying in a chorus, "Just one spoon."

From kids' lunches and store shelves and desk drawers and airline meal packs, in every country of the world: Canada and the United States and Nicaragua and Uruguay and Argentina and Ireland and Burkina Faso and Russia and Papua New Guinea and New Zealand and very probably the Antarctic. Where wasn't there disposable cutlery? Plastic spoons in endless demand, in endless supply, from factory floors where they are manufactured and packaged in boxes of 10 or 20 or 100 or 1000 or individually in clear wrap, boxed on skids and trucked to trains freighting them to port cities and onto giant container ships plying the seas to international ports to intercity transport trucks to retail delivery docks for grocery stores and retail chains, supplying restaurants and homes, consumers moving them from shelf to cart to bag to car to house, where they are stuck in the lunches of the children of polluting parents, or used once each at a birthday party to serve ice cream to four-year-olds where only some are used but who knows which? So used and unused go together in the trash, or every day one crammed into a hipster's backpack to eat instant pudding at his software job in an open-concept walkup in a gentrified neighbourhood, or handed out from food trucks by the harbour, or set in a paper cup at a Costco table for customers to sample just one bite of this exotic new flavour, and so they go into trash bins and dumpsters and garbage trucks and finally vast landfill sites or maybe just tossed from the window of a moving car or thrown over the rail of a cruise ship to sink in the ocean deep.

It could be a billion spoons. But it must be more. Seven and a half billion people on Earth. What if everyone used an average of two spoons in their lifetime? That's all it would take to reach 15 billion. Of course for many it was none, but for others — for others, it would be hundreds, even thousands. How many spoons had she herself used? Yesterday she stirred her coffee with one. Every army-issued Individual Meal Pack contained a spoon. How many IMPs had she consumed in her life: 500, 1000? It was 60 in just the last few weeks.

This could be 100 billion, 200 billion. Is this what 200 billion spoons looked like?

She suffered a dimming of her vision, a kind of dilation, and the ground seemed to pitch like the deck of a capsizing ship. She put a hand against the carpet wall to maintain her balance. Her mind slipped into a kind of fugue as it fought to compute something so absurd it could not be processed.

"Sarge? Are you ill?" Virago asked, and Sharpcot shook off the feeling, straightened up.

"I'm all right, Private," Sharpcot lied.

But before her stood that block, and she had to turn away, step into the intersection and gaze down the south passage the way they'd come, hiding her face, her expression, for she feared that it betrayed terror at what she'd suddenly determined. That these were *all the white plastic spoons in the world*. Every one of them. And because of the persistence of plastic, aside from those that had been catastrophically destroyed, this stack contained *every white plastic spoon ever made.*

And when she shifted her vision to the right, she saw transformers, millions of them, stacked here, sequestered, arranged in a block, superficially like a city block, with streets around it, but much larger. The transformers of humankind, of civilization? If all the spoons, why not all the transformers? All of them, here, in one spot. Which meant they had been removed from wherever they'd been, in whichever township or city or hydro substation, and placed, neatly, diligently, here. In this place. Which meant those places were now completely without electrical power.

And plastic spoons.

She was vomiting. It happened just like that — she was standing, facing away from her troops, looking down a corridor with transformers on the right and all the wool carpets in creation on the left, and she was throwing up her granola bar breakfast, spewing on the ground before she'd hardly had a chance to bend forward. She leaned and spit. Someone was at her side, holding back her braids.

"You okay, boss?" Virago asked.

Sharpcot nodded, wiped a sleeve across her mouth, straightened up. She looked down her front and saw that mercifully she'd missed her CADPATs, though not her boots. She rubbed them in the grass, hunted her pockets until she found a pack of tissues, and as she cast a look back, she met Wakely's eye. Gave a nod to show she was okay. But it was all show. She was decidedly not okay.

Wakely knew it, got everyone lined up, and they set forth, northwards along the barrier-spoon corridor. He maintained a good pace, concentrated on the task, and she wondered what he was thinking, if he'd reached the same conclusion about the blocks, that they weren't each just some of a thing, they were all of it.

She lifted her eyes to escape the confine of the walls, the concrete of the jersey barriers on the left, spoons on the right.

Focused on a cloud illuminated along its fringe by sunshine. She knew it was around 12:45, could look at her watch to check, but somehow it wasn't important. Lana still at summer school, finished lunch, starting the afternoon math session. Probably. Probably not. Probably skipped out to find her friends and now doing god-knows-what. Smoking weed. Or worse. Sharpcot was cursed with a vivid imagination, and she could imagine worse. She indulged in it because Lana doing something, anything, even if it was bad, was better than the alternative.

She looked at the prairie grass, which produced a tranquillizing sibilance against her boots. She focused on that sound, like the wind, like the surf, to calm herself. She knew deep down she'd gone into full panic mode, and this was the only way to hold it at bay. It worked for a few minutes, until it was shattered by a voice ahead, a voice she rarely heard, which made it all the more unnerving. Private Tse. "Grass," he called out. "Grass! The grass!"

The procession ahead stalled and the section bunched up. Annoyed at the procedural breach she pushed through to where Tse squatted, gazing at the ground. Prairie grass transitioned abruptly into domesticated turf of a lush, deep green. It went on for 40 metres, then shifted back to course grassland.

"What do you make of this?" Sharpcot asked Tse.

"I don't know. I had a notion, but now I'm not sure," he replied.

"Yo, guys," said Loko, who had stepped ahead of the group and stood with his neck craned, peering up the passage. "There's more ahead."

Tse rose and walked past Loko and the rest of the section fell in behind. He treaded a dozen paces and stopped and looked to his right to see that the spoons ended at an eastbound passage followed by a new block made of housekeeping carts, the type used in hotels, in black, grey, beige, brown, and blue, some flanked with rectangular waste bags. They were stacked upright, shelves that would hold fresh linens and towels and toilet paper empty, mounts for mops and dusters and spray bottles vacant.

He checked the side passage and continued northward with determination until Wakely ordered him to hold and joined him. They saw the grass change again to the same species and quality they'd encountered previously. Immediately following it lay a zone of cropped grass of a paler green. Beyond it, trees filled the passage, wall-to-wall.

The brush made Wakely lift his arm up to halt the section. He waved everyone down, spooked as he imagined tracer rounds flying out of the trees. He and Tse went flat and peered through their scopes into the foliage.

"On your belly, Bronski," Sharpcot hissed, and the private flopped from hands and knees to prone.

"How's it look?" Wakely whispered to Tse.

"Pretty dense."

"What do you got, Jack?" Sharpcot called.

"Can't see much. I'm taking Tse in with me."

"We'll cover."

The pair rose and advanced across the cropped grass. The trees ahead looked forlorn in the shadow of the block, showing in wilt and paling colour their distress at the shade they found themselves in. Wakely and Tse came to the perimeter and treaded between the trunks. Birds flitted around them, and branches cracked underfoot. They went in 20 metres and stopped, and Wakely experienced a moment of calm among the trees. Crickets maintained a constant chorus. He breathed the good air. But to his left through leaves and branches he could see concrete barriers, climbing into the sky, and to the right, housekeeping carts.

"Clear?" Wakely said quietly.

"I guess," Tse answered.

"You okay, Corporal?"

"I know where we are," he replied. "I knew when the grass changed. We're at the thirteenth."

55

"Yeah," Wakely replied. "I think you're right."

They came out of the trees and Wakely gave the all-clear, and he followed Tse to the middle of the crop-grassed area, where the corporal stopped and looked down.

Sharpcot arrived with the rest of the section trailing.

"What are we looking at?" she asked.

"Thirteenth hole," Wakely said.

"The first grass we crossed was the third fairway," Tse said. "We're standing pretty much in the middle of the course."

"The golf course?" she asked, but obviously that's what he meant. She'd never understood the appeal of golf, had never visited Shilo Country Club, which lay east of the base. But when she looked at the grass she recognized it as a golf green that hadn't been maintained in some weeks, unmowed, blighted with bald patches. She went to where Tse stood over a round hole.

"Cup's gone," Tse said, then kneeled and lay his machine gun on the ground and put his hand into the hole, felt around. "Just dirt." He pulled some out and cast it on the green. He picked up the gun and stood.

"It means Shilo is right there," Wakely said, pointing west. "Less than a klick."

"So this is all built on top of the course?" Deeks wondered, looking at the walls.

"Messed up. This is so messed up," Bronski muttered, walking in a circle.

Sharpcot gazed at their faces and saw mounting panic. Private Boyko pivoted away, his head down, and as she grabbed his arm and pulled him around, he tried to hide his phone. He looked at her in fear, but instead of a reprimand she asked quietly, "Signal?"

He shook his head.

"Right, everyone," she called. "Let's keep at it. Stay alert. We're going to make our way through those trees. We'll be at the base in short order. We are close, so if they're planning a surprise, it'll be now."

They went into the trees, stepping among fallen logs, trying to go quietly. Partway through the forest, they arrived at a new intersection. When Wakely looked up through the overstory he saw countertop kitchen blenders stacked to the sky. They were all similar in design: base with motor in a variety of shapes, in various colours (black, white, grey, silver, some red, blue, green, turquoise, purple), controlled with buttons or knobs or dial or touchpad, each topped by a transparent jar, also in various shapes, and capped with a lid colour-coordinated to the base. They stood upright in neat rows, with no attempt to group like models or designs together, making the wall look simultaneously orderly and chaotic.

Wakely passed the corner of jersey barriers and pushed through foliage until he arrived at this new wall. He reached for a blender, a silver-cased KitchenAid, prodded one of the buttons, which clicked loudly. He almost expected the machine to spin up, but it didn't. He raised his head and scanned the wall, reading nameplates: Oster, Krups, Black+Decker, Philips, Russell Hobbs, Smeg, Electrolux, Vitamix. He moved sideways, saw Hamilton Beach, BioChef, Sunbeam, Ninja, Moulinex, Breville, Cuisinart, Wolf, Tribest, L'Equip, Kuvings, Blendtec, Omega, Dash . . .

"Oh mang, this gets more and more fucked up," Bronski grumbled.

Sharpcot heard the sound of the others pushing buttons and turning knobs, and wondered vaguely if they shouldn't be doing that.

She saw Virago tilt back with her phone raised to photograph the block's corner, was about to issue a rebuke, but caught sight of the northeast corner of the intersection, and a new collection formed from black and silver objects each the size of a shoebox, with vents and small protrusions. She pushed through the brush and when she reached the wall could still not determine what they were, labelled T-400, Chauvet, Rosco 1700, Moka, Martin,

Look Solutions, Antari Z-1500II Series II. She studied them, trying to discern their function, when Bronski spoke beside her, "Whoa. The motherlode."

"What are they?" Sharpcot asked.

"You kidding?" he said, then turned and looked at her. "Uh, ma'am. They're smoke machines."

"Not 'ma'am,' Private Bronski. Just 'Sergeant.' Smoke machines for what?"

"You know, stage shows. Oh, look here, we have one of these, actually the newer model," he said, tapping a black box on which was printed "American DJ MINI FOG Portable Fog Machine."

"Who's we?" Private Deeks, who had moved up beside them, asked. "Like, your family? To make holiday gatherings more atmospheric?"

"Funny. My band."

"You're in a band? You play lead triangle?"

"Synth. Look, you put on the fog alongside a really deep synth pad," Bronski said, uttering a low note, "mwoooo," while illustrating with one hand. "Smoke rolling off the stage, lit by red lights. It's like the apocalypse." He stepped back, gazing up the wall. "Mang, there are some high-end ones here. We should come back and grab a few." Someone coughed in a way that wasn't a cough, and Bronski said, "What?"

"Jack," Sharpcot called, and Wakely stepped through the brush to meet her. "Get us home."

"Three section, gather," Wakely called, and the section assembled around him. He looked them over, adjusted Loko's helmet, told Leclerc to straighten her vest. "We are a thousand steps from base. Bring it together, stay sharp for surprises, and let's arrive in perfect shape. Same formation." He and Tse moved to the front, and the rest fell in. They went west through the trees.

A dozen metres on the trees ended and they found themselves passing along an open corridor between concrete barriers and blenders. Wakely had his map out, glancing at the view ahead, hoping to spot the first of Shilo's low-rise buildings. His skepticism mounting as the walls ahead tapered towards the horizon. They trod along verdant fairway grass, followed by more rough, then crossed another green. Wakely glanced at Tse, who knew the course better, asked, "The fourteenth?"

"Fifteenth," Tse stated in a daze.

They crossed the green, stepping over the empty hole, and returned to the rough. Wakely squinted down the passage, saw that they might have to run through more trees, and he slowed and lifted his rifle and peered through the scope. While he looked, Tse said, "Master Jack." Wakely lowered the rifle and saw that the blenders on the right ended at a northbound alley, and the next block, actually more of a tower, was made of what looked like millions of horizontal blades. Its footprint measured only a dozen or so metres square, and when Wakely raised his head he felt queasy at its proportions, a slender spire nine storeys tall. When they closed on it, they saw it was made from packets of some kind. They checked and crossed the new passage to reach the tower. Other blocks stood to the north and west. With the caution of a Jenga player, Wakely plucked out one of the packets and looked at it: framed in silver, with the word KIMLAN in large letters, and smaller, SOY SAUCE and "no preservatives." Reaching for a different part of the wall he pulled another and read the familiar name KIKKOMAN against a red background. The next said Yamasa, and the pack after that was clear and filled with brown liquid and labelled Yi Pin. Tse drew some too, and the section came up behind and no one spoke. Sharpcot had one in her hands, with Lee Kum Kee on it. She tore it open and drizzled some on the grass and the scent of soy sauce filled the air.

Bronski started to say, "Hey Corporal Tse" before Tse shot the private a look.

"I guess you're going to ask me about Chinese food now, Bronski?" Tse sighed.

"Uh, no. Why would I do that? I just . . . hey, when's your birthday?"

"Why? You going to bake me a cake?"

"Do you people even eat birthday cake?"

"For fuck's sake," Abby Deeks said.

"What? Being curious about the Chinaman's rituals makes me racist?"

Sharpcot looked up the passage and saw that beyond the narrow soy sauce tower lay another passage and block, somewhat larger, hard to tell from this distance, but could be rubber stamps, each with a handle in red, black, woodgrain, other colours. Past that stood another block of a composition she couldn't discern, something very small and dense, colourful, shiny. Maybe glass figurines. She wanted to investigate, but they had to get to Shilo. A sudden thought about Lana. She had to talk to Lana.

She clapped her hands and called out, "Right, Three Section, let's move. Take us in, Jack."

Wakely and Tse checked the alley past the soy sauce tower and looked briefly over the next block, which appeared to be made up of paddles. "Cricket bats?" Loko wondered. They were stacked in orientations both horizontal and vertical, some new, handles and upper paddles colourfully decorated in brand names (GM, Thrax, BAS, Bradbury, Gray-Nicolls, Adidas, Spartan, Malik, Genius MRF, some with a bird on them — "a kookaburra," Loko explained), but many more older: varnished, taped, warped, battered, chipped, splintered, some embossed, a few autographed.

"So many," Virago said as she gazed up the wall.

"The rest of the world plays cricket," Leclerc answered.

"My mom is into it in a bad way," Loko said. "Her team is Sydney Thunder. She'd leave my dad for Chris Gayle in a heartbeat."

Wakely and Tse continued along cautiously, and Tse said, "Road." Wakely looked down and saw dirt under his feet in a wide strip running diagonally across the passage floor.

"You know it?" Wakely asked Tse.

"Yeah," Tse replied. "Second fairway ahead."

Wakely saw a long stretch of good grass that ended at trees. If this was a hoax, a fabrication, some kind of remarkable illusion, it would all happen here, the revelation, the action, and likely, considering how the brass regarded Three Section, the humiliation. He behaved as if everything from this point forward was being recorded to be immortalized on YouTube. It would all be wretched and embarrassing and possibly career-ending, but he wanted it more than the alternative — the end of civilization. He'd make that sacrifice.

He straightened his sunglasses and snugged his rifle against his shoulder and set his mouth into a flat line and stepped into the brush ahead of Tse. He found himself holding his breath as he passed between the trunks, had to let it go, had to breathe. Suddenly thinking about Daisy. Remembering her small hand in his. How she was supposed to help him rebuild the ruin of his life, and instead had become part of that ruin. Swiftly taken by cancer three months after they'd married. The trees reminded him. The first time he'd taken her camping in the bush, how scared she was, explained that growing up in Japan she'd never been in a wild forest. How her fear had turned gradually to comfort, to a love for deep woodland. Almost an addiction. They used to go east, past Winnipeg, into Ontario around Kenora, seeking the deep woods, and she'd make him drive the truck down the worst roads, branches lashing the doors, and then they'd walk. Daisy standing under a cluster of white pine, eyes shut, lost in a trance, listening to wind soughing through the needles. He let the memory in, let it go deep. He and Tse stepped forward with the section behind and he saw the trees thinning ahead.

"What you got, Jack?" Sharpcot called from behind.

He stepped out of the brief forest and turned slightly and called back, "More of the same." He got out the map and looked, then walked on and saw a four-way intersection ahead, the end of the vast block of jersey barriers on the left and cricket bats on the right. The passage ahead continuing indefinitely like a drawing exercise in perspective. They stepped over rough grass and came again to what must be a fragment of a road, this one perpendicular to the passage. As Sharpcot crossed it she called out, "Hold up. Tracks!"

She squatted and looked at the dirt and Wakely returned. They saw tire tracks among their own bootprints. The tracks followed the road, running north, came from under the concrete barriers on the left and disappeared beneath cricket bats on the right.

"This must be one of the dirt roads on the east side of Shilo, west of the exercise area," Sharpcot said.

"LAV tracks," Wakely said. "Bison or Kodiak."

"What's it mean?" Bronski asked.

No one answered. What did it mean? That at some point before the landscape changed a light armoured vehicle had travelled along this road. But under what circumstances?

The question hung there while Wakely turned and approached the new intersection. He paused before he crossed it, stood looking at the new blocks. Some kind of metal things, most around six centimetres long, many silver but also coloured metal: orange, blue, green, purple. On the right, flat clubs of some sort, but distinctly different than cricket bats; the majority were black or grey with bold lettering in yellow or orange, all 40 or 50 centimetres long, handles with a paddle at the end. He walked towards the first block, glanced up and down the north-south passage, disregarding potential threats, which it occurred to him is exactly the kind of situation in which threats were most likely to manifest. But he felt hopeless and reckless, eager for a resolution to all this.

"Clear," he called as an afterthought. He pried one of the metal strips out of the wall. It was a carabiner, D-shaped, made from red pressed steel, with a non-locking solid gate. He nudged its gate with a finger before pocketing it. He saw the others gathering around the block opposite. Deeks pulled one of the objects out and looked it over. The name "Garrett" was emblazoned in yellow across the back of the paddle. She waved it briefly over Virago and her rifle. The device chirped.

"Ma'am, would you happen to have any metal objects on your person?"

Sharpcot threw a look of annoyance at Wakely, which he saw was fringed by panic. He called the section to order, and they set out, passing between carabiners and metal detectors. He kept his eyes down, alternating between map and ground, and after a hundred metres they reached a new crossroads, with a block of machines on the left that Loko said looked like vegetable oil pressers — he recognized them from a documentary on Netflix about oil — each distinct in design and shape but all topped by a wide hopper into which olives or soybeans or sunflower seeds would be cast. The air coloured by a greasy scent. And on the right stood a mass of integrated circuits. Virago took one into her palm, a matte grey beetle with pin legs that plugged into a circuit board socket, on its back, a round window showing a tiny chip in a matrix of silver wires. Others they sampled from the wall were similar, varying in length but most of the same colour, some with gold legs or square windows. Wakely and Tse checked the passage and they continued west for a brief distance. Wakely observed the quality of the ground, and just where he expected it, the grass ceased at a boundary that ran perpendicular to the passage, another dirt road, but this one a foot below grade, its floor an expanse of unmarred dirt. He and Tse stopped at the verge and stood looking at this trough like at a river they had to cross.

"Dorking Road?" Sharpcot asked.

Wakely poked the map. "Looks like it."

"Why's it so deep?"

"Paved. Asphalt and gravel bed have been pulled up."

He could have used a more violent term — "torn" or "ripped" — but it wasn't like that. The pristine edges and smooth soil made it look as if the asphalt and its underlying aggregate had been delicately lifted, leaving an impression of the road, 30 centimetres deep and six metres wide. Where it emerged from the walls on both sides, the block material filled it.

Sharpcot stepped down into this trench and walked around, bootprints stark and clear.

"If this really is Dorking," Wakely said, looking at the map. "We walk a hundred metres we'll hit Edinburgh Road."

She put out her hand for the map and took the lead, holding it flat against her forearm, as if she needed it to navigate, as if she had options other than moving west between walls. They stepped across the roadbed and up the far ridge back to the prairie and began to walk and soon arrived at another block intersection. The composition of the monument on the left corner wasn't obvious from where they stood — a block of metallic edges, superficially similar to the soy sauce packs, but these were larger, thicker — but the right corner drew their attention, not just because it was made up of millions of alarm clocks, all of them of the same basic shape: round, topped with twin bells, yet diverse in colour and design, but because it was emitting a massive and layered din of unsynchronized ticking.

Unlike the blenders, the clocks were set at every orientation, upright, inverted, base or top outwards. The proliferation of varied clock dials invoked a startling effect, an abandonment of timekeeping, these instruments of time's measure recklessly stacked.

"Like an art installation," Virago said quietly.

The group slowed, studying the wall as they passed. White dials predominated, with many in other colours, while some were elaborately decorated with illustrations and words. Here was one that advertised Guinness, another for Air France. Numbers, roman numerals, stripes, dots. Most were the expected size, but some were novelty big — embedded near the top of the wall was a clock with a face two metres in diameter. Virago stepped close to examine a dime-sized one, made from brass, highly detailed.

The cases came in every finish and colour: copper, nickel, painted steel, coloured plastic. Hands varied in style, from conventional to ornate to abstract, all in myriad colours. Here was a Smurf with arms outstretched, index fingers indicating a time of 12:57.

While many had stopped, others, presumably battery-operated, or handwound with long springs, continued to run. The latter recognition brought a pulse of despair into Virago's chest. Thinking of the people who wound them. The people — where were the people?

The motion of second hands produced an eerie effect, the twitch of movement across the wall accompanying a chorus of ticking. Slow progress of minute hands around a million clock dials.

As they moved along, a new sound grew apparent. Among the ticking came a distant rattle. Wakely stalked forward, stopped. He stretched up and pulled a blue clock from the wall, and the rattle became ringing as the bells were liberated from the damping of neighbouring clocks. He silenced the alarm and pushed the clock back into its place.

"Hey, anyone got the time?" Bronski called.

"Time for some loser to state the most obvious joke ever," Deeks said.

Wakely did look at his watch. It read 1:58. He scanned the wall, and some of the clocks, those that were running, showed a more or less accurate time — at least to the minute. Gazing at eye level he picked out 9:58, 11:58, 7:58, 2:58, 4:58.

"What do you got, Jack?" Sharpcot asked as she came to his side. Before he could answer, a new rattle started, high up the wall, then another and another. But more than that, a muffled clattering began from inside the wall, and as a minute passed, the sound mounted, multiplied.

"We're hitting the hour," Virago said over the din. "Most people set their alarm on the hour. You get up at five or six or seven or eight."

"Get up at eight? Luxury!" Bronski cried.

"Right, right," Deeks said. "People wake up on the hour or half hour. Plus this kind of clock is a bitch to set to anything else, like 6:45 or whatever."

Across the face of the wall, many of the minute hands had reached 12.

Cheree Leclerc poked a clock face that showed 4:30. She could see the second hand moving.

"That one's way out," remarked Loko, who'd drawn up beside her.

"Not if you live in Newfoundland," Leclerc said. "Two and half hours ahead of central."

"How long will these ring for?" Bronski cried, looking crazed.

Sharpcot went to the wall opposite and plucked out one of the objects, a blister pack of pills, with a dozen bubbles, each holding a blue and white capsule, three of the cells empty. When she turned it over she saw pits of ruptured foil. She got down another, and this one had been plundered but for one cell, and inside it a lozenge of gum. Another, this one fully intact, filled with blue gel caps. Wakely beside her.

"We should get moving," he said.

"To what?" she wanted to say, looking past him down the corridor of blocks that stretched ceaselessly into the west. But she nodded, and they went on.

They went 60 metres and another trench a foot deep crossed the passage. Edinburgh Road. Sharpcot stood on its rim, gazing at the dirt. Edinburgh had just been repaved, maybe six weeks ago. She remembered traffic cones, steamroller, oily stink. Next day, an easy drive on a surface formerly potholed and fissured. Scent of fresh asphalt wafting through her open window.

Now it was a groove in the prairie.

She and Wakely exchanged glances.

66

"We should be looking at Gunner Arena," Wakely said, pointing. "Right there."

Sharpcot stepped forward with her eyes down, studying the ground. The sound of clock alarms began to subside. She stepped up from the roadbed, watched the ground under her feet pass through grass and dirt until she spotted a stark line. She went to a knee and touched the surface where two kinds of earth, subtly different in grain and colour, met in a perfectly straight line. Somebody came down beside her, and she glanced to see Virago looking too. Wakely moved past, walking where new grass and wildflowers sprouted.

"You see this, Private?" Sharpcot asked, tracing the line with a finger.

"I see it, Sarge," Virago replied. "Like a building was pulled up and infilled."

"Wiped off the map, Shilo's wiped off the fucking map," Bronski muttered.

"There's nothing left, Jack," Sharpcot said to Wakely, who was staring down the west passage. The clocks had returned to a clicking din, most of the alarms silenced.

"Yeah," he said.

"What do we do?"

He looked at her. She always knew what to do. It unnerved him right now that she didn't.

He lifted his rifle, switched off the safety, raised the barrel to the sky, and fired a single round. A shock ripped through the group as the noise of it resounded in the tight passageway and carried on for a moment before it faded.

"If there's someone around they'll hear that," Wakely said, but it was more of an excuse for action borne out of frustration and fear.

"So we wait?" Sharpcot asked.

Wakely wanted her to stand up. She looked small and vulnerable on her knees in the dirt. She wasn't a tall woman, but she carried an authority that repelled the disrespect she often endured as an Indigenous woman in the infantry. Kneeling, with that expression on her face, she had none of that. And he needed it back.

Sharpcot was too busy trying to manage the cascade of thoughts that followed the fact that a Canadian Forces base no longer existed, that its buildings and roads had been peeled off the surface of the Earth, while homogenous blocks containing billions of random products were set down in its place and the surrounding area to a distance she dared not guess at. Six kilometres to the southeast, past the bunker, but how far beyond? If they walked to the next crossroads and looked north would they see open prairie spreading to the horizon, maybe telephone poles and grain silos and cell towers?

She put a hand in her pocket and gripped her phone. Was there any point in taking it out? But she took it out and turned it on and stared at the screen as it powered up, her eyes fixed on the upper left where the words "No Service" were sure to appear, and did appear.

She heard a crackle of foil and looked to see Bronski and Loko picking blister packs out of the wall, the ground at their feet littered. Loko was sucking on a throat candy, and Bronski studied a package and asked, "What is Seroquel? If I take some what will happen?"

Wakely squatted in front of Sharpcot. "What next, Sarge?"

"They must've been evacuated," she said, not meeting his eye.

"Yeah," Wakely said.

"I mean we just need to locate them. Or what if they come looking for us?"

"Right. At the bunker."

She met his gaze and nodded. "Yes. The bunker."

"Where all our stuff is," Wakely added, thinking about supplies. Like him, everyone was hungry. He needed a bathroom break, had been holding on for a toilet at the base, and he was sure the others had to go.

As sunlight struck the top of the north wall at an increasingly acute angle, his mind moved towards night.

"Round them up, Jack," she told him.

"Let's get you to your feet first," he said, and stood, reaching out a hand.

She looked down, surprised to discover that she was still on the ground. Ignoring Wakely's hand, she climbed hastily to her feet, dusted her knees.

"Right, everyone," Wakely called loudly. "Hot showers and fresh food are going to have to wait. We are heading back to the bunker for possible rendezvous."

Sharpcot felt a stir of optimism at his words, despite the groundlessness of his speculation.

Before they set out, Wakely split the section by sex and sent them down separate passages to do their business. After quips about "why didn't you go when there were a million toilets?" and negotiation for tissues — of which Leclerc was well equipped, and begrudgingly shared, "But what if I have an allergy attack?" — the task was completed.

The section headed back through the maze, treading east between blister packs and clocks, computer chips and oil presses, metal detectors and carabiners, along the monolith of jersey barriers right and cricket bats left. Through the brief woods and past soy sauce. Blenders came on and they went into trees and reached the intersection of barriers, blenders, fog machines, and housekeeping carts. Turned right and came out of the trees and crossed the thirteenth green and continued south past plastic spoons, carpets, transformers, paperboard tubes, and toilets. A neighbourhood both familiar and foreign. Discipline unravelling as they increased the pace and Sharpcot saw the Christmas trees ahead, anticipating the corner, the left turn, preparing to enter the east-west corridor where she fully expected to meet a welcoming party, Lieutenant Blake and a group of others, maybe even Lieutenant-Colonel Wenz, hailing them as they approached, with big grins and cold beers, Man we really had you guys going, can you believe it? All this? Yeah, it's really something. So real! But look, it's all just an illusion which is achieved by . . . But here she had to halt the thought because she couldn't fathom how it had been achieved.

She watched Wakely and Tse round the corner ahead, caught their body language as they looked eastward, and knew by the droop of Wakely's shoulders, the way his pace slowed before he picked it up again, that he faced an empty passageway. That the same thoughts — the platoon waiting for their return — had likely crossed his mind, and been dashed. Even so, as she turned the corner and looked, disappointment slammed her. They passed wristbands, saw the sloppy protrusion where Virago had crammed them back into the wall a few hours earlier. All that seemed like days, weeks ago. Here were brake lathes, and ahead a small mound of dirt. As they drew up and stopped they saw that nothing had changed: the grass pressed flat where they'd stepped, and the hole into the bunker as they'd left it.

"What do you think, Sarge?" Wakely asked as he knocked a cigarette out of a pack. "What do we get?"

"Everything we can carry," she replied. "Rations, water, shelter, radios. All personal effects. Anything that might come in handy."

He lit the cigarette and took a drag, murmured, "Bit late to be setting out. You want to overnight here?"

Sharpcot considered the sky, saw sunlight glazing the tops of the toilets, the shadows acute as the sun fell into the west. At least day and night functioned as previously.

"Good point," she replied. "Make it happen."

Wakely moved in front of the six soldiers, looked them over with a sense of hopelessness. Corporal Tse didn't concern him, but rest were an inexperienced, fussy bunch he'd worked hard without success to mould. He believed firmly in folding misfits in with regulars — it's how he himself had succeeded, entering the Forces as a moody, dark youth unable to tolerate mainstream education, who got whipped into shape by placement in a tough section of serious soldiers, most of whom had faded out of the Forces after a few years while here he still was, a master corporal on the move.

But he knew that despicable motives — racist and sexist — had brought this group together. Elsie Sharpcot, a rising star of the Princess Patricia's Canadian Light Infantry, could not be ignored. She'd made sergeant, and needed to command, so they handed her the worst to watch her fail. "That'll show you can't put an Indian in charge." He'd heard that phrase more than once, and not muttered either. White men cackling over beer. He hadn't spoken up against that; it's not what you did. But he should have.

Bronski looked at him with expectation, rejecting reality, wondering when he'd see his wife and new baby. Virago, squinting, thoughtful, skeptical, storing it all up for social media. Leclerc, short, vulnerable, but alert, always absorbing. Loko, a man out of place wherever he went. Deeks, vaguely amused, inscrutable otherwise. And Tse, taking it all in stride.

"I know this is the last place any of you want to be," he told them in an even, reassuring voice, a style he'd learned from the best commanders in Afghanistan, who stayed steady while bullets flew and shrapnel rained down. "But it's just tonight. We're gone at first light. Prep your kits now for travel: hydration, food, bedding — as much as you can carry."

"Do we have to go below?" Loko asked. His face had blanched to the complexion of a corpse.

Wakely glanced at Sharpcot, who stepped forward.

"We'll need to post sentry. To guard this exit. You volunteering, Private Boyko?"

"Wait, you mean up here alone?"

"Jesus, Boyko, make up your mind," Deeks said.

"Quiet," Sharpcot snapped. "Anyone else? Private Virago, you're interested?"

"Yes, Sergeant."

"What are you grinning about, loser?" Bronski said to Loko, who suppressed his smile.

"Don't get all worked up, Private," Virago told him. "I came out of that hole pledging never to go back in."

"Well, you are going in, both of you, to get your rucks," Wakely said, and when Loko moaned, he added, "You're in the infantry, soldiers, and don't you forget it! At oh six hundred tomorrow we will assemble here with full kits, FFO. Orders will be disbursed at that time. Move!"

4

An old gooseneck desk lamp aimed at the ceiling illuminated the little office in which Sharpcot and Wakely sat. They'd reactivated the batteries, which immediately complained about their low state. Flashlights at the ready if they faded tonight. Bracing for darkness, they passed a flask back and forth.

"Is this stuff good or bad?" Sharpcot asked after a swig. "I don't know whiskey."

"It's the worst," Wakely replied, taking it back from her and drinking, making a face.

"Same effect, though. You know, you're the only white guy in the world I'd drink with."

"We've been through some shit," he said.

"Nothing like this," she replied, lifting her eyes to the ceiling.

He laughed, short and sharp. "It's ironic. The worst we've seen, yet nothing like the second worst. Moshtarak. Fire and lead." He looked lost, and Sharpcot knew where his mind was, but he shook himself free, said, "What are we gonna do, Elsie? What the hell is that up there?"

"It feels like the end of the world."

"That's what got you when you threw up?"

Sharpcot gripped the sides of her steel chair, a relic from the 60s. She pushed herself upright.

"That and . . ." she said, looking into his eyes.

"What?"

"The spoons. So many. Dor, what got me is it looked like all the spoons."

"All of them?"

"Yeah. In the world. Like, every plastic spoon *ever made*. Every one of them that could still be called a spoon. And the same with everything else. The housekeeping carts. The alarm clocks."

Wakely sat with that for a moment, then drank and passed the flask.

After a time, Sharpcot said, "We'll go west."

"Brandon?"

"Yeah."

"You figure towns and cities were spared?"

"Spared. Spared. That's a weird word, Wakely."

"Is it?"

Sharpcot leaned forward and put her head between her hands. She stayed like that for a long time.

"Elsie," Wakely called.

"What is this? What the hell is going on? Say it like it is. What do you see up there?"

"Stuff. Arranged."

"You ever seen anything like that in your life?"

"Just Costco," he replied with a grin, but she didn't see it.

"And who would do that? Who does that?"

Wakely thought it over. "Terrorists?"

"Terrorists destroy things," Sharpcot said. "They blow things up. This is organization. What kind of terrorist organizes shit? And that is some kickass arranging. I mean it's obsessive. It's like the work of an OCD lunatic."

They passed the flask. Sharpcot leaned forward and stared at the floor.

"You okay, Sarge? You're thinking about Lana."

"Course I am. Why don't the phones work, Jack? Why is there no GPS?"

"You want to go east? To Winnipeg?"

"I can't justify that. Too far. Brandon's closer."

"And if there is no Brandon?"

"Well, then Winnipeg."

"And if there's no Winnipeg?"

"Toronto. Ottawa. Washington, DC."

"How much stuff can there be?" Wakely wondered. "Maybe—" he said, sitting forward on the chair. "Maybe you go in a few feet and there's nothing there. The blocks are hollow inside. Who says it's spoons, or toilets, or alarm clocks all the way through? Maybe these are just facades with a space in the middle. A courtyard."

"We'd have to get up top to look."

"Even so, that's a lot of toilets. That is a lot of toilets up there."

"Yeah," Sharpcot said. "But there are a lot of toilets. Maybe it's like you say, some kind of local art project."

"Yeah. Except the base . . ."

"Just some crazy concept."

"And set up so fast. I don't know any project of that scale could happen so fast."

"Someone making a point about overconsumption. Like Greenpeace or something."

"Sure, it's something they'd do. But at that scale. And done in, what, three weeks? Less than that. I can't imagine any labour force or technology on Earth that could do that."

"What are you saying?" she barked.

"Shh. Keep it down."

"I know what you're saying. And I don't buy it."

"Jesus, Elsie. Easy now. At least keep your voice down."

"It doesn't make sense," she hissed. "It just doesn't."

"I know."

"It's just. You know. Lana. My mom. Everyone on the base. What the hell happened to Shilo? Where are the people?"

"I don't know, but there is an answer. There is an answer, and we're going to find it."

"Find Lana. Find everyone?"

"Find everyone. Find Lana. Find the platoon, the whole damn regiment. Find everyone in the goddamn world."

A groove of starry sky shot between the toilet wall and the brake lathes. Virago lay on her bedroll with her boots off and ruck beside her as she stared into the deep sky. The night moonless and warm.

Loko, a few metres away, muttered something in his sleep, something about chickens. Didn't his parents keep chickens? Or maybe he said Chiclets. Virago had fallen asleep earlier and slept deeply once she'd made it clear to Loko this wasn't a genial camp-out. He'd wanted to build a fire.

"With what fuel?" she'd demanded. "Toilets? You going to burn your boots?"

He started to say something about going off to collect firewood, silenced himself. He'd grown sullen after that, as his mind spiralled, and Virago drifted. Now he was out, and she lay awake, fresh from her own dreams. A concrete building, navigating corridors that grew increasingly constricted, leading a group of children, trying to escape.

It was godawful quiet. Crickets sounded on and off according to some unknown cue, and sometimes the wind whispered through the passage, curled through toilets and the frames of brake lathes, but she longed to hear something else: a transport truck sailing along a distant highway. A cross-country jet. She liked silence. But not this.

She'd never encountered a situation so completely unambiguous, yet totally senseless. Every time she tried to pursue those thoughts, they ran into a loop: What was this, who did it, where was everyone? What was this, who did it, where was everyone? She had to interrupt the cycle, or let it accelerate into a whir that pressed against the inside of her head with a centrifugal force that prefaced a headache. It was the kind of thinking she'd previously managed with alcohol, or worse. Trees were good for that too, or open water, or the prairie she was now lying on, which she could feel spreading away in all directions, to the forests in the east and the mountains in the west, which she had to reassure herself still existed. Because when her mind tried to navigate past toilets and carpets and blenders and alarm clocks, it just met more stuff, more of the junk of humankind piled up and sectioned in a maze of endless corridors.

She thought about her mother, who'd worked in a hotel during Virago's childhood. Pushing one of those housekeeping carts.

She felt abruptly scared. She'd thought the situation hypothetically frightening, but it didn't actually scare her until now. Her mind on her mom, who now worked as a receptionist in a physio office in Calgary. Her crisp voice, tinged with West Highlands accent, answering the phone with, "West Calgary Physiotherapy Clinic. This is Emma."

Virago thought about waking Loko. She envied him in his slumber. Wanted to talk to somebody. Wanted to hold somebody, or have somebody hold her. She was a hugger, but for a woman in the military there was no hugging. Too easily misinterpreted, as it would be now, if she asked Loko to hold her for a minute. He might be respectable about it now, understanding, might need it himself, in a platonic way, but it would never be the same between them. She'd have to stay on guard. If only it was Deeks or Leclerc or Sharpcot. Even Wakely or Tse would understand and be cool about it. But never Loko or Bronski.

An impulse to phone her parents overcame her. She half rose to grab her phone when she thought about the late hour. The fact that phones didn't work. Thoughts beyond that terrified her, so she fell back and fixed her eyes on the heavens. Waiting for the transit of a red-eye between Vancouver and Toronto. Spine rigid, hands balled into fists as she stared wide-eyed at a vacant sky.

Loko sat up, baffled at where he found himself. On the ground in a dark hallway under a night sky that blushed red in the east. Virago slumbering nearby. Her face coloured by dawn light. He got out his phone and turned it on. No signal, but it gave him the time: 5:46 a.m. He rose and shook out his boots and pulled them on, stood at the hole. Heard activity below, faint voices.

"Hey," he called.

"Hey," a voice replied, Bronski's, and a flashlight lanced upwards. "Coming up."

Bronski climbed the stepladder hauling his rifle and rucksack, teetering under the weight. When he got to the top, he threw it all down on the crater's brink.

"Don't help or nothing," he said to Loko.

"Didn't want to spoil the comedy."

"Hey, Virago," Bronski called. "Rise and shine."

"I'm awake, jerk. Some jerk just woke me up," Virago said as she got to her feet.

"Am I the jerk or you?" Loko murmured to Bronski.

"You're both jerks! What the hell time is it?"

"Coming on six," Loko replied.

She heard someone on the ladder and went to the hole and in the meagre light saw Deeks climbing up.

"Reinforcements. Thank god," Virago said.

"Hey, sister disco."

Deeks passed up her rifle and mounted the stepladder and when she saw Bronski and Loko facing away to the glowing east put her arms briefly around Virago and let go.

"You okay?" Deeks whispered.

"Nope."

Leclerc emerged next, and the three women convened away from the men until Tse and Wakely arrived.

"Pack up this shit," Wakely ordered, and Bronski scooted over to collect his things while Virago and Boyko rushed to roll their sleeping pads.

"Where's the sarge?" Bronski asked.

"I'm here," Sharpcot called from the bottom of the shaft. "Need some help."

"Bronski, help the sergeant," Wakely ordered, and when Bronski opened his mouth to complain Wakely jabbed a finger

78

at the ladder. He went down and returned carrying a hard-shelled case like a piece of carry-on luggage. As he swung it up it slipped from his grasp and struck the ground.

"Bronski, really?" Wakely said.

"Congrats on acing the Air Canada baggage handler test," Deeks announced.

Sharpcot reached ground level and granted permission to check devices. Phones appeared, but the situation remained unchanged. She left her own stowed. She'd charged it below and wanted to conserve the battery.

Once phones were away, Wakely lined everyone up for a rapid inspection, kits on the ground at their boots, heels together and feet turned out, backs straight, shoulders squared, rifles at rest. He'd never seen them so competently arranged. When shit gets real.

By now the sun had risen but lay concealed beyond blocks. Another warm, clear day.

Sharpcot went down the line. She cited small violations — magazines poorly arranged in pouches, a shirt untucked, a smoke grenade in a bad spot, and saw each instantly corrected. Looked into Cheree Leclerc's unwavering stare, studied Bronski's pursed lips. Loko swallowed as she stepped before him. Deeks's expression atypically unsardonic. Virago's expression verging on despair. Tse, eyes narrowed, intense, primed. Wakely took his spot at the end of her line, and she looked him over, brushed dirt from his shoulder. He did not react, gazed into the distance, despite no distance to gaze into.

She let them hold for two minutes until she could feel the strain, then spoke a casual, "Stand at ease."

They relaxed, feet moving apart, a collective exhalation. She'd been too blithe with them yesterday, unnerved by what they'd discovered. Not today.

"As you know, we are in a situation which no one can satis-factorily explain," Sharpcot said. "I want to remind you that you are soldiers, first and foremost, and you signed up to protect the sovereignty of Canada, however that job manifests. Today, and over the next few days, that means exploration and travel. You will stay alert and do as you are told. Protocol does not change. For soldiers, it does not change. Clear?"

"Sergeant Sharpcot!" came the united reply.

"I don't know if the situation is hostile, but we are going to treat it as such. Take care of each other. No one fires their weapon without my authorization, or that of the 2IC. Got that?"

"Sergeant Sharpcot!" they called again, louder.

As they marshalled for departure, Virago called to Sharpcot, "What about this, Sarge?" Sharpcot glanced at Virago, who stood beside the hard-shelled case carried up from the bunker. "I'm pretty sure I know what's inside. Might be useful."

"Open it up."

Virago kneeled at the case and tripped the clasps, raised the lid. Pieces of white hardware, some kind of disassembled device, rested in foam cutouts.

Virago sat back. "It's what I thought. A drone."

"Can you fly it?"

"Sure. My previous CO sent me to a class. Thought I'd be good at it."

"Because you're an Instagram queen?" Deeks said.

"Just my interest in photography, I suppose."

Sharpcot glanced at Wakely, now standing beside her and regarding the hardware in the case.

"How long to assemble and get it airborne?" Wakely asked.

"A couple of minutes."

Wakely peered into the east where the sun glanced off toilets and cast light along the avenue. "How's the light? Good enough for the camera on this thing?"

"Sure."

"Right," Sharpcot said. "Let's get it in the sky. Survey the area."

Virago went to work on the machine, fit four rotor booms into a central pod, extended the legs, locked the battery into the top, and latched a spherical camera gimbal into the base. She pulled what looked like a tablet computer from a slot in the case, powered it up.

Sharpcot and Wakely watched over her shoulder as she activated the camera, which transmitted a blurry closeup of grass and soil. She tapped the screen and the camera swivelled. She fiddled with settings along the right margin, called up a map.

"This is a stored overview of what would be the battlefield, the zone around Shilo. But I'm not getting a GPS fix, can't determine our actual location."

"Can you still fly it?" Wakely asked.

"Sure. I can centre the map manually where we are, about here." She tapped a location to the bottom right of CFB Shilo, and the map reoriented itself.

"What about all the RF interference," Sharpcot asked. "Preventing us from communicating, blocking the radio and cell service and GPS?"

Virago took a few steps back from the drone while studying the screen. "No effect at this range. The signal is strong. Where to?"

Sharpcot regarded the sky. "Send it straight up. Maybe 500 feet? But stop the ascent at the first sign of signal loss."

Virago tapped the screen, and the drone's rotors flicked on, cutting the air in the enclosed space with a sharp whine. It kicked up a cloud of dust and everyone took a reflexive step back. Virago tapped a slider and the motors pitched higher. The craft rose. Wakely started to caution her about clipping the walls, but Virago sent it up, vertical and true. He saw in a small window at the corner of the screen a view of themselves, the section, standing there, himself and Sharpcot and Virago observing the screen, the others with heads raised to watch.

The drone cleared the walls, revealing an overhead view of toilets and brake lathes, and between them, the dark channel of the passageway, their own figures faint in shadow as the camera's aperture cinched to accommodate the dazzle of sunlight.

"Can you make it fullscreen?" Sharpcot asked, and Virago tapped a button, swapping out the map for a camera view. Sharpcot glanced at the rising drone, then looked at the screen and saw the scene expand, confirming that the stacks of toilets and brake lathes were solid through their cores. So much for the theory of walls of stuff surrounding empty courtyards.

The drone continued to rise, and on the screen, the avenue shrank as toilets and lathes swept outwards. At the lower left, a southbound corridor appeared, with two rectangles of different textures: the dense, multicoloured lattice of wristbands, and south of that, below another canyon of precisely the same width as the one in which the section stood, a disorganized matrix of squares, each of roughly the same size, but in silver, black, red, and yellow: measuring tapes.

The toilets resolved into a wide but narrow block, bordered on the north by a corridor, then a huge matrix of multi-sized holes: the tops of the paperboard tubes, running a good distance north and followed by the carpets, their patterned tops like icons for rugs, traditional designs laid out in an immense grid. The eastern boundary of tubes and rugs lay directly north of where they stood, and east of that rested a new block comprised of a dense, pixelated grain of small objects, impossible at this altitude to determine what. The view widened to show a mass of dark green at the bottom left — fake Christmas trees — and above that the larger slabs of electrical transformers. Still the craft rose, showing jersey barriers, plastic spoons, some kind of round-cornered rectangles in muted colours adjacent the spoons. To the east, areas unexplored came into view, and it was the same matrix of rectangles that varied in size and texture depending on their composition, pixelated when composed of tiny objects, tiled when they were mid-sized, and varying patchworks of still larger items. One of the latter could have been trampolines, mesh squares and circles.

Sharpcot noted that every block's corner formed a perfect right angle. She also saw that four-way intersections predominated, but there were ample T-intersections too. Most importantly, she saw no dead ends. Every corridor, without exception, joined with another. They would not have to worry about blind alleys.

Virago swallowed her nausea at what she saw unfolding, the vastness of it. "Holding at five hundred feet AGL," she announced. The entire section clustered behind her, straining to see the screen.

"Mang, this is completely fucked up."

"Shut it, Bronski," Sharpcot ordered. "Nobody say a thing for a minute."

All fell silent, listening to the vexed whine of the drone's rotors. It was a dot in the sky, awash in yellow light.

Sharpcot cleared her throat. "Nice work, Virago. Can you pan the camera up?"

"Which way?"

"Out towards Shilo."

Virago worked the controls and the scene shifted, the grid sliding past and expanding as the camera took in fresh landscape. They could see housekeeping carts and then the breathtaking expanse of jersey barriers. Smaller blocks surrounded it, and Wakely got out his notebook and named a few off: fog machines, blenders, soy sauce packs, cricket bats. Nothing demarked CFB Shilo's location, but Wakely indicated blister packs and alarm clocks, where they'd found evidence of the hockey arena's foundation. And beyond that, an infinite continuation of the lattice, rectangles enormous and small, like farm fields growing sundry crops of disparate texture and colour.

Virago stilled the camera on that angle, asked, "You want me to keep going?"

Sharpcot felt sick. She didn't want to see more but thought of that time she'd felt a lump in her breast while showering, the bolt of fear it had prompted. She'd lost an aunt to breast cancer. She chose to ignore it, probably nothing, why get worked up? But then sitting at breakfast with Lana, watching the girl eat toast, how she hoped her child would never ignore a symptom for fear of truth, and it was like the girl read Elsie's mind, for she stopped eating and cried, "Oh my god, what is it? Tell me right now!" Sharpcot spilled it all, and Lana cried and pleaded for her to go to the doctor. A biopsy revealed a small, malignant tumour, which had been removed and treated. Knew she'd be dead now if it hadn't been for Lana. Dead for evading reality.

"Take it as high as it'll go."

Virago tapped the controls and the drone rose, the whine of its motors diminishing as it gained altitude. A minute and a half passed before it reached a thousand feet AGL, and the sound of it was a mild buzz, an insect. A dot in the middle of the sky.

On the screen a large area lay visible, and it was nothing but rectangles of different hues and textures, and the black grooves of avenues separating them.

"Pan about 10 degrees and up. Let's see if we can spot Brandon."

The lens shifted, and everyone hoped desperately for a break in the relentless grid. But the small city failed to appear. Sharpcot searched her memory for its tallest structure, probably the tan Scotiabank building at 10th and Rosser, and ascertained that at 11 or 12 storeys it stood only slightly taller than these blocks. The top, if the building still stood, would represent a small, obscure protuberance in the landscape.

"Wait, what's that?" Wakely asked, pointing at the screen. "Zoom in there."

Virago manipulated the controls; the scene enlarged until a squiggle that cut across the grid became distinct against the rigid geometry of the landscape.

"What is it?" Sharpcot asked.

"The river. The Assiniboine," Wakely said. "Private, bring the camera up and around to the north."

The camera started panning. Haze made it impossible to determine if the grid continued all the way to the horizon.

"Stop," Sharpcot ordered, and Virago halted the pan. "There, does that look like Sewell Lake?" She pointed at a dark, irregular shape cut out in the grid.

"I'd say so," Wakely said. "How about a full, 360-degree pan?"

Virago sent the camera pivoting clockwise, and the latticed landscape, broken by straight, black lines, stretched away everywhere as far as they could see. In the east, the sun hove into view, a huge blot of white that dimmed the landscape as the camera's aperture contracted and hexagons scattered across the image. Something glinted below the sun's orb, and Wakely called out, "Might be more water. Or something shiny," as the camera continued its scan. The land here was immensely flat. Sharpcot asked, "Anyone know how to calculate distance to horizon based on altitude?"

Cheree Leclerc cleared her throat. "It's basic Pythagoras. I can do it with my phone's calculator."

Leclerc bent to her pack and came up with her phone. She powered it on and keyed in numbers, muttered as she computed, "Drone at a thousand feet, let's call that 304 metres, plus Earth's radius six point four million metres ..." She worked the numbers, announced, "Sixty-five thousand metres."

"Right. So distance to horizon is about 65 kilometres," Sharpcot said. "Double that for total view, horizon to horizon, and you get 130 klicks. The maze is at least that big."

Bronski emitted a blurt of deranged laughter.

"Shut it, Bronski," Wakely warned.

"Can you take it higher?" Sharpcot asked.

"Software limits it to 1000 feet. But I know the trick to override that."

"How much flight time left?"

"Just under 10 minutes. Battery had only a partial charge to start."

"Take it higher," Sharpcot said, and Virago worked the controls, sent the craft up. As it rose she continued to swivel the camera, taking in an increasingly broad view of the land-scape. Altitude brought into view no respite from the matrix. It extended continuously in all directions.

"How high can you go?" Wakely asked.

"I don't know. I'll just keep sending it up. Horizontal range is three kilometres."

"Leclerc, at 3000 metres, what's the distance to the horizon? How far in theory could we see?"

Leclerc did the calculation. "Almost 200 kilometres."

"To Winnipeg. Or almost," Sharpcot stated.

Wakely nodded, frowning. "Except for this haze. Lit by the low sun. Make more sense to try later, midday." Sharpcot gave him a hard look, and he added, "Sergeant."

"Steady as she goes, Private. Keep climbing."

They could no longer hear the drone, and when Wakely stared skyward the machine appeared as a single pixel in the sky's lush indigo. To the left he spied a raptor pitching about, unconcerned by the drone. The snub of its head swivelled about, making Wakely think of the drone's camera, both of them seeking something of consequence. For the bird, prey. For the drone, civilization.

He looked at the ground, wondering if mice or other rodents roamed these passageways, and if the bird — he didn't know birds, if it was eagle or hawk or falcon — could spot them down here, and swoop into the narrow passageways to nail them. Mice. Rats. Voles. How did the maze impact wildlife? It had to be devastating. Maybe not at the micro level, for microorganisms, worms, bugs. But what about prairie dogs, rabbits, foxes, wolves, deer, caribou, elk? Migration routes. Access to plants, prey. To water.

Sharpcot's voice snapped him back. "What are those? Swing the camera back!"

On the display, a sparse scattering of what looked like towers, each of identical height, some covering vast areas, dotted the maze at the horizon. They leaned closer to look, but the vista was growing increasingly unstable as the drone's propellers dug into ever-thinning air and stabilizers fought to steady the image.

"Can you zoom?" Sharpcot asked, and Virago tapped at the controls. The image abruptly shuddered as the craft pitched sideways.

"What's happening?" Sharpcot demanded.

"Battery's almost dead. Looks like enough to transmit video, but the motors are failing."

Sharpcot squinted at the sky, initially saw nothing but flat blue, then spied a speck, careening northward. The screen displayed a blur of sky-grid-sky as the craft tumbled. Everyone silent for minutes as they switched attention between screen and sky. The final view before the screen went dark was a sea of banjos. Red text showed the words "Contact Lost." An instant later, they heard from far off the crack of the drone's impact, accompanied by a dissonant twang.

Wakely watched the effects ripple through the group: Loko shook his arms out and paced, while Tse fiddled with the scope on his weapon. Leclerc powered off her phone and tucked it away. Bronski glared at the heavens, while Deeks stuck a cigarette into the corner of her mouth, muttered, "Mind if I?" Virago kneeled at the drone's case and carefully slid the tablet back into its slot, closed the lid, secured the latches.

Wakely saw Deeks smoking and wanted one himself, thought he shouldn't, then thought fuck it. Sharpcot gave him a hard look as he put one in his mouth. He held the pack out. She shook her head and nodded for him to follow her down the passage.

"You okay, Sarge?" he asked as he lit the cigarette.

"You saw that landscape, what we're facing. You tell me if you're okay."

He looked at the ground, shook his head. "Have to be. And so do you."

She nodded. "I know it."

They were silent a long time. Wakely studied his cigarette, said, "We're going to run out of these."

"We're going to run out of everything. Which way, Jack? Where to now?"

Wakely considered the question. "Brandon's out. North there's nothing. South will get us to the border, about 85 klicks, but it's just more prairie."

Sharpcot wished he would say it, make it his idea, not hers. But he didn't. "Winnipeg in what, five, six days?"

He nodded, then saw her expression. "Hey, El, it's good. It's not just about Lana and we know it. Winnipeg makes sense. Closest major city. The capital."

"Thank you," she replied, placed her hand briefly on his forearm. She glanced at the soldiers, saw that most had succumbed to fiddling with phones, aimlessly prodding apps, adjusting settings, hoping to find the key to acquiring a signal. But she understood now why they had no contact. Interference, like deliberate jamming, would've affected communication with the drone, but that hadn't happened. Even at peak altitude it had operated and broadcast flawlessly.

The cell phone radio band wasn't jammed — it didn't exist. There were no signals because there were no transceivers. All the world's cell towers lay stacked and idle in some block somewhere. Likewise for radio and TV transmitters, police and fire and aviation and marine radios. Radar and aircraft VOR beacons. Wireless access points. Bluetooth speakers. Remote control toys. Microwave ovens.

Those who hadn't figured this out would soon. And they'd need discipline to hold it together. She looked at Wakely and narrowed her eyes. "Round 'em up, Jack."

Wakely finished his cigarette, crushed it under a boot, and strode to the section. Sharpcot watched him whip them into shape. It took two minutes, and he barely raised his voice. Only Bronski, panicked about finding out if his kid had been born yet, gave trouble, and he paid in pushups.

"You are still members of the infantry," Wakely reminded them. "And will remain so, until I tell you otherwise. Is that understood?"

"Master Corporal!" they responded.

Sharpcot approached, and Wakely stood aside.

"Three Section," she said. "Things look bad. The base is gone. So is Brandon, as far as we can tell. And you saw the drone's view: these blocks go on in every direction.

"We have two priorities. Number one is survival. We've got food and water. Some. But we'll have to conserve. Looks like rivers and lakes have not been—" Sharpcot hesitated, searching for the right word. "Compromised. That water should be potable, at least with the use of purification tablets you should all have in your kits. Hold steady, Private Leclerc. We'll take inventory shortly. We don't know what we're going to encounter in this maze. Maybe we'll find food. And maybe we won't. Rivers and lakes should have fish in them. Maybe we'll encounter animals we can kill and eat. We will do whatever we must to stay alive.

"Second priority is to find somebody, anybody, who can tell us what happened while we were in that bunker. And we need to find our people, and by that, I mean those in authority, but also those important to us. Our — families and friends."

She paused to suppress the emotion clouding her voice.

"People we care about are out there somewhere. And they're wondering about us too. Survival, and finding our people. Anything that gets in the way of pursuing those two goals will not be tolerated. You are still in the army. You still, every one of you, belong to me. And I will not take bullshit from any of you, for any reason. Is that clear?"

"Sergeant Sharpcot," the section replied somewhat in unison.

"Is that clear?" she bellowed.

"Sergeant Sharpcot!" they shouted back.

"Each of you will report to Corporal Tse an inventory of your supplies. We move in 10 minutes."

She stepped back and the soldiers broke up, and Tse went among them as they emptied rucksacks on the ground, and he took it all down on a notepad. When he finished with Private Virago she gathered her pack and rifle, donned helmet and sunglasses, came to stand beside Sharpcot.

"So which way are we going, Sarge?" Virago asked.

"East," Sharpcot replied curtly.

"If I may ask: What's our actual destination?" Leclerc queried as she repacked her supplies.

Wakely stiffened and said, "Winnipeg, soldier. The provincial capital."

In a few minutes they stood in a neat row, buttoned-down, kits donned, rifles at patrol carry.

"This is what it's come to," Loko muttered to Bronski.

"Humping to Winnipeg," Bronski murmured back.

"Title of the worst Canadian film ever," Deeks whispered.

"Quiet," Wakely shouted.

"Three Section, let's roll," Sharpcot called, and they set off into the rising sun.

5

The righthand wall of brake lathes ended at a southbound alley, which they checked according to protocol, and crossed. The edifice on the corner opposite stood massive and metallic grey and formed from billions of tiny objects: cotter pins, "split pins" if you were British, or so Leclerc explained. Metal fasteners made from a length of stiff wire, bent to form a small ring at one end, two tines that would be kinked to retain the pin in a hole, as at the end of an axle holding a wheel in place. Steel, brass, bronze, aluminum. Some were new, most old, corroded, twisted, broken. The majority were small, a few millimetres in length, many a centimetre or two, making the wall dense with texture. A scattering of larger ones, five or six centimetres long, lay embedded like fossils in the matrix of finer pins.

Objects like these stacked in such a fashion would have to subside, cascade like a thick fluid into the passageway, but the wall stood flat and solid and perfectly vertical. Something held it all together, yet the pins were easily prized out.

"Feels magnetic," Leclerc said as she pulled one out, then set it back in place. "The attraction that diminishes rapidly when you come away, then draws back when you're near. Inverse cube rule."

"But with that kind of magnetic force, shouldn't it be pulling other metal, like our rifles?" Virago asked, as she held her C7 to the wall and pulled it back without effort or effect.

"Then what is it? Static?" Deeks asked.

"Feels like invisible Velcro," Bronski said. "Invisible, *silent* Velcro." He tore open one of the pockets on his vest for effect.

"Maybe something we don't even know about. Military secret," Deeks said.

"But we're military," Loko remarked.

"Bottom end of the military," Deeks said. "Nothing but boots."

"What if it's something not even from Earth?" Virago said. "Some kind of alien technology."

"Shut that crap right now," Sharpcot barked. "I don't recall giving you permission to stop. Move it!"

The section resumed their eastward march, and the cotter pin block soon ended, while on the left the toilets also ceased, and they came to a crossroads. Wakely and Tse checked it north and south, Wakely noting that the cotter pins ran only 50 metres down before ending at a new block formed from some featureless objects in black and grey. On and on down the distance, he saw walls and breaks and more walls, each of some new material and quality.

He slipped out his notebook, wrote "cotter pins," then looking at the new monuments that formed the opposite corners, "coat trees," and after a moment examining the other, "calculators," which he erased and wrote, "mechanical adding machines." These were antique computers, with steel cases in black and grey and dark green, or bare silver, or textured with grey or black wrinkle paint, some in brown or black Bakelite, others in wood. They had nameplates or stencilled manufacturer names: Victor, RC Allen, Sundstrand, Barrett, Olivetti, Precisa, Remington Rand, American, Burroughs, McCaskey. A few emblazoned with a letter B on a red disc. They assumed inconsistent orientations, tops out showing the ivory and black keys, bases with rubberized feet, some with their backs cradling a scroll of yellowing paper. Where a machine's right side faced outwards there sometimes protruded a steel lever with a worn handle, to be pulled to stamp figures onto tape. The block, not large — it went only 60 metres in each direction — smelled of machine oil but also old paper, a library scent.

"These must be worth a fortune," Bronski muttered.

"They're beautiful," Virago said, snapping photos with her phone.

"All right, troops," Sharpcot bellowed. "Get a move on. This is not a sightseeing tour."

She glanced at the objects opposite, coat trees, all laid out horizontally, rods of wood or steel, with splayed bases and hooks. Looking ahead she saw an increasing variance in the terrain, and that the corridor sloped downwards, with the blocks ranging off into the distance following the ground's contour, maintaining with eerie precision the nine-storey height above the ground.

The section picked up the pace. Coat trees continued on the right. Adding machines were replaced by thousands of vertical columns in varying widths, from a few centimetres to a metre wide, with the majority in the 20-centimetre range, and all faced by masses of steel teeth of varying density. The section gazed up at this lethal bulwark, which extended for a hundred metres.

"What are they?" Virago wondered, snapping photos.

"Stacked circular saw blades," Loko suggested.

Wakely nodded. "Makes sense. Most are the standard seven and a quarter inches." He jotted it down.

They continued at a steady pace, passing many blocks, some built from masses of objects they could not identify: a narrow stack of plastic wafers, circular with a corrugated surface, and then a million metal brackets in silver and black that might've been bicycle handlebar risers, followed by flexible carbon fibre rods with steel mounts, holes drilled for rivets, their function unknown until Corporal Tse had one in his hand. "Static wicks. Fixed to aircraft to discharge static electricity."

A wall of chalkboard erasers spiced the air with a scent that brought Sharpcot's thoughts to Lana in her summer school classroom. She desperately tried to imagine her there, at a desk, scowling at her teacher.

From the next block, Bronski pulled out a small tool, a digital caliper with an LCD screen. He flicked the power switch.

"Hey, this thing works," he cried. "Whatever the fuck it is."

"It's a micrometer," Leclerc explained. "Used to precisely measure minuscule objects."

"Finally something that can detect your brain, Bronski," Deeks said.

"Fuck you, Deeks."

"I'm sure he has other tiny parts it can measure," Virago said.

Bronski wound up to deliver another stinging rebuttal, which Wakely silenced with a glance.

An enormous monolith, mostly red, followed the slender caliper tower: fire extinguishers, stacked upright in orderly rows, most following the standard morphology: red tank, black hose, silver discharge lever with a pressure gauge, and a dataplate with instructions, warnings, supplier phone, who to contact for service and replacement. The plates in every language: English, French, German, Japanese, Thai, Chinese, Korean, Cyrillic, Arabic. Some extinguishers were tagged with a service card showing a handwritten date, initials, punchcarded by year.

A few of the canisters were antique, made from nickel or copper or brass, some with intricately embossed nameplates. The block went on for a kilometre, while on the left they passed a conglomeration of smokers' poles, the kind set at a building's entrance to accept cigarette butts. After that came a smaller mass of what Deeks stated with authority were orange juice machines — she'd worked in a café where the thing ran all summer, consuming vast quantities of oranges and yielding comparatively little juice. The air as they walked past seasoned with a scent of oranges.

Past noon and the heat stifling, complaints suppressed only by Wakely's warnings, Sharpcot called a stop in a passageway between jet turbines — cylinders ranging in diameter from a foot to over 12 feet, stacked every which way. The soldiers gaped into turbofan blades or nozzles, or viewed them in profile: silver, white, blue, warning labels, British Airways, KLM, FedEx, a couple with access doors gone or shells stripped away and compressor blades visible, nests of wiring and tubing. Mount points where the engine would be bolted to the aircraft, feeds for control systems and fuel. Some damaged, dented, scorched, one with a smashed cowling, others old, corroded.

The wall opposite was formed from pool noodles: narrow polyethylene foam cylinders, some stacked in profile, others in cross-section, creating a sickening array of pastel. Somebody said it looked like Froot Loops breakfast cereal. The air stank of kerosene and oil, like an airport tarmac.

Sharpcot remembered stepping off the plane in Afghanistan, fresh from the chill of Manitoba autumn, slammed by the heat, stink of jet fuel, the thud of helicopter blades as an American Blackhawk lifted off and thundered low overhead. She'd been on the ground five minutes, trying to orient herself, gathering gear and succumbing to the realization that people here wanted to kill her, when the world rocked with a massive concussion that turned out to be Canadian artillery firing on a Taliban position six klicks away.

She watched these young soldiers shuck their kits, sip from water bottles and canteens, light cigarettes as they spread out on the grass. An easy deployment, superficially. But at least Afghanistan existed in a world they had known still existed.

Loko, chewing on a Snickers bar, said, "I heard in England they call those 'woggles.'"

"What, in England a jet engine is called a 'woggle'?" Bronski asked.

"No, you idiot," Virago said. "Pool noodles.'"

Deeks spoke up in a convincing British accent: "Captain, I'm throttling up the woggles. Let's get this bird in the air!"

95

Sharpcot walked to Wakely, who was pacing the corridor, smoking, still fully kitted, studying the engines. "Jack, you should eat and rest."

"I could say the same for you," he replied.

"Not hungry."

"Me neither."

"I see. We're going to out-tough one another."

"We always do," he replied.

"I always win."

"True," he admitted. "That Indigenous spirit."

"Sit down and eat something, white man."

She put up her fist and he tapped it with his own, and he walked further down the row to investigate a huge engine. He could manage heat and hunger. This was a cakewalk compared to Afghanistan, where they trudged in full gear through terrific heat, tracing the footprints of the guy in front to keep from stepping on an IED. Everything in life was easier than that. Everything except losing Daisy.

He arrived at an enormous cylinder three metres in diameter containing a fan surrounding a dome painted with a white spiral. The lip of the cowling stood above waist height, and he propped his rifle and hopped up and sat with his legs dangling like a kid in a highchair. He set his helmet and ruck beside him, took a drink of warm water from his CamelBak before he threw it off and wriggled out of his jacket and vest until he sat in his T-shirt, armpits sweatstained.

He got a strawberry applesauce from his pack, peeled back the lid, rummaged around until he came up with a white plastic spoon. Studied it thoughtfully: another plastic spoon. He peered down the corridor at the section, saw that Sharpcot still hadn't sat down, was stepping among the section.

She stopped in front of Loko, who was using a flameless ration heater to warm a pork chow mein sachet.

"You planning to waste an FRH for every meal, soldier?"

"No one said not to, Sarge."

96

"'You didn't order me not to be an idiot, Sarge,'" Deeks said, mimicking his cadence.

Sharpcot narrowed her eyes at Deeks, returned her attention to Loko. "Private Boyko, Deeks is right. I need you to be autonomous, not just follow explicit orders. To independently make wise choices. Consider the circumstances and behave accordingly."

"Yes, Sergeant."

"I'm not talking shit, Private. I'm being very specific." She addressed the group, "All of you. You've spent your lives consuming resources and chucking the waste without a thought. We can't afford that now. Everything you consume has a consequence. It always did, but now it'll affect you directly."

She continued along the passage a distance from the group, set down her rifle and squatted, got a cereal bar from her ruck.

"That there's some fine Indian wisdom," Bronski muttered.

"Shut the fuck up, Bronski," Virago said.

Perched on the engine, Wakely got his notebook out. He added pool noodles and jet engines. He wrote them small, as the first couple of pages were already full. It sent his mind outward, into the expansiveness of the maze. The endlessness of it, the claustrophobia. Pool noodles four metres from his face.

He let Daisy into his mind. The way she would throw away nothing that could be mended, and she seemed capable of mending anything with needle and thread. He ran the ball of his thumb along a line of stitching on his TAC vest, where she'd sewn a tear. He could think about her and feel good, but there was a price: her absence. She'd been spared all this, though. Whatever this was.

Thank god for the infantry, or he would've offed himself the day of her funeral. He'd come close, knew he could do it right — he'd seen enough death in Afghanistan to know how death operates. Two close friends had done it. Darren Grainger put a gun in his mouth in the basement of his parents' house in Calgary six months after coming home. And Shane LeBlanc had scaled the anti-suicide barrier on the Bloor Viaduct in Toronto and tossed himself into the Don River. That was Shane to the end, determined to illustrate design failure through practical demonstration.

He'd coped through focused meditation of what his death would look like. Imagined it as a film sequence. Medium shot: a man walks into the woods carrying a shotgun. A late spring morning, sun shining. We think he's going hunting. He moves among the trees, spots a doe frozen in a clearing, watching his approach, ear twitching. He sees it, pauses and sighs, maybe smiles a little, but then continues through the brush until he finds a clearing beside a stream. Sits against the bole of an oak and puts the shotgun's barrel into his mouth. Here he conjured it with unflinching detail. He did not cut away. The closeup of his finger on the trigger, the explosion of buckshot blasting through his head. A fountain of gore. The deer sprinting away.

The film goes time-lapse: body slumped against the tree, invasion of maggots and microbes. Decay and dissolution. And in the end, nothing but a clothed skeleton with a shattered skull, a rusting shotgun across its lap, discovered years later by a lone hiker.

By imagining it forcefully, in shocking detail, over and over, he stopped wanting it. Whenever the impulse intervened, he would play that film in his head, and the feeling would cease.

He looked into the notebook in his lap. Pool noodles. Jet engines. It was important to document all this, but he couldn't think why. To inform someone coming the other way?

Would they meet someone? He took a breath and closed his eyes, imagining it. Squinting down the corridor at an approaching group. He puts up a hand in greeting. It's a schoolteacher and her class of six-year-olds. Each gripping a yellow rope as they wander the maze. A class trip to the end of the world.

He opened his eyes. Down the row, the section was chatting, ribbing one another, theorizing. Bronski going on about his kid, this potential baby that should have arrived by now — his hope and dread at the thought. But aside from the local noise, Wakely sensed silence. Not an audio silence. An existential one. Immense and superlative.

Or an electromagnetic one. He thought about broadcast energy, from radio and TV stations, signals beaming from towers and satellites. Every person with a phone, a transceiver in their pocket. Photons slicing through our bodies, every minute of the day. He felt different, physically different, in his skin, in his bones. A tension to which he'd grown accustomed now absent. Despite everything, despite the state of the world, possibly ended, he felt a kind of relief. Relief at the end of some futile enterprise. Civilization.

Sharpcot came up the passage.

"You ready to move, Jack?"

"When you are."

"Just talk to me a minute."

"All right."

Sharpcot glanced away, hesitating, something she rarely did.

"It's a shit show," Wakely said.

"Yeah. Though we've been in shit shows before. This is more than that. This is a radical world transformation."

"RWT." This was a thing they did, a military thing: collapse phrases into acronyms.

"Right, yes. RWT. So who's responsible?"

He thought the question rhetorical, until she met his eye. "Well," he replied, and paused. "Let's call it a crime we're trying to solve. Who are the suspects?"

"That's just the thing — there are none. No one could collect everything in the world and organize it like this. Not in three weeks. Or ever," she replied.

"Right. So we've got an MO that no one we know could pull off."

"Correct."

"What are they saying?" he asked, nodding towards the section.

"Aliens," she replied.

He laughed, but without humour. "Sounds crazy to say it out loud."

"They're calling them 'Accruers.' They started with 'Collectors' but Deeks said it sounds like they bug you to pay your phone bill. Leclerc went through synonyms until they landed on Accruers."

"So the MO is a big unknown. Think of the way the stuff in these walls sticks together. It's like an advanced alien technology."

"AAT," Sharpcot said with a smirk. "Robots and algorithms. That's how you do something on this scale, this fast. A lot of programmed robots."

"An RWT achieved through AAT, using R&As. And what about motive? And why like this?" he said, waving at the stacks of goods.

"Gather resources. Harvest the manufactured creations of humanity. The MCHs."

"Meaning they'll be back. To collect said MCHs."

Sharpcot involuntarily snugged the rifle to her shoulder but kept the barrel lowered.

"We won't be able to do anything about it, Elsie. If all the armed forces of Earth couldn't prevent this, what can we do?"

"Yeah. Well, they'll still have to deal with me if they come back. So what did they do with the people?"

"They left the bugs and birds alone, far as I can tell," he replied. "I saw a prairie dog down one of the alleys we passed."

"But the animals didn't fight back."

He was going to suggest that maybe there was no fight. Technology this sophisticated could probably neutralize any human threat. Missiles gently subdued. Fighter jets tenderly overcome. You wouldn't want to damage resources you intended to collect. But she didn't need that right now. Right now she needed to know that Lana and all the people she cared for were safe and alive somewhere. But he didn't say it. Because he didn't think it so.

She turned and strode down the corridor, calling, "All right, Three Section, pack it up, we are moving. Where the hell is Boyko?"

"Up here," Loko called, and Sharpcot looked to see him 10 metres above, clinging to one nacelle of a corroding dual-turbofan engine.

"What the hell, Private, did I give you permission to climb?"

"No Sarge, sorry Sarge," he replied as he made his way deftly back to the ground.

Wakely gathered himself and stood in the passage, gazing east, away from the group, listening to Sharpcot's eroding patience as she urged them to assemble. He should assist, not that she needed it. Though she did sound less cool than usual.

He fidgeted with his rifle, dropped the magazine and ran the top of it against his pant leg and snapped it back. He looked at sky, ground, pool noodles, engines, trying to suppress an image infiltrating his brain, one fuelled by films of Nazi concentration camps and Khmer Rouge killing fields: bodies, bodies, naked and dead, seven billion of them, neatly stacked into a block nine storeys high. How big would that block be? A block seven billion cubic humans in volume.

Loko stood helplessly, foil bag, spent ration heater, and plastic spoon dangling from his grip, and asked Sharpcot what to do with them.

"Just drop it all, Private," Sharpcot told him impatiently.

"You could hike back to the spoon block, jam that spoon in. We'll wait," Deeks quipped, and Sharpcot spun on her.

"Enough, Private," she snapped. "Everything's a joke to you."

"I'm sorry, Sergeant," Deeks said, and took a breath to manage an emotion.

"All of you," Sharpcot called. "Stay alert, and keep up. I'm taking point. Virago, you're with me."

They set off towards Wakely, and when they passed she grimaced, and he joined Tse at the tail of the column.

The next intersection — steel cookie tins, empty, and ant farms, plastic and glass, big and small, filled with different types of sand — interrupted their momentum, for a bathroom break which might not have happened had Sharpcot herself not needed to go. Wakely stood at the wall, peeing, while at eye level harvester ants navigated a sand maze sandwiched between sheets of acrylic, as if nothing had changed. He felt a kinship with them as he zipped and joined the group moving down the corridor.

They went at a hard pace for an hour, passed multitudes of blocks: stanchions used in airports and museums and other public spaces, with a retractable belt that notches into its neighbour, and branded from places all over the world, Charles de Gaulle airport in France, Kingsford Smith airport in Australia, the Hermitage in St. Petersburg; soon after, a small tower of dental x-ray bite blocks; a monument almost two klicks of flattened and torn industrial shrink wrap, used to shroud boats and buildings; balance scales in brass, steel, and wood, which Leclerc described as Roberval balance scales, and for which she explained the advantages over a standard balance, and to which no one listened. After those, napkin rings in wood, steel, pewter, brass, gold, some with rhinestones, pearls, zirconium.

They passed along a massive wall of cash registers set at every orientation, most in muted business hues: beige and black and white and grey plastic, pushbuttons and cash drawers. Wakely watched Bronski ahead of him butt a couple of registers with his rifle stock until a drawer popped open. He glanced into it and walked on, and when Wakely passed he saw it was empty. Bronski hit another, and another, until Wakely ordered him to stop. All the drawers were empty.

Opposite the registers stood a monolith of rubber formed from a snarl of thinly compressed objects of muted blue, yellow, grey, black, beige. Sharpcot asked Virago to pull one out and she withdrew a light blue latex glove, and Sharpcot looked up the wall and muttered, "Hell."

"I guess hospitals and clinics," Deeks said. "Every exam a new set of gloves. When my dad was in hospital the garbage was full of these."

"That guy at the CANEX, he puts on a new pair every time he uses the cash," Virago said. "You know, the bald guy?"

"Germ freak?" Deeks said. "Sniffles a lot?"

"They wear them when they make you a sub. Like at a Subway," Bronski said.

"My car mechanic wears them," Tse said.

"There's got to be a hundred billion here," Loko said.

They continued, and up ahead Sharpcot saw water crossing the passage, a stream, and as they approached she saw that fissures roughly a metre wide opened in both walls, the rubber gloves on the left and cash registers on the right. She stopped at the stream's edge and regarded the breaks in the blocks, narrow canyons with towering walls, perfectly vertical, but meandering with the stream's course, so she could see in each direction only as far as the first bend. The section stood on the bank and looked into the muddy water, its surface streaked with greasy rainbows.

"Something leaking upstream, like the transformers," Wakely said.

"I wouldn't drink it," Leclerc said. "Even filtered."

"Means there'll be more water," Sharpcot said. "We should be able to find something clean."

They stepped through the stream and went on. The blocks ended at a new intersection, corner built from pulleys packed in different orientations and showing a staggering variety of size, type, style, composition, and condition. At ground level sat a pulley two metres in diameter in a housing of peeling yellow paint, with four wheels grooved for cables an inch thick, and packed above and around it smaller pulleys in silver and grey and black and brown, and as they cast their vision higher they saw other large pulleys set among common ones in sizes from a dime's width to a handspan to a foot to a metre. They were made from iron, plastic, ceramic, wood, galvanized steel, composites, carbon fibre. They saw antiques in iron, rusting, with elegantly curved spokes; some with a running hook; some geared for toothed belts; they were made for compound bows, dining room lamp height adjusters, exercise machines, industrial hoists, oil derricks, wooden blocks from the rigging of sailing vessels, elevators, flagpoles, window blinds, theatre curtains, clotheslines, ladder extenders.

The right view presented a variation in the arrangement of stuff: not a single, massive block, but a series of slender towers, each of a different composition, with a 10-centimetre gap separating each, stretching off into the south and east. The stack at the corner of the intersection was a tangle of small figurines wrapped in plastic and string. Sharpcot pulled one of the strings and a figure in dark green emerged, a plastic soldier, attached with a web of thread to a polyethylene parachute of red, white, and blue.

"At last, the airborne arrives," Deeks said.

A tower of parachute guys.

Sharpcot held the toy at eye level, dropped it, and stepped down the righthand passage.

Bronski snatched up the figure and tossed it in the air, watched it descend on its chute. He picked it up, did it again, and again. "Stay put," Wakely ordered, and followed Sharpcot down the passage. They gazed up at the next stack, narrower than the first, and made from bobbleheads, all of them of Vladimir Putin in various outfits: shirtless, in a suit, wearing a karate outfit, riding a bear. They walked on, and the tower that followed, of roughly the same width as the Putins, was made up of accent lamps shaped like silver teapots. Next, another block of the same width, white plastic dust cover caps for HDMI cable ends. Tubes of antiperspirant foot lotion. Countertop mushroom growing kits. Plastic strips designed to go into car seat gaps to catch dropped items. Electromagnetic devices that allegedly repel insects. Stainless steel pineapple corers. The towers continued on, hundreds of them, thousands, fading into the haze of the distance.

Wakely jotted in his notebook. They returned to the intersection where the section stood watching Bronski jogging along the passage, tossing the parachute guy into the air and watching it drift down until he caught it and threw it again.

"He's kind of lost it," Virago murmured to Wakely.

Sharpcot observed for a moment before calling out, "Private Bronski, if you're done here, we'll move on."

Bronski squatted and with a tremendous effort sprung up and launched the toy high into the air, but as it descended it snagged on the pulley wall, and he stood staring up at it, chute dangling from the hub of a pulley. He turned and came back towards the group, evading eye contact, and when he arrived at the parachute man block he withdrew another, unwrapped the strings, and prepared to launch it in the air. Wakely placed his hand on his arm.

"Private," Wakely said quietly.

Bronski tried to shake his arm free, but Wakely held firm.

"Will you please let me throw one more time," Bronski said through gritted teeth.

"We are moving out."

"All right," he replied, but when Wakely let go he dashed away and tossed the figure. The parachute failed to deploy and the figure struck the ground at his feet. He bent to pick it up, but Wakely signalled to Tse, and they stepped forward and each seized one of Bronski's arms.

"Please, sir," Bronski moaned. "Sir, please, one more time."

Wakely and Tse hauled him backwards and Bronski thrashed, eyes fixed on the toy. Sharpcot stepped into his line of sight. He strained to see past her, and she said gently, "Private Bronski, I need you to meet my eye. Please."

Bronski ceased struggling and looked into Sharpcot's eyes, and as he did so he returned from a distant place.

"Thank you," Sharpcot said. "Are you all right?"

"I'm fine," he replied as he tried to shrug himself out of Wakely's and Tse's grip. Sharpcot nodded and they released him. He shook his arms, and as he stepped over the toy muttered, "You let me down, mang."

Pulleys continued on the left while on the right they counted 417 mini stacks, each between one and four metres in diameter, most composed of unknown parts: rods, spars, spacers, fasteners, joiners, separators, isolators, reinforcers, adjusters, along with varied baubles and gewgaws. Among them were readily identifiable products: headlight restoration kits containing a polishing tool, buffer rags, and liquid polish; aromatherapy dispensers; spoon holders that clamp to the side of a pot; canned silkworm pupae.

"So there is food," Leclerc said as she studied a label.

"That's not food," Bronski said.

"Technically it is," Leclerc replied calmly.

"Technically barf!" Bronski cried.

"Oh, Bronski, you really must captain our debating team," Deeks pleaded.

The mini stacks ended at a full-sized block of fabric shavers: Perfect Solutions Sweater Defuzzer, Just Care's Lint Remover, Conair Defuzzer CLS1, Sunbeam S20 Deluxe, Just-F-Rechargeable, Philips GC026, Evercare Shaver.

And on they want through grand blocks of gas duster cans, barbells, squash balls, leather martingales (identified by Virago, who had a spell in her teens as an equestrian), Tibetan Buddhist hand prayer wheels — spinnable metal cylinders with a weight on a chain atop a handle, many beautiful and ornate with complex designs. Followed by foil turkey roasting pans, wooden pestles from mortar and pestle sets.

Late in the afternoon they encountered a river a dozen metres wide crossing the passage, and like the stream it cut a canyon through the blocks on each side: woodchippers on the north, child car seat boosters south. The chippers varied in shape but all had wheels, couplings for towing, and many included a steerable chute to direct chips into a collector, such as the back of a truck. They sat jammed together, one atop another, in yellow and green and white and grey, stencilled with Carlton, Vermeer, ChipMax, Morbark, Timberwolf, many branded with the name of a tree management company or utility or government agency, and they came from everywhere: Slovakia, New Zealand, Argentina, Liberia, Venezuela, Finland.

This water ran clear and moderately deep, with a sandy bottom and weeds stretched out like pendants in the current. Its burble echoed in the canyons of boosters and wood chippers. It smelled fresh, alive. Tse spotted a frog in the greenery of the bank, which leapt into the water when he approached it, and Loko claimed to see fish.

Leclerc squatted at the edge and filled her canteen and added a purification tablet. She capped it and shook it longer than seemed reasonable, then took a tenuous sip.

"Tastes okay, whatever that means," she said. "Could be all manner of furans and heavy metals in there."

"Won't the tablets help?" Deeks asked.

"Only for pathogens. Bacteria and amoebas. You won't get giardia — beaver fever."

"I always got beaver fever," Bronski muttered, and nudged Loko.

Wakely put out a hand to Leclerc, accepted the canteen. He sniffed and then took a drink. "It's all right," he said. "A little chloriney, but that's the tablets. I've had worse. Okay, everyone should have tablets in your kits. Private Leclerc will instruct you on their use; follow what she says exactly. You do not want to be shitting your guts out with the only toilets we know of 30 klicks back thataway."

They filled bottles and prepared to cross the river. Bronski suggested backtracking and finding a way around.

"How do you figure that?" Deeks wondered. "It runs north-south, and we're travelling east."

"It's not the last we'll meet, so get used to it. I'll go first," Sharpcot said.

"Shouldn't Tse go?" Bronski said. "He's tallest."

"Shouldn't Bronski go?" Loko echoed. "He's scaredest."

"Oh hey, haw haw," Bronski replied. "Why don't you—" and he punctuated the final word with a shove that sent Loko staggering into the shallows before he scooted back onto the bank, kicking water at Bronski. Bronski tensed to retaliate when Sharpcot shouted, "Stop before I lay you both down like logs and use you for a bridge!"

Sharpcot sat on the hitch of a woodchipper and unlaced her boots, pulled them off, and tied them together. She hung them around her neck and stood and got her rifle and stepped into the water. The river deepened until it went to her waist, and she lifted her rifle to keep it dry, but it didn't get much deeper and she shuffled across and mounted the far bank, where she called, "Don't just stand there, you saw how it was done. Move!"

Once they'd all crossed — Loko managed to slip and thrashed until Tse fished him out by the scruff — they got back into their boots and continued eastward, each wet to the waist, Loko soaked to the chin and his rifle and ruck wet too. They dried fast in the heat, and the boosters and woodchippers ended at a wall of drums that blocked eastward progress. The soldiers spilled into the north-south passageway, regarding the wall. As with every collection they'd encountered, it produced its own micro-climate, one of artisanship and musicality after the outdoorsy pragmatism of woodchippers and the depressing collection of child car seats. Drums of every conceivable type comprised the block, from African and Australian and American and Asian Indigenous instruments made from wood and gourd and skin and bone to modern drums with synthetic heads and composite shells. The collection exuded a museum-like quality, a monument to lost peoples. Surdos and snares and tympani and dhaks and congas and bongos and djembes and tom-toms and tablas and bara and doumbeks and karyendas were arranged almost aesthetically: heads outward to display ornamentation or brand names, others with sides visible, not stacked with the abandon of other objects, but arranged with care and precision. As if to give an effect. Which it did: a drum museum, tall and broad.

Sharpcot regarded the wall before she went to a Japanese taiko two metres in diameter, packed among smaller instruments, chendas and crowdy-crawns and madals. She turned her rifle and swung it so the butt struck the centre of the drum.

It boomed, and a tremendous pulse proliferated deep within the block, the throb propagating, each drum reverberating sympathetically with the taiko's voice and then each neighbour's. Everyone took an involuntary step back, except Sharpcot, who watched the wall with defiance, rifle poised, waiting for the noise to diminish, 10 seconds, 20, before she swung again, *boom*, and again the drums in the stack responded, setting the air and Earth atremble as if the foot of a giant had come down. She hit it again and again as the section stood watching, in awe and not without fear for Sharpcot's sanity as she struck the taiko's head.

When the final strike diminished like a roll of fading thunder, she said, "If there's anyone within a few klicks, they know we're around. Be ready." Then she set off northwards, and the section fell in.

Wakely wondered about the wisdom of alerting the neighbourhood, but he understood the impulse, remembering how he fired his rifle at the site of CFB Shilo. Was that only yesterday?

The woodchippers ended at a westward passage, and ceramic teapots all of the same muted red hue constituted the northwestern corner.

"These I know," Tse said as he moved close to the wall and ran a palm along the belly of one of the pots. "Yixing zisha teapots. It's named for the clay. My grandmother collects them."

They were struck by the diversity of shapes of the pots: round, cylindrical, shaped like fish or pigs, but all of the same zisha clay.

"Their taxonomic proclivities are curious," Leclerc remarked.

"Who do you mean when you say 'they'?" Deeks asked.

"The Accruers. If that's what we've settled on calling them."

"Have we even settled on a 'them'?" Virago asked.

"Private Leclerc is right," Sharpcot said as she regarded the wall. "These are widely different shapes, but made from the same material. The drums are the same basic shape, but made from different stuff."

"So how are they classifying things?" Leclerc asked.

"Who cares," Loko said. "It's just junk."

"It isn't, though," Tse said as he moved from pot to pot, evaluating them against what his grandmother would tell him as she showed the shelves that held her collection.

"Hey, Tse, maybe some are your grandma's," said Bronski, who stood beside Tse, squinting at the pots. "You recognize any?"

Tse turned and looked at Bronski with a despondent expression. "What?" Bronski said.

"Bronski, you are a shit," Deeks said, as Sharpcot called for them to move.

Bronski paused a moment, said, "What. What did I say? Something happen to his grandma? How would I know that?" before Wakely came from the rear and ordered him to march.

The drums continued and Sharpcot saw greenery ahead and that the passage broadened. She raised a hand and they slowed as she scanned the foliage. As they eased forward the walls fell back to further accommodate what looked like a forest, larger than the copses they'd encountered at the golf course. The wall of Chinese teapots ended at a passage, followed by plastic shipping pallets, most black but some grey, blue, white, towering over the trees and shrubs crowding against it. The forest spanned

300 metres, and though evening was coming on, drums and much of the foliage yet received sunlight. The woods stretched an indeterminate distance north. Birds chirped and flitted through the branches, and Virago spotted a red squirrel. They passed through a mix of conifers and hardwood deciduous, then crossed a small meadow fringed by a marshy zone alive with rushes and a buzz of frogs. They re-entered the trees, Sharpcot leading with little reduction in determination except to keep up a scrutiny of the surroundings.

Wakely called from the back for Sharpcot's attention, and word went up the line until she stopped and turned, impatient. Wakely made his way through the brush.

"Hey, Sarge," he said. "Suggest we stop here."

"We've got a lot of ground to cover, Jack."

"All due respect, they're pretty worn out," he replied, nodding to the section as they stood waiting among the trees. "Three weeks immobile in that bunker and then humping all day. Not just that — there's the emotional toll."

"Who exactly are you referring to?" she asked defensively.

"Everybody. Me. You. Look, tomorrow will be better if we're rested. And this is a pretty good place to spend the night. I'd rather be here than trapped in a corridor somewhere, nowhere to go if the . . . if the situation should change."

Sharpcot looked away from him and took a deep breath.

"El. We're not getting to the city today," he said softly.

"Yeah," she replied. "Yeah, okay." She called, "Three Section, we're calling it quits early today. We pushed you hard. Pretty good progress. Tomorrow will be better. Spread out a little, find a place to overnight, but stay alert and within earshot."

The soldiers looked at each other in stunned exhaustion, then moved off, each taking to their own territory in the wood: Sharpcot to a shaded grove, and Wakely at a strategic position close enough to protect her, but far enough for privacy. Downwind, too, a conscious choice, because before he did anything he sat against a tree and smoked a cigarette.

111

Bronski and Loko headed to a spot they'd seen on the way in, a stand of white pines with the ground bedded in soft needles, while Leclerc settled beside a pond carpeted by lilypads. Tse picked a swell of ground above the pond. The place Deeks chose stood equidistant from Wakely, Sharpcot, and Tse. She didn't much like the outdoors, at night, alone.

Virago took the furthest point, 50 metres north of Wakely, beneath equal parts sky and overstory. She dropped ruck and rifle, kicked off boots and socks, and sat cross-legged on a grassy patch and closed her eyes, limbs humming from exertion. She listened to the forest. After a minute she unrolled her sleeping pad and blanket and lay back, gazing through leaves to sky. A prairie sky, but this was no prairie. On a prairie, you can see everything. Nothing takes you by surprise. Here she was boxed in, trapped in a maze with a bunch of people she wouldn't voluntarily spend 20 minutes with. She thought about her phone, resisted the temptation to turn it on and see "No Service." For a photo, though? This view of sky and trees, one corner of it interrupted by the crest of the drum wall. #SkyTreesDrums #Apocalypse #WhereIsEverybody

She peeled off jacket, vest, armour, shirt so she was down to a tanktop. The air sweet on her shoulders. She could smell herself. Next time they found water she would swim. It had been two days since her last shower, a pathetic trickle in the bunker. She wondered if there existed in the world any more showers. Working showers, not stacked in a nine-storey block. She took a drink of water and pulled the elastic from her hair and shook out her ponytail. She ate and tried to read from the book of poetry she'd read and reread in the bunker, but the words were meaningless. Felt a distant crampy twinge, tried to compute if her period was due, thinking with dread of managing that while travelling. A cloud of bruised emotionality usually presaged it, but who wasn't feeling that right now?

She thought about Terrance. He must be worried about her. Alex too.

112

"Huh," she said aloud, as she analyzed this sequence of thoughts, the first about her cat, under the care of her parents in Calgary, and second about the semi-ex-boyfriend who had moved to Portland. Cat first, Alex second. Maybe she and Alex really were through. Her mind drifted to Calgary in the distant west. Her parents settling in front of the television. Terrance between them. She almost reached for her phone, didn't, then did, and powered it on, eyes fixed on the screen. No Service. She waited, sometimes it took a minute. No Service. Battery at half, so she shut it off and tucked it away.

A shadow climbed the wall of drums and the sunlight turned gold and night came on under a revolution of stars. She smelled woodsmoke and heard the others gathered at a campfire. If she looked south she could make out the flames among the foliage. She thought everyone must be there and she should go too, decided not to. But the voices and firelight cut through the vast and silent dark, and after a few minutes, she went.

Loko and Bronski had dragged logs and brush from the forest, and one by one the section members, each satisfied or haunted by the solitude of their camps, collected at the fire. The conversation stayed light and avoidant, talk of the day's fatigue (despite which Loko couldn't resist climbing a couple of trees), critiques of the campfire, complaints about the food. If talk ventured to things current — Deeks wondered if the Blue Jays had maintained top spot in the American League East, and Bronski mentioned that a Jason Stratham action film he'd been looking forward to opened that day — it was quickly diverted to immediate concerns: solicitations from the machine gunners to share ammo carry, complaints about the TAC vests, complaints about the Individual Meal Packs.

"Look on the bright side," Loko said. "Imagine being vege-tarian."

"Imagine that," Virago muttered.

"I guess vegetarian is for lesbians," Bronski laughed. "No wieners."

"I heard wieners are your favourite," Deeks said.

"They are. What?" he said to the laughter. "I meant the beans and wiener meal packs. Fuck you guys."

"I love the salmon IMPs, so I must be lesbian," Loko said.

An outcry of disdain rose about the salmon IMPs, and in a few minutes, Loko had traded everything he had for salmon.

The talk trailed off into fatigued silence, and they passed long moments staring into the fire, until Leclerc cast her eyes at the starry sky and said, "I wonder when they'll be back."

An agitated silence followed, and Loko hissed, "Who?"

"The Accruers. Everything's in stacks, ready for pickup. Though it's possible they're still here and working somewhere far away."

"Can you shut up now, Leclerc?" Bronski said. "Can you just, you know, shut up?"

"Well it makes sense, doesn't it?" she persisted. "You don't do a job like this and leave it. If the collecting theory is correct, they'll be back."

"Not tonight," Bronski insisted.

"Why not?" Leclerc asked.

Bronski got up and disappeared into the darkness, returned to the edge of the firelight wearing his helmet, C7 at ready. He dropped the rifle's magazine, rapped it against his helmet, and punched it back in place.

"Private Bronski, what are you doing?" Sharpcot asked firmly.

"We have to be ready, Sarge. Shouldn't we be ready?"

"You going to fight them off single-handed, Private?" Wakely asked.

"If they want a fight, I'm up for it," he replied.

"And what do you bring to the battle that's superior to the combined firepower of the planet's armed forces?" Wakely asked.

"Attitude, that's what," Loko said. "One look at that face and they'll flee."

"I want to flee just sitting here," Deeks said.

"You guys are funny. This is serious," Bronski said.

Wakely stood and said, "Private's actually right. It is serious. We'll post sentries tonight. There are other considerations. Wild animals, displaced people."

Sharpcot stood too, dusted off her pants. "Good call, Jack. I'm wiped out. Need to get an early start. Bronski, you're up first. You and Leclerc."

"That's just great," Bronski said, glaring at Leclerc. "Don't try to scare me by saying they're coming back."

"I won't. I'll only say it because it's true."

Wakely interrupted Bronski's frustrated shout with a glance. "We'll do two-hour watches. Deeks and Virago next. Me and Loko will take the dawn shift."

"I'll do one," Sharpcot said.

"We're covered. You and Tse can take first watch tomorrow night."

"I'm going to hold you to that," she said. "Thanks, Jack. Good night."

When Tse woke he knew two things: the Accruers hadn't returned, and today it would rain. Rain hard, and thunder. He always knew, didn't know why. He lay on his side, looking at the grass, the soil. Ants moving among the plant stalks. Like the ones in the ant farms, they had no idea how the world had transformed. For an ant, the world was always changing. You build your anthill under a car, and one day it moves. What does the ant do? The ant has no choice but to accept. So Tse accepted. He'd accepted from the moment he'd emerged from the bunker. He'd known instantly, the way he knew it would rain today, that the whole world had changed. Could he do anything about it? Could he do anything about the coming thunderstorm? In the old world, he could take shelter. Here was a fundamental truth about the new world: there was no shelter. They were going to get rained on today, and there was nothing they could do but get wet.

He looked at the sky. Blue above, but at the horizon it thickened to bronze. The air ponderous.

He rolled onto the ground beside his pad and did 60 slow pushups. His arms burned. He did 60 more, slowing at the end, making each harder than the last. On the pad again, on his back, he did crunches until he saw stars. Lay on his back with a hand on his belly. A bird began to whistle a tune of remarkable clarity, and the sharpness of it rent the air like the trail of a meteor. Tse saw sound. Like when Sharpcot pounded that drum yesterday — that had looked to him like exploding hay bales. The kind you spot on drives in the country, rolled up in farmers' fields, each like a giant cinnamon bun. Exploding. Boom. Boom. Boom.

He kneeled and got out his rosary and with closed eyes made the sign and whispered, "Lord, I offer You this day." Also, he thought, but didn't speak it aloud: let the world and everyone in it be okay. It seemed like a big ask, something he didn't usually do in prayer.

He brought the C9 onto his lap and ran a cloth over the barrel, opened the feed tray cover and inspected the rotary bolt mechanism. He'd cleaned the gun in the bunker — yesterday? — and it didn't need it, but he worked it anyway, methodically, his thoughts on the components, how each fit crisply into place, every click a yellow spark. He'd only ever fired this weapon on the range. He didn't like to think of it being used against people, even bad ones, because he knew what it could do.

When he was done he smelled camp smoke and decided he'd take his breakfast at the fire. He packed everything in a few minutes, was trudging in the direction of the campfire when Sharpcot called to him through the trees.

"Morning, Sarge," he replied. "How did you sleep?"

"Up a bunch, but deep when I was out. What about you?"

"It's going to rain today."

She gazed at the sky. "You sure? Doesn't look like it."

"It is."

"You eat?"

"Thought I'd heat mine up. If there's time."

"We'll need calories today. Round everyone up and meet at the fire."

"Sergeant." Tse set off through the forest.

Sharpcot found Wakely on a log by the fire, drinking instant coffee from a tin cup, Bronski and Boyko across from him, lounging on their sleeping pads. They were all about to leap up when they saw her, but she waved them down. She set her ruck on the ground and dug until she found a breakfast IMP. Wakely had set a small pot in the coals, with IMPs heating in the boiling water. He fished them out with pliers, tossed one each to Loko and Bronski, who both exclaimed and dropped them.

"Coffee?" he asked her, and she nodded, handed him her cup. He filled it from the pot, dropped in her IMP. She poured instant coffee crystals into her cup and stirred.

Tse stepped out of the woods, said, "Deeks and Leclerc are coming. I'm on my way to find Virago."

"Throw your breakfast in the pot and sit, Corporal," Wakely said as he drained his cup. "I'll get her."

Wakely picked up his rifle as Deeks and Leclerc arrived. He nodded to them and stepped north through the forest.

"Ah, the weekend," Deeks said as they found spots at the fireside. "Always a brunch rush."

Fifty paces out Wakely paused to light a cigarette. He relished solitude, and last night only his responsibility to the sergeant prevented him from seeking a more secluded bivouac. The forest comforted him. He'd grown up with a city ravine behind his house, where he and his friends had spent the seasons hidden away from parents and responsibility. Now, his duty to Sharpcot and the mission briefly prorogued, he finished his cigarette and slipped contentedly through the brush.

He thought he should call for Virago but didn't want to disturb the silence. He took off helmet and ballistic glasses, closed his eyes, drew a deep breath. It was good at first, fresh, but then he detected something beneath it all, a smell of gasoline from the wood chippers, and a scent like the inside of a mall, along with other misplaced odours. He trudged on, eyes lowered, found Virago's boot prints and followed them along a sandy crest.

Stopped dead and dropped to a squat, sweat breaking on his brow, nerves triggered. It was like Afghanistan, it always became Afghanistan. He sank to a knee and listened, suddenly fearful that something had happened to her. He heard a low moan, then panting. He pushed silently forward on his knees, parted the greenery.

He couldn't understand what he was seeing. She was stretched out horizontally, facing the ground, and appeared to be levitating, until he saw her hands pressed to the sleeping pad, forearms braced against her belly, a strenuous yoga pose. She was clad in white shorts and sports bra, and it took him a moment to recognize that the dark areas covering her body were not injuries, not bruises, but tattoos. Birds and foxes, feathers and fish scales, lush foliage, all in an intricate Japanese style. Her arms quaked as she held the pose.

It felt intrusive to discover the fact of this body art without her consent, as if he'd seen her naked, and he turned away, put his back to her, sat on the earth, and called out, "Private Virago."

She gasped, and he heard her tumble out of the pose. "That you, Master Corporal? Where are you?"

"Over here," he said, lifting his rifle, making it visible through the brush. "Sorry for the startle. We are rallying to leave."

"Understood," she replied, and her voice sounded small. But then it firmed up, and she said, "I just need a minute. Will you wait?"

"I'll wait."

6

They went east until they met the drum wall, set off north along its face. Twice Loko struck drums, both times to punctuate a bad joke, and Sharpcot ordered him to desist. The woods ended, and the corridor funnelled down to the standard four-metre width. It felt constricting, and departure from the greenery cast a dispiriting effect.

Shipping pallets gave way to birdhouses in wood, steel, plastic; bare or painted in subtle or lurid colours; some with a single hole in the face, others with dozens of openings.

"Bird condos," Deeks said. "Wonder what the fees are like."

They saw birds arrive and depart from some houses, reminding Sharpcot of a nature show she'd watched with Lana a week before the bunker, about a river in Borneo, or was it Burundi? Swallows darting to and from cliffside nests. The thought of Lana beside her on the tattered sofa filled Sharpcot's chest with desperation. As it threatened to overcome her, birdhouses and drums ended at a four-way intersection. On the left, electric hotplates, each with a single spiral burner: Elekta, Brentwood, Master Chef, Breville, in white, stainless, black powdercoat, Bakelite. On the right, paper cone party hats stacked in dense columns, only the lower rim of each visible, colourful strips showing polka dots, Happy Birthday, stars, Paw Patrol, squiggles, glitter, rainbows, SpongeBob, monkeys, metallic, stripes. A cheerful, cheerless monument.

They rounded the corner and went east between drums and party hats, and as they approached the next crossroads Leclerc

119

commented that like the toilets, the drum block's length far exceeded its width.

"They're using an algorithm to ensure fit, and where to position intersections, while computing the proportions for each block," she mused. "I'd love to view that code."

"Shut up, shut the fuck up," Bronski muttered under his breath.

Sheets of corrugated tin formed the left corner, with stuffed toys, all of them horses, zebras, or unicorns, to the right.

The temperature and humidity climbed, and Wakely considered Tse's storm prediction. He suffered a thought of heavy rain, not even here, it could be somewhere far off, causing a flood that would produce a massive wall of water bearing down the corridor, rolling relentlessly towards them. They'd see it coming, but there was nowhere to go. He glanced at the wall of tin to consider its climbability, saw the precision with which the sheets were stacked, each corrugation nested within the one below. No protrusion for hand- or foothold.

It got him to thinking that they should, at the next opportunity, when there was a wall with sufficient purchase, send someone up top for a survey. Wishing they still had that drone.

He watched the column ahead stumbling along in the heat, wondered how long this arrangement could be maintained. He was glad to have Sharpcot in charge. She ran a tight ship, but at some point, without a higher command structure to enforce consequences, someone was going to stop following orders. And then what would Sharpcot do? What would he do?

When he glanced down he saw his hand on the butt of his sidearm. Would he? If it came to that?

The tin kept on, while stuffed horses ended, followed by a red and yellow electronic toy with a keyboard: Speak & Spells.

"Hey, Deeks," Bronski called as he prodded a button on one of the toys and a synthesized voice said "U," to which he added, "are an idiot."

Deeks leaned in and keyed "M," then after a pause, "U-R."

Looking at the tin wall, Sharpcot thought about Kabul, its dusty, stinking streets, smoke and gasoline and propane and rotting food and feces, with its corrugated tin shops selling phone cards, goat meat, oranges, car parts, handbags, spices. Her mind went to images of other countries of the Global South, tin shacks rising, tier upon tier, up hillsides, or constituting vast city slums, walls and roofs all made from this stuff, corrugated tin, the building block of poverty. Were these stacked sheets from those walls and roofs in Afghanistan, in Africa, Asia, South America?

The tin went on and on, while on the right they passed jars of rubber cement, fanny packs, and then a big block of mismatched knitted green mittens, their presence obscene against the day's heat and humidity. After that came clear plastic bottles — hundreds of billions of them. Water bottles, clear or tinted plastic, most with familiar labels: Aquafina, Dasani, evian, Fiji, Nayan, Nestlé Pure Life, along with obscure brands, Odwalla, Arrowhead, Calistoga, Ice Mountain, Nongfu Spring with Chinese characters, others in French, Spanish, Thai, Arabic.

"Polyethylene terephthalate," Leclerc declared.

They were all empty, set upright, packed in disciplined rows and columns, a devastating ledger of waste, and when the sun cut through them, a glow of undersea blue burned within the block's heart. Sounds within a specific pitch range, Tse's voice in particular, resonated to the point that he became even more taciturn, suppressing the low, mournful thrum it caused when someone asked him how he was for cigarettes, and he answered, "I've got some." "Sommmmmhhh," the bottles responded, the thrum persisting for seconds before fading. Wakely had to keep his own voice above pitch to avoid creating a disruption, but the women's voices, and Loko's (Bronski noted with glee) did not resonate significantly.

"Why not crush them to save space?" Virago wondered.

"Maybe packing them isn't the goal," Leclerc answered.

"What's that mean?" Loko asked.

"We don't know the reason for all this," Leclerc said, waving a hand at tin and bottles. "Maybe the goal is to illustrate a problem."

"What problem?" Bronski said. "It's a bunch of bottles. Big deal."

"You buy bottled water, Bronski?" Virago asked.

"Course."

"Then you're an idiot," Virago replied.

"What the fuck?" Bronski replied. "I can't drink water?"

"Can you get water for free?"

"Sure."

"What would you call someone who pays for something they can get for free? And the free thing is of better quality?"

Bronski didn't answer. "I'd call them an idiot," Wakely called from the back of the column. "Wouldn't you, Bronski?"

"Bottled water is safer," Bronski said.

"Nope," Virago said. "Unlike tap water, it's unregulated. It's dirty and it contains plastic, from the bottles themselves. So why do you buy bottled water rather than drinking it out of the tap, Bronski?"

"Everyone does it," Wakely suggested.

"Only idiots," Virago said.

"Well, then the world is full of idiots," Bronski cried.

No one disputed this fact.

Some bottles appeared to have been crushed and reconstituted. Many were cracked, some had missing fragments. Others had fogged with age. Some still held a little water.

They pushed on, corrugated tin on the left, dark, ponderous, and on the right, translucent, lightweight bottles. The difference in density created a disconcerting aural effect, dense and silent on the left, hollow and airy on the right.

For Sharpcot, the objects themselves presented an unsettling commentary: a vast quantity of a cheap, low-grade material required, due to chronic widespread housing crises, to shelter much of the world's people. Here it was, set beside a vast quantity of vessels made to contain water, to which much of the world has no safe access, and the wealthy can get practically for free, yet they choose instead to purchase it at inflated prices in containers made from an unrenewable, non-biodegradable resource that blights the planet.

What kind of shit society would allow that?

They plodded down this corridor for four kilometres, without interruption. The only breaks in the monotony were a series of gentle rises and falls in the landscape, the blocks on both sides following each contour. Corrugated tin finally ended at a northward passage, with shopping carts at the next corner, a mesh of chrome and steel, wheels and pushbars labelled with grocery stores familiar and foreign, but the bottles persisted on the south side, six kilometres, seven kilometres. It seemed they would go on forever. Finally, when they'd walked 15 kilometres, they spotted the end of them and the next intersection.

At the northeast, anvils: cast iron and steel, most with a single horn, most black, some painted teal, blue, red, bronze, many rusting, some embossed with manufacturer names and weights. The sight of them spurred conversations about Wile E. Coyote and Road Runner, and Loko went on about the importance of anvils in *Minecraft*. On the southwest, a spaghetti of glass tubes, each bent and kinked, which at first glance appeared as a random cluster, but after inspection revealed words: Open, Welcome, Live Girls, Casino, All Day Breakfast, No Vacancy, Pabst Blue Ribbon, Movieland Arcade, Central Café, along with signs in other scripts, Arabic, Thai, Greek, Cyrillic, a lot in logograms, grids of glass Chinese characters, in one place a giant SEGA spelled out among kanji and hiragana. Pictures too: a turntable, a dragon, the state of Texas, palm tree, crown, rose, flamingo, ace of spades, turtle, crocodile, cloud, electric guitar, rocket, nude woman, Saturn, cocktail glass, Sae Woo Chop Suey with a giant rooster. They were neon signs, plucked from building fronts and store windows, some broken, glass tubes cracked or snapped, but most intact, oriented every which way.

In their unlit state, tubes of clear glass, colourless, anemic, one had to imagine the florid magic they would exhibit if a current were applied to their electrodes.

Each mass of objects they encountered prompted discussion, but Sharpcot cut it short, got them moving, and on they marched, through the heat and humidity, the passage stretching off without obstruction as far as they could see. They crossed intersections, continuously encountering new blocks, new materials, much of it mundane, collections of obscure parts, but then something surprising. Here stood a tremendous block of disposable cigarette lighters of every hue and size and design, astonishing in its scale. "This can't be right," Bronski muttered as he regarded it. "Too many."

"Forty thousand per hour," Leclerc stated. "That's how many disposable lighters are thrown away in the United States alone."

"How do you know this shit?" Bronski demanded.

"Environmental exhibit, Science World, Vancouver, BC," Leclerc replied. "I was there on October 18th last year with my niece."

"You just try to memorize stuff like that?" Virago asked her.

"I don't try," Leclerc replied.

"Freak," Bronski said, pocketing a bunch of lighters. Others did the same.

"But where are the cigarettes?" Wakely muttered to Sharpcot. He was on his last pack, didn't know where things stood with Deeks and Bronski and Tse, but by Bronski's level of irritation he'd probably run out. Tse could hardly be called a smoker, it seemed more of an affect, and Deeks said something about wanting to quit, and the situation offering an opportunity. "Nothing like the end of the world to get you motived."

Across from the lighters, a soft block of fabric objects, which when Virago pulled one turned out to be leg warmers, in black and grey and pink and lurid neon. She held it up in a way to invite comment and ridicule, but no one possessed the energy or verve to attack such a broad target.

They passed between scuba masks and window air conditioners, their grilles and control panels mostly white or beige, and they persisted when the masks ended and next came sections of waterslides, stacked to the sky, made from aluminum and fibreglass and some of concrete, painted light blue, but in some cases purple, lime green, fluorescent orange. Disassembled, nested together, trough within trough. Next on the right came hand-operated ice drills, and on the left, Adirondack chairs in wood and plastic, many colours. From the head of the column, Virago suggested quietly to Sharpcot that they pause for lunch and rest. Sharpcot declined, but after they passed another southbound passage and met a block of grout floats, and Deeks and Loko spoke up from behind, pleading for a break, Sharpcot relented.

They scattered lethargically along the aisle, sinking to the grass, taking up poses cross-legged or reclining, until Bronski got up and gripped the arms of one of the chairs set into the base of the wall and began to tug it out. Everyone watched in a kind of dazed exhaustion until Deeks asked in a lazy drawl, "Bronski, if you get that chair out, what do you think is going to happen to all the ones above it?"

Bronski stopped and gazed up the wall, nine storeys along its sheer face, before he turned around and perched himself on the lip of the chair and scrunched himself beneath the one immediately above it. "I never planned to pull it right out."

A growl of thunder rolled across the sky.

Sharpcot sent Leclerc down the line to tally rations and then listened expressionlessly as she read the stock numbers from a notepad, nodded Wakely over.

"Food will soon be a problem," she stated quietly.

"Yeah, well we knew it would be. None of this has been food," he said.

"Except canned silkworm pupae and soy sauce," Leclerc reminded him.

"Right," Wakely replied stiffly. Though she wasn't wrong. "Take a rest, Private."

125

"Do we have enough to get to Winnipeg?" Sharpcot asked after Leclerc settled among the others.

"What makes you think we'll find Winnipeg, that there even is a Winnipeg?" he replied, pulling on a cigarette, until his eyes circled back to hers. "Oh crap. Sorry."

"Just because you've got shit to live for in this world."

"I said sorry."

"I need you to believe in something, Jack. I can't do it alone."

"I know, I know. I just think that from what all we've seen, all of this—"

"Stop it. I need hope. They need hope. And you do too, probably, somewhere, in your blank soul."

"Is that what you think? My soul is blank?"

"You act like there's nothing left in this world. But there is. There's me, and there's them. This, all this," she said, sweeping her hands at the towers. "It's just stuff. Our crap. This is not the people. We are going to find our people."

"Shh, Elsie. Keep it down," Wakely said, glancing at the section, where heads had turned. "Okay, okay. I'm sorry. We're going to find them. We'll find Lana. We'll find everyone. I'm sorry."

"Goddammit, Jack. Goddamn. I'm sorry too. I'm sorry," she said, gripping his forearm.

"Yeah, okay. Jesus Christ, El. Our first fight."

She released his arm and punched his shoulder.

"Maybe we've been travelling the housewares and hardware aisle. What if I scout down that south passage a spell," Wakely offered. "See if we can find the pasta aisle, or snacks and confections." Thunder again, and Wakely checked the sky. "And something we can use for shelter."

"Split up? I don't know. Could get lost in this maze."

"I won't get lost. But yeah, I wouldn't trust everybody. Let's keep a base here. First foray. I'll go on my own."

"Take someone. Virago. She patrols like she's walking at the mall. Her fieldcraft needs work."

"We can keep radio contact. Try yours?"

Sharpcot fished her headset from a pocket and put it on, swung the mic into position at her lips, activated the push-to-talk.

"Test test," Wakely called into his mic, and she nodded, pushed her own transmit button, replied "Test test."

A roll of thunder, stronger, boomed through the passage. She looked at the sky, still blue. "Go now. If it rains, I mean really rains, come on back. Otherwise, you got one hour." She looked at her watch and he looked at his. "Be back by 13:10."

"Sergeant."

Wakely moved down the line of soldiers finishing their meals, Bronski still tucked into his chair niche, Loko picking his teeth. Tse and Leclerc and Deeks chatting quietly. He stopped in front of Virago, who was reading a slim book. "Short patrol, Private. You're with me."

She got to her feet, put on her helmet and began to repack her kit. "Just your weapon," he said.

Wakely briefed Virago before they rounded the corner, told her to picture an urban setting, the passages as city streets. He'd hold back while she advanced so he could observe and critique. It made her self-conscious and shy.

"Go on," he said, and she set out. She stepped cautiously to the next crossroads where she snugged up against grout floats and checked each passageway.

"What do you see?" Wakely called.

She swung her rifle to the northeast block, studied it before taking in the southeast one. "Some kind of spoons on the left. Small jars on the right."

"I meant is the passage clear?"

"Clear," she said, and he moved in, took the wall opposite, against the chairs.

"Go in," he said, and she rounded the corner. He followed, crossed the intersection, glanced at the northeast block and saw it was all melonballers. When what they needed were melons. He crossed south and leaned into the wall there. Jars of anti-aging cream: frosted glass, black, red, grey, green. Olay, Estée Lauder, Eucerin, Pond's, Swisse Origins, Vichy, Lancôme, Age Perfect, L'Oréal, Lotus, Marcelle, Sephora, Juvena, Kiehl's, Brickell, Kate Somerville, Wow, Algenist, Babor, Caudalie, Bel Essence, Neutrogena, Nuxe.

"Move up," he ordered, and she advanced, hugging the righthand wall, rifle raised, scanning, moving in fits and starts. "Sniper check," he called, and she swept the high walls before pushing on, so tight to the block she dislodged a bunch of grout floats, turned to look as they fell around her boots and he called, "Forget those. Eyes up!"

It was only superficially urban: uniformly tall and wide, no cover such as garbage cans or newspaper boxes, no parked or moving vehicles, no actual windows from which fire could come, few intersections. No civilians. No people. Wakely thought: What was the point? Why train this soldier to fight in an extinct environment? Who was she fighting? Who was she protecting?

They should be retraining the section specifically for this, for maze and block warfare. To fight the Accruers. Whatever the hell they were.

Thunder rumbled, and when he glanced up between stacks he saw a line of ashen cloud. The light grew sombre and the temperature dipped. He smelled rain, saw another intersection coming up, T-shaped, with a passage leading right, and it became apparent they'd reached another area populated by slender towers, larger than the ones they'd encountered previously, these ones three or four metres wide, separated by narrow gaps. Wakely couldn't identify the objects that comprised the corner block, but he could see they were small, mostly white or off-white, beige, brown, some grey or light blue.

Wakely crossed and recrossed the aisle, and in a few deft moves got ahead of Virago, maintaining coverage up and down the street. He stopped at the corner and signalled Virago to take position against the face cream jars opposite. He flicked around the corner and studied the empty passageway and saw short blocks stretching away, and beyond them the south face of the air conditioner block they'd passed previously. Dropping the pretense of an urban patrol, he crossed the passage and removed his sunglasses and regarded the corner block.

Hearing aids, millions of hearing aids, of varying shapes and hues, packed tightly together, nine storeys tall.

"Jesus Christ."

"What are they?" Virago whispered.

Wakely told her. "My dad wears one. He's been through a dozen different models, different styles, in the canal, in the ear, behind the ear, trying to find one that works for him. He's never happy, we still have to repeat everything we say. I think he just doesn't want to hear it. Says it's nothing but bad news anyway. The last one he had was like—" he stepped towards the wall, prodded one of the devices with an index finger "—that one."

Virago looked; it was powder blue, the curved battery case that sits behind the ear, with a switch and a slider along the rear edge, plus an ear hook and a tube running to an ear mould. Virago recoiled. She'd looked too closely, saw the mould stained with yellowish earwax.

"You see?" he asked.

She nodded. He looked at what she saw, that hearing aid, and stepped back to take in the tower, this block of equipment, the possessions of how many millions of people, clustered here, arranged, and he endured a wave of nausea, just as Sharpcot had when she'd contemplated the plastic spoons. But this was different, it was worse, because these objects held an intimacy beyond spoons: hearing aids, plugged into people's heads, to facilitate listening — to conversations, laughter, babies, birdsong, crickets, symphonies.

And what if the hearing aid he'd indicated was his father's.

He dismissed the thought — there were probably a hundred million devices in this stack, what would be the chance? And

129

yet — that didn't much matter, if it was here, somewhere in this tower.

He had to stay on track, remain clear on their purpose — find food, find something to protect them from rain. That was his impetus, not to consider the horror of what may have happened to humanity. To his family.

He was about to push on when Virago whispered, "What's that sound?"

They heard a low, fizzy hum.

"Bees? Is that bees?" he wondered.

"It's not bees," she replied, stepping in, tilting her head. "It's the hearing aids. Some still operating. How long does a hearing aid battery last?"

"I don't know. A couple of weeks?"

They listened. Wakely's stomach churned: bees, all these hearing aids, his father's hearing aid.

Lightning strobed nearby, followed by a strong crash of thunder, and when it subsided, the entire obelisk was growling, the sound of the bang fed into the receivers, spit out of ear moulds not into human ears but into the receivers of neighbouring hearing aids, where it was amplified and sent through the tower in a kind of groaning, shivering wave. It gradually subsided and the previous beelike hum resumed.

"Oh god," Virago said. "Let's move."

They continued south, scouting the narrow towers that followed. Among the stacks of hard-to-identify replacement and assembly parts, they encountered mechanical tally counters, clip-on studio microphones, spiked dryer balls, keyboard cable adapters for an obscure computer platform, stainless steel cake-decorator icing tips, some kind of quasi-paracord bracelet with a cheap compass, and a bunch of something Virago identified as "cable bites": hollow plastic phone cable protectors shaped like animals with wide jaws.

On the left, face cream ended at pet grooming mitts, each arrayed with silicon bristles. They passed them for 20 metres while towers of miscellany continued on the right.

Wakely thumbed out his notebook and jotted in a tight, graphite scrawl everything they'd encountered. While writing "hearing aids," he mused that his father's inability to listen to others far predated his need for a hearing aid.

"Master Jack?" Virago called, startling him from his reverie.

"Private," Wakely replied, tucking away the notebook and making rapid study of the passageways around them.

"I was wondering something."

"All right."

"When you got me this morning."

"Yes."

"Well. I've been wondering what you saw."

"You were doing yoga, if I'm not mistaken."

"Mayurasana."

"What?"

"The name of that pose I was doing. It's a hard one."

"Is it."

"Thing about having a lot of tattoos is people always have something to say about them. You know? I guess I'm like, 'When's he going to say something about them?'"

"All right."

She waited, then asked, "So . . . what did you think?"

"I think we need to stay focused."

They edged forward, and after a time she asked, "Have you got any?"

"Any what, Private?"

"Tattoos."

"No. But I guess I'll get one at some point."

"Oh. Any idea what it would be? What image?" she asked.

"A daisy," he replied. He turned and looked briefly into her eyes, and she tried to summon a reply about the Calgary studio that had done hers, their long waitlist, she could put in a word to get him in, but emotion froze her voice in her throat.

He returned his attention to the passageway. "What are those?"

Virago followed his eyes past the pet mitts. They ended at a corridor, after which stretched away a block comprised of millions, or more like billions, of white or clear cylinders, most five or six centimetres in length and a centimetre thick.

Sticking close to the wall, which smelled faintly of dog, she edged towards the intersection.

"Check that passage," he reminded her before she crossed it. She peered around the corner and gasped, then drew back.

"What?" he asked. "Is it safe?"

She nodded and he stepped into the corridor and beheld what she had seen: on the right, stretching 400 metres into the east, a wall of protruding needles. Billions of them. She stood beside him and they gazed in awe. She imagined falling into that wall, ten thousand times impaled.

The staggering quantity made sense: for each vaccine — measles, mumps, rubella, polio, tetanus, HPV, chickenpox, shingles, hepatitis, diphtheria, typhoid, seasonal influenza — a new needle, every time. That didn't include other injections: saline, B12, antibiotics, anesthetic, epinephrine. Insulin too, all the world's diabetics, and not just the human ones; an old boyfriend's cat needed a daily insulin shot. Vets inoculated pets against rabies, kennel cough, parvovirus, adenovirus, distemper. And what about the vaccines and antibiotics used on billions of cows, pigs, chickens, and other animals raised for food?

She thought about IV drug users. Heroin and she didn't know what else.

Reflecting on the rubber gloves they'd just seen, she concluded that medicine's "a-new-one-every-time" doctrine was an environmental curse.

"How many would you guess?" Virago asked Wakely.

"I don't know. How many needles in a lifetime? I mean I've probably had a hundred."

"Not everyone gets needles."

"Well, yeah. Less in developing countries. And not if you're a stupid-ass antivaxxer. Or your stupid-ass parents are," Wakely said.

"Ouch. Some history there?"

"A girlfriend, a few years ago. Her six-year-old got measles and then I found out why. She started to explain, got halfway through the word 'autism' when I ended it. 'Vaccines cause aut—' And at that instant, I walked away. I can tolerate a lot of shit, but not intentional stupidity."

"You think it's intentional?"

"When you decide to trust unqualified, dishonest people, while dismissing those who've clearly done the work, that's intentional."

She wanted to photograph that nightmarishly barbed wall, but his bitterness made her reticent to ask. They continued south, studying the syringes with their graduations and brand names spelled out in black. Many held residual liquids, clear, some cloudy, some filled with a serum of red or blue or amber, but most had been used, plungers deployed. They talked about gathering a few, but for what?

A squawk in Wakely's ear, and he thumbed the radio button. "What's up, boss?"

"Turn around you'll see me," Sharpcot answered, and Wakely pivoted and saw Sharpcot far up the passage. "I tried you back at the camp, you couldn't read me?"

"Not a thing. These blocks — I guess they impede radio. Need line of sight."

"Anything to report?"

He listed the objects they'd encountered, and she told them to continue their recce.

Thunder growled in the distance as they continued south, syringe barrels to the left and various stacks on the right.

Porcelain figurines, each the size of a dime, and every one of them a toucan. Compact electronic sensors, each with a blue motherboard and the words DUST SENSOR. Metal desk grommets: discs with a cutout for computer cables, for insertion into a hole cut into a desktop. Esoteric tools and fasteners, parts and products.

They reached the end of the syringes, and the southern face of the block was a field of plungers. Every syringe oriented like a compass, needle pointing north. Across the aisle stood a monument of pedestals found on marina wharfs, used to supply moored boats with power and water. And on the right the smaller towers ceased at stacked wooden snowshoes, a mixture of authentic and reproductions. They passed between both until they reached a new four-way intersection, with postless aluminum mailboxes occupying the southwest corner, all of a tunnel-top design and of the same approximate size, most in bare aluminum, many painted. Some with the words U.S. Mail stamped into the door. On the left, slabs of stone of varying lengths, two or three metres, a few centimetres thick, in a wide variety of muted colours or naturally variegated patterns. Not stone, Virago reported after examining them, or at least not natural stone. Engineered quartz countertops. Edges of different profiles: bevelled, cove, ogee, bullnose, demi, crescent, chiselled, forming a vertical, stratified face.

Wakely peered along each passage, thumbed the push-to-talk. "Sarge?"

A moment later Sharpcot's voice came in, "What's up, Jack?"

"We're going east a spell. It'll cut off the radio. Won't be long."

"Roger that. Out."

Wakely nodded to Virago, and they proceeded left, between marina pedestals and countertops. Virago took in the pedestals, the water and electrical ports, their finishes in aluminum and stainless steel and wood. Some appeared fancy and sophisticated, and she thought of them feeding million-dollar yachts. Wakely's attention fixed on something past the pedestals, his pace quickening as more of that corner came into view. In a moment they arrived at a T-intersection where the pedestals ended. Across the aisle stood a block made of cans.

"Bingo," Wakely said. "Let's get back."

"Oh yeah, that's more like it!" Bronski cried as he dropped his rifle and, like a supplicant, placed his hands against the wall of tinned lobster meat.

The section regarded the stack, cans labelled Rocky Point, Bar Harbor, Baxter's, Sogel, Homard, Trader Joe's, Indian Island, some in Chinese, Greek, Russian, Thai. Various renderings of lobsters. The block stood only 30 metres wide, but it relieved Sharpcot to know that food existed in the maze, even if she couldn't stand lobster.

Wakely reported that after notifying her by radio, he and Virago had reconnoitred further to investigate the possibility that they'd entered a food zone, but the mix of materials remained random. The next stack was pewter belt buckles: elk and mountains and dragons and trucks and marijuana leaves and Celtic knots and American states ("Why is Texas fetishized?" Virago wondered) and beyond that they'd found woodburning stoves.

Sharpcot feared that like the water bottles these cans might be empty, and she tapped a few and confirmed otherwise. She tried to pry one out, but they'd been stacked with the bottom of each set into the recessed top of the one beneath it, like in a grocery store. Tse got out his entrenching tool and stood with it poised, watching Sharpcot with expectation.

"Let's back everyone off first," she said, and the section stepped away, leaving a semi-circle around Tse that she realized would protect none of them if the cans came down.

Tse jabbed the tool lightly into the wall, piercing a can, and glanced up to see the effect before drawing it out and pulling with it the one he'd impaled, along with a few above it. Either the friction with which they were packed or that alien force prevalent in all the blocks maintained the wall's integrity, and he stooped and picked up the liberated tins and passed them around.

Sharpcot had a can opener and fork ready and she opened the tin and sniffed, tasted the meat. It was wretched, as expected, but she faked a smile at the expectant faces and said, "Delicious. Go ahead."

Only Loko abstained — shellfish allergy — and watched them eating before he regarded the passage in each direction. He turned attention to the countertop block, jammed fingertips into a gap and scrambled a few of metres up before letting go, landing on his boots.

"Do it, mang," Bronski said.

"Fuck off. Anyway, it's going to rain."

"Tse says not for hours."

Wakely watched as he ate. "Private Boyko, you think you could climb to the top of this block?"

"If you want me to, Master Jack."

"What do you say, Sarge?" Wakely asked. "You want an area survey?"

Sharpcot came over, gazed up the block face.

"Why this one?"

"Pretty good for handholds, plus it'll be flat up top," Wakely said. "Can't say that for most of the stuff around here. He can roam to different corners for views in all directions."

"I don't know. I wouldn't order it. Be strictly voluntary."

"I'll do it."

"You understand the risks?"

"I fall, I die," Loko replied with an eager grin. "Standard climbing risk."

Before any more could be said, he propped his rifle against the wall and threw off his pack, jacket, vest, armour — ballistic plates clacking as it struck the ground — dropped his helmet. He stepped out of his boots, pulled off his socks. In a moment he was on the wall, scurrying up like a squirrel.

"Jesus, Loko," Deeks said, a forkful of lobster paused halfway to her mouth, eyes following his rapid ascent.

They backed into the alley between the lobster cans and the marina pedestals for a better view. Sharpcot had to unclench her jaw as he flew up the wall, expertly locating hand- and footholds. In the sky behind him, blue when he'd commenced his ascent, oily cloud began to congeal, and thunder, which they hadn't heard in some time, rumbled. She thought about lightning. With the blocks all the same height, Loko up top would represent the tallest thing around. And what if it rained?

"Private Tse," she called. "Are we going to be hit by that storm while he's up there?"

"Likely, Sarge," he replied.

"Wait. Didn't you tell Bronski not for hours?" Wakely asked.

"I did not. I told him definitely within the hour."

"Heh. What?" Bronski asked as Wakely stepped towards him. "It's not like the guy's always right. Okay, okay, so I told a white lie. How many, sir? Twenty?"

"Fifty," Wakely barked, and Bronski groaned and went to the ground and begin doing pushups, neck craned to watch his friend's progress.

The new information made Sharpcot consider calling him down, but he was nearing the summit. Let him take a quick glance around and come down. She mused that he climbed with a confidence he lacked while walking.

But there came a strobe of lightning, and an immediate clap of thunder, and he slipped. It all happened simultaneously, flash-boom-slip, and he fell a brief distance before he jammed his fingertips into a gap. He hung there, feet scrabbling for purchase, and Tse darted to the wall's foot, body tilted and arms uplifted, ready to catch him. Sharpcot calculated that a fall into Tse's arms would mean two injured or dead men. Leclerc cried, "He's okay," as Loko resumed the ascent, apparently unfazed.

After a minute he flipped over the edge and stood and pivoted and waved down. Sharpcot suffered vertigo as she imagined herself at that railingless brink, gazing nine storeys down. He smiled triumphantly as he lifted his head, then strode confidently along the verge, heedless of his footing. Sharpcot wished she'd provided clearer instruction: what he should look for, how far to go, how long to stay up.

"Loko," she shouted through cupped hands. "Look east!"

"What?" he called, cambering harrowingly forward with hands on knees.

"East!" she cried, waving her hand. "The direction we're travelling!"

Loko straightened and gazed eastward. "Big stuff!" he shouted.

"What kind of stuff?" Sharpcot yelled.

"Big! Really big!"

He stalked along the ledge towards the northeast corner, and he stood, a heroic figure against the stormy sky, hands on hips, surveying the distance. He broke his stance and shouted down through cupped hands, "Should I take a picture?"

"What? How?"

Loko drew his phone from a pocket and powered it on and began to snap photos.

Bronski continued his punishment, moaning, "If that little fucker falls . . ." but the rest was lost in a boom of thunder.

"Checking other directions," Loko shouted, and disappeared from view.

Sharpcot dropped her head and rubbed her neck and met Wakely's eye. More lightning, followed by a crack of thunder, and a drop of rain smacked the top of her helmet. She raised her eyes again, hoping to see Loko descending, but he was nowhere in sight. More rain, fat drops like glass marbles.

"Loko," she called up. "Private Boyko!"

He did not appear, and she called again.

"Help me out, soldiers," she shouted.

"Loko!" they called repeatedly in unison. Lightning answered, strong thunder. More rain.

And suddenly Loko was there, at the top of the wall, smile gone, urgency in his motions. He turned and lowered his naked feet to the countertop face. The rain came on. Sharpcot looked up and with a bomb of fear ticking in her gut watched him descend. The rest of the section stood frozen, shielding their eyes from the rain, watching. They should be running for cover, but there was no cover, there was only their colleague climbing down the wall in a thickening rain. Lightning struck close, followed by a sudden, deep boom that shook the earth, rattled the lobster tins. He descended fast, falling more than climbing, a controlled descent where by luck or skill he reached a handhold to slow his descent enough to keep him from accelerating to the point where he could not keep hold. The rain intensified and she couldn't keep looking, water filling her eyes, blinding her. She lowered her head to stare straight at the wall, rain running off the rim of her helmet in a beaded curtain. She heard voices around her, but didn't turn, didn't look, just tried to will a cocoon of safety around Loko, alone on the wall. A kind of fugue overcame her, one that she hadn't experienced since Afghanistan. Moving through the landscape outside the wire, soldier in front, soldier behind, keep your spacing, land your boots in the prints of the guy ahead. A trance of motion at the threshold of death.

Then Loko's big, pale feet — she hadn't realized how big they were, disproportionate to his body size — slid into view below her helmet's brim. The rest of him descended into view, short legs, tiny butt, back, arms, hands making impossible grips into the wall.

He landed and turned, grinning, utterly soaked.

"Good work, soldier," Sharpcot shouted over the storm.

He saluted, then dropped to his knees, and was overcome by a fit of shaking.

She knelt, put a hand on his shoulder. Someone threw a rain poncho over them, and the rain abruptly ceased, became a crackle against the vinyl.

He put a hand in his pocket and pulled out his drenched phone, thrust it into her hands.

7

They squatted in a circle at the intersection of marine pedestals, lobster tins, and countertops, wearing their CADPAT ponchos, the rain falling hard and steady. Loko, who'd declined to put on his socks and boots while wet, had drawn the hood over his head and pulled the drawstring tight.

"You look," Bronski said in an Eastern European accent, "like Czechoslovakian refugee lady."

"You look like Polish asshole," Loko replied in the same accent.

Sharpcot hadn't looked at the photos yet, concerned about rain hitting the phone, though it was already soaked when Loko handed it to her. She'd drawn the hand that clutched it into her sleeve and was running a thumb against the screen's glass like a worry stone. Bronski asked Deeks about the Blue Jays' chances in their weekend series against the Yankees. She didn't reply.

Tse stuck a hand out from under his poncho, said, "It's stopping."

The thunder ceased long ago, and Sharpcot had settled into the idea that it would rain for the rest of the day, as was the pattern for the region: wind and thunder at the start, which settled into an interminable rain that rarely broke before nightfall.

It occurred to her that only a massive alteration of the landscape — hundreds of square kilometres of varying objects, with unique thermal signatures and reflectivity — could influence local climate. If the change was affecting the regional meteorological patterns, that demonstrated the tremendous scale of the maze. It meant it spread further than she feared. She hadn't stopped hoping to abruptly reach its border, to step between a pair of blocks onto prairie. She closed her eyes and saw it: yellow grass stretching away under a blue sky, wind stroking her cheeks.

"Sunshine," Virago said, and Sharpcot opened her eyes and looked up to see a sunbeam lance through the clouds and strike the lobster tins high up.

The section rose and cast off ponchos, though a light rain continued to fall, raindrops like descending fireflies, charged with sunlight.

"Hey, maybe a rainbow," Bronski said, looking towards the sun.

"Wrong way," Leclerc said, pointing, and everyone turned to see a fragment of rainbow between countertops and lobster cans like an archway into the east.

Wet from rain before they'd sheltered under the ponchos, Sharpcot longed for the bitter dust of Afghan summer, to be hot and dry, for a few hours at least. Sunlight reached into the maze's narrow passageways only at midday, and that was hours ago.

She threw off her poncho and pushed the power button on Loko's phone. At first nothing, and she thought the rain had killed it, but a white apple appeared, and it booted to the lock screen. She glanced at the upper left, the spark of hope extinguished by "No Service."

"Private Boyko, unlock please," she asked.

Loko stood glumly with a wet sock in each hand and was glad to delay the enterprise of putting them on. He dropped them and punched the code and opened the photos app and scrolled to the first one. He handed the phone to Sharpcot.

"Really? A selfie?"

A grinning Loko stood in the frame, but in the far distance, obscured by the haze of approaching rain, she saw the "really big stuff" he'd reported: a block four times the height of the surrounding ones, and vastly wide, running out of the frame.

141

He'd taken another shot, minus himself. She zoomed in. Might be ships, by the line of superstructures. Cargo ships. Oil tankers. Cruise liners. In the deeper distance and further south another massive block, equally tall, wide enough to escape the image, its composition obscure. She scrolled through the other photos which showed the expansive top of the countertop block and a few images of the neighbouring block tops, the lobster cans, belt buckles, wood stoves. She flipped back to the first photo.

"Jack," she called, and handed him the phone.

"I see he included himself for scale," Wakely murmured, squinting at the first image. "Huh. I guess not everything fits in the standard block. And does that look like ships to you?"

"Yeah. How far away do you think that is?"

"I don't know. Fifteen clicks? I wonder what this other tower is."

"It'll be off our track, pretty far south."

Wakely flipped through the photos. One shot illustrated the top of the block, countertops: right-angled, odd-angled, curved, two-tiered, and most with sink and tap cutouts, trip-hazards over which Loko would've had to step.

"That was brave work, soldier," Wakely told Loko.

"Master Jack."

He handed back the phone. "Now get your gear on." He called, "Three Section, kit up. Wet or not, we're moving."

They headed east until sundown, packs heavy with wet and lobster cans, passed through a landscape of brass and stone sundials, battery-powered milk frothers, stainless steel soup ladles, multi-bladed windpump fans, ironing boards, front-loading washing machines, wooden picnic tables. They bedded down after dark in a canyon with orange traffic cones on the south side, stacked neatly cone-upon-cone in fluorescent spires, and dog crates, plastic, big and small, to the north. It smelled like roadwork, it smelled like dogs. Deeks said it made her miss her dog, Lasha. They all knew about Lasha, an Australian shepherd who did tricks, gone six years, still a source of grief.

The night fell clear and cool. Sharpcot took first watch, and Wakely relieved her at midnight. He sat on a Chihuahua crate, rifle across his lap. He thought about the things they'd passed that day, looked into the stuttering fire fuelled by boards they'd snapped off picnic tables, longing for that woodland nestled between drums and teapots where they'd spent the previous night.

He got up and fed table fragments into the fire, squatted there nudging them about, trying to make something happen. The splintered ends sparked and caught. He looked each way along the passageway, soldiers sprawled under their rain-damp ranger blankets, saw Leclerc on her side nearby, watching him. He nodded and she lifted herself on an elbow and looked at the sputtering fire.

"Can't sleep?" he whispered.

She shrugged.

"Ask you a question?"

"Sure."

He paused as he constructed the query. "What uh ... what proportion of the Earth do people occupy? Cities and suburbs. Office buildings and malls and warehouses. Apartments and houses. I mean how much land do we actually cover with our stuff?"

She sat up and crossed her legs, drew her blanket over a shoulder, firelight illuminating her pale features. She thought a moment, and Wakely imagined her consulting a database in her brain. "On the spectrum," Sharpcot once said once of her. He'd previously only heard that applied to kids.

"There's not much agreement," she replied.

"Ballpark. Is it like, 20 percent?"

"Oh no. Nothing like that. The dispute is whether it's one percent or two percent."

"That's all?"

"It's a big place."

"How much would one percent be?"

"Approximately one million square kilometres."

"Sounds like a lot," Wakely replied.

"It's a square 1000 kilometres per side."

"Is it?"

"Of course. One thousand squared equals one million."

"Right," Wakely replied. He decided she wasn't trying to make him feel stupid.

"How big is Canada?" Virago asked. She'd sat up to listen.

"I actually know that," Loko's voice called from the darkness. "From grade nine geography. Weird what sticks with you. It's ten million square kilometres."

"Wait, that's all?" Wakely said.

Sharpcot spoke: "So, one-tenth."

"Sergeant," Wakely said, trying to make her out in the darkness.

"Don't mind me," she said. "Carry on."

"One-tenth what?" Bronski asked. "What are you talking about?"

"If you took all the cities," Wakely said. "All the urban and suburban areas in the world, and put them in Canada, how much space would it take up?"

"And what's the answer?" Bronski asked.

"One-tenth of Canada," Leclerc said.

"Not much," Wakely replied.

"Are you kidding?" Virago said.

"I'm not," Wakely said, his voice rising now that it was clear no one was sleeping. "Imagine all the cities. Major ones like New York, London, Moscow, Mexico City, Tokyo, and every little one too. Winnipeg. Brandon. Plus every little town and hamlet in France and Pakistan and Peru. Take all those huge Chinese manufacturing towns. You stick them all together, cluster them in one spot. It covers one-tenth, *one-tenth* of Canada. Ninety percent empty. While the rest of the world is nothing. Or not nothing: nature. Trees and mountains and deserts."

144

"Is that what's happened?" Loko asked in a soft voice. "Is that what we're looking at? This," he said, raising his hands and taking in the blocks. "All of this?"

"I don't know."

"Nine storeys," Virago said. "If you figure nine storeys is taller than the majority of the world's buildings. And if this is everything, packed together . . ."

"Right," Leclerc said. "The way things are packed means higher-than-native density."

"Like your apartment seems crammed," Deeks said. "But you arrange it right, pack it tight, you can fit it in the small U-Haul."

"Meaning a million square klicks might be an overstatement?" Virago asked.

"Even if it's everything," Wakely said.

"What are you guys saying?" Bronski demanded, his voice edgy.

"Even if this maze contains everything, it might not be that big," Deeks said.

"Seems big to me," Bronski replied. "From down here. Hauling our asses through it."

"So it'll have a boundary," Sharpcot said. "What's beyond it?"

"We saw trees," Loko said with mild panic in his voice. "There are still trees, right?"

"Looks like trees have been . . . respected," Virago said.

"So let's say forests are still out there," Wakely replied. "This is everything created by mankind, arranged in a square. It's a thousand klicks per side. Give or take."

"Okay. So who's responsible?" Sharpcot wondered.

"Not this again," Bronski cried. "Why does there have to be a who?"

"Then what?" Wakely asked.

"Can we agree for Bronski's edification that *someone* or *something* did this," Deeks pleaded.

"No way," Bronski replied. "I'm not agreeing to that."

A long pause while everyone tried to reconcile Bronski's logic.

145

"The Accruers," Tse's deep voice spoke in the darkness.

"Fuck that shit!" Bronski shouted, rising to his knees. "I never signed up for this!"

"Stand down, Private," Wakely said calmly.

"I'm not standing!" he cried, flapping his hands.

"First true thing he's spoken," Deeks muttered.

"If there are aliens, where are these fucking aliens?" Bronski demanded. He shouted to the sky, "Show yourselves, mother-fuckers!"

"We have evidence of their existence. We're surrounded by it," Leclerc explained calmly, oblivious to Bronski's agitation.

"Trav," Loko said in a gentle voice. "If your garbage cans get knocked over, do you have to see raccoons to know they did it?"

Bronski was on his feet now, they could see his pacing silhouette. "It's not fucking aliens. This is our stuff. Someone — people — have simply arranged it this way. Maybe it's a corporate thing. Or maybe the Chinese did it, or Russians. You know, to fuck us up."

"I've seen stuff from Russia here. And China," Leclerc stated.

"What's not from China these days?" Deeks asked.

"Whatever it is, it's going to take a while to clean up," Bronski said.

"Who's going to do that?" Loko wondered.

"People. I bet the army or whatever's working on it right now."

"We're the army!" Loko cried, bolting upright. "We're the fucking army!"

"Like the Americans or whatever," Bronski persisted.

"Dude, grow up. The world is done!" Loko cried. "We're the last people on Earth."

"No we're not," Bronski said, sitting down on his sleeping pad, suddenly calm.

"What makes you say that?"

"It just wouldn't make sense. It wouldn't be right."

"What the hell are you saying?" Loko persisted. "You're living in a dream world. This is the end of everything. This is Armageddon."

"This?" Bronski said. "Well it's a pretty tidy Armageddon, isn't it."

"What does that even mean?"

"Armageddon is like a nuclear holocaust or asteroids, right? Cities wiped out. Everybody incinerated. Or a plague that kills everybody. Or zombies."

"You're the zombie," Loko cried.

"But this stuff. It's nice and neat. I never seen an apocalypse like this."

"Never seen? What does that mean?" Deeks asked.

"Like in movies."

"Dude," Loko replied, striving to sound calm. "Trav. Look. All this stuff, the way it is right now, is useless. I mean we might get lucky and find stuff to survive on, like lobster or hopefully something I'm not allergic to, but civilization is done. It's over."

"It's not over. It's right here."

"Fine, smartass, define civilization?"

"What do you mean?"

"How about this: If this is civilization, then make me a sandwich."

"What are you talking about?"

"Make me a goddamn sandwich."

"Do I look like a chick to you?" Bronski sniggered.

"Whoa there, fuckhead," Deeks growled.

"What I mean is," Loko persisted, "civilization is kind of like making a sandwich. The luxury of making a sandwich. Whenever you feel like it."

"That's your definition?" Bronski sneered.

"He's kind of right," Virago said. "You're sitting in your apartment. You think: Hey, I want a tuna sandwich. You've

147

either got the stuff to make one, or can go to Sev and pick one up ready-made, or buy bread and tuna and mayo. Point is, in 20 minutes you're eating a tuna sandwich."

"Wait, I want mine with scallions," Deeks muttered.

"Right," Loko said. "Exactly!"

"Whatever," Bronski replied.

"What do you say, Trav," Deeks said, and continued in a breathy southern drawl, "I'd do just 'bout anything if you made me a tuna sandwich."

"How about you suck my dick?"

"I'd rather not get tetanus," Deeks shot back.

"Bronski and Deeks," Wakely snapped.

"Tell them to stop making fun of me," Bronski whined.

"We're trying to help you see a point," Virago said.

"And what point is that? That the world is over? It's not over. It's all — right — here!" He jerked his arms about, pointing randomly.

"And useless," Loko hissed. "All this is useless. If this is civilization, find us shelter for the night. Or get me a popsicle. Or fly me to Argentina. It's almost like wilderness. Worse than wilderness. Out there we'd have berries and mushrooms to eat. Here we got shit. You want a traffic cone or a crate for your dog, I can help you out. But if you want anything else, anything necessary for survival, this is a desert. The world as we knew it is over, buddy. It's over!"

Bronski chuckled, said, "Hey mang, chill out. You're going to pop a vein."

"You are such an idiot. You are such a fucking, fucking idiot!" Loko shouted. He might have been crying.

"Private Boyko," Wakely said in a calm voice, rising to his feet and stepping to where the private stood. He put a hand on his shoulder. "Easy there, Kyrylo."

"Yeah, where's the pile of valium, mang?" Bronski said.

"All of you, shut up," came Sharpcot's voice from the darkness. "Shut up with this speculation. We only know what we've seen.

Anything else is conjecture. Our job as members of the armed forces is to stay disciplined, and find out what's happened and — more importantly — fulfill our duty. That's what I want you to think about as we travel over the next few days — and we are going to travel, hard, make our push and get to the city — is what can I do, as a soldier, to support my section, and support my country. Is that understood?"

There was a grumble of ascent.

"Is that understood, Private Bronski? Private Boyko."

"Yes, Sergeant," Bronski replied promptly.

After a few moments, Loko sniffled and answered, "Yes, Sarge."

Sharpcot rose before sunrise, found Tse asleep on watch, tipped against a dog crate with the machine gun across his lap. She kicked his boot, and loudly deprecated him for dereliction of duty, waking the others. He sat there and took it without apparent emotion, but Deeks saw his expression as he bent to collect his ruck, punched his shoulder lightly.

"How'd you sleep?" Wakely asked Sharpcot, but she didn't reply.

They ate a cold breakfast and set out in the nascent dawn, shivering and damp from yesterday's rain. Wakely had done worse, humping through the furnace and freeze of Afghanistan, death ever-present, shadowing you, waiting to pounce, but these unseasoned rookies, exhausted from yesterday's push and late-night chat, plodded along like prisoners.

They passed among paint rollers and water skis and stainless steel tiffin boxes and toy jellyfish made from stretchy gel. A wide stream emerged on the right from a block of tractor-pulled disc harrows and crossed the passage and entered a wall of toasters. Beyond the rift where the stream entered the toaster wall they saw that it drained into a large pond contained within the toaster block. Vertical walls of toasters towered above the pool, most of them silver and black, some coloured, all set upright, displaying faces or flanks, levers, doneness dials, sliders, buttons or switches for frozen, for bagels. Vintage streamlined or boxy modern, a name or logo on a face. A few novelty ones in iconic shapes: Mickey Mouse, Darth Vader, Volkswagen bus. They were steel and plastic and chrome, and all of them, from what they could see, of the two-slice, top-loading type.

The pool reminded Sharpcot of a quarry where'd she'd once in her teens skinny-dipped with a boy she couldn't remember, at least not beyond the squeaky nakedness of his skin against hers as they grappled tentatively before parting, embarrassed and awed at what had almost happened. The experience forgotten until this moment.

This pond sustained an ecology, stunted plantlife beneath a surface creased by water striders, rushes clustered along the eastern edge, a dorsal flash of fish beyond the reflection of toaster walls. Toasters visible in the underwater murk around the pool's perimeter.

They filled their water bottles and flasks. Leclerc pointed out a spotted frog and Bronski joked about frog legs for lunch.

"It is an option," Wakely said. "Or fish."

"Are we eating frogs, or moving on?" Sharpcot exhorted.

They forded the creek and pushed east, hit walls that obstructed their progress (chest freezers, enamelled Dutch ovens, soldering irons), forcing them north or south to seek the next eastbound pass.

They paused for lunch, and Loko, who was out of IMEs, ate two cans of lobster.

"Thought you were allergic," Deeks said.

"Well, you know the army. Only way to avoid a thing is pretend it will kill you."

"So you're full of shit," she said.

"Full of lobster, actually," he replied with a grin. "Never tried lobster cuz they're basically giant bugs. But it's great. You going to eat that?"

The day warmed but humidity remained low and they made good progress, and in the afternoon, a white pilothouse bristling with masts and radar — first sign of the megablock of ships — rose beyond a wall of something they couldn't identify, a mosaic of brightly hued pebbles that they approached between a nine-storey medusa of extension cords (black, brown, white, green, orange, yellow) on the left and on the right cat trees made from wood and wrapped in carpet and sisal all in grey and white and tan and black.

As they neared the coloured wall they detected a sweet smell, fruity and fermented, pleasant until it turned poisonous with its potency.

"Jellybeans!" Deeks declared.

Along the block's top they saw the effect of yesterday's rain: an oozing rainbow of melted candy. Below it, intact beans formed a polychromatic field that Virago mused could've been arranged, like pixels, to portray an image. For some reason, she imagined the iconic Barack Obama "Hope" poster. But there was no hope. Arranged as they were stochastically, the effect was of a jumbotron screen tuned to a dead channel, a fatiguing, multicoloured noise.

They bunched in the intersection and looked each way to determine the shortest route to the next eastbound passage, but could see neither corner. Loko stepped forward and jammed a hand into the wall, pulled out a handful beans, and brought it to his mouth.

"Loko, are you kidding me?" Deeks said.

"What? There's plenty for everyone," he said, and crammed a few into his mouth, chewing, nodding.

They went north, some scooping jellybeans as they passed, stowing them in ziplocks. When they reached the next intersection, they discovered large stainless steel tables with tops made from rollers — fruit and vegetable graders — and opposite, jewellery beads of all kinds: seed beads, rocailles, toho beads, wooden beads, semi-precious stone beads, Swarovskis, chatons, rivoli crystals. The wall exceeded jellybeans in dazzle for their broader range of colour and size and shape and faceting. Looking east down the corridor of beads and jellybeans, a psychedelic nightmare, they saw, half a kilometre away and towering 40 storeys high: stacked ships.

Wind soughed down the passage, carrying with it the scent of ocean.

Sharpcot drew a deep breath, reminded of the sea, crash of surf, bleat of wheeling gulls, but the candy reek intervened, and as they approached the stacked ships at the end of the corridor between beads and beans, the ocean smell turned fishy and rancid.

A nameless anxiety impaired their progress. These were not beads, or toasters, or toilets, these were oceangoing vessels of overwhelming scale. In the water, at the quayside, at anchor in a harbour or coasting along the horizon, they appeared graceful, resolute, but here their enormity was unsettling. Stacked against the prairie sky, they exhibited a precariousness, and Sharpcot acknowledged an urge to flee even as she pushed on.

They heard wind whispering through masts and rails, slipping between the packed hulls. A creak of something swaying, and then the slap of a cable against steel.

The hull of the ship at ground level, black above the waterline and russet below, stood with its rail lower than the bead and jellybean blocks. Hull plates barnacled and rimed with salt, a path of rust streaking the paint below a tug bitt.

On top of this ship rested a smaller one, azure, set with its keel on the deck below. And atop that ship, another, a medium-sized ferry with yellow, white, and blue striping and Arabic script painted along its flank. Hulls and masts of other ships were visible beyond those forming the block's boundary.

They emerged from the bead-bean passageway and halted, gazing up at the ship before them. Its bilge, red paint pocked by rust and barnacles, curved down to meet the keel, which lay buried in a metre of soil. Above the waterline, a vertical expanse of scratched and peeling black. The ground here was muddy, air salty, rank of rotting fish and seaweed. Loko squatted and poked one of the puddles and licked his finger. "Salty," he reported.

"Gross, mang. That's fish pee," Bronski muttered.

Sharpcot glanced north up the passage, wall of beads on the left, ship hulls curving up from keels and forming a continuous rampart on the right. She squinted south, knowing from Loko's photo that the block's terminus lay nearer that way.

She set off, with the section falling in.

They reached the bow of the ship, saw its name painted there, MSC *Ingy*, passed next along an orange-red ship *Arctic Princess* with four steel domes rising from its deck, then an enormous Maersk Line container ship in light blue — a third of a kilometre long — with two smaller cargo vessels stretched end to end on its deck ahead of the bridge, and a couple of fishing trawlers, a billionaire yacht, and a littoral combat ship on top of those. Clusters of disoriented seagulls populating rails and rigging. Next a black tanker with a red and teal smokestack, the whole thing emitting an oily reek, and when they reached the prow they read the name *Sifa*. On top of that, black and red *Century Melody*, with smaller vessels packed around its loading cranes. On and on they went, passing container ships, bulk carriers, LPG carriers, each topped by two or more levels of smaller vessels: coast guard ships and destroyers and ice breakers and one named *Queen of Cowichan*, its freeboard emblazoned with "BC Ferries."

The block exuded a miasma of shifting smells — crude and refined oil, diesel, rotting fish, iron, seaweed, salt water. On the right, jellybeans had ended to give way to rag mops, followed by beams of extruded aluminum; some kind of exotic vehicle gearboxes; computerized industrial knitting machines, all of the same model, in black, with a Chinese nameplate. The distance between the righthand wall and the flanks of the ships remained consistently four metres, the passage providing more space at ground level where the ships' hulls tapered inward to their keels.

The undercuts formed murky caverns where drips of bilgewater ran down the curved hull plates to form salt-rimmed pools.

"We could shelter underneath, you know, if it rained," Deeks said to Loko.

"There's no way," he said, face betraying panic. "No way I'd go under there." He kept glancing up at the ships and wincing.

"You think they're going to fall over?" Deeks asked with a half smile.

"What the hell keeps them up?" he groaned. "Nothing."

"Probably that weird force that holds everything else together," she reassured him.

"Oh, so magic? Magic keeps them from rolling over and crushing us? Thank you. I feel so much better."

They crossed a foot-deep recession, flat with sharp margins, like the fragments of roadways they'd encountered near Shilo, but wider, and walls showing signs of erosion, some sections crumbling, weeds and grasses taking root on its floor.

"Two-lane highway," Sharpcot said.

"Trans-Canada," she heard Tse say at the back of the line.

A soft red block on the right, winter parkas in various styles, hoods lined in faux and real fur. Virago pulled one down in a rage, cursing the brand, Canada Goose. "Murder coats!" she exclaimed. Bronski taunted her by picking it up and attempting to pull it on (impossible without removing his gear and ruck) before Wakely barked at him to drop it and get back in line. Sharpcot lifted a tag dangling from a sleeve: 129 Euros, from a store she'd never heard of. Wakely half-thought to grab a coat, thinking ahead to autumn, and the brutal prairie winter. He jotted in his notebook, "red parkas," and added: "near SW corner ships."

They paused for a bathroom break in an alley between coats and cake platters before forging ahead.

Transparent suction cups, then white votive candles — they grabbed a few, useful at night, when flashlight batteries died. Then ballpoint pens.

"There's my goddamn pen!" Bronski cried as he tugged one from the block.

They were Bic Cristals, or knockoffs, "biros," Deeks called them. The sun pierced the clear barrels along the block's edge, scattering rainbows against a massive white and blue vehicle carrier across the aisle. Like everything else, their condition varied widely, from shiny new to worn, clouded, cracked, splintered, gnawed, hemorrhaging ink inside the barrel. Reservoirs full, half, empty.

"Guess the caps are someplace else," Deeks said.

They collected a few. As they moved away, Bronski wiped ink-stained hands against his pants.

After the vehicle carrier lay a cruise ship, with a red bulbous bow and keel, glossy black hull, gold anchor, and a gold stripe that started with a design flourish at the bow that ran above a double row of portholes to the stern, the stripe interrupted a third of the way back with the ship's name: *Disney Fantasy*. A trio of bow thrusters abaft the waterline marker. The superstructure with stateroom balconies dominated the deck, towering over the ballpoint pens and the big block that followed, round-tube chrome racks from every clothing store on Earth.

Craning their necks they could make out the green sides of the ship perched on the top deck, but little more than that beyond the glass galleries protruding above the staterooms.

"Lifeboat berths are empty," Leclerc noted.

"Maybe everyone went overboard," Virago suggested.

"And then where?" Sharpcot wondered.

After walking its 340-metre length, they discovered abutting the liner's sloped stern the prow of the bulk carrier *Callao Express*. The *Fantasy*'s hull retracted where the screws, half-buried in earth, emerged from the hull, and in the gap between the two vessels they saw the side of a tanker, with more ships piled on top. High above them, on the cruise ship's stern, hung a minivan-sized sculpture of Dumbo the elephant gripping a paint can in his trunk, and perched in his yellow hat, a mouse in ringmaster's garb stretched out with a paintbrush, apparently completing in gold paint the embellishment around the ship's name.

An air of abandoned cheeriness pervaded, and the ship's stillness, its silent bulk towering above them, was haunting.

"Could be food up there," Wakely said. "In the galleys. Should we send someone up?"

"I'm not climbing a ghost ship for Mickey-shaped pretzels," Loko stated, then added, "Master Corporal, sir."

On the deck above the "Hapag-Lloyd" emblazon along the *Callao Express*'s side lay a smaller ship, a literal wreck raised from the sea bottom, every surface and spar jacketed in crustaceans and sea flora, all of it bleaching and crumbling in the dry prairie air. Seashells, chunks of dead coral, and desiccated anemones lay scattered on the floor of the passageway. They saw an enormous rent in the hull behind the bow — "Torpedoed," Tse suggested — which had clearly broken off and now lay forced into its original position. Smaller ships lay on top, and only by that mysterious repulsive force did they not crush the fragile hull.

The clothing racks ended, were followed by rubber hot water bottles, most in a red that matched the antifouling paint of ship keels, but in other colours too, beige, white, green, blue, some shaped like animals, the stink of rubber barely registering above the reek of the sea.

As they neared the *Callao*'s stern they made out the flat-decked vessel that followed, and Sharpcot pointed to indicate clear sky beyond it, stated, "Last boat." Many mid-sized ships lay sprawled along the ample deck, its steeply sloped freeboard painted grey. An aircraft carrier.

They passed the *Callao*'s rudder and bronze propellers and moved under the tray of the carrier's flight deck, which was fringed with horizontal mesh fencing. The ship was set back to maintain the protruding landing deck at the prescribed four metres from the blocks opposite — hot water bottles, then bowling pins, then cereal bar wrappers (Sunbelt Quaker Clif Sante Kellogg's Nature Valley Corny Free Uncle Toby's Iron Vegan Kirkland Selection Kashi Kind Fibre1 Great Value Made Good Nature's Path Atkins President's Choice Tesco Carman's Cascadian Farm), foil-lined polypropylene, torn open and flattened and packed to form a huge, sweet-smelling monument.

"Sea-wiz," Tse said as they passed beneath a platform ahead of the carrier's landing deck.

"In English we say 'gee wiz,'" Bronski corrected him.

"It's how you pronounce CIWS, dope," Tse responded. "That thing there is the Phalanx Close-In Weapons System. This is a supercarrier, Nimitz class."

"Obviously," Bronski replied. "My dad served in the navy. Mang, if he could see this." He slipped off his rucksack and rooted about, dug past a towel, bag of jellybeans, dirty underwear, pulled out the signalman's manpack radio and set it on the ground, finally located his phone.

"What's that beeping?" Wakely said. "That someone's phone? Bronski, that your phone?"

Bronski was snapping photos of the carrier, shook his head.

"I think it's you, Master Jack," Tse said.

Wakely padded his TAC vest and pulled from a pocket the portable dosimeter he'd found in the bunker's armoury. Panic blossomed in his gut. The display showed red and the device chirped insistently.

"Oh shit. Three Section," he cried. "This way, no questions, move, move!" He waved them back up the aisle and ran with them into the passageway between cereal bar wrappers and bowling pins. He held the counter in front of him as they rushed down it, watched the numbers fall, warning colours cycling from red to yellow to green, before he called a stop.

"What the hell?" Sharpcot called, panting. "Jack, what just happened?"

"This," he said, holding up the counter. "Dosimeter. Measures radiation. Just went nuts."

"From what?" Sharpcot asked.

"Nimitz class are nuclear," Tse said.

"Right. Reactor on that ship must be compromised," Wakely said.

"How much of a dose did we get, Jack?" Sharpcot asked.

"I can't read this thing, I don't know. It was in the red for a minute."

"Whoa, what?" Bronski asked, his hand covering his crotch. "Did my boys just get radiated?"

"I'm sure your ovaries are fine," Deeks shot.

Wakely silenced Bronski's rebuttal with a glance, bent his head, and fiddled with the device. "I think there's a way to get a history. Someone else want to look? Virago, you're techy."

Virago accepted the dosimeter and worked the buttons. "This graph here — dose over time. It spikes, then drops sharply, I guess as we ran. And this is accumulated dose. In the green. Looks like we're okay."

"We'll have to avoid that carrier," Sharpcot stated. "This way."

They headed away from the ships, between bowling pins — some new, but most yellowed, grimy, scuffed, and battered — and cereal bar wrappers, until they reached a four-way intersection, obscure steel assemblies, each three metres long, stacked in vertical columns, and the block opposite made from millions of municipal parking meters.

"Keep an eye on that thing," Sharpcot ordered Virago, who held the dosimeter aloft like a talisman, as if it could ward off radioactivity rather than detect it.

"All good," Virago reported as they moved south. They reached a new intersection, the righthand corner a block of dark, fist-sized stone oblongs.

"Bunch of rocks, finally something interesting," Loko grumbled.

"They are interesting," Leclerc insisted as she pulled one out, examined it. "This is pure flint. And it's been shaped by chipping." She held it in her palm with a sharp point exposed.

"What is it?" Tse asked as he towered over her.

"Prehistoric hand axe." She mimicked a chopping motion with it. "These are really old. From museum collections." Then quieter to Tse, "Or excavated by the Accruers."

She handed him the axe and he gripped it, studying its knapped faces. He set it gingerly back into the spot where Leclerc had pulled it.

The other block was AA alkaline batteries arranged in vertical columns, dominated by the major manufacturers — Duracell, Energizer, Rayovac, Panasonic — along with constellations of less common brands and re-brands: Sony, Fuji, Toshiba, Daewoo, Kirkland, Monoprice, GP, Kodak, GoGreen, IKEA, Camelion, Tenergy, VARTA, Fusion, ACDelco, Allmax, Toys "R" Us, Maxell, Fujitsu, Philips, Sunbeam, and more, printed in a variety of languages and scripts. New, scratched, dented, crushed, some ruptured and leaking, all oriented upright, positive terminal up, and Leclerc stood looking with a hand pressed to her helmet.

"You're figuring something out," Tse observed.

"Each column is batteries joined in series. Twenty-eight metres high, and a battery is, what, five centimetres in length ..." She thought a moment, then said, "Five hundred and sixty batteries. Each with a full charge, that's 840 volts."

Deeks tentatively touched the wall, then shuddered and yodelled. Bronski seized her arm and pulled her away, and she shook him off, cried, "Dude, get your hands off me."

"What? I saved your life!"

159

"You didn't save my life, shitpump, there's no charge without a circuit. Plus you never touch a person who's being electrocuted — you'll die too."

"Fuck, mang! Last time I try to be a hero."

Far down the corridor between cereal bar wrappers and batteries Sharpcot saw ships towering against the sky, the stern of the aircraft carrier standing high above the intersection.

"What's your reading?" Sharpcot asked Virago.

"Yellow," Virago reported.

"We'll keep going south until we can pick up a safe east-bound passage."

They travelled between batteries and hand axes, the latter brief and soon followed by cartons of instant mashed potatoes. They grabbed a few. Batteries ran for another 200 metres and both blocks ended at rolls of plastic lawn edging right and guitar effects pedals left, boxes in lurid colours with knobs and switches, names like Fuzz Unit, Leviathan, 7th Heaven, Big Muff, Carbon Copy, Metal Zone, Sneak Attack, Flashback, Triple Wreck.

They turned left, and Sharpcot led them between batteries and stompboxes, Virago continuing to monitor radiation levels. The guitar pedals gave way to a tangle of spoked wheels, pedals, and seats. Sharpcot experienced a rush that they'd found bicycles, but her vision of them tripling their pace was dashed when they turned out to be unicycles: black tires, frames and rims in various colours, randomly arranged.

"So what we do," Deeks said, "is all learn how to ride, and roll into Winnipeg one-wheeled and victorious. The Princess Pat's Unicycle Review."

As they approached the end of batteries and unicycles Sharpcot took the dosimeter from Virago and proceeded ahead. When she reached the end she extended it into the corridor. The unit began to chirp and indicators rose into the high yellow.

"Shit," she said, withdrawing her arm as the section collected behind her. The detector returned to green.

"Batteries are dense," Leclerc said. "Good blocking. I wonder how that reactor was shut down."

"Twin reactors," Tse said. "They're designed to auto-scram if something happens. Like if the ship takes a hit and sinks."

"How many nuclear warships in that block?" Sharpcot asked.

"Not just warships," Leclerc said. "Icebreakers too. And subs. Though subs will have their own block."

"So we're fucked wherever we go," Bronski moaned.

"Should we head further south?" Wakely asked.

"Takes too long," Sharpcot replied. "We've already lost an hour."

Wakely lit a cigarette to suppress an insubordinate impulse to question their haste to reach a city he didn't believe existed. He saw her annoyed expression from the corner of his eye and regretted his irritation. Lana was there. And he hoped like hell they'd find both her daughter and Winnipeg itself.

"Whatever dose we get will be negligible. Like a chest x-ray." He stuck the cigarette into his mouth and lunged across the corridor, and the rest followed.

The new passage had a futuristic aesthetic, lined on the left by fluorescent tubes set lengthwise, forming a wall of horizontally-ribbed white glass, and opposite that, a steel rampart of galvanized standoff post bases. They followed it for some distance before they reached a T-intersection with a corner of underarm deodorant, a monument of sticks and coloured caps and labels: Secret, Axe, Arm & Hammer, Arrid, Suave, Clinique, Degree, Camay, Dove, Ban, Speed Stick, Neat Feat, Melao, Essential Palace, Gillette, Rexona, Green Beaver, Blica, Lynx, Nivea, Shield, Lcosin, Bioderma, Mitchum, Old Spice, Clarins.

They continued east through a floral/ocean/powder/vanilla/ lavender/coconut/sage/lime/arctic-fresh miasma until they reached a passage running north along ice cream cones, each with a base that tapered to a point, stacked upside-down in packed towers, #1 cake cones, according to Loko, who once worked in an ice cream parlour. A mass of police riot shields formed the southeast block.

Cones collected for snacks were stale and proved inedible. Looking north they saw the ships and with the dosimeter showing green Sharpcot headed towards them.

They passed north between batteries and cones, approaching a tremendous red stern, above the screws and rudders the name *Bu Samra* in Latin and Arabic script, then "Majuro" and a registration number. On its fantail and extending across the space between the ship adjacent sat the Canadian icebreaker *Terry Fox*, and packed on top of that, various yachts, trawlers, ferries, and patrol boats. The dosimeter continued to show green, and they stocked up on batteries for their flashlights before rounding the corner and continuing east along the ships, a different scene with prows and sterns instead of ships' sides forming the boundary. They passed the bow of the USS *Missouri*, which Bronski, remembering a postcard from his father, explained served as a Pearl Harbour museum.

"The Japanese signed their surrender on its deck," Leclerc stated.

"I *know*," Bronski rebutted.

They passed bulk carriers, container ships, a cruise ship named *Allure of the Seas*. Along the right, household gas meters, wooden stir sticks, spring mousetraps, floor heat diffusers in steel. A great yellow ship named *BigLift Barentsz*, then a flat, rust-red stern showing the name MV *Paul R. Tregurtha* and Willington Del.

The proliferation of masts got Sharpcot thinking about the radio, and she called Bronski over.

"Turn around, Private," she ordered, and as he pivoted she opened the flap on his ruck. After rifling around, she asked with forced calm, "Private, where is the manpack?"

Bronski went rigid. "I think it's over by the— over by the—"

"What?" Sharpcot demanded.

"The aircraft carrier," he whimpered.

"Are you kidding me?"

"I was taking pictures of the ship for my dad. I put it down but then Jack — I mean Master Corporal Wakely — made us run. It's not my fault!"

"You will go back and get it, Private Bronski."

"Wait — what?"

"We need that radio, and you are responsible for it. You'll just have to go back there and retrieve it. We will wait."

Bronski staggered sideways and Tse caught him and set him upright like a malfunctioning toy.

"Sarge," Bronski moaned. "I can't. I can't do that. The radiation . . ."

"You will do it, Private," Wakely said.

"I'll go," Loko said, but no one heard him.

"And you'll be quick," Sharpcot added. "We can't wait around. I'm determined to get us to Winnipeg in two days."

"I'll go get it," Loko said, louder.

"Why should you do that, Private Boyko?" Wakely asked.

"I'm quick. I'm not a coward."

"Hey, whoa," Bronski objected, then after reconsidering, "Wait. Yeah, he's right. He should go. He's not a coward."

"Bronski left it. Bronski gets it," Sharpcot stated.

Loko wriggled out of his ruck, removed his jacket and TAC vest and armour. He took off his helmet and handed it to Bronski.

"Buddy," Bronski said.

Loko took off his boots and socks. "I'm quicker barefoot."

"Private Boyko, you are not our signalman," Sharpcot said. "You are not responsible for the loss of equipment. Private Bronski goes."

Bronski walked a circle with his forearms pressed to the sides of his head before sitting heavily on the ground.

"All due respect," Loko said. "Look at him, Sarge. He can't go. I can. So I will."

"Sergeant," Wakely said. "Write this man up for a commendation."

Loko performed a few leg stretches. "I just feel like running. And when this is done we can get going."

"Fine," Sharpcot replied. "You go, Private. But Bronski here will pay for his insubordination later."

Loko took a drink of water and handed his canteen to Sharpcot.

"Kyrylo, you remember the way we came?" Wakely asked. "To get back, go left at ice cream cones and fluorescent tubes, then hang a right at deodorant. Here, wait." He sketched out the route in his notebook, tore out the sheet, handed it to Loko.

"Hey, buddy," Bronski said from the ground, his face wet with sweat, possibly tears. "Be careful, mang."

Loko nodded at Wakely and Sharpcot, then sprinted away. But he didn't turn down the passage between cones and tubes — he ran straight on, down the passage alongside the ships, directly towards the aircraft carrier. Sharpcot and Wakely shouted after him, but he did not slow, and Wakely ran a few steps before he recognized he would never catch the small runner.

Everyone watched through rifle scopes as he ran the two klicks back to the carrier. Wakely reminded them to check safeties and keep fingers off triggers. It took under 10 minutes, and when he vanished around the corner, Sharpcot held her breath, imagining him withering in the radiation.

"Come on, come on," she muttered, staring through the scope, her arms beginning to quake from the rifle's weight. She lowered it and asked, "What if it knocks him out? What then?"

"It would take at least eight grays to render him unconscious," Leclerc explained lightly. "He'd only get that from direct exposure to the core. He'd be dead in a day."

"That's reassuring," Deeks said.

"There he is!" Tse reported.

Loko reappeared, flinging his arms in the air in triumph or despair, and headed back, running hard.

164

About halfway home he stumbled and fell, raising a cry from the group, and Wakely bolted a few steps forward before the private rose and came on.

"Where the hell did that kid find courage?" Sharpcot wondered.

"End of the world will do that to a person," Wakely mused. At last he stumbled into their midst and fell to hands and knees, wheezing. Sharpcot kneeled beside him, tenderly lifted each arm to free the radio's straps. She threw it at Bronski, who barely managed to catch it. Loko flipped onto his back, struggling to catch his breath, grinning madly at the section clustered over him.

"Good job, Private Boyko," Wakely said. "Nicely done."

"Hell yeah, what a sprint," Deeks said, leaning down to grip his hand.

"You okay, buddy?" Bronski implored as he crawled over. "Could you feel it? The radiation?"

"Yeah," Loko replied. "Like being cooked in a microwave."

"Whoa, mang. Whoa," Bronski replied, recoiling.

"You bonehead," Loko laughed through gasps. "You can't feel it. Gets inside and wrecks you."

"Why'd you do it, mang?" Bronski asked, his voice wavering. "We're dead anyway."

"We are not."

"Dude, the world is done. Do something with what's left of it."

"Shut that bullshit," Bronski cried. "What do you call all this?"

"I call it ships two thousand miles from sea. Real useful, buddy. Make me a goddamn sandwich."

"Fuck you guys," Bronski said, standing up and brushing off his knees. He slinked off to smoke a cigarette under the bilge of a ship.

8

They continued along ships to the left and on the right, oscillating lawn sprinklers, two-wheel pulled rickshaws, jugs of tile and laminate floor cleaner, IKEA Allen keys (the type with two bends), vintage rests for clothing irons. In the distance they saw that the ship block, which had extended over seven kilometres, ended at a variegated wall of ivory. They passed the stern of a massive wreck raised from the seabottom, saw through its incrustation of sealife a hull possibly white, with a green stripe wrapping the stern and a fragment of its name visible — *itan*. This sent Bronski into a frenzy that they'd discovered the *Titanic*, deaf to the fact that while it matched the scale and form of that ship, the paint scheme was wrong, and it seemed, according to Loko, who'd seen an IMAX documentary about the famous wreck, in significantly better condition.

"But the *Titanic* is here somewhere," Leclerc reminded them.

As they approached the white wall, shapes and shadows began to resolve into a horror show: it looked like bodies. Was this it, where humanity would be found, in a mass of decomposing flesh? And was it white people only? Sharpcot suffered a shameful moment of elation at the thought, then considered that people of colour might be segregated into their own block, or blocks. These thoughts and their implications were too harrowing to pursue.

As they neared the wall she saw that these were indeed human forms, but rendered in pale marble: women, men, children; philosophers, warriors, artists, politicians; gods, angels, demons, cherubs, Zeus, Athena, Apollo, Cupid, Venus, Bacchus, Jesus, Moses, Buddha, Vishnu; Augustus, Lincoln, Lenin, Mao, Thatcher; figures sleeping, hunting, wrestling, battling, playing, blessing, reading, orating, dancing, kissing, fucking, killing, raping, grieving, all of them in pale or yellowed marble and set in a random jumble of extreme density. Idealized bodies, sculpted breasts and pectorals, backs and bottoms, muscular biceps and thighs, with hands gesturing, bunched into fists, or gripping daggers, swords, quills, books, parchments; faces expressing ecstasy, rage, serenity, astonishment, horror, resolve, mirth.

The section moved into the new passage and spread out, gazing at the wall of entangled bodies, and as the sun fell the shadow of the block forming the right corner — sewing machines: Singer, Brother, Pfaff, Consew, Sendo, Juki, TechSew — crept up the statues. Some of the faces seemed incredulous, traumatized at what had befallen them: collected from temples and museums and gardens and plazas and private collections around the world, where they had been free, revered, here compressed into this terrible monument. They were shocked at what their marble eyes saw: tens of millions of sewing machines in white and grey and tan and black, and for those on the left already in deep shadow, the broad hull of a teal and red liquid natural gas carrier, with tenders and freighters and crane barges and corvettes piled on its deck. All of these brought together and made to stand as objects of equal value.

"Stop looking at me, dude," Bronski grunted at a statue of Apollo at ground level, the god's left arm extending from the wall, hand clutching a fragment of a bow, carved cloak draped over arm and shoulders, face serene, white eyes simultaneously ardent and vacant.

"Dude," Bronski persisted. "Like I said, look at something else."

Loko said, "Probably wants you to stop staring at his dick."

"I'm looking at his stupid face."

"Leave it alone, Bronski," Sharpcot said.

Bronski had unslung his rifle, now lifted it to his shoulder and aimed it at the statue's face.

"Private Bronski, stand down," Wakely ordered.

Bronski let out a long, slow breath.

"Soldier, lower your weapon!" Wakely shouted.

Bronski held his stance for two seconds, then dropped the rifle. He looked at Wakely, close in at his shoulder.

"Kidding," Bronski laughed, but he was sweating profusely. "I think radiation affected my brain."

"If only you had one, Scarecrow," Deeks said.

"Really, bitch?" he cried, pivoting, rifle swinging towards her belly.

Wakely seized the barrel and forced it downward.

"Private, I would relieve you of your weapon," he growled. "But someone else would have to carry it. For now I will take your magazine." He put out his hand and Bronski glanced at Sharpcot.

"Follow the order."

Bronski staggered a little, recovered, then thumbed the catch and removed the magazine, placed it in Wakely's open palm.

"Show me," Wakely ordered, and Bronski pulled back the cocking lever, held it to the rear, and lifted the rifle so Wakely could inspect the receiver and chamber. "Continue," Wakely said, and Bronski let the bolt carrier go forward, set the fire control selector, squeezed the trigger, and closed the ejection port cover.

"And the rest," he said, and Bronski tugged magazines from his vest pockets, handed them to Wakely, who distributed them to the section.

"What are you looking at?" Bronski demanded of Apollo, and threw a punch into the statue's jaw, then gripped his hand and yowled in pain.

They marched north between the enormous white ferry *Stena Hollandica* — "Connecting Europe, for a Sustainable Future" painted down its side — and the wall of statues in their poses of constricted agony.

Near the stern of the *Hollandica* they rounded the statue corner, leaving the ships behind, and entered an eastbound passage with handheld hairdryers on the left. Sharpcot thought of her own hairdryer, a purple Conair Infiniti Pro that Lana would consistently leave plugged into the lamp fixture above the sink, ignoring pleas not to leave it dangling like that.

As they walked, Leclerc lectured Bronski on how the maze represented organization carried to an extreme, no less destructive than randomly scattering the creations of humankind across the globe, or incinerating them in a nuclear fireball.

Sharpcot found herself averting her eyes from the hairdryers, recognizing that her own must be here. What if she saw it, or one like it? What would that mean about the fate of humanity, and the fate of that girl who failed to unplug the thing and put it away?

If it was here, where was Lana?

But looking to her right, with its vast audience of startled statuary, was no better. We are all in a predicament, she wanted to tell them. And then she spotted, looming high up in the wall, someone she recognized, someone famous: Michelangelo's *David*. The giant face peered out from the orgy of snarled bodies with that pensive expression, in preparation for his confrontation with Goliath. But this goliath was a million tons of plastic hairdryers stacked nine storeys tall.

They pushed on, statues ended, hairdryers ended, and they ran past loafs of pink fibreglass insulation; Honeywell thermostats, round with Fahrenheit scales; trailers that carry baggage to jets waiting on tarmacs; a soft block of hair scrunchies; muffin baking tins; electric rice cookers; and then highchairs, which compounded Bronski's agitation.

169

"Jeez, I still need one of these," he muttered as he rubbed his chin. "For the baby." He backed up against rice cookers — Panasonic, National, Zojirushi, Salton, Black+Decker, Imusa — and gazed at the chairs. "Mang, I could just take one and be done."

"Move it, Private," Wakely said as he and Tse came up from the rear of the column, and Bronski scuttled to catch up with Leclerc.

They were passing between a wall of coloured chalk — slender sticks for blackboards along with chunks of road chalk and everything between, and across from them empty acrylic cases for swimming goggles, when they encountered the cows. A black and white Holstein stepped into the aisle, intending to cross and enter the southbound passage. The motion of the soldiers halted her mid-stride, and she was promptly rear-ended by another cow. The struck bovine bellowed and staggered and the cow behind it veered into the aisle and more followed, filling the passageway.

"Oh my god, oh my god," Bronski cried.

"Right everyone, stay calm," Sharpcot ordered.

"Back up, give them space," Wakely said. "Don't spook them."

"Wow, the smell," Loko moaned into his sleeve.

More cattle filled the intersection, bawling and mooing, grinding against the chalk wall, summoning a billow of coloured dust, ploughing into the corner of goggle cases and sending a cascade onto the passage floor where they splintered under hoofs.

Wakely regarded the blocks past them: clipboards and French horns.

"What do we do, boss?" Tse asked in his deep bass, sweeping the Minimi along the line of crowding cattle.

"If they rush us," Sharpcot said, "You, and only you, have permission to open fire. Wait on my order."

"Understood."

170

"Hey, no ammo, I got no ammo!" Bronski cried, backing away through the group.

"Cow phobia, Bronski?" Deeks asked.

"Bovinophobia," Leclerc said.

"Damn right. They step on you you're dead."

"If we shoot one we can eat it," Loko suggested.

"Hell yes!" Bronski said. "I'd kill for a steak or burger or bacon."

Deeks and Virago exchanged glances, both silently mouthing the word, "Bacon?"

"Who's going to butcher it, Bronski? You?" Tse wondered.

"Deeks. She grew up on a farm," Bronski said.

"I milked cows, asshole. I didn't slaughter them," Deeks replied. "These are dairy cows."

"Then we could get milk," Loko said.

"These haven't been milked in a while. They're sick."

Deeks was right: the cows were suffering, udders distended, infected, some ruptured. They were miserable, lethargic, eyes and muzzles crusted with yellow deposits. They mooed and brayed pathetically, besieged by flies.

"It's awful," Virago said. "The poor creatures."

"You have to milk dairy cows every day," Deeks moaned. "Several times a day. You have to."

The cattle surged closer and the soldiers continued to retreat, hugging the wall, chalking their uniforms.

"Maybe they got tired of their block. Standing on each others' backs," Loko said.

"They don't stack animals, jerk," Virago said.

"I'm kidding."

"Aren't cows essentially manufactured through breeding?" Leclerc wondered.

"No tags," Deeks said, touching her ear. "They get their ear tagged for ID."

"Those tags are in a block somewhere," Virago said. "They were removed."

"By who?" Bronski demanded. "Who removed them? Who is this whoever who is doing whatever with all this everything?"

"Whoa, Travis," Deeks remarked. "You should print that on a T-shirt."

Bronski scoffed, then turned his head and cried, "Holy goddamn fuck, a wolf!"

"No, that first thing you said."

"I'm not crying wolf! There are goddamn wolves coming this way!"

A quartet of white and grey wolves approached from the east, heads lowered, attention fixed on the cattle. The cows began to bawl and bumble into each other in an effort to retreat. Bronski crashed into the midst of the section, arms flapping. "Shoot them! Shoot them!" he screamed.

"Quiet, you fool," Sharpcot hissed. "No weapons without my order."

"Why the hell not? Is that your sacred spirit animal or whatever the fuck?" Bronski rasped, and Sharpcot slammed him into the wall.

"Shut your mouth, Private, and maybe we won't leave you behind to fend for yourself. Nobody move. These wolves are after the cows."

The wolves came on, oblivious to the soldiers, stalking the cattle, but as they came abreast of the section they slowed and lifted their heads and sniffed, hackles rising. Bronski whimpered, "Oh shit oh shit."

Sharpcot unholstered her sidearm, but the wolves remained fixed on the cattle, skimming the wall opposite, and only when they were past did the last one lift its head and inspect the soldiers with yellow eyes before returning its attention to the cattle.

Sharpcot signalled to the soldiers to edge towards the previous corner, and at that moment the wolves rushed and the cows emitted a collective moan and began to panic and collide. The wolves recognized the danger of trampling, held back, darting back and forth, waiting for an opportunity.

The chalk block stood 70 metres wide and they soon reached the previous corner, where home saunas smelling of raw cedar faced jugs of windshield washer fluid. They paused, watched the wolves cut one of the cows from the herd and surround it. The cow lifted its head and bellowed as they snapped at its flanks. The rest happened fast — the cow went down with a groan, and in moments wolves were gorging themselves at the cow's belly as it shuddered and died.

"That's how you butcher a cow," Deeks exclaimed as they left the intersection and headed north between chalk and saunas.

They humped for two hours, driven to escape the proximity of wolves and cows, until the light failed and they came upon stacked pregnancy test sticks and wooden foot massage rollers. They camped by a stream which cut slender canyons through the blocks and was so crammed with fish they could catch them with bare hands. Shrieks of laughter as a bass squirmed from Deeks's grasp and struck Loko in the chest. Wood from broken up massagers built them a fire, and they fried fish in Wakely's cookpot. Only Virago abstained.

"Smells a bit like piss here," Bronski commented.

"Most of these sticks have been used," Deeks said, examining one, adding, "And . . . we're pregnant!" as she held it up to show the display.

"So why does it smell like piss?" Bronski asked.

When they explained, he dropped the stick he'd been examining and rushed to the stream to scrub his hands.

They settled around the fire, which crackled madly when the flames consumed a shellacked piece, the noise more than once startling Bronski or Loko to their rifles. At some point Deeks shed her boots and socks and rolled her soles against a foot massager. Virago saw what she was doing and followed suit, and soon most of them were soothing their weary feet.

"Soldiers," Wakely said after a long period of the crackling fire and the squeak of foot rollers. "Today we survived cows and wolves. This" — he held up a small silver flask — "is my reserve of 16-year-old Lagavulin single malt. It's eight ounces, so everyone gets exactly one ounce. Be conservative in your swigs."

"Be conservative. Should be easy for Bronski," Loko said as Wakely took a short drink and passed the flask to Sharpcot, who deferred.

"My troops drink first," she said. "I'll catch it at the end."

"Rude to talk politics at the dinner table," Virago muttered.

"Trav still thinks Trump will win," Loko persisted. The flask came to him and as soon as he put it to his lips and tipped, Bronski screamed, "Way to hog it, Loko!"

"I haven't even had any!" Loko replied, and took a quick sip.

"Two sips, did everyone see that?" Bronski bellowed. "And he is going to win. He's going to beat Hil-liar-ly."

"He's not going to win," Wakely said.

Virago took a swig, passed the flask to Leclerc, who wouldn't drink anything but white wine. She took a tentative sip. "Smokey," she coughed, handed it to Deeks.

"So you think it'll be Crooked Hillary?" Bronski asked.

"Nope," Wakely said. Deeks took a nip, then another. She held the flask out for Bronski, who failed to notice as he demanded, "Who then?"

"Nobody, you fool," Tse said in his low voice.

"There isn't going to be an election, Bronski," Loko said. "Because the world is fucking done."

Bronski seized the flask, leapt to his feet, and tossed it back for a long drink, paddling a hand to fend anyone off. Tse rose and clamped a hand around Bronski's wrist and yanked the flask away. Whiskey spilled down the private's chin and uniform and Loko rammed a shoulder into his belly. The two went down in the grass, scrabbling and grunting.

Tse lifted Loko by the back of his belt, while Virago and Deeks pinned Bronski against the wall of foot massagers. With Loko suspended in his grasp, pawing the air, Tse shook the flask, frowning. He passed it to Sharpcot. She put it to her lips, then held it inverted and shook it. A single drop fell. She screwed on the cap and handed it to Wakely.

"Nice work, Bronski!" Loko cried. "You selfish son of a bitch!"

"Shut it," Wakely ordered. "Private Tse, put him down."

Tse let go and Loko thumped to the earth. He didn't rise immediately, moaned, "Ow."

Virago and Deeks released Bronski, who dusted himself off and wiped his eyes with his cuff. He sat and glared into the fire.

Loko rose to his knees and was about to speak when Sharpcot said, "You've said enough, Private Boyko. You too, Bronski. Time for sleep. We start early tomorrow."

"Wolves and cows on the loose," Wakely said. "I'll take first watch."

"I will," Sharpcot said. "I'm the only one who hasn't been drinking."

"Denied the pleasure, spared the duty. I'll take first, then Loko. Last is the worst, so it's Bronski's."

"With my ammo?" Bronski implored.

"Without," Wakely stated.

The section unpacked bedrolls and ranger blankets and spread out. The sky was a torrent of stars. Sharpcot watched Wakely at the corner of her view, lit by firelight. He sat very still, looking into the flames. Thinking about the kid with the artillery shell, or Daisy, who had fixed him, or started to, before he lost her. Sharpcot thought: how lucky. To have definitively lost his beloved before all this came down. Not wondering about, fearing for, Daisy's fate.

Where are you, Lana?

She listened to the crackle of the fire and the mutter of the stream, looked hard for the beacons of aircraft, and when she saw none, for orbiting satellites, those elusive pinlights her father showed her scooting across in the sky when she was a child. Looked for a long time. Saw none.

They ate breakfast in the dark, concern increasing over dwindling IMPs. After a rapid redistribution of gear — "If we're saddled with Bronski's rifle mags, he carries the C9 ammo" — they set out towards the blushing eastern sky in such haste Leclerc had to spit toothpaste and pack her brush on the move.

Around 11 that morning they encountered canned peas. They'd been passing through stacks of obscure or quotidian stuff, rolls of self-adhering air- and water-resistant barriers, braces for some kind of shelving, various mysterious gadgets and machinery, along with identifiable things: plastic tags printed with CAUTION: FIBRE OPTIC CABLE, a mile-long wall of microwave ovens, a toxic monument of urinal deodorizer pucks reeking of surfactants and pee, and historical plaques made of brass or zinc with raised lettering on painted backgrounds, which Sharpcot's haste prevented them from studying in detail. They skimmed them as they hurried past, read chronicles of the Old State Capital, ERECTED IN 1852; Pass Manchac, S. Boundary of Tangipahoa Pashish; The Waving Girl, for 44 years, Florence Martus (1868–1943) lived on nearby Elba Island with her brother, the lighthouse keeper; Juan Cailles (1871–1951), MAKABAYAN REBOLUSYONARYO, ISINILANG SA NASUGBU, BATANGAS, 10 NOBYEMBRE 1871; Jolliffe Island, The City of Yellowknife is not confined to the mainland alone.

The peas faced a wall of aerosol oven cleaner, and with Easy-Off, PowerHouse, Oven Bright, Mr. Muscle, and Big D on the left and Green Giant, Del Monte, Plein Soleil, Libby's, Green Garden, and Nature's Promise on the right, they found themselves in a grocery aisle of extreme proportion.

Tse smashed pea tins from the wall and carved one open with a tool from his vest. He sniffed, fished a few out with his fingertips, tasted.

"Seem okay," he said.

"Ugh, why peas?" Loko wondered.

"It must be hard to have so many allergies," Deeks quipped.

"You have no idea."

They stopped briefly for a lunch of cold peas and lobster.

Mid-afternoon they saw when they passed a southbound passageway between cafeteria serving trays on the west and green tank tops on the east another stack as tall, if not taller, than the ships. Wakely scanned it with binoculars.

"Bridges," he said.

"For crossing rivers?" Sharpcot asked.

"Dental bridges."

"Seriously, Jack."

"Well, there's a block of those somewhere. These all look steel."

He handed the binoculars to Sharpcot, who glassed the stack. She took a sharp breath at what she saw through the softness of the haze: suspension and truss bridges painted in blue, black, grey, orange, red, some unpainted, corroding, all of them tangled and blended to occupy a minimum volume, creating a moiré of terrible density. She panned the matrix of cables and buttresses, lifted the binoculars, following the pylons of an enormous structure, steel trusses painted in grey-blue crowned with saddle housings through which the top cables descended to the deck, with vertical cables fanned along them, binding the platform to a causeway with red trusses visible inside the matrix of the span. Towers from other suspension and cable-stayed bridges stretched off into the background, rising high above the stack, some approaching 300 metres.

"Any you recognize?" Virago asked.

Sharpcot handed her the binoculars and she looked.

"Well?"

Virago spent a long time panning the block, lifted them along the towers of the big bridge in the foreground, then lowered the glasses, wiped her eyes with her sleeve, and handed the binoculars back. Wakely asked her what it meant, what she had seen. She muttered and picked up her rifle and moved on.

"What did she say?" Sharpcot asked.

"I don't know. Sounded like 'Williamsburg.'"

"Let's move," Sharpcot said. "We've got ground to cover."

9

They made excellent progress, endured a brief but intense thunderstorm under rain ponchos which they joined using the embedded snaps to form a large tent, under which they remained mostly dry.

"We're getting good at this," Wakely said as they dismantled it and the sun came out, heat and humidity immediately oppressive. They lunched on reconstituted mashed potatoes they'd collected near the ships, plus new items: blue corn tortilla chips and Korean Jjolmyeon noodles. They'd passed along furnace filters, earmuffs, and uppercase letter Es — lead type; metal and glass from signage; acrylic and translucent in many colours; on clear vinyl rectangles for roadside and letterbox signs; with embedded lightbulbs for marquees; in aluminum with retroreflective coatings; for letterboards; in cast iron, felt, ceramic, clay, fabric, nickel, pewter, brass with screw holes for mounting, carved wood; from slats of reclaimed lumber; cast in cement; in a variety of scales, from dime-sized to colossal, the latter from warehouses, buildingtops, hillsides. One Virago recognized by its font and yellow tone from an IKEA store's exterior. Another appeared to be the blue skewed E in "Dell." There was one that came from "Lego."

"I wonder if that big white one there is from the Hollywood sign," Bronski said.

"Bronski, spell Hollywood," Deeks demanded.

"It's not hard, Abby," Virago said. "Sound it out: Holl-EE-wood."

"Right," Deeks replied. "Silly me."

As they ate lunch, Virago said she'd kill for a carrot or apple. "Something, anything unprocessed."

"Don't count on it," Leclerc said. "The maze's composition is defined by the fact that everything in it is processed."

"Luckily we're active," Deeks remarked. "Or imagine our cholesterol."

They trudged on into early evening, and Sharpcot sensed they were nearing the city, might be only a dozen or so kilometres away. An impulse of urgency overcame her, and she wanted to dash ahead, to reach it tonight, but today's pace had been relentless, and her troops were flagging, stumbling along, glassy-eyed, so spent they'd lost the energy even to complain.

She decided to press them for another hour, would tell Wakely at the next crossroads. He'd protest the extension, not for his own sake — he'd walk all night if she asked — but for the soldiers under their care, arguing that pushing them might lead to injury, or rebellion, or worse.

The intersection was a long time coming. They were passing a vast collection of trolleys, trams, and streetcars, stacked one upon the next, pantographs crushed beneath wheels and undercarriages, their shells painted in the originating city's transit palette: Sapporo green, Cincinnati white and green and blue, Hong Kong double-decker red, Sofia orange and white, Lisbon vintage yellow, Belgrade white and red, Kolkata white and orange, Tashkent white and green, Toronto red and white, many wrapped in advertisements for theatre performances, colognes, tourism destinations, underwear, pork, liquor, cars, condos, morning radio shows — and on the right, steel pencil cases, painted and bare, stamped, new, dented, crushed, rusting. All empty, their contents, pencils and protractors, compasses and erasers, stacked elsewhere.

Sharpcot spied ahead something different: rather than new blocks infinitely extending the corridor, there was open sky, and for an instant a surge of hope possessed her, and the atrophied muscles of her cheeks tightened, prelude to a smile, until she saw in the golden light a long distance beyond the passage's terminus more blocks, blocks, but for the first time viewed from afar. Not the end of the maze, but a clearing, like the zone of drums and woodchippers and teapots and shipping pallets, and significantly larger. She accelerated, leaving the others behind, noting a decline in the land, and she reached the end of the passageway and encountered an abrupt downgrade. Below her spread trees, stretching into a shallow valley cut by a river, with more brush on the far side, then a wide river that snaked north and south. Beyond it, a kilometre away, the land climbed to fresh blocks, bordering the valley like a rampart, dark slots indicating the passages between them, stacks too distant to make out, but from their complexion, the standard wild variety, objects large and small, some of nearly uniform colour, others tiny, complex, multifarious.

A smell rose from the valley, of trees and wildflowers and river, and Sharpcot heard the soldiers breathing it in as they arrived and spread into the passageway's mouth.

"The Assiniboine River," Sharpcot stated. "I know this place. Dwight and I used to come here with Lana when she was a baby. For hikes and picnics. Beaudry Provincial Park. We're standing 10 klicks from the edge of Winnipeg, 25 from the city's core."

She felt winded, from the day's exertion, from speaking after hours of silence, from recognition they could make the city limits in under two hours if they pushed. But her legs burned and back ached from the weight of her ruck and gear, and a glance at the section told her they had nothing left, certainly not enough to reach their destination, and to what? If they found the city intact, if she could locate Lana, if she was sure, or even suspected that it might all still exist, that they wouldn't find more of the maze where the city once stood, then she would've insisted they push on. But uncertainty allowed civilization to persist as possibility, and she wasn't ready to extinguish that. In any case, here they could rest, and breathe, and bathe in the river, which god knows they needed, considering the body odour miasma accumulating around them. Maybe find something fresh to eat, raspberries perhaps, she didn't know what else you could safely eat in the forest, so she fixed on that: wild raspberries.

"Let's go in, but stay wary. Remember the wolves."

"And cows," Bronski said. "Don't forget the fucking cows."

Sharpcot stepped from between the walls into the open, and the section followed her down the slope and into the forest.

They moved cautiously, turned at every sound, birds flitting through trees, Tse swinging the C9 towards a chipmunk on a log. The absence of walls unnerved them, made them feel exposed, vulnerable. The sound of a redwing blackbird up ahead, at the river. Sparrows. Frogs. Mosquitoes. They were on a narrow pathway, beaten flat by footsteps. Used by animals, maybe people. Basswood, cottonwood, maple. They looked in the grass along the trail for anything — for pop cans and candy wrappers and plastic bags, the inescapable detritus of humanity — and discovered none of it. Not a scrap.

They spread out, eager for personal space. Recognizing the area as unsecured, Wakely kept track of everyone: Sharpcot ahead, Bronski and Loko to the left, Deeks, Leclerc, and Virago spread out on the right, while Tse brought up the rear.

They came to the river where they collected and stood looking at its flat, slow-moving surface. It might've been idyllic but for the blocks looming beyond it, obscuring the horizon, like a city, but nothing like a city.

"A heron!" Deeks called, pointing to a large white bird stalking through shallows on the far bank, 60 metres away.

"Aren't herons grey?" Virago said.

"Whatever. Big water bird with pointy beak," Deeks replied.

"How are we getting across?" Bronski added. "Cuz I'm not swimming. There is no way you'll get me in that."

Loko gave him a shove and Bronski staggered into the mud along the river's edge, arms flailing. He managed to step back and screamed at Loko, "What the hell, are you trying kill me?"

"Quite possibly," Loko replied calmly.

"Well how'd you like it if I did the same to you . . ." Bronski moaned, trying to get behind Loko, until Wakely shut them down.

The heron had taken flight at the sound of Bronski's cry, went downriver, its wings beating slowly.

"We'll make camp here, figure out how to cross," Sharpcot said. "Don't go far. Stay vigilant and keep a firearm close at hand."

"Hello, still without ammo over here," Bronski stated, but was ignored.

They spread out along the riverbank. Sharpcot got a fire going to repel mosquitoes, which grew fierce as daylight faded. She invited Wakely to set up on the bank beside her. Cottonwoods arching overhead. They heard a splash 50 metres downriver and saw Virago and Deeks in the water, swimming and whooping, calling to Leclerc, who stood on the bank in a tank top and tights, swinging her arms to beat away the bugs.

"You going in?" Sharpcot asked Wakely.

"Absolutely."

"Wearing what?"

He ducked into the brush, and after a moment emerged wearing a black Speedo. He said almost apologetically, "I carry one. Just in case."

"It's small enough."

"To save packing space," he said quickly.

"Jesus, Wakely, I don't think I ever seen you blush before."

He turned and sprinted into the water and dived, spent a long time under before popping up some distance out.

Downriver Leclerc waded, flapping at the bugs as she worked in until her thighs were submerged. With a sudden shriek she flopped into the water. Deeks and Virago began to swim towards Wakely and he watched them come. They stopped a few metres away.

"What's up, Privates?" he asked, not unkindly.

"Don't go inquiring about our privates, Master Corporal," Deeks laughed. "That's harassment."

"Do we call you 'master corporal' when none of us are in uniform?" Virago asked.

He didn't reply, instead slipped beneath the water, and after 20 seconds the women began to glance about. At 30 their scanning grew frantic. Sharpcot had risen, was searching the surface for wake or bubbles when he breached explosively between the two women, who shrieked in fear and relief, paddling in opposite directions. He pursued Deeks, who had a strong crawl and briefly evaded him, but when she realized she could not escape she stopped and faced him, wondering what he intended when he reached her. At the last instant he flipped and set off for Virago, caught up in a dozen crashing strokes, but dived before he arrived.

Sharpcot stripped down to sports bra and panties, smelled her own stench — last shower was in the bunker, four days ago, and they'd travelled hard in the heat — and stepped into the water, feeling the beaks of mosquitoes against her skin. She plunged, and it was a glorious, cool immersion, the water velvety against her skin, and she stroked out, but not so far that her feet lost contact with the bottom.

"Sergeant in the water!" Leclerc called from downstream, and was startled into a shriek when Wakely torpedoed out of the depths nearby. She splashed madly at him with both hands until he submerged again.

"We're going to need a bigger boat," Deeks cried.

Sharpcot treaded water, watching Loko and Bronski labour to start a fire, and shouted, "Boyko and Bronski, in the water, now! That is an order."

"All due respect, Sarge, I can't swim," Bronski called.

"I'm not ordering you to swim. I am ordering you to bathe. You both stink."

"Is it cold?" Loko asked. "It looks cold."

"It's refreshing," Virago called.

"That means cold," Bronski said. "That always means fucking cold. Can we get our fire going first? So we can warm up when we get out?"

She chose to enjoy the river instead of arguing, swam a few strokes on her belly, didn't like the vertigo prompted by gazing into the dark water, turned onto her back and kicked along, studying the sky. Worried about venturing into the deeps, she stopped and put her feet into the soft loam. Watching Wakely swim among Virago and Deeks, she experienced a pang of something she couldn't name as he pursued them then feinted, always arcing away at the last instant. That white dude confidence. Plus there was something irksome in the lazy way these young women evaded him, as if daring him to catch them.

Leclerc herself didn't go far, and Sharpcot spotted Tse swimming alongside, whom she hadn't noticed go in. The mutter of conversation floated indistinctly across the water.

Wakely shot past on Sharpcot's outriver side, leaving a long, spreading wake as he curved towards Bronski and Loko. He stopped in the shallows and stood to his waist and repeated her orders. A tendril of smoke hung above their nascent campfire, barely established and in need of tending, but they instantly complied, pulled off fatigues, stripped to underwear, and in seconds stood in the water to their knees. These two always resisting her directives, slow to respond, brimming with attitude. It was a thing she talked about with other women in command. She recalled the day Major Brenda Carston invited her into her office after Sharpcot's promotion.

"You'll work twice as hard, and get half the credit," Carston had said.

"Like always."

"It'll be worse, Elsie, worse than being under their command, worse than being their peer. Some men will never accept your position."

Sharpcot wondered what worse could be like. There'd been anonymous rape and death threats, notes slipped under her door; there were two sexual assaults, one reported, the second not, because the fallout of reporting the first was almost as bad as the assault itself.

She and Carston maintained two seconds of eye contact, and that glance communicated much. The major knew, and yet she didn't know. Sharpcot asked, "So what can I do?"

"Find a good man to be your right hand."

"That's bullshit. Ma'am. Sorry. No disrespect."

"It is bullshit, actually, Sergeant. And I hate to say it, and you'll hate me saying it, but it's going to be even harder for you."

"Because I'm an Indian."

"I'm afraid so."

"You're right."

"About what?" the major asked.

"I do hate you saying that, ma'am. Again, no disrespect."

"I have no idea what it's been like for you, Sergeant Sharpcot. And I have no idea what it's going to be like. Only — difficult. It's going to be awfully difficult. So, in terms of your 2IC. Have anyone in mind?"

Sharpcot did not hesitate. "Yes."

Wakely swam back and forth in front of the two men, taunting and insulting them, until at last they submerged to their necks, but that wasn't enough, Wakely wanted their "greasy heads" under, and finally they both dunked and came up sputtering and complaining. Loko could at least swim, took a foray into the current, but Bronski remained in the shallows, glowering.

Even with Wakely at her side, it was bad. She experienced constant sexism and racism, both subtle and not. One visiting Van Doo captain called her "Pocahontas" in front of a roomful of officers and enlisted during an exercise briefing, which garnered an enormous laugh from the assembly. And Three Section got, without exaggeration, the worst assignments, like the one that had brought them here, to this outpost at the end of the world.

186

Stuck in a bunker while the rest of the army battled the Accruers. And lost, apparently, but at least they went out fighting.

Disrespect from subordinates was harder still, and it wasn't only the men. While Leclerc seemed oblivious to everyone's sex or race, and Virago had warmed quickly to Sharpcot as sergeant, she'd sensed distrust from Deeks, a disingenuousness at the start, like she intellectually recognized Sharpcot's competency, but couldn't emotionally accept her as commander. Her father was an army colonel, if Sharpcot remembered correctly, so maybe that was it.

And Corporal Tse had always shown respect, she assumed because they were neither of them white, until she learned his family was ruled by a long line of matriarchs. The little he spoke of his family concerned the women, especially the aunt who'd served in the Royal Hong Kong Auxiliary Air Force, "a multi-talented pilot of various fixed wing and rotary aircraft," as he put it more than once. It was she who had inspired his love of flight, taking him flying on family visits. Sharpcot once asked why he'd joined the army and not the RCAF, and he said he'd tried, but never explained what happened, and she suspected he'd met a barrier, probably racist. Once when she pressed, he'd shrugged and stated, "I'm too big to fly the CF-18," as if that was the only craft in the Forces.

In a way the punishment she'd received for her sex and race, to command this section of misfits, was a gift, at least when it came to the three women and the corporal. She had to congratulate the brass on their stupidity — handing her a bunch of awkward, unconventional outsiders was kinder than forcing her to manage a group of military diehards who would harass her and question every decision. While neither Bronski nor Boyko represented the worst she could imagine, they typified the hell she'd experienced through her entire military career, and they represented the bulk of her anxiety and distress. She loathed and feared their resistance, those dark looks when she issued orders, the way they muttered conspiratorially to one another. At least she could trust Wakely to enforce discipline; on occasions where other soldiers required reprimand for offences, like when she'd been blatantly disobeyed by a couple of male recruits during a live fire exercise, she'd seen the rebuke from their sergeant delivered with a grin and a wink.

Bronski and Loko began savagely splashing each other until Bronski jammed his hands under the water to hurl gobs of mud. Loko swam into the deeps, out of range.

A few minutes later there came an abrupt change in the light as the sun dropped behind blocks. The water seemed to chill, and in minutes the three women, who may have been waiting for the shadow's concealment, emerged from the river and dressed while fighting off mosquitoes. Tse stayed in, swimming a series of lengths while the women dressed, and then rose from the river like a mighty Neptune, silhouetted by sunlight on the far bank and the blocks beyond it.

Wakely got out, dressed, built up a large fire, and Sharpcot paddled to shore as the sky darkened. She could hear Bronski and Boyko 50 metres up the shoreline, trading homophobic insults as they laboured to revive their ailing campfire.

Wakely used his utility hatchet to pare branches from a fallen tree, fed them into the fire, his back to Sharpcot while she dressed. She came to the fire's edge and stood with hands extended. The swim had chilled her. He rose and kicked a fat log into place, rolled it to set the good side up, started to mention spiders and woodlice until she gave him a hard look. She sat and he moved to the far side of the firepit and squatted, prodding the fire with a stout branch.

"Marshmallows?" she asked.

"Didn't pass that block yet."

"How are we going cross the river?"

"Build a raft for our stuff and swim towing it."

188

"What about Bronski?"

"On the raft. If that no-swimming thing isn't bullshit," Wakely replied.

"Where the hell's the rowboat block?"

"I'd take anything: canoe, dinghy, punt, zodiac. Standup paddleboard."

"Ocean liner. We know where to find those."

"You wanna drag one down here?"

"Someone dragged them up there. All of those ships. I'm trying not to think about it, but I'm thinking about it."

"Mind if I join you?" Tse asked from the edge of the firelight, carrying branches.

"By all means," Sharpcot said, making room on the log. He tossed the wood onto the woodpile.

They turned to a sound from the brush, Sharpcot's hand on her sidearm, and the three women came out of the forest, each carrying wood.

"We can't get a fire going," Virago said.

"Though we didn't really try," Leclerc said.

"Always so bloody honest, Cheree," Deeks said. "Anyway, we thought we'd hang out with the last humans on Earth. Call me nostalgic."

"We're flattered," Sharpcot replied.

"Plus it's a hell of a fire," Virago said.

Wakely and Tse ducked into the brush to drag in another fallen tree. The women tossed down their wood and lined up on the log.

An awkward silence as everyone looked into the flames, rattled by Deeks's joke, until they heard a curse from the bush, and the sound of someone struggling through vegetation.

"Where's your wood, losers?" Deeks called.

"I told you," Loko said to Bronski. "Can't show up empty-handed."

"We brought charming personalities," Bronski replied.

"Sit down and keep them to yourselves," Sharpcot growled. They sat and Loko pulled off his boots, yanked off socks, and held them to the flames.

"Christ, Boyko, we don't want to smell your feet," Deeks cried.

"I bathed," he said with a frown. "They're clean. See?"

Deeks recoiled as he lifted a pale foot towards her.

They unpacked foodstuffs they'd collected during the day's journey: blue corn chips, jars of artichokes in oil, and Wakely set his pot in the coals to boil, tossed in Korean noodles.

"So, Winnipeg tomorrow," Bronski said. "I've never been to 'Winterpeg.'"

"What do we do if it's not there?" Loko asked. "What? It's a valid question. What?"

"No tact, Loko. You have no tact," Virago said.

"I'm going to have a burger," Bronski said. "And fries."

"There won't be any burgers and fries, dumbshit," Loko croaked. "Can someone tell this asshat the world is done?"

"I'm sure we'll find the city right where it should be," Bronski sighed. "Anyone want to wager otherwise? Anyone?"

"What's the wager?" Tse asked, eyeing Bronski. "You lose, burgers on you?"

"Yeah. If I'm wrong burgers are on me."

"You are such an idiot!" Deeks said, drawing her hair into an elastic. "Let me explain it to you. Aliens came. They saw all our shit. Blenders and battleships and alarm clocks. They brought it all here. They stacked it for some purpose."

"For what?" Bronski asked.

"How do we know? They're aliens!" Deeks cried. "Look, I've been thinking about this," she continued as she lifted a flap on her ruck and took out a sketchbook. "Look, okay, just look," she said as she flipped through.

"Wow," Leclerc said. "Abby, you can draw!"

There were pictures of people, horses, birds, mountains, expertly rendered in pencil, but she flipped past to a radically different image. She held up a page that showed the maze from above, like they'd seen through the drone's camera. In the sky she'd sketched an enormous craft of alien design, with pipes and vents and portholes and gun turrets. It had partitions emerging from its rectangular belly. Below the vessel lay unicycles, formed into a block identical in dimension to the hold below the ship, those partitions shaped to fit into the passageways, to encompass the block. When Sharpcot leaned forward she saw more craft in the background, one settled onto another block. And far off, a rising ship, a block clutched in its partitions, and below it a rectangular crater in the maze.

"Harvesting," Sharpcot said quietly.

"Right," Wakely said. "Everything we know has been put to the curb for pickup."

"We are in the beginning phase of some kind of alien operation," Deeks said. "I mean that's my theory."

"Aliens? Come on!" Bronski said. "What, like *The X-Files*? Like *ET*, but an ET who wants our shit?"

"Manufactured stuff, all components pre-refined?" Wakely said. "What's not to want?"

"We have a hard enough time disassembling our own creations," Leclerc said. "Look at our landfills."

"Only because it's not important to us. Our shit, once we're done with it," Virago said. "Think of the energy we're willing to spend to rip metals and oil from the ground and refine and process it to build stuff. But when it comes time to take things apart, suddenly it's too hard?"

"No money in it," Tse said.

"Their technology's obviously advanced if they built the maze in three weeks. From everywhere on the planet."

"We're fucked," Loko said.

"But where are the people?" Sharpcot asked. "We see natural things, like trees and wolves, that have been left more or less intact. But what about the people? How do the Accruers classify

191

human beings? Are they animals? Or are they also the collectible products of humanity?"

No one had an answer to that.

They spent the night clustered close along the riverbank, out of concern for wolves and other animal threats, but also unnerved by Deeks's drawings, and the conclusion that the Accruers might yet return to collect their plunder.

Wakely took first watch, followed by Leclerc, Tse, and Deeks, whom Sharpcot relieved early when she awoke in anticipation of what the day might bring. Dawn began with a whip-poor-will sounding across the river, followed by a glow in the east. The sight of it made her gut founder, not for what it was, but for what it made her recognize had been missing from the ending night: light pollution. If Winnipeg stood alive and vital 10 kilometres away, its luminescence would've obscured half the sky. But when she'd risen in the night to relieve herself, stars had painted the vault from rim to rim.

She sat clutching forearms across her abdomen while the light grew, a deep saffron that intensified and obliterated the stars before the rim of the sun appeared above the stacks that walled the park to the east.

They paracorded logs together and lashed their packs to the top, set Bronski up there like a king on a litter, and floated it across the river, Wakely and Tse kicking and pushing. They dried and dressed on a spit of land from which they could see the river looping north. They followed it as best they could, knowing it led into the heart of Winnipeg. As they walked Sharpcot remarked that the park trails had been well-marked, but the fluorescent orange arrows nailed to trees were gone. They encountered along one section a series of eroded holes a handspan in diameter. Sharpcot stopped and looked into one. When Wakely stepped up beside her, she stated, "There was a line of wooden posts. To separate the trail from the marsh."

He said nothing and they continued north until the ground rose to a wall of stiletto-heeled shoes, all of them in tones of blue. They worked their way east along the shoes — new, old, destroyed, worn, in hues ranging from baby blue to periwinkle to powder to ice to navy to teal to sapphire to ultramarine; in PVC, suede, leather, leatherette, plastic, glitter, sequin, satin, silk; strappy, slingbacked, open-toed, point-toed, zippered; with bows, ribbons, stars, feathers, pom-poms, tassels, fur trim, encrusted with rhinestones, crystals, pearls. They were unpaired, and Deeks found on one a label stuck to the sole with a price: $1,250.

"You could fund a school for a year in Malawi for that. Civilization deserved to end," Virago said when she saw it.

They smelled sea, familiar after the ships, found entry into the maze along a wall of tetrapods, concrete constructions used for coastal erosion protection. Leclerc called them Akmons, each like a capital letter *I* with a twist, so top and bottom serifs ran perpendicularly. They were stained and weathered, fringed in seaweed and other sea life, arranged for compactness.

The section stepped reluctantly back into the maze. The smell of shoes and sea followed them up the passage. The shoes ended, were followed by small, aluminum rings of varying widths with a split down one side and engraved with digits, letters, and addresses. They puzzled over these until Bronski stated, "Bird bands."

"The Eagles?" Deeks wondered. "The Black Crowes? Flock of Seagulls?"

"My cousin's an ornithologist," he explained, ignoring her. "I helped her a couple times with banding. They are weird little fuckers when you got them in your hands."

"Cousins?" Deeks asked.

"Birds, you moron!"

"The Housemartins?" she persisted as Wakely stepped between them, his hand on Bronski's chest.

They walked between sea barriers and bird bands, Loko wondering how they'd been removed from the birds.

"If we find a parrot we'll ask," Deeks suggested. At that point Sharpcot had to bring Deeks up front with her as Tse and Wakely held back a snarling Bronski.

They ended at another westbound passage, Akmons continuing right, and on the left, metal casting robots, foundry robots, a tangle of thick, complex arms of heavy steel in yellow and red. Robot arms and Akmons ended at an east-west passage, on the left corner a pile of armoured motorcycle jackets, mostly black, some grey or white, some trimmed in red, all arrayed with hard plastic plates and protectors for chest, spine, elbows, forearms. A meaty, salty smell came from the block adjacent, rough-textured and a deep, variable carmine in colour, made from short sticks: dried meat, jerky. Beef sticks.

"Now we're talking," Loko said as he stepped to the wall and prised one out and took a bite. "Fuck sake bugs!" he yelled, spitting out the piece, tossing down the stick, sputtering.

Tse pulled one and studied it, said, "This one looks okay." He took a tentative bite.

Wakely and Sharpcot each collected a few and examined them.

"These look fine," Sharpcot said. "A good find. They're preserved, full of protein. Load up!"

"But the bugs," Bronski said.

"I think it was only one bug," Loko replied, drawing out another, and looking it over before taking a small chew, then eating the rest and eating another and then another.

They harvested handfuls and filled their packs — even Virago took a few, for "protein emergencies" — and continued east. Wakely updated his notebook with the latest finds. The jerky ended at spectrum analyzers, complex devices with a screen on the left and buttons and probe ports on the right. Virago nudged the power button on one as she passed and it came on, a welcome message and brand name (Keysight) lighting up the display. These ended alongside the Akmons, and they faced an avenue with steel rails of some kind, for railroads or subways, and on the left, McDonald's signs, iconic golden arches fixed to a red trapezoid on which the name appeared in white. These were affixed to their posts, some with additional signage below: Drive-Thru or Restaurant or Open 24 Hours or McCafé or Hamburgers or 99 Billion Served or Billions and Billions Served, some with the name in Japanese, Chinese, Arabic, Thai, Cyrillic. Some dirty, cracked, missing their glass and showing the stark mounts for fluorescent tubes — which would be found in the stack by the aircraft carrier.

The signs darkened their mood as they pushed eastward.

They crossed a series of creeks that fed the Assiniboine, most shallow and easy, one of them crossed using steel toolboxes, each rectangular with a handle and a latched ring for a padlock, pulled from a block and arranged to form a stepping bridge. At other times, they got soaked to the waist.

While the land remained flat and grassy, they encountered increasingly diversified flora, places where the blocks retreated to accommodate individual trees or thickets or groves, many of a clean geometrical shape, or with a linear boundary, some of them bordering roadbed trenches of varying depth.

Virago was thrilled to pass through an orchard of apple trees, the fruit ripe and luscious. They ate apples while crossing areas where mismatched soil in rigid lines suggested building infills. They hit a long trench, dotted with sprouting weeds.

"There was deep asphalt here," Wakely said, squatting to study it. He squinted ahead. "Goes on a good way."

"Highway 1. The Trans-Canada," Sharpcot said. "Runs more or less straight into the city."

They followed it for several hundred metres, past wire baskets, ultrasonic jewellery cleaners, grommet presses, empty fabric softener jugs, sextants (which turned out on closer inspection by Leclerc to be octants), vertical meat smokers, swimming pool skimmers, along with an array of mysterious parts, building materials, objects, novelties, before the roadbed banked north and disappeared under a block of wooden boxes.

"Oh my god. Oh my god, are those . . ." Bronski stammered, lifting his eyes to take in the enormous stack stretching away north and east.

They were coffins. Someone said "caskets" but Leclerc made a correction: caskets are rectangular, with four sides; the boxes stacked here each had six sides, wider to accommodate shoulders, tapering at each end. They were all of unfinished pine, rough, knotted, some with handles in rope, wood, iron, chain. A few new, pale and fresh, but most filthy, rotting, cracked, split, smashed, some crushed to half their original depth.

"Do you think they're—" Loko said, before going silent.

"Occupied?" Deeks appended. "Is this where everybody went?"

"Most are old," Sharpcot stated firmly. "They've been in the ground for years. Centuries, some."

Tse liberated his entrenching tool and studied the wall of coffins before dishing a hole in one. He drew out a flashlight and peered into the hole.

"Empty," he stated. "Smells bad though."

He chose another and did the same. "Empty." Another. And then another. All empty.

"So they're just coffins, without bodies?" Deeks said. "Oh god, why is that worse?"

"Because it means the Accruers pulled the bodies out. Every one of them," Virago said.

"But why?" Sharpcot wondered.

"They just want the coffins. Not the bodies," Leclerc said.

"Oh fuck," Loko moaned. "Fuck this shit."

"You said it, mang," Bronski cried.

"This is fucked up," Loko added.

"It's fucked beyond all fuckness," Bronski called.

"Enough!" Sharpcot shouted.

196

They pushed east, the wall opposite composed of plastic cards, banking and credit cards, membership cards, access cards, all of the same dimensions, all with a magnetic strip. Bronski drew a handful, read each before he tossed it down: "VISA: Michelle Wren; American Express Platinum: Hank G. Foxley; Bank Maspion: Nikita Soetoro; VISA Gold: Mr. Egon Kessel; Diners: Jill Takemoto; Sampath Bank: Chanaka Prasad . . ." until Wakely told him to stop.

Wind chimes comprised the next block, the kind with metal rods and a wooden clapper in the middle, all silenced in their packed state, and across from them, boxes of hair colour. A million, million pictures of women photographed to show hues of brown, red, blonde, blue, silver, pink, purple; L'Oréal, Revlon, Garnier, Clairol, ColorSilk, Nice'n Easy, Nutrisse, Excellence, Hydrience, Féria, Natural Instincts, Préférence, Ultime, Vital, LIVE, go Intense!, Herbal Essences, Texture & Tones, many in Korean, Japanese, Chinese, Arab, Thai.

"This is basically the drug store experience," Virago said. "Only slightly exaggerated."

"I wonder if the Accruers are looking to dye their tentacles Light Intense Auburn," Deeks said.

They crossed roadbeds, a golf course, then weedy ground with infilled soil showing geometric patterns where buildings had stood, followed by a wide north-south trench from the Perimeter Highway. After that, more infilled buildings, another golf course.

"Who knew Winnipeg was a golf capital," Virago quipped.

"When it's not a frozen hellscape," Sharpcot said.

After that came a zone gridded with roadbeds, plots of dying grass that had been cultivated lawns, elm and ash in orderly rows, their crowns intertwined. Blocks arranged to accommodate them.

"A subdivision," Leclerc said.

"Where'd they put the houses?" Deeks wondered.

"If we find them we can move in," Virago said. "One for each of us. We'll be neighbours."

"Do you think they'd have furniture?" Bronski asked as they walked along.

"Obviously not," Leclerc said. "Anything not fixed together was removed. We'd have to find the coffee table block, couch block, the bed block . . ."

". . . the dishwasher block, the 75-inch 4K TV block, the washing machine block . . ." Deeks continued.

"We saw that: front-loading washing machines," Leclerc stated.

"Right, hey, Master Corporal, when was that?" Deeks queried.

Wakely thumbed through his notebook. "Sunday. After Loko climbed the countertops."

"Who said my name?" Loko asked from behind.

"You're a hero, Loko," Bronski grumbled. "A goddamn hero."

"Maybe time to climb again, Private Boyko," Wakely said over his shoulder. "Get you on top for a fresh survey."

"Any time," Loko said. "Anything to get out of these canyons."

"If that was Sunday, what is today?" Leclerc asked.

"Tuesday," Wakely said.

"That was only two days ago?"

"When the fuck we get paid?" Bronski asked. "I got a credit card payment due in two days."

"Oh, Bronski," Loko sighed.

"Mail your payment here," Virago called.

They'd reached a monument of public mailboxes: red, yellow, blue, white, black, square, cylindrical, rectangular. Slots for local and international mail. On their shells, printed or embossed: Letters, Pósturinn, Poczta, Poste, Postes, Pošta, Postur, Postbriefkasten, Brieven, Post Office ER, U.S. Mail, Canada Post, Post with white kanji characters above.

On the north side: jigsaw puzzle tiles, a wall formed from tens of thousands of strata of pieces, each layer producing a unique, jagged edge. An upward glance showed protruding grey or brown backs, or a fragment of an image, producing a stochastic haze of tone and colour and texture. Leclerc tried to thumb out a piece but could not, found it joined to the pieces adjacent. When she looked closer she was astonished to discover that the layer, and every layer in the block, was assembled from pieces from disparate puzzles, yet perfectly assembled into vast sheets. It made sense: manufacturers used a limited number of die cutters, so two puzzles with different images might share the same pattern, making each piece interchangeable. These giant puzzles were assembled according to shape and without regard to image. She saw no edge pieces. Another block for those?

She managed to pluck from the wall a few pieces, saw a castle turret, a bird's webbed foot, a sailboat's prow, the eye of a cartoon cat. She felt a blend of nostalgia and nausea. Between ages seven and ten, jigsaw puzzles alone would tame her rampant thoughts, her mind a dervish of ideas driving her frantic, exasperating her parents and teachers. The school social worker had initially rejected the use of them, citing the recent adoption of jigsaw pieces as the symbol for autism. He didn't want the girl to be stigmatized without a diagnosis.

"Et après que je sois stigmatisé?" she called, seven years old, having overheard the conversation between social worker and parents, glaring at them from the low table where she kneeled, glumly drawing icosahedra with an orange crayon.

She glanced up at the wall and imagined spending the rest of her life disassembling this block, solving it into their respective puzzles. It was not an altogether bleak prospect.

They trudged on, past speaker cones, wheelbarrows, canister vacuum cleaners, spring doorstops in brass and nickel.

This wall continued along the righthand of the corridor, with nondescript black rubber cylinders in various sizes on the left — spacers? cushions? — and those ended at a mass of cameras, every type imaginable: digital SLRs and Bakelite Holiday Brownies from the 1950s, Polaroid OneStep Land Cameras and Rolleiflex twin lens reflex, green Imperial Satellite 127s and

Soviet Leicas and yellow Olympus Trip 35s and green Kodak No. 1 Pocket Junior with lens barrel bellows, along with ample Canon and Nikon and Olympus and Pentax and Hasselblad and Sony and Panasonic and Fujifilm and Vivitar.

The Accruers' classification system was a baffling thing, for at times it isolated a single type, shape, form, composition, or colour of object: clear ballpoint pens, red parkas, blue stiletto heels, while in other instances, like here, it grouped together a broad category of multifarious objects by function. Sharpcot wondered aloud how one would describe the block, and Leclerc posited, "Handheld instruments for recording images upon a variety of media." Deeks noted the stack was, at least in the area they surveyed, devoid of other objects that incorporated cameras, things like phones, laptops, tablets, refrigerators, teddy bear spy cams. Also apparently absent were devices like webcams and security and surveillance cameras. From what they could see, the block was composed entirely of single-purpose consumer and professional cameras, constructed from wood, plastic, steel, brass, leather, Bakelite. Lenses, all of them uncapped, constituted a million eyes gazing out. They caught the mid-morning sunlight and cast it into the wall behind them (cocktail shakers) and onto the ground like shining coins. The section moved along the wall in a kind of retail awe. Cameras were valuable, a thing people saved for, gifted, locked in the trunk out of sight, insured, accessorized, upgraded, coveted in the BestBuy flyer or a shop window. But the older cameras among the new ones and those from various periods in history — from the nineteenth century, from the 20s and 40s and 50s and 90s, along with the very latest, shining and unmarred — created an unsettling effect, as each type dragged the mind into a different era, and a shift of the eyes instantly summoned a fresh age.

A scrambled camera museum, Wakely thought as he reached for a black Olympus OM-2, changed his mind and stretched for a high-end Canon EOS 5DS that he'd read about only weeks before and had considered buying, even though it was far out of his price range. Daisy had been an avid photographer, skilled but always learning, studying, improving. It would've been ridiculous to buy such a fine camera for himself, and he recognized it as a fool's impulse, one which he could not resist. He'd honour her by assuming the task of capturing the sights of the world. He tugged the camera out. It felt good in his grip. He hadn't held one before, had only seen it on websites. He slid a palm under the body, took the lens ring between his fingers, and rested a finger on the trigger. He thumbed the power switch and the camera turned on. He pressed the shutter, took a photo of the wall of cameras before him. The image appeared briefly on the display, then switched to show various settings.

He impulsively touched the button to show images stored on the camera's media card, and saw the photograph he'd just taken. He pressed the back button and saw a picture of an infant in a highchair holding a sippy cup in one hand with her other hand splayed in an awkward wave. The child's mouth open, eyes joyful.

He immediately shut the camera off. But it was too late, the image had burned itself into his mind. Somebody's kid.

He saw Virago beside him and when their eyes met he recognized that she had seen the image too, and it had affected her similarly. He stashed the camera back into the hole it had come from and walked on.

"Whoa, look at this," he heard Loko saying. "Sarge, look at this!"

Sharpcot returned to where Loko held another camera, a compact with a retractable lens. He showed her the image on the display, the last image in the camera. It was a shot of the afternoon sky, brilliant blue with high cirrus cloud, and arranged in the sky, a grid of black dots.

"Can you zoom it in?" Sharpcot asked.

Loko futzed with the controls until he found a way to enlarge the photo. A series of diamond-shaped objects filled the sky, perfectly spaced, and blurred by motion.

Some of the others had clustered around to look, and Tse said, "Fighters. Looks like F/A-18s. Super Hornets."

"Big deal," Bronski said. "It's an airshow."

"That many?" Tse said. "That's a squadron. A couple of squadrons."

"Scroll back. Show other pictures," Sharpcot said.

Loko went to the previous image, but it was a photograph of a red dog taken too close, blurred. More pictures of the dog, then a picture of a garbage bin knocked over and trash spilled on the road. The same trash can from different angles.

Leclerc plucked out another camera and found it dead, tried a couple more before she discovered one that worked. She panned through images of Asian girls flashing peace signs in front of the Louvre, the Eiffel Tower, other Paris landmarks. A camera Bronski pulled down produced pictures of a band at a club, while another showed a retirement party for an ancient man in a brown suit. Cameras the section tested yielded a wedding in Pakistan, damage to a car's fender, a sunrise, a deer in someone's garden, a birthday cake (Happy Bday Maury), people at a protest holding signs with Korean lettering, shots of mountains with an airliner's wing in the foreground.

"I got video here," Deeks said. "Look at this."

She played footage shot through the windows of a tall building. The view panned along fragments of sky between neighbouring skyscrapers. They could hear jets, loud and sharp, which went on for a time before they abruptly halted. The view tilted upwards but an intense light overpowered the image and washed it out. The sudden cessation of the jets suggested a failure of the audio, but then they heard a woman moan, "Oh dear god." The video ended.

The section stood stunned. Bronski asked Deeks for the camera and watched the clip again and again, the repetition of the voice at the end, "Oh dear god," sounding increasingly desperate, until Sharpcot ordered him to stop, and Bronski dropped the camera before they moved on.

They came to a block of wire fragments, most a centimetre long, some of varying thickness and finishes: brass, copper, a small number coated in plastic of different colours. Virago fit a thumbnail between them, pulled out staples: for paper, paper-board, cardboard, upholstery, panelling, roofing, wood, and flesh; they were all unused, legs straight; narrow or wide, short or long, fine or thick, most flat-crowned but some rounded, many bonded in rows, ready to load into staplers, but vast quantities of free, individual ones too, endless billions, held in place by that curious force. Across the aisle on the south, chairs for dentists and barbers, for massages and gynecological exams, packed in a compact, tessellating pattern.

The density of soil lines, which indicated former building foundations, roadways, and sidewalks, increased as the soldiers moved deeper into the city's core. The blocks continued to accommodate trees or shrubbery, often situated in rows where roads and walkways had been.

They passed between empty yogurt containers and bags of cheese puffs — Cheezies, CheeWees, Crunchys, Cheetos, Cheez Doodles, Twisties, Kurkure, Wotsits, and other brands in English, Thai, Japanese, Arabic. They grabbed bags, snacked as they walked, fingertips stained orange.

Newspaper boxes next, in many colours, new and shiny, old and rusting and crushed, covered in stickers and graffiti, labelled by newspaper brand. From cities and towns across the globe. They peered through the scratched acrylic windows, opened those that didn't require coins to unlock, found them all empty, those newspapers collected in some vast and distant pile.

"Oh hell," Deeks said from the front of the column, and stopped abruptly. The wall of newspaper boxes terminated at a northbound passage with what looked like flexible dryer exhaust pipes forming the south wall, while the north was built from objects flesh-coloured and black and pink and red and purple and clear and silver.

"Dildos!" Bronski cried triumphantly.

"Private Bronski," Sharpcot said. "You will keep your mouth shut, and march with discipline and according to protocol past this entire block, and when you are past it you will never mention it again, is that understood?"

"Fuck that shit," Bronski said, and in an instant Wakely was on him, shoving him into newspaper boxes.

"Private, you were issued a direct order by your sergeant, and you will obey that order."

"Get off me! Okay! But get off me."

"If Jack won't get off you, maybe the dildos will," Deeks cracked.

It was an impressive wall, some of the items manufactured from glittering rubber, some in glass and steel and hard plastic, and they varied in size and shape, length and thickness, style and texture, smooth, ribbed, nubbed, simple, abstract, realistic.

Bronski did his best to obey orders, walked upright and square-shouldered, trying to keep his eyes ahead. Loko muttered from behind, "Smells like pussy, but I think that's just Bronski."

Bronski stiffened, half turned, but saw Wakely's eyes on him, threw his head forward and marched.

Unlike other products they'd passed, no one seemed inclined to handle these. There were a lot of them, like there was a lot of everything. And if there was a scent, it was of latex rubber.

They could see up ahead that the eastward passage ended at something dark grey, couldn't tell what. They continued along; dryer pipes and dildos ended at stacked steel plates, each about a foot wide, with hospital beds on the right: frames, no mattresses or bedding, piled in every orientation, horizontally, vertically, upside-down, all chrome and cream and blue and fake wood trim, castors and retractable side rails, cranks or a power cord from the motorized adjustment system, handheld keypads on cables tied to the rail or dangling free. Wakely pulled one of the sheets of metal on the left to reveal a licence plate, blue with white lettering, a Chinese character followed by numbers. He next drew a plate with the European Union symbol on the right edge and a letter D for Deutschland. Another EU plate, with EST: Estonia. Then one from Delaware, United States. One from New Zealand, another in Arabic. There were plates from Ecuador and Malawi and Suriname and Tajikistan and Eritrea and Brunei Darussalam. They were, like everything else, new and old, polished and glittering, some rusted through and little more than a brittle frame and fragments of letters that fell away when handled.

Wakely passed them out to the section and they studied them, and when they departed they left plates lining the base of the stack in a display representing a large fraction of Earth's nations and territories.

The deep grey wall ahead of them was tires, all of them laid flat and stacked in perfect columns. The soldiers stopped at the wall and looked up and down the passageway. It ran north and south as far as they could see.

"Well, this wall is rather *tiring*," Deeks quipped.

"Oh god," Virago said, a hand pressed to her mouth, oblivious to the pun. "It's terrible."

"We'll go around it," Sharpcot said.

"Due respect, Sergeant," Virago said. "If this is all of them, that could take months."

"Come on," Bronski sniffed. "It's a bunch of tires."

"Every tire ever," Virago moaned, her face pale. "Every car and truck, every spare and set of winter tires. Tires in stores, tires in landfill. Did you know some tire dumps are visible from space?"

"Tires don't biodegrade?" Loko asked.

"Of course they do, Loko," Deeks said. "When shopping for a tire I look for one that decomposes rapidly in rain, snow, and sunshine."

"Last basically forever," Virago stated.

"You seem awfully invested," Deeks said.

"In grade seven my class toured a tire dump. It was a . . . profound experience," Virago explained, but didn't add that the scale of the operation so upset her she suffered nightmares for months about tires replacing everything: houses, trees, food, people. Her father becoming the Michelin man, that rotund rubber mummy.

"If this block is not square," Leclerc muttered, who had been computing in her head, "and there are in this block 40 billion tires . . ."

"At least!" Virago interjected.

Leclerc studied the wall's expanse, then viewed a tire at eye level, measured it with her hand, and began to speak in a drone, like an incantation, a prayer, "Say for common tire average width 22 centimetres makes 127 tires per column with average diameter 72 centimetres equals a volume of about 114 litres per tire minus the inside but wait keep the inside since that space is trapped and so 114 litres per tire times four gets you 456 append to that 10 zeroes for total volume . . ."

"Go, Cheree," Tse quietly exclaimed, watching the dart of her eyes as she calculated.

The hymn of her words continued, ". . . fit into the 28-metre height leaves you with an object with equal sides of 12,727 metres per side . . ."

"What is actually happening?" Bronski wheezed.

"Math is happening, Bronski," Deeks said. "Keep up!"

". . . recomputed to one thousand metres on one side gives us . . . gives us . . . 160 kilometres," she concluded.

"What?" Bronski demanded.

"I theorized a block width of one thousand metres. If that were the case, and there are 40 billion tires in this block, it will have a length of 160 kilometres. Approximately."

"Whoa, so you're saying one kilometre wide means a hundred miles long?" Wakely asked.

"Right?" Virago said with a mix of triumph and dread.

"We'll go south around it," Sharpcot stated.

"How do you know it goes north? Why not south, or east?" Tse wondered, and added, "Sergeant."

"The rivers," Sharpcot said. "If the Accruers stick by their model, the rivers will be clear. There's the Red to the east and the Assiniboine to the south. So the block must run north. This way." She turned and strode down the passage between hospital beds and tires, and the rest fell in.

After a time they reached a trough across the passage, which Sharpcot declared Portage Avenue, and they passed through a band of trees and reached the river where they stood in the brush and mud of the riverbank and looked at the trees fringing the opposite bank. Rising beyond them towered a rampart of blocks, the one opposite constructed from blue curbside recycling bins, with moulded styrofoam packing to its right and on the left some kind of endlessly repeating multicoloured product, a toy maybe. The view west revealed continuous walls bordering the river's meander, the river canyoned between them, vanishing beyond a bend.

Sharpcot led them left through the trees lining the bank between tires and river, their progress eased by sparse underbrush and well-trod pathways. Tires towered above the treeline, and Sharpcot eyed them through the leafy canopy. Birds bolted through branches, and they saw a fish leap in the river. They spotted mallards, a female and her adolescent offspring, paddling in the shallows.

Their formation opened up, discipline relaxed, but Wakely remained alert, remembering wolves, cows, and wondering suddenly about cats and dogs, snakes and turtles, cockatiels and canaries. What happened to pets?

Virago paused ahead to tie a bootlace and stood when Wakely passed, walked alongside.

"Never thought I'd be depressed to see no garbage along a path like this," she said. "I keep looking for a Coffee Crisp wrapper or a Bud can."

He grunted, and she lowered her voice and asked, "Master Jack, why are we here? Why did we come to the city?"

"To see what's here."

"We knew there'd be nothing. She knew it."

"I don't know if she still doesn't believe she'll find something."

"A waste of time," Virago grumbled, added hastily, "Master Corporal."

They walked silently, until Wakely said, "Well. Hope isn't reasonable."

"Hope is dumb."

He said nothing and she tried to read his expression with a sideways glance, wondered if she'd offended him. He got out a cigarette pack and offered her one, which she declined. He lit one and smoked.

"When Daisy got sick I *hoped* she would get better. She didn't, but without hope it would've been unbearable.

"Hold fast to dreams,
For if dreams die
Life is a broken-winged bird,
That cannot fly."

"Is that a poem?" Virago asked, then quickly, "Dumb question. Of course it's a poem."

He continued,

"Hold fast to dreams,
For when dreams go
Life is a barren field
Frozen with snow."

After a moment she asked, "Did you write that?"

"Langston Hughes. I tacked it up over Daisy's hospital bed. I thought she'd like it because she loved birds. But she pointed out the only bird in the poem has a broken wing and can't fly."

They walked silently, and then he added, "One of the last things she said to me was: 'Keep flying.' I'm going to do that. As long as we're not erased, as long as there's hope for humanity, I'll keep flying."

"We should make a pact."

"What kind of pact?" he said, looking at her.

"Just that: keep flying."

He jammed the cigarette into the corner of his mouth and put out a hand. She reached out and took it, squeezed it, hard. They walked on.

10

They followed the river's twists, the trees and bush along its bank varying in density but maintaining a band 50 metres wide, sometimes wider, often showing the remnants of neighbourhoods, straight lines and roadbed trenches and infilled soil. In some spots only a few trees separated tires from river, and they had to squeeze through a gap or step into the shallows, but the brush persisted, allowing steady progress. Leclerc's calculation haunted Sharpcot as she led the section, imagining a hundred miles of this, but knowing the Red River to the east, wider than the Assiniboine, had to interrupt it.

Their luck ran out a couple of kilometres in. The riverbank trees that resisted the tire wall ended, and the tires surged not just to the river's edge, but into the water itself by a half-dozen metres, cutting off eastward progress.

"I know this spot," Sharpcot said, nodding at a small, elongated island that ran parallel to shore. "We're at the tip of Assiniboine Park. There was a footbridge across the river connecting the park below the river. This section was treeless."

Wakely looked across the water, trying to imagine a bridge here across which people once ambled with their kids and dogs and hopes and dreams. A park for frisbee and catch. He imagined the frisbee block, the baseball block, the mitt block. Towers directly across the river sat far back, beyond a band of trees, and he saw long beams of aluminum stacked horizontally, shining in the afternoon sunlight, bleachers or shelving. More forest amassed to the west, beyond which stood other blocks, their composition difficult to discern, and west of them one made from ski lift chairs. The block adjacent might be cereal boxes, hard to tell. He wrote in his notebook: stadium bleachers (?), ski lift chairs, cereal boxes (?).

"You done?" Sharpcot asked with a hint of annoyance. "What now?"

He gazed at the river. "I don't like the idea of getting everyone and everything wet again. Not to mention the Bronski problem."

"What?" Bronski asked.

"You can't swim. You're a problem," Loko told him.

"What about going over the top?" Virago suggested.

"Climb?" Sharpcot asked doubtfully, panning her eyes up the tires.

"Or go back and take the long way," Wakely said.

"The park is a hundred metres wide," she recalled. "The riverbank treeline likely picks up after that."

Wakely scratched his chin. "It's either a hundred across the river or a hundred over tires."

"So we're climbing?" Loko asked eagerly.

"Looks that way," Sharpcot replied, yet uncertain.

Loko clapped his hands and moved through the group, reassuring everyone that it will be easy, easier than countertops. He set down his rifle, shook off his ruck, indicated hand- and footholds between tires, showing how to dig fingertips into gaps.

"Go barefoot, better grip," he explained, unlacing and kicking off boots, peeling socks. In a few quick moves, he scaled to a point 10 metres up, imploring others to follow.

Virago removed kit, jacket, armour, boots, and socks, and pulled herself up the wall to meet him. He raised a hand to high-five, which she acknowledged with a nod, unwilling to relinquish a handhold.

"I'm not taking off my boots," Bronski said.

"Thank god," Deeks said, and went up the wall too, with less skill than persistence, panting as she rose.

"It's fine for you skinny ones," Leclerc said. "I'm not sure I can do it."

"Come on, Cheree," Virago called. "You can!"

"I don't know," Sharpcot said, looking at the climbers. "Private Leclerc is right. Fine for fit and thin, and there are rucks and rifles to consider."

Leclerc said, "I have an idea."

"You gonna use math to get us over?" Bronski sneered.

"Geometry, actually," Leclerc replied. "We can build a simple machine: an inclined plane. Those who can climb can throw down tires, which we use to build a staircase." Leclerc went on to describe in detail a design, which entailed excavating a rising section within the block and relocating it outside, against the foot of the block. "Staircase to the sixty-third tire, and then 64 tires inside the block."

"I still don't get it," Bronski declared, crossing his arms.

"Well, Private," Wakely grunted. "Luckily that won't stop you from helping."

"What about getting back down?" Virago called. "Same deal on the far side?"

"Privates Virago and Boyko," Sharpcot called up. "You understand the plan? Get to the top and start dropping tires from one of the columns. Deeks, you game?"

"Hell yes," Deeks replied. "Sick of walking. Let's build something."

"Incoming!" Loko called, and a tire landed among them before it bounded into the trees and struck a trunk and flopped over.

"Goddamn it, Loko!" Bronski cried.

"Everyone okay?" Loko called. "Here's another."

He tossed a second tire and everyone scattered.

"Stop!" Sharpcot shouted, then to Wakely, "Jack, get up there and guide them before they squash someone. Bronski, grab those tires and bring them here."

Wakely stripped down and went up. Heavier and less adept than the others, he tried not to rush. When at last he reached the top and threw his arms over the highest tire, sweating from exertion and the day's heat, he made the mistake of looking behind him, saw treetops near enough to touch, and he abruptly appreciated the height of the stacks. He would never in his old life have scaled a nine-storey building, not without a safety harness and training, yet here he was, untethered, clinging to a wall 90 feet above the ground. When he peered over the rim of the tire he gripped he found himself gazing into a black hole nine storeys deep. Smell of hot rubber.

"You all right, Master Jack?"

He looked up to see Loko standing with his feet braced across a tire's opening. Wakely tried not to think what would happen if he fell into that rubber chimney. Virago and Deeks were sitting on the wall's edge, feet dangling. He hauled himself up and adopted a similar pose but with his feet inside a tire, braced against its inner rim. He told himself he was too big to fit, or if he fell he could extend arms and legs and halt his descent.

Then he lifted his head to regard the landscape. Looking north lay a wasteland of tires to the horizon, a landscape of holes. It was a terrible thing to see, and he felt any hope of escaping the situation, this new reality, evaporate.

He looked south, and this view revived him. The brown river rippled in sunlight as it flowed east, oblivious to this abomination of tires on its north side, banks elsewhere fringed with trees and bush. The view west took in the treetops of the woods through which they'd come. Along the south bank, where forest covered the southern stretch of the park, blocks stood sparse and irregular to accommodate trees. In the distance, as far as he could see in any direction, the maze persisted.

The sky itself, normally confined to a narrow groove above passageways, spread out vast and blue, embellished with a high cirrus, foregrounded by a vaporous mist drifting rapidly east, seeming very close, the motion inducing vertigo, so he had to glance down and grip the tire.

When he lifted his eyes the three privates were watching him, and he wondered what his expression had betrayed.

"Let's get to work," he said.

The day's heat further complicated a difficult and perilous job, high up on an uneven surface punctuated by holes, sun bearing down, the objects they had to move heavy, unwieldy, filthy, dropped with care to avoid crushing those below. They stripped to T-shirts, Virago in a tank top that showed her tattoos. She put a finger up to silence Loko when she first exposed them, certain she didn't want to hear whatever he had to say.

After some discussion and a call-down to those on the ground to stand clear, they began pulling up tires in a straight line inward from the wall and sending tires down into the clearing. As they worked further back, they developed a technique for rolling them along the junction between the rows to avoid the holes. Their skill improved as they progressed, and soon they were firing them down the line to the wall's precipice.

They cut a channel one layer at a time, accelerating as they went, the length of each layer decreasing by one tire, so the second groove went in 62 tires, the third, 61. Progress slowed, however, when they got a few tires deep, making the tire rolling within the channel they'd cut less practical. The walls also prevented the breeze from reaching them, increasing heat and fatigue.

When finally they finished, they had carved a neat staircase, 63 tires high, 63 tires deep, one tire wide, its lowest step halfway up the wall, 64 tires up.

They scaled down the wall and surveyed the litter of tires filling the area, stunned with exhaustion.

"Nice work, troops," Sharpcot told them.

"You guys stink," Bronski said to Loko.

Loko, panting and sweating, put a hand on Bronski's shoulder, muttered, "Your turn now, buddy."

"What?" he asked.

"He still don't get it," Deeks said. "Listen Bronski, all these tires? It's now your job to build a staircase with them. To reach that spot right there." She pointed up the wall to the first step of the staircase they'd just completed.

"Oh shit," he said, looking at the mess of tires among the trees.

"I'm going for a goddamn swim," Virago said.

"I'm with you," Deeks said.

"Come on, Loko, Jack," Deeks said, tugging Wakely by the arm. He glanced at Sharpcot and she urged him to go. They jogged through the trees until they reached the far end of the little island, and before they could think it through stripped down and plunged naked into the cool river.

The others set to work, rolling displaced tires to the foot of the wall below the staircase, where they began stacking them. Tse suggested making each step two tires high, building a steeper staircase and improving the construction pace.

The work was backbreaking. While construction within the block involved excavating tires in a descending fashion that allowed them to roll tires down, the outer staircase required lifting them, stacking them one by one. After a time Sharpcot assigned the task of rolling the tires to Bronski and Leclerc, while she helped Tse, with his considerable strength, to stack them. The staircase gradually took shape.

Wakely went deep in the river, wondering vaguely about pollution, chemicals, and pathogens that could make them ill, something he hadn't considered when they'd bathed at the provincial park, only a few klicks upstream. Swimming where the city had been spawned these thoughts, that and all those tires. He'd already forgotten the sweat, felt cool and calm in the river's depths, surrounded by columns of golden light.

He broke the surface some distance from the others, Loko dogpaddling close to shore in his underpants, Virago and Deeks naked in the middle of the river, sculling and chatting, fragments as their voices drifting across the water, ". . . natural impulse because society trains us to fix broken men. It makes him compelling."

He put his face in the water and swam away, against the current, digging deep with his arms, kicking hard. Escaping gossip and speculation, things he loathed about human nature. Trashy magazines at the grocery checkout. Pointless obsession with royals and celebrities. All of it gone with the apocalypse. Good riddance.

Deeks and Virago turned at the sound of Wakely's crashing stroke, watched him swim away. "Do you think he heard us?" Deeks wondered.

"Oh right. Voices carry out here."

After a time, Deeks asked, "Adonia . . . Addy, how do you stay calm? I mean through all this?"

"Calm? Goddamn, Abby, every minute, every step we walk, I am silently freaking out."

"Oh god me too," Deeks whimpered. "But I don't show it. Don't bloody show it."

"The stuff, the maze. Missing people." Virago pivoted slowly to take in the towers lining the banks. "Brief, intense flashes of recognition about what's happened. But they never go far. Too surreal to be real."

"Yeah. Yeah, except. It's like I'm walking along, hum hum, la-di-da," Deeks said. "And then it just fucking smashes me. When we encounter a new thing. All the . . . whatever in the world. Hula hoops. Wine corks. Travel mugs. And then I think, Oh god, this is all of them. Ever. Made. That will ever *be* made."

"Once owned by a person, a human," Virago added. "A mother, a child. A friend. Who held it in their hand. Who drank their morning Starbucks from it."

216

"Yes. Jesus, yes," Deeks replied, and tears spilled from her eyes.

"But no one else seems to notice at that moment. You're alone with the thought. Everyone just soldiering on."

"Yes," Deeks sobbed, reaching underwater for Virago's hand.

"Guys. Yo, guys!" Loko called. He stood on the riverbank, dressed, combing fingers through wet hair. "I'm just — I wanted you to know I'm going back to see if I can help."

"Whatever," Deeks replied.

"See you there, Loko," Virago said.

"Little asshole," Deeks muttered.

"He's all right. If you can get him away from Bronski," Virago said. "Anyway, I'm done too. You coming?"

"I — I need a few minutes," Deeks replied and watched Virago swim back to shore, watched her tattooed body rise from the river, then spun and paddled upstream, maintaining her position relative to shore. She turned on her back, regarding the quiet sky, imagining it crisscrossed by aircraft jetting towards distant cities. When she checked the bank, Virago was dressed, pulling her wet hair into a ponytail. She lifted a hand and Deeks waved, and Virago went into the woods.

Deeks looked for Wakely, who had swum vigorously upstream, spotted him drifting on his back, idle. The current would carry him past her, and she vectored to intercept him, kicking silently. As he slid past she extended a hand, and his head collided with it. He flailed and splashed before he turned and saw her.

"Jesus Christ, Deeks, what the hell?"

"I thought you heard me."

"I didn't," he said, and ran a hand down his face. "I was thinking of the Accruers, had this thought that they're lurking in the river, waiting to grab our stuff and carry it away to the piles of helmets and Kevlar and army boots."

"And what about us, our bodies? What happens to them?" she wondered.

"That the biggest question of all," he replied. "Loko and Virago go back?"

"Yeah."

"We should too. Help."

"We should," she replied, but kept looking at him, both of them sculling against the current.

"Something on your mind, Private?"

"Just. I think Adonia has a thing for you. Master Corporal."

"A thing. You're telling me your BFF has a crush on me?"

"Something like that."

"Such a bad idea," he said.

"Because of rank structure, because you're not interested, or because the end of the world?"

"All that and more."

She swam closer and he backed away. "Private?" he said.

"Sorry. I'm sorry. This is awkward," she said, looking away.

"Indeed," he replied. He was about to swim for shore when he saw she was crying. He sighed, said, "Private Deeks," and she shook her head. "Abigail. Abby."

"Just touch me," she whispered, meeting his eye, reaching out. "Just my hand. I need some human contact. It's a thing for me. I haven't been touched in a month. It's killing me."

He moved tentatively towards her and extended a hand. His fingertips brushed against her palm, then moved along the inside of her wrist. She pushed her arm towards him, sliding in until they were gripping forearms, skin to skin, looking into each other's eyes. They each had to paddle with a free arm, causing a slow pivot, legs churning, the motions drawing their bodies closer together, until the back of his arm grazed her breast, and at that instant he broke free and swam, making for shore. She'd seen a flash of anger or fear before his eyes left her, but he glanced back and called gently, "Let's see how the work is going."

He stayed ahead of her and without self-consciousness rose naked from the river and went to his clothes and swept the water from his skin and began to dress, and she followed and he did not once look as she dressed, and they went wordless through the trees towards the sound of voices.

Sharpcot led the way up the tire staircase. The lower portion rose without railings, a single tire wide. The curved sidewall of each tire flexed with each step, lifting on the far side if she didn't plant her foot right. She found it safest to crouch and press a hand on the opposite rim as she stepped. Her heart hammered as she rose, until at last she passed into the block itself, walls on each side. The remainder of the climb, while equal to the lower half, seemed brief, and she found herself abruptly up top, gazing at a landscape of holes. It made her think of *Yellow Submarine*, the animated film. The Sea of Holes. She'd watched it only months before, with Lana, certain her teenaged daughter would mock and ridicule it, but that didn't happen: the movie charmed the girl, and she could be heard in her bedroom singing "Hey, Bulldog" for months afterward.

Sharpcot pulled an arm across her belly, as had become habit when thinking about Lana. Holding her guts in. Eviscerated by the apocalypse.

She looked across the river at the park with its trees intact and the open spaces infiltrated by blocks. The city overrun. The city gone. The people, her friends, her child — gone? Or relocated? She had to retreat from a vision of stacked human bodies, as she'd seen in high school films about the Holocaust. For which they'd needed a signed parental permission slip. She wondered if her mother had imagined what signing that form meant, what her teenaged daughter would see and how it would change her forever. Make her want to be a soldier, one who fought against tyranny.

"You okay, boss?" Tse asked as he arrived beside her. She turned, watched Leclerc rise from the staircase.

"Bronski's still clinging to the lower bit," Leclerc reported.

"You game to check out the other side?" Sharpcot asked, and the three of them stepped diligently across tire holes until they reached the block's far side. They gazed over the precipice, saw trees below following the riverbank in a wide swath. The tire block ran eastward along the treeline, but they could see its end, and beyond it a new stack formed from an indeterminate product: short, colourful planks with gaps between.

"What next, boss?" Tse asked.

"We'll spend the night on the west side of the tires, build the down staircase in the morning, and continue into the heart of the city."

They met Bronski, face pale with fear and exertion, in the enclosed portion of the staircase as they prepared to descend.

"Private Bronski reporting for duty," he announced, offering a mock salute.

"We're done up here, Private," Sharpcot snapped. "You'll get your chance tomorrow."

"Great," he sighed and began to work his way slowly backwards.

Sharpcot waited, then said with annoyance, "Let us by."

He pressed against the tire wall as Sharpcot, Tse, and Leclerc crushed past. When they reached the lower section they descended feet-first, like climbing down a ladder. A hasty camp had been assembled, Wakely stretched out on his bedroll, eyes shut, Deeks resting on her side and Virago cross-legged, spine straight. They'd set up a pyramid of firewood. Sharpcot sensed tension there, between the three of them, dismissed it. The light was waning and she took Tse and Leclerc to the river to bathe. When Bronski arrived, Wakely sent him to join them.

Sharpcot returned 10 minutes later, hair wet, furious.

Wakely rose. "What happened?"

"Bronski happened. I was swimming when he took a bad step and went down thrashing like a maniac. I tried to help but he pulled me under. If Tse hadn't been there we'd both be drowned."

"Dammit," Wakely barked. "What do you want me to do?"

"What can you do? Teach the little weasel to swim." She went to her kit and unloaded it, dropped to her bedroll, began brushing her hair roughly.

After a time Tse and Leclerc returned with more firewood, and Bronski staggered to the edge of the camp where he stood panting, hands on knees. When no one noticed he exclaimed, "Almost caught a rabbit!" He went to where his stuff lay, picked up his rifle. "With ammo I could shoot us one for dinner."

"Drop your weapon, Private Bronski," Sharpcot growled. "You will blow that rabbit to bits, or shoot one of us, or yourself."

He sat hard on the ground and sighed.

They got a fire going and distributed the last of their IMPs, supplemented them with canned peas and flour tortillas with a best before date six months in the future. Loko read the date out loud, laughing, but it raised the spectre of expiration for all the maze's consumables. Then they'd have to slaughter rabbits and fish and possibly ailing, feral cows.

The day's labour brought quick sleep to most. Sharpcot lay on her side, watching the fire, tended by Tse on first watch. Tse, usually calm. Only now he could not leave the fire alone. With a pronged stick, he poked at the junction of two logs, set new pieces into the gap, while pushing other branches and logs to the side where they began to smoke. He continued to make adjustments, and her eyes closed on the scene, and she fell into fitful sleep.

Wakely lay awake for a long time, despite fatigue. His arms hummed from hauling tires, and he traced a sense of accomplishment to the labour: dismantling the Accruers' work. An act of defiance. They were the resistance. With the cotter pins and jelly beans and licence plates they'd liberated from the stacks and scattered in the passageways they were breaking down the destructive order the Accruers had imposed.

He jerked awake with a snort, wondered if he'd been snoring, turned onto his side to avoid more of that. The sleeping pad

221

wasn't thick, and the ground felt hard against his hip and shoulder, but he slept nevertheless.

Sharpcot squatted on the tire plateau in the morning sunlight beside the nearly complete descent staircase, this one hastily built, steeper, less precise than the first, uneven in places with double and sometimes triple-tire steps, but adequate. She'd just sipped warm water from her CamelBak when Bronski came careening across the tire field towards her, stepping madly against sidewalls, tripping once before scrambling up and resuming his sprint, tripped again, and twisted trying to find footing. His ruck, thrown loosely over one shoulder, slid off and went instantly into a hole, fluttering as it slapped past tire beads, falling deep.

He kneeled above the hole, gazing into the abyss, then lifted his head. His eyes met Sharpcot's.

"Oh shit," he said.

Some minutes later, after Sharpcot's lengthy excoriation, the section stood around the hole into which the pack had fallen, discussing strategy.

"Do we even need it?" Deeks asked.

"It's got my stuff," Bronski said.

"Just your crap," Deeks rebutted. "You obviously don't use deodorant or a toothbrush."

He made a move at her and flailed as his foot slipped into one of the holes, and Tse seized him by the back of the collar.

"It's got the radio in it," Sharpcot said.

"What good is that anymore?" Loko said.

"We need it," Sharpcot replied firmly.

"I can't see a way to retrieve it," Wakely said.

"What about a hook and rope or something?" Bronski wondered.

"You'll go find the hook block? The rope block?" Virago asked. "We won't wait. You'll have to catch up."

"I'll go," Loko said.

222

"Even if we had the equipment," Wakely continued. "You can't fish around at the bottom of a hundred-foot tube."

"I'll go down," Loko said. "I can do it."

"You can't, Loko," Leclerc said kindly. "What if you get stuck?"

"I won't get stuck. I'm small."

Deeks shook her hands, put one to her forehead. "Oh god the thought of it. Nope nope nope."

"You don't have to," Loko said. "I'll do it."

"You brave little bastard," Deeks shuddered. "I don't get how the bunker made you crazy but you'd go down a dark pipe like that."

"Easy. It's open at the top. The bunker was a closed box."

"Kyrylo," Sharpcot said, stepping across tires to stand close. "You don't have to do this. I won't order you to do it."

He nodded, unlaced his boots, pulled off socks and tucked them inside, laced the boots together and handed them to Bronski, who refused them.

"Take my boots, jerk. This is your fault."

Bronski glanced at the faces around him, then accepted the boots. He pretended to sniff them with an expression of disgust, but no one noticed. Loko took a long drink of water, handed his canteen to Wakely, who passed him a flashlight, which he tucked into a vest pocket.

He put his feet into the hole. "No big deal. Lots of foot- and handholds on the tire edges. Easier than countertops in rain."

He lowered himself and was gone. Then called up, "Bronski, you sure this is the right hole?"

Everyone looked at Bronski. "Pretty sure," he replied with a weak smile.

"I'm only doing this once," Loko called, and they heard the flap of tire beads as he descended.

"You okay?" Virago asked Deeks, whose face was pale and sweat-drenched. She shook her hands like they were wet.

Wakely kneeled over the hole, watching Loko's sandy hair vanish into the dark.

"Keep talking, Private Boyko," Wakely said.

"Air's not great," Loko called back, his voice muted. And after a minute, "Just a circle of light above. That you, Master Jack?"

Wakely waved.

"Can we — can we work on the down staircase?" Deeks said. She didn't wait for a reply, stepped across the tire field to the descending staircase. Virago and Tse followed.

Wakely stared into the darkness. He cupped his ears and listened, heard the flap of hands and feet on rubber. Then silence. He leaned forward to call down when Loko's voice rose faintly. "Pretty hot down here," he said. "Pretty hot."

"Tell him not to faint. If he faints he's dead," Sharpcot said.

Wakely put up a hand to silence her, called down, "What was that, Private? You say something?"

"Sound reaches me loud and clear. No dying talk, please? I think I'm almost at the bottom. Feeling around with my feet. There better be a kit down here. Oh, what are these?"

A long pause, and Wakely called down, "Loko?"

"Yeah, I just lit the flashlight and there are spiders. Like, a lot of them."

"Oh god," Bronski muttered, hugging himself.

"How are you with spiders?" Wakely called.

"As good as anybody. One is okay. Ten thousand, not great."

"Are there 10,000?" Sharpcot asked.

"More or less," Loko replied. "I'm continuing down. Like being in a chimney. Not that I've ever been in a chimney. Though more like a smokestack. Hey, what's the difference?"

Wakely looked up, "Leclerc. Difference between a chimney and a smokestack."

"Oh. Uh. It's a matter of scale and purpose. Houses have chimneys. Factories use smokestacks. Though the terms are interchangeable. On a ship, you call it a funnel."

"You hear that, Loko?" Wakely called down. "The *Titanic* had funnels."

224

Wakely waited for a reply. He wiped his brow. At least the breeze cooled him. He couldn't imagine conditions deep in that rubber hole.

"Loko?"

A lengthy pause, then his voice, far off, rose from the depths. "I got it. Tell Bronski I got his fucking pack. And he owes me a blowjob or something."

"You tell him when you get up here."

"On my way."

Wakely sat back, mopped his brow with the hem of his shirt. The sun was beating down on them now, heating the black rubber field. He could hear Tse and Deeks and Virago, tossing and stacking tires, calling to each other. He gripped Loko's canteen like it was tethered to the man. Shook it to ensure it had enough to hydrate him when he emerged. He wondered how long their water purification tablets would last, how many were left. They'd have to start boiling their water. But at some point, he thought soberly, it would no longer be necessary, or less necessary, in a world without polluting humans.

Sharpcot watched Wakely hunched by the hole. She'd worked with three master corporals, three "Master Jacks," and none was like Dorian Wakely. The other two used aggression and cruelty to enforce discipline — MC Kirby was a screamer who frequently lost his voice, and MC Reznikov liked to grab and shake, by the arm, by the shoulders, by the neck, to make himself heard. Wakely commanded a hundred times their respect.

They'd heard nothing from Loko in minutes. Wakely leaned to call down when he smelled something that panicked him. A wisp of smoke rose from the hole.

"Smoke," Wakely called.

Sharpcot stiffened. She'd seen media coverage of tire fires — they burned for months, years, even decades. Tires burned madly, and released toxic, oily smoke, but worse still, Loko was in that hole. Fire down there would kill him fast. Wakely was

225

thinking the same thing, prepared to lower himself into the hole when he sniffed the air, fell back, and laughed.

"What?" Sharpcot demanded. "What happened?"

"Private Bronski?" Wakely queried.

"Sir?"

"You didn't happen to have, uh, illicit botanicals in your ruck, did you?"

"What do you mean?" he asked, looking uncomfortable. Then he sniffed the air, and bounded across the tires to the hole, put his hands on both sides of it and shouted, "Loko you asshole are you smoking my weed?"

And from a few metres inside the hole came a low chuckle.

Wakely led a stoned and sweating Loko to the tire staircase. As Bronski began to follow, Sharpcot called him to halt.

"This about my weed, mang?" he asked. "Uh, Sergeant."

"Enough with that mouth, Private. I'm an inch away from disciplining you in some unpleasant way I haven't even conceived of. And yes, this would be about your weed if I didn't have a thousand other things to concern me. But right now I want you to turn around."

"What?"

"Turn the fuck around, Bronski," she said, seizing his shoulders and forcing him to pivot. "When you're ordered to do something, do it. I can't make it any more simple."

She opened his ruck, flinched at a sour odour, and dug past filthy laundry and ballpoint pens and lobster cans, located the antenna and screwed it in place, turned on the radio.

"This is the highest we've been since leaving the bunker." She slipped on the headset and ran through the frequencies, pausing when she heard an errant crackle, maybe a voice, but it always resolved into static. When she'd done a thorough search, she tuned to a random band and thumbed the mic. What to say? Released the button, thought, "Is there anybody out there?" Haunted by memories of a song.

She listened to the static that blew into her ears in a wind of nothingness. Then pressed the button and spoke evenly into the mic, "This is Elisabeth Sharpcot, Sergeant, Three Section of Two Platoon of B Company of the Second Battalion of the Princess Patricia's Canadian Light Infantry, broadcasting from ... from Winnipeg, Manitoba. Anyone copy?"

She looked at the sky and watched a raptor corkscrew through the air, hunting, while she hunted the pitted spray for something human. But the static was barren. In the past the signals of distant transmitters, of radio and television stations and walkie-talkies and CB, ham, police, ambulance, taxi two-way, of airband and marine, of satellites and cell phones and engine spark plugs and microwave ovens and hard disks and buzzing fluorescent lights and freezer compressors and garage door openers and game controllers and moose-tracking radio collars had tinted the frequencies. Even if the content was unintelligible, it added a structure to the noise, a structure that was now, she recognized, entirely absent. The sound she heard was universe, lonely universe. And yet this thought collided with the possibility that some other race, an alien race, was responsible for the end of human civilization. So it came together as a bitter triumph: we are alone, we are not alone. And whoever is left in the universe is not us, and not for us.

"Anything?" Bronski asked, and when Sharpcot didn't answer, "Yo, Sarge. You get anything?"

She turned off the radio, stowed the antenna, then made her way down the staircase where the rest of the section was waiting, Bronski too close behind her, as if he feared being left behind. They scanned her expression, and she knew she could conceal nothing, despite an instinct to maintain optimism.

"Let's go," she barked, and they pushed on.

They stuck by the river, past the block of planks (skateboards) they'd observed from the top of the tires, then Robertson screwdrivers, copper Jell-O moulds, wooden milk crates, flattened chicken wire, some kind of small individually wrapped balls, and ran into a wall of baseball caps that went to the water's edge. They could probably step through the shallows past them, but they reasoned that hats being smaller and less copious than tires meant the block wouldn't run excessively far north, so they could circumnavigate it without soaking their boots or risking Bronski's life. They still expected a large block of caps because, to quote Deeks, "Every fucking redneck owns a shitload."

As they walked north Loko discovered through sampling the composition of the left wall: individually wrapped candies with an array of flavours, everything from peppermint to green tea to blueberry anise to lychee to curry-mint. The baseball caps came in myriad colours, and they celebrated not just baseball teams but hockey, basketball, football, lacrosse, cricket, rugby, as well as monster trucks, films, television shows, bands, brands, superheroes, video game characters, countries, cities, political views, and there was a proliferation of slogans too, some clever, some opaque, most annoying. They were nested together, creating a compacted wall that absorbed sound and silenced their footsteps. About 400 metres up the candies ended at a vast monument of copper pipes like some enormous Victorian steam engine, most of the pipes tarnished and patinated, but some fresh and polished and dazzling in the sunshine.

They gazed at the block, and Sharpcot couldn't help but see it as beautiful, which seemed all wrong, considering that she stood in what was essentially the ruins of the city where her child had lived, where friends had lived, where she had lived. All gone. Not actually a ruin, but still, a kind of ruin, a gorgeous, homogenous ruin.

"What are you thinking?" Wakely asked as he gazed up.

"Copper on blue. So lovely it hurts."

Virago had her phone out, powered it on for a photo. "Dammit," she muttered. "It just died."

"Last time I turned mine on it was at four percent," Deeks muttered.

After a long moment of studying at the stack, Wakely asked quietly, "Where we going, Sarge?"

"We're here. The city. Winnipeg."

"So now what?"

"I don't know. It makes sense to get to the heart of it. To a landmark that will confirm it."

"And that would be?"

She looked at him. "Indulge me."

The section went north along pipes and caps until the latter ended at an eastbound passage with a block of wooden cases of some kind, most painted white, some bare wood, others grey, light green, yellow, and a sweet scent in the air. Tse said, "Honey."

"Right. Beehives," Virago said, placing a hand against one.

"Oh god," Bronski cried. "There aren't bees in there, are there bees?"

"What's the matter, Bronski," Deeks asked. "You allergic?"

"No. Just fucking hate getting stung."

Virago put her ear up to one of the cases and listened, then slapped the box with the flat of her hand. "I don't hear anything. If there are bees inside they're dead."

"But is there honey?" Loko wondered.

"Yeah, you'd ask that," Bronski grumbled.

"Who doesn't like honey?"

"I don't like things made by crawlies," Bronski muttered.

"So what I read in the tabloids is wrong — you don't wear silk underwear?" Deeks gasped.

"Like I'd wear something made by spiders," he replied, flinched at the laughter that followed. "What?"

"Silk is made by worms, moron," Loko said.

"Same difference: insects, worms."

229

"Except spiders aren't insects," Leclerc stated.

"Dude, you know what has bugs in it? Hops," Deeks said. "You love IPA, but hops are loaded with aphids."

"I'm off IPA," he replied. "As of now."

"Don't forget the beetles they crush to colour raspberry Jell-O," Virago said.

"Dactylopius coccus," Leclerc said.

"I don't eat raspberries," Bronski said. "From now on."

"Can we crack one open, get the honey?" Loko asked.

"Whoa, what if it's full of angry bees?" Bronski said.

"The bees aren't here," Virago insisted.

"Where are they?" Sharpcot wondered. "I guess it's the same question we keep asking."

"Free in the world," Virago suggested.

"Isn't that going to fuck them up? Like the cows?" Loko asked.

"Bees haven't been bred to rely on humans the way the cows have," Virago stated. "So they're probably okay. They can build hives. And maybe now they stand a chance. Without Bayer and Monsanto murdering the fuck out of them."

"You almost sound happy for bees," Deeks said to Virago.

"I am," Virago mused. "And for Earth."

Sharpcot tapped one of the boxes, wondered, "How do you open them?"

"You have to go in through the top," Virago said.

Sharpcot nodded to Tse. "Can you crack one open?"

Tse got out his entrenching tool and took a swing, splintering the wood on the front of the hive. Bronski bolted back, while Virago came forward and swept away a ridge of dead honeybees that lay against the frames. They were slotted to be pulled from the top, but Tse's blow had broken the runners and she managed to draw a frame out. She brought it to Sharpcot, who studied it.

"Is that honey?" she asked.

Virago dipped her finger into the comb and tasted it. "Oh god so good."

Wakely stepped forward and ran his index finger through the honey and tasted it. Sharpcot did the same.

"Any way to collect some and take it with us?" she asked. "That's really good."

The others tasted it too, collected hunks of honeycomb.

"We'd need jars," Wakely said. "This is the problem — everything is here, but not where you can find it. Need a jar? Too bad. But here are a literal billion fucking baseball caps." He looked around. "Let's just kit up and move on."

"Guys. Guys?" Bronski said.

"What now, Bronski?" Sharpcot demanded.

"Uh. Bear?" Bronski said.

A distance down the passage a black bear stood on hind legs, head bobbing as it sniffed the air.

"Nobody move," Sharpcot ordered.

She noted that the wind blew from the west, carrying their scent — and the smell of honey.

"Set down that frame, Virago. Everyone fall back behind me, slowly," Sharpcot ordered, raising her rifle and chambering a round, clicking off the safety.

Wakely's gun came up, and he said, "I'm on it."

"Fall back, Jack," she snapped.

She peered through the scope, put crosshairs on the bear's head, knew it was an easy shot, wind from behind, range 300 metres.

"What's your plan, Sarge?" Wakely asked.

"Shoot it! Just fucking shoot it!" Bronski hissed. "Why doesn't she shoot the fucker?" he said to the others. "Is it her spirit animal or some bullshit?"

The bear dropped to all fours, and began to lumber towards them.

"Three Section, you heard the sergeant, assemble around the corner now! Slow and orderly," Wakely instructed in a controlled voice. The rest of them complied and Wakely shifted

231

to the middle of the passage and backed after them, his own rifle up to cover Sharpcot. He waited at the corner as the bear advanced, pausing momentarily to sniff the ground along the edge of the beehives, before progressing towards them.

Without turning around, Sharpcot called with annoyance, "You too, Jack. I got it."

Wakely lowered his rifle and swept around the corner, waited close, back pressed to the hives, ready to return to the passageway if needed. He looked at the section, and when the first shot came, they all started. Five more followed, in slow succession.

He hazarded a glance and saw Sharpcot advance backwards, rifle up, and far past her the bear down in the dirt. He regretted the necessity of her action, but then saw the bear's head come up, its nose testing the air. He raised his rifle, amazed that six shots had not finished the animal, when he saw that the hives halfway between Sharpcot and the bear had been blasted open, with honey leaking from their shattered faces. The bear was recovering from fear, rising, began working its way towards the honey.

Sharpcot turned, gave Wakely a half smile before rounding the corner and moving towards the section with him trailing.

"Is it dead?" Bronski asked.

"The bear is in fact not dead," Wakely said. "The Sarge here came up with a better solution than deadly force. Blew open a bunch of hives so it has all the honey it can eat. Nicely done."

"Figure out what your threat wants," Sharpcot explained, "and if it's something you can give up, then give it up."

"Whoa, Sarge, is that like an Indian saying?" Bronski asked.

"An *Indian* saying, Bronski?" Sharpcot bellowed. "I wouldn't know, I'm not an *Indian*. How about, 'Let's prepone lunch.' That's an Indian saying. 'An eye for an eye makes the whole world blind.' Mahatma Gandhi said that. So that's an *Indian* saying."

"Never mind, Bronski," Deeks said to Bronski's dumbfounded expression. "You'll never get it."

They went north between the pipes and beehives, reached an eastbound passage lined with stainless steel beer kegs. They remained wary of bears and anything else that might want honey, reached an area where a cloud of yellowjackets swarmed a few metres above their heads, sending Bronski into a panicked run ahead, despite explicit orders to remain with the group. He was about to cross the next intersection when he remembered the bear, and he held there, paralyzed, until the section caught up.

When Sharpcot arrived, she seized him by the shoulder and barked into his face, "Private, you are way out of line, and have been since we left the bunker. You have a serious issue with discipline, and I've had enough of it."

"I don't care what you think," Bronski screamed. "Because I fucking quit!" He threw down rifle and helmet, squirmed out of his ruck and let it drop behind him, tore off his jacket. Sharpcot watched the tantrum with a neutral expression, and when Wakely moved to intervene, she raised a hand. They watched him toss off vest and armour. He stood in boots, pants, and a stinking T-shirt, panting and sweating and casting his mad eyes about.

"So you'll return to civilian life?" Sharpcot asked calmly. "Hockey and Netflix and playing in your band? Maybe Walmart's hiring?"

He nodded, hands balled, trembling. He held the pose for an instant, then something broke and he uttered a sob, and began to cry, tears streaming down his face. It went on for a minute, and when no one moved, the crying shifted to bawling. He covered his face as it all came to him, that despite his resistance to the idea, despite the unharmed presence of everything ever made, the world had ended, completely, definitively, and that without Three Section, these seven people, he would be alone. And he would die.

He cried until he felt someone touch his shoulder, and he shrugged away, but when the hand returned he leaned into it. An arm, he didn't know whose, curled around his back, and in a moment he was surrounded, arms around him, holding him, and when he realized he was the nexus of a group hug the hopelessness surged deeper, and he bawled loudly, accepting the embrace. The despair began to subside, and he let his hands fall, and made out through a prism of tears the faces of those who held him, Virago close up, probably the one who started it, and Loko beside her, and he felt behind him the towering presence of Tse, and Deeks and Leclerc were in there too, and Wakely, and somewhere further back Sharpcot. He felt a sudden unclamping inside, between his shoulder blades, in his chest, an unwinding of the furious tension that had gripped him since the bunker, since before that, since he'd joined the army, since he'd left childhood and adolescence.

"Okay," he whispered. "Okay. I think I'm okay."

Then shame inundated him, and he felt an urgency to reassemble himself. He churned out of the embrace, kneeled beside his ruck and dug out a wad of tissues, blotted his face. He began to draw his gear back on, armour, vest, jacket. He perched the helmet on his head and got his rifle and climbed to his feet, stood regarding everyone with a crooked smile. He felt the anguish resurge and sucked air through his teeth, bottling it up.

Wakely lit a cigarette and passed it over. Bronski took a drag.

"How's that, Travis?" Wakely asked.

Bronski nodded, lips clamped on the cigarette, because if he spoke he'd cry again.

"Keep it," Wakely told him. "I got one left. And seeing as there are bears and wolves and wild cows around, you'll need this."

Bronski accepted the proffered magazine and popped it into his rifle.

Sharpcot stepped over, asked, "We all good here? You ready to move, Private Bronski?"

Bronski narrowed his eyes at her as he took another puff on the cigarette, then nodded, and Sharpcot checked the intersection for bears and led the soldiers across it and east.

They passed the great rubbery mass of machine belts, and on the right, paperboard drink coasters, used to protect the table from a cold glass of beer or other beverage. Bronski remained uncharacteristically incurious, failed to yank out coasters, and gave only a cursory look when Loko showed him a few, with images of windmills or sailboats or pictures of Paris or printed with the names of beer and liquor brands: Heineken, Left Field, Everards Daredevil Traditional Winter Warmer, Campari Red Passion.

"These making you thirsty, Trav?" Loko asked, but Bronski looked straight ahead and marched on.

Sharpcot in the lead noticed at the far end of the passage, still some distance away, a break. She increased their pace.

Belts continued on the right, predominantly black, some grey, white, orange, even pink, printed with model numbers and specifications and tolerances and barcodes and "Do Not Crimp," some toothed, others multi-grooved, some with a V cross-section. They were leather, rubber, neoprene, polyurethane, chloroprene, polyester, PVC. For sewing machines and bread makers and engine pumps and grinders and air compressors and washing machines and printers and money counters and saws and lathes and combine harvesters. On the left the coasters ended, and something clear and gelatinous comprised the next block. Sunlight punching down into the block illuminated it from within, invoking a haunting, undersea blue. Sharpcot's determined pace subsided as she gazed at it, something drawing her in, and she stopped.

Loko suggested blueberry Jell-O, Leclerc submitted the goo they put in gel insoles, but Virago stepped up and ran her palm along the wall and held up her hand and found it covered in clear disks each smaller than a dime. She studied them for a few seconds before she brushed them to the ground with a shudder.

"What?" Loko asked. "What's wrong?"

"Contact lenses," Virago groaned.

235

"Oh god," Bronski said, stepping back to take in the entire blue block. "Oh god, those — those were in people's eyes?"

They regarded the block with fresh recognition.

"It's like looking at eyeballs," Deeks said softly.

Bronski walked a circle, gripping his head.

"Let's move," Sharpcot said.

"Gimme a sec," Bronski said, leaning with hands on knees, huffing.

The others set out, but Bronski remained rigid. Sharpcot waited, patience thinning.

"Private Bronski," she said after a minute. He lifted his head and glared, his expression so full of hate that she flinched. Furious at the insubordination, she stated flatly, "Stand at attention, Private Bronski. That is an order."

He continued to glower, defiant.

It triggered the desperate helplessness she felt when Lana grew recalcitrant, forcing Sharpcot to strip privileges — give me your phone, forget seeing your friends this weekend, no dinner, go to your room — and everything failed, the girl accepting the mounting consequences with greater resistance. Sharpcot panicked as she drained the pool of penalties. Meanwhile she suffered sorrow for the girl's forfeiture of recreations and pleasures. Sharpcot was not one to relent — a consequence could not be retracted. She would not be the permissive wimp the girl's father had become, caving to her whims. Maybe Lana would grow to prefer her father, but she would respect her mother.

All this brought fury to her voice. "Private Bronski, if you don't immediately straighten to attention as I have ordered, we will leave you here. I will forbid you from continuing to serve with my section, and you will not be permitted to accompany us further. You will be on your own. Do you understand? Do you understand what I'm saying? Private Bronski?"

Bronski narrowed his eyes and growled, "Yeah, I understand. And y'all can go to the devil, you drunk fucken Indian."

Sharpcot gave him a look of disappointment, and he knew he'd lost. He was ready to comply. But he needed a minute, to compose himself, to straighten to attention. He wanted with all his might to comply, to follow the order, to do what he needed to do, and if he had five minutes, two minutes, he could do it, but right now a dark emotion paralyzed him, the same black feeling that got him kicked out of high school, estranged from his parents, lost him jobs, friends, girlfriends. It's why he'd gone into the army in the first place, or why he'd told himself he had. And here it was, that feeling, never to be evicted.

Sharpcot walked away, following the section down the passageway. He watched them go, saw them approach the intersection where watering cans stood on the left across from something he couldn't discern. As they left him behind, he felt tears on his cheeks, and his back began to ache from the stance, hunched forward, hands on knees. He put a hand to the small of his back and straightened, gazing at the sky as it fragmented into shards of tear-broken light.

Sharpcot passed Loko as she headed for the front of the column.

"Sarge?" he said, but she did not turn.

He spun just as Bronski lifted the rifle to his shoulder and pressed his eye to the scope. Loko heard the click of the safety and took a swift step forward while raising his right hand towards Bronski. The muzzle flashed and the bullet crossed the distance and came in below his arm, nicked the top of his Kevlar vest and drove across his chest cavity, passing through both lungs and grazing the heart before it lodged in his left humerus.

He heard the crash of the shot and felt something like shocked sorrow, as if hearing of a loved one's death. Abruptly remembered a morning when he was eight and woke to find his hamster had died in the night. The bundle of russet fur that never stopped moving oddly still.

His body jolted sideways from the shot, and he went down hard on his left shoulder.

When Sharpcot reached him, he was on his back, struggling for breath, a pink foam on his lips. The rest of the section clustered around him, unsure of what to do — there were always admonishments about not moving an injured person, but they could see he was floundering.

Virago looked down the passageway to where Bronski was standing, a hand pinned to his jaw, the rifle in the dirt where he'd dropped it. He stumbled forward, tripped once and went to his knees. He rose again and came towards the group clustered around Loko.

"Is he — how is he?" Bronski asked quietly. He heard a low wheeze and gurgle. "It hit his armour, right? He's only winded?"

Sharpcot lifted her head and looked at him, and more terrifying than anger was her entirely neutral expression.

"Sarge, you have to believe me. I was aiming for your back plate. It wasn't a kill shot. I only wanted to knock you over. It hit Loko's armour, right? He's just winded?"

She held up a bloodstained hand.

"No," Bronski heard himself say, putting a hand to his eyes. When he looked again, Sharpcot had gone back in, and he could see only the top of her head. Wakely was kneeling in front of him and Bronski began to reach for his shoulder, he had to explain it to someone, that he hadn't meant to shoot to kill the sergeant, and he certainly hadn't wanted to harm his friend.

He saw where Wakely's jacket had ridden up the sidearm in the holster on his hip. Bronski reached in and loosened the snap and tugged the piece out. Wakely turned.

"What the hell, Bronski?" he cried, standing, and the private racked the slide and thumbed the safety and aimed the gun at Wakely's face. "Give it here, Trav," he said gently, a hand out.

Bronski started to back away, the pistol raised. He got a dozen paces away before he turned and ran.

He thought no one would pursue, but a quick glance showed Wakely behind him, running hard. Bronski got to the intersection and hooked right, ran between the drink coasters and contact lenses.

When he looked again Wakely was no closer, but Bronski hadn't opened the distance either. He was 10 years younger than Wakely, but Wakely jogged and lifted, while Bronski spent a lot of time on his ass, as much as possible in fact. He only had to get a little lead to do what he needed to do, but when he recognized he wasn't going to get that, he made a quick decision.

Wakely saw Bronski's hand with the gun go up, but he didn't know what he intended until the barrel went to the private's head and he heard the shot, and Bronski went down, crashed raggedly into the dirt.

Wakely stood over him, panting from the run, thinking irrationally that Bronski should be out of breath too after that sprint along the passageway. But he lay there, immobile, a piece of his head gone and gore and blood everywhere, painting the wall of coasters, filling the soil, absorbed passively by the soil, in the same way it would take the rain.

He knew it was pointless, but he kneeled and put two fingers to the private's neck, adjusted them. There was a momentary flutter, but it faded. Bronski was dead.

Wakely raised his head and for a panicked moment could not fathom where he was. A private, from his own section, curled dead in the dirt before him, a massive wall of blue jelly on one side, and an equally tall rampart of coasters on the other, and it was so like a dream that he briefly wondered about the symbolism it represented, as if it could be submitted to his therapist for analysis, and from it she'd tease some canny truth.

"Jack?" a voice called from the distance. He turned and saw Virago at the intersection. She jogged up the aisle and he bolted towards her and when they got close and it was clear she was going to check on Bronski he caught her arm, and though she struggled to get past him, he would not let go. She thrashed in his grip until he said, "He's dead, Adonia."

She sagged against him, and moaned, "Loko too."

He pulled her to his chest and she wept, and he started to tell her what happened, how he was trying to catch Bronski because he knew what the private would do, and how he thought if only he could grab the gun, or tire him out, the thing that happened could have been prevented, but Bronski was determined, and had done what Wakely had never expected: shot himself at a full run.

But Wakely got only a few words into this explanation before he trailed off, and just held her.

11

Sharpcot regarded Wakely squatting in the dirt with his back to the watering cans, smoking his last cigarette, gaze vacant. She took a drink from her canteen and heard the last honk from a vee of southbound geese that had just passed overhead, and went to where Tse crouched in a hole a metre deep and big enough to accommodate two bodies. He was digging hard. She hopped down beside him and unfolded her own entrenching tool and worked beside him for a while and took off her jacket and vest and kept working until Wakely relieved Tse. The two declined offers from Virago and Deeks and Leclerc to help, and they dug until they'd doubled the grave's depth.

Their shovels turned up nothing but soil, not a pottery fragment, stone tool, nail, bottle cap, or tin can, objects you would expect from an excavation at a river junction used continuously for 6,000 years, by Assiniboine, Cree, Ojibwe, Oji-Cree, Dakota, and Métis, where Fort Rouge, Fort Gibraltar, and Upper Fort Garry had stood, and where a modern city had bloomed. The earth was clean, cool, and fragrant.

When they finished they climbed from the hole and sat and drank water and ate a few rations and a can of peas. Then working together they laid the bodies of Private Kyrylo "Loko" Boyko and Private Travis Raymond Bronski Jr. side-by-side in the hole alongside their rifles, firing pins removed and magazines emptied, loose ammo distributed. Wakely set Bronski's helmet on his head to conceal the gore, wiped blood from Loko's lips.

They'd gone reluctantly through the men's rucks and extracted a few essentials — from Loko's, a bottle of ibuprofen, a sewing kit, a Vonnegut paperback; from Bronski's, a baggie of marijuana and a glass pipe and the manpack radio. Among other personal effects, toiletries, collected objects, they found curiosities: in Loko's, a tiny notebook in which he'd jotted brief and spare poems, some only a dozen words, and all of them about nature, and in Bronski's a threadbare stuffed puppy, its floppy ears worn. They set these objects in the grave, the notebook in Loko's shirtpocket, the puppy in the crook of Bronski's arm.

They stood above the grave gazing down at the men, and Virago made them hold hands while Sharpcot offered a brief, awkward eulogy.

They worked together to fill the grave, and it was done quickly. They left nothing to mark the spot but the turned earth.

Walking east brought them to the Red River, wider than the Assiniboine, flowing north. They stood looking at the blocks on the opposite bank: shiny, dull, colourful; fine objects, large ones, none explicitly clear, though one stack of squarish, wheeled vehicles may have been Zambonis. They moved upstream along a path of packed earth. Sharpcot said it was the River Walk, and she was here with Lana at the start of June on a radiant afternoon, and she felt sick and empty retracing those footsteps of three months previous.

The path rounded to the west and they arrived at the Assiniboine River and looked to the south bank, which was richly treed and devoid of blocks, and they looked at the water where the currents collided and sediment from the rivers whirled and blended.

"The Forks," Sharpcot said with a kind of finality. On a cloudy morning she and Lana had visited the Human Rights Museum, which had stood a few hundred metres north of this spot. They'd emerged after an hour to blue skies and sunshine, walked along the riverbank to this place before they'd crossed the old railway bridge to South Point Park and back again. No evidence now of that bridge.

They were six now. And Sharpcot had failed, utterly. Failed to keep the people under her care safe. Failed to find her daughter. Failed to save the world.

She saw Wakely watching her, knew that look of expectation. She was supposed to come up with a plan. A way out of this. Like she always had. Like she had that morning in Panjwayi when they were pinned down in a ditch along a poppy field and she'd led an LMG fire team 200 metres through a trench to set up a flanking position where they peppered the Taliban and broke the attack.

"We could camp here," Wakely said. "Figure out where next tomorrow. Just, you know, we could go north along the river, do a recce with . . . well Tse and I could . . ." He trailed off, so drained he couldn't finish the sentence. What was the point of anything? They'd made it to the city only to confirm that the city was gone. Which meant every city was gone.

They made camp, built a fire. Virago went through the trees to investigate the block that stood beyond them, and when she came back Wakely asked her without interest what it was.

"Come look," she said, putting a hand out as he sat staring into the fire. He looked at her hand and in that instant it seemed the only thing left in the world, this hand extended to him, to help him to his feet, requesting his companionship. He felt a need to give something, and he could give this, so he set his hand in hers and she pulled him to his feet and they went together through the bush still holding hands and came to the wall. It was unlike any they'd seen, beautiful, curving elegantly to follow the shape of the river, composed of irregular strips of brass and nickel-silver and steel and aluminum lying flat and stacked nine storeys high. A metallic wave.

Wakely put both hands against the wall and ran them along the jagged surface.

243

"What is it?" he asked, throwing his gaze up the stack to detect any protruding object, but the construction was flawless.

"Guess," she said.

"I don't know," he replied, not at all inclined to play this game. "Do you know?"

"I know."

He stepped back and glanced each way along the curve, not wanting to make an idiotic suggestion. As if there could be one.

"Saws? Pocket knives? That can't be right."

She held up a closed fist, turned it over, but did not open it. He tapped it with a forefinger. "Come on."

When he looked at her face she was staring at him intently, and he noted without wanting to that her eyes were an extraordinarily pale blue. When he realized he'd spent too long looking he stepped back and turned to the wall. She sighed.

"Okay, look," she said, and opened her hand to reveal a key, an ordinary brass housekey. It said Ilco on it, Made in USA, with a numerical code.

"Jesus Christ, keys?" he said, looking at the wall again, panning its width. He closed his eyes and took a slow breath.

"Master Jack?" she said, and when he didn't answer she cleared her throat and tried, "Dorian?"

"I can't get my head around any of this." He nodded at the wall. "Keys. Every key ever produced, ever owned. How many keys have you owned in your life? Your parents' house. Every apartment you've rented. Maybe two or three for each. The back door, the garden shed, a cupboard, the garage, the padlock on the gate, your desk drawer at work. Multiple copies, one in the kitchen drawer, one on the keyring hanging from a nail in the basement, one under the flowerpot on the back porch. Every key you've ever lost. For locks that were changed. A hundred billion keys. All the keys in the world, Addy. All the keys in the world." He pressed his palms against the wall and pushed. He was crying.

244

She lifted her hands to press them to his back, to comfort him, but hesitated, didn't know how he would react to the contact, held her palms close without touching. She saw his muscles strain as he pushed against the wall. Then he backed away, into her hands, and he bent forward and she stroked his back as he leaned on his knees, sobbing.

He turned up his palms and she saw they were red and dimpled from where he'd pushed on the wall. Then he stood and wiped his eyes and without looking at her turned and walked back through the trees and down to the riverbank.

Sharpcot woke to a cool dawn and lay shivering, watching the stars wink out. Shaking not from cold, but fear. She'd slept after her watch, listening to the confluence of the rivers, exhausted by grief. For an instant when she awoke, they were all alive: Loko, Bronski, Lana, her parents, her sister, her friends, all the people of the world. Then consciousness ripped them away, as it had every morning for the past week. Had it been only a week? They emerged from the bunker last Thursday, and today was Thursday. It felt like decades. Or she'd dreamed civilization, and the world had always been thus.

She sat up and saw Wakely on a log a dozen paces away with his rifle across his lap. Watching the two rivers. Listening to the birds as they remarked on the sun's rise. She looked at her watch, saw it was just after seven.

They ate and discussed options. Deeks spoke a single word: "South."

"You're scared of a Winnipeg winter," Sharpcot replied.

"Yeah," Deeks replied. "It scares me when there's housing and central heat and Netflix. We should follow the birds."

"It'll mean crossing the border," Virago said. "Do you think things are different in the United States?"

245

"They were conquered like everyone else," Sharpcot said. "Despite their bloated military. If not, there'd be something on the radio. We'd see aircraft. The stuff in the stacks is as much from America as it is from everywhere else: Japan and Russia and Bangladesh."

"Right," Virago replied, dropping her head. "Dumb question."

"Just optimistic," Deeks corrected her kindly.

"If we intend to go south, we'll need to swim," Tse said.

They gathered their gear and moved a hundred metres up the Assiniboine to a point where it narrowed. The block of keys ended, and they came to the eastern end of the baseball caps.

"Not a great morning for swimming," Leclerc said, shivering.

"I've got an idea to float us across," Tse said. "Just need a hand."

He led Wakely, Deeks, and Virago up the passageway between keys and caps. Wakely drew his sidearm and checked the beehive passage for bears, but it was vacant. They reached the intersection of coasters and beer kegs, liberated a bunch of 50-litre kegs, and selected the lightest ones. They each hefted a pair and began to carry them back.

"This guy's not empty, sloshing like mad," Tse said, and tipped the keg on its side. "Master Jack, have you got that tool you carry? Need a screwdriver and pliers."

Wakely plucked the tool from his belt and passed it to Tse, who jammed the tip of the pliers against the keg's ball, releasing gas and a quantity of yellow beer. He set the keg upright, pried out the retaining ring, then rotated the cap and pulled out the spear.

"I was keg guy at the Storm Crow in Vancouver," he explained.

Wakely said, "It's probably gone off, but those suds smells damn fine."

Tse told Wakely to cup his hands, and Tse lifted the keg and poured them full of beer.

Wakely sniffed, sipped, then drank it all. He shook beer from his hands, ran a sleeve across his mouth. "A little skunky.

246

Warm, of course, and almost flat. But Christ. Right now I'll take what I can get."

Deeks and Virago dropped their kegs and Tse filled their cupped hands. Wakely took the keg from Tse and poured into the corporal's palms. Then they stood rubbing their hands and grinning.

"Beer in the morning," Virago said.

"At the end of the world," Deeks added.

"There still some for the sarge and Cheree?" Tse asked, and Wakely shook the keg and nodded.

"The last beer we'll ever drink," Deeks sighed, and they picked up their kegs and headed back to the river.

After floating across on kegs they lashed together with paracord, they headed southwest, following the forested western bank of the Red. Through the foliage they spied cat figurines in black, white, gold, and red, made from ceramic and plastic. When struck by the morning sunlight, some began waving a paw.

"They're maneki-neko," Wakely explained. "For good luck. Not actually waving, more like beckoning. Come in and buy something. They're Japanese but popular in China."

"Whoa, suddenly you're Leclerc?" Virago asked.

"Yeah, what gives?" Leclerc called.

"Daisy's parents," he explained. "Ran a paper store in Sannomiya, near Osaka. They had a bunch of maneki-neko set outside, in the window."

"In China they sometimes call it jinmao or zhāo cái māo," Tse added.

Tuxedo jackets followed the cats, most black, some in white, burgundy, red, pink, navy, and turquoise, until the river curved eastward and they came out of the brush and re-entered the maze, passing between a massive block of three-wheeled baby strollers on the left across from an equally impressive tower of printer ink cartridges, Canon, HP, Epson, Brother, Samsung,

247

Kodak, Lexmark, G&G, Sophia Global, Silo, many empty, many not. By noon the day was warm and getting warmer, and they passed through a variety of blocks and met a wall of coffee pods, Keurig and Nespresso and Tassimo, plus lesser-known types, showing coffee brands from Starbucks to Illy to Folgers to Bialetti. Most were used, tops punctured, cases filled with dry, used grounds, some still wet, mouldy. But plenty were new, and the section filled their kits, the coffee-addicted among them, Sharpcot and Wakely and Deeks. They debated heating water and making some, but Sharpcot wanted to find a better spot to enjoy her first cup in days, and they pressed on. The coffee pod wall continued across from jugs of vegetable oil: Wesson, Simply, Crisco, Saporito, Great Value, Mazola, Unico, Takta, Saffola Gold, Golden Core, Sotong, NNS, Rosa, King Rooster, Knife, Rivoc, Swad, Rostlinka, Oki, Pride, Envoy, Saber, Mamador; there were Russian brands, Korean, Indonesian, Polynesian, Croatian, Argentinian, Kuwaiti; Halal, Kosher, light, low acid; sunflower, safflower, cottonseed, soybean, corn, canola.

They stepped through an oily mud along the passage from bottles that had leaked, moved with care to keep from slipping.

"Bronski would've fallen," Deeks said, almost wistfully.

"And pulled Loko down with him," Virago added.

No one spoke for a time as they continued southwards.

It was 100 kilometres to the border, and after five days of walking they reasoned they had crossed it, moved from Canada into the United States of America. Nothing indicated the fact, not the sky's hue, the weather, the smells, the birds, rodents, insects, the creeks or rivers or the fish in them, the stout grasses growing in the passageways, or the nature of the maze itself. During their southern transit they'd passed blocks of crib mattresses, boxer briefs, CRT televisions, theatre popcorn machines, empty toothpaste tubes, eight-inch floppy disks, drafting tables, harbour buoys, lipsticks, hand-cranked pencil sharpeners, as well as miscellaneous packaging materials and all manner of unidentifiable parts for the maintenance and manufacture of cars, trucks, aircraft, kitchen cabinets, refrigerators, septic systems, conveyor belt mechanisms, eyeglasses, seed milling machines, rock crushers, picture frames, trampolines, trade show kiosks, purses, web printers, malt mixers, milking machines, shortwave radios, aquarium pumps . . .

"The goddamn border is gone," Wakely growled. He was struggling with nicotine withdrawal, had to admit an apocalypse was a hell of a way to enforce abstinence. "Even the *idea* of the border is gone."

"That's all it ever was," Virago said. "An idea."

"A colonial idea, which severed Indigenous groups," Sharpcot added.

"Hey, you know what no border means?" Deeks said. "Patriotism is done too. The way I see it, you can be proud to climb a mountain or, better still, cure a disease. Being proud of where you come from is for losers who can't accomplish things. Like I'm sure that pile of rocks there is proud to be American."

"Like the way Bronski was proud to be a Polish-Canadian," Leclerc stated factually, which the others answered with a silence she didn't register.

Tse broke the quiet by stating, "You know what else is gone with the border? Border agents. Surly, powertripping, 'you've been randomly selected for additional security screening,' waste-of-DNA border agents."

After a pause at the uncharacteristic venom in Tse's tone, Deeks added, "Also gone: Astroturf."

"It's in a block somewhere," Wakely said. "We could make it a quest — find the Astroturf. Burn that shit."

"And frozen yogurt," Virago said. "I will never have to eat frozen yogurt again."

"Parking tickets," Sharpcot said. "No more of those."

"Being on hold with Air Canada," Tse said.

"Yeah, I'll bet they're no longer experiencing higher-than-usual call volume." Deeks laughed.

"Police brutality," Virago said. "Police. Also politicians. And billionaires."

"Billionaire politicians," Deeks said. "Too many of those."

"We don't know where the people are," Sharpcot reminded them.

"Yeah, but even if they're still alive, they're no longer billionaires," Virago said.

"Wouldn't you just love to come across the Walmart family right now?" Deeks cried. "I'd make them crawl behind us carrying our rucks."

"CEOs. CFOs too, and CTOs, and earnest but clueless human resources people: all gone," Deeks said. "And lawyers! Oh my god."

"Money too," Sharpcot said. "It's here somewhere, but its value is lost. Just stuff now. Matter."

"Which is all it ever was," Leclerc reminded her.

"A concept we all agreed on," Sharpcot noted. "Loans, debts. Anyone owe on their credit cards? Student loans? Behind on mortgage payments? All gone and done."

"Taxes," Deeks noted. "Oh my god we never have to file another tax return. Maybe the apocalypse was worth it!"

"So it's no longer death and taxes. Just death," Tse said. "Half our certainty lost."

They walked south, deeper into what was once America, passing among hitch-mounted cargo racks and switchplate covers of plastic and steel and wood and brass, then batting cage pitching machines and chafing dishes, beyond which they saw some distance to the west the top of an unusual stack, constructed from cylindrical towers, smokestacks maybe, arranged short to tall, forming a kind of bell-curve, out of place among the flat-topped blocks, and they changed their vector to investigate. They walked past upright pianos, all glossy black. Deeks popped the lid on one and played two minutes of boogie-woogie then shut the lid and continued along without comment.

They passed between old steamer trunks facing a wall of backyard hot tubs, scenting the air with chorine and sweat, and at the end of the aisle arrived at the mid-block of those clustered towers, which turned out to be lighthouses. They stood bunched, shoulder-to-shoulder like refugees, far from any lake or sea, a few metres taller than the surrounding blocks, their columns round, square, octagonal, made from stone or brick or concrete or welded steel, painted white, red, grey, yellow, blue, or candy-striped. And they smelled of the sea, a salty, fishy smell, some with their bases stained with grime, soot, green with seaweed, moss, others barnacled where they'd stood in the surf. When the section looked up they saw the lightrooms, all with glass intact, a testament to the assiduousness of the Accruers. But their beacons forever dark.

Deeks stepped towards the closest lighthouse, a red one, with a door of dark copper and a latticed peaked window framed in black arches. She rapped the side with her knuckles and Leclerc pronounced it a dodecagon: 12 sides, formed from plates of cast iron. Deeks read haltingly from a black plaque with brass lettering:

"ONDER DE REGERING VAN
WILLEM III,
KONING DER NEDERLAND,
ENZ. ENZ. ENZ.
TIJDENS HET BESTUUR VAN DEN
MINISTER VAN MARINE,
W.F. VAN ERP TAALMAN KIP;
VOOR DRAAILICHT TWEED GROOTTE
1875."

"Danish?" Wakely asked.

"Dutch," Leclerc replied.

"So this thing is from Holland," Sharpcot said. "Now standing in North Dakota."

They looked up its column, a trio of windows leading to a gallery bristling with masts and antennae. This structure crowded by neighbours where once it had stood alone, gazing out at the North Sea.

Deeks tried the door and found it locked.

"Let's keep moving," Sharpcot said, nodding left along the passage. "Get to the tall end. If we can climb to the top of one we'll get a good vantage. Help us determine which way to go next."

They moved along a passage with lighthouses on their right and steam trunks, then cell phone cases, to the left, counted 70 or so lighthouses until they reached the one at the corner, more than double the height of the Dutch lighthouse, this one a truncated cone constructed from granite blocks.

Sharpcot found the door unlocked and opened it and went inside. She looked up into a cylinder circumscribed by a winding stone staircase. She glanced at a red bust of a man on a granite pedestal, didn't bother to read the plaque on the wall. She mounted the first step and began to climb. The tile walls echoed with the sound of boots on stone, light increasing as they rose. She passed a big window deeply recessed in the thick walls and surrounded by granite and pale blue tile. Neighbouring lighthouses obstructed the view, and as they rounded upwards gripping the iron railing they passed another window with a prospect of the cell phone cases. Up they went, looking through windows as they passed, momentarily seeing an improving vista of surrounding stacks, but they didn't pause long, anticipating the prize at the top. Nearing the summit, the steps changed to iron, and they rose through a curving staircase into the lightroom, a cluster of fresnel lenses in the centre and views in every direction through the tall windows. The sun falling into the west, a red globe, and above it a streak of cloud like a neon strip, which Sharpcot mistook for a jet contrail, her heart fluttering. But it was only cloud.

The lantern room was hot, a greenhouse cooked all day by sunlight. Sharpcot saw through the windows a descending spiral staircase to an outdoor gallery. She found a handle and turned it and a hinged section in the glass swung outward and she stepped into the evening air, descended the stairs to a narrow gallery. She propped her rifle against the wall and rested her arms on the granite railing and looked out at a sea of blocks.

The land was a patchwork quilt, each block precisely the same height, but each of different area, some tiny, others vast, and each unique in pattern and texture. To her left, the cell phone cases, black, grey, silver, blue, hot pink, all of them stacked neatly and resting face-up, some with screen protectors reflecting the pink sky, a broken glitter scattered across acres. The lighthouses spread over an area perhaps two kilometres square, with the tallest clustered at the northeast end, neighbours partially blocking the view south. A lighthouse of a design similar to this one stood nearby, its domed roof topped by a sphere, and she considered while she regarded it that lighthouses rarely received close study because by nature they always stood alone. Shorter lighthouses fell away to the right in a kind of gradient, like a live, three-dimensional infographic documenting lighthouse heights of planet Earth, sloping from the tallest on the left to the smallest, two klicks away, on the right.

She moved around the gallery, lifting her field glasses to study the distance, but as the sun fell, visibility diminished, made the passageways between the blocks into black canals. Something fabric over there, something beyond it shimmering like glass, over there a dark, flat material in large fragments the size of coffee tables. Maybe coffee tables. She completed her orbit at the staircase and found the rest of the section standing at the rail, regarding the landscape, Virago and Wakely close together, indicating features, trying to guess what each block contained, maybe that's roller blades — no, not roller blades, roller skates! — bread clips, the type they use for loaves and milk bags, and I'll bet that's soothers, that you stick in a baby's mouth to shut up the crying."

Sharpcot looked towards the sun sliding beyond the Earth's rim and spotted something to the right, above the horizon, an abrupt reflection of sunlight in a vertical strip, a tapered spire, and clustered around its base other objects, shining with evening light. Glass and stone.

She held her breath, watching the sun's descent wipe the scene away from the bottom up. In a moment it was gone. "What the hell was that?" a voice exclaimed beside her. Deeks.

"You saw it too?" Sharpcot asked. "It was like . . . like . . ."

". . . a city in the sky," Deeks concluded.

"Yes."

In an afterthought she raised her binoculars and scanned the area but saw nothing.

"Smoke!" someone called from the south quarter. She hurried to where Tse stood, pointing. Sharpcot glassed the distance.

"I don't see anything."

"I'm pretty sure it was there. Gone with the light," Tse replied as he squinted into the fading landscape.

"Could just be something on fire," Wakely said from behind Sharpcot. "Who knows what kind of volatile stuff is out there. Lithium-ion batteries. Astroturf."

Sharpcot nodded.

After a moment he asked, "What next, Sarge?"

She began to speak, but hesitated, turned away, a look of despair clouding her features.

"Elsie," he said softly.

"It's just . . . for an instant I thought they were up here with us," she said quietly. "Loko and Bronski. Standing at the railing on the far side making inane comments."

"Yeah," Wakely replied. "I get that while we're walking. Like they stepped down a passage and will be right back."

She shut her eyes for a few seconds, then opened them. "Let's stay the night here. We can bed down in the lightroom. It's not a lot of space, but it's sheltered. We can look around in the morning and choose a direction."

They stood side-by-side along the gallery railing and watched the dawn. Sharpcot had roused them from their beds on the lightroom floor and assembled them here.

"I ... I need to explain some things," she stated. It was a cool morning, but the day, like those before it, would be warm. The sun had just stepped off the horizon and hung suspended in an orange gauze. A fishy ocean smell mingled with the prairie wind.

"I've failed you," she stated. There were immediate protests which she silenced. "It's my fault you're here."

"No one believes that," Virago stated firmly.

Sharpcot pushed on: "You need the full story. *They* knew something big was about to happen."

"Who?" Deeks asked.

"The top brass. Lieutenant-Colonel Wenz. Maybe Lieutenant Blake. I mean not specific details. Certainly no one predicted this." She swept the maze with her hand. "But an order came to mobilize for a potential threat.

"If our theory about the Accruers as aliens is correct, I figure somebody looked through a telescope and spotted an object or objects. Inbound. Moving fast, because there was virtually zero time to prepare. The world leaders, some of them anyway, probably knew. The prime minister, maybe Cabinet. The president. NATO and NORAD. Possibly the United Nations, though maybe not."

"So why are we here? Today," Tse asked. "Why us? Why Three Section?"

"Blind luck," Sharpcot replied. "But ... there's another reason." She looked uncomfortable, stared out into the morning. "We're here because they hated us."

"What does that mean? Who hated us?" Virago demanded.

"The brass. The army. Wenz. He stuck us in that bunker. It was decided. For each base, for every base around the world, to hide a reserve of troops in a secure location. They knew something big was going down. So they prepared to greet these . . . visitors. Meanwhile, the world's military was put on high alert, ground, sea, air, ready to defend the planet from an invasion, if that's what it turned out to be. NATO decided to hold troops in reserve. To hide our hand, our full strength. Wenz told me as much."

"Why would he tell you?" Wakely asked, added, "Sergeant."

"Because he loathed me. And all of you, too, I'm sorry to report. Look, I'm the first to admit we were not Shilo's best and brightest. But Wenz considered us an embarrassment. To be stashed away, hidden. He tolerated us only because he was ordered to. The directive to promote me to section commander came from the minister of defence. Possibly the prime minister. To fulfill an election promise. Diversity in the Forces. To show how they were reforming the military, making it more inclusive. Putting women, people of colour, in command positions. Tokens."

"How do you know this?" Virago asked.

"Wenz took me aside after my promotion, felt 'compelled' to inform me that everything I thought I'd earned had been handed to me because of my sex and race. 'Bonus you're a woman *and* an Indian. Saves me from promoting one of each.'"

"That son of a bitch," Wakely grunted.

"That's not the worst of it," Sharpcot said, her voice rising. "How do you think I ended up with you lot? Half of us are women! Among sections dominated by white dudes."

"We had Bronski and Loko," Tse reminded her.

"They were trouble. Disgraced themselves in basic. Well, Bronski did. Had a list of infractions a mile long. And Loko wasn't motivated to distinguish himself until, well, until the end of the world. So it was those two, three female privates, an

Asian corporal, and their Cree female sergeant." She looked at Wakely. "I don't know how you got into this mess."

"I do," Wakely replied. "About 10 months ago I wrote a letter. See, Daisy predicted I'd be getting a promotion. When I asked why, she said that I'm a good soldier. But then added: and a white man. We argued. Had a pretty bad fight, actually. White privilege. Patriarchy. All bullshit. But it got me thinking. It got me *looking*. I started noting the gender and race of everyone in a command position. And it was 90 percent white men.

"So I wrote a letter to Wenz, about equality, about giving others a chance, the value of alternative perspectives. And instead of a promotion, I got transferred to Three Section. He thought it would be a punishment to be under your command. But it's been an honour, ma'am. I mean that sincerely."

Wakely dropped his eyes and she gripped his shoulder and stated, "The honour is mine, Master Corporal Wakely." She drew a breath to govern strong emotion and continued.

"So they stuck us underground, while the world greeted the visitors. Tanks and warships on station. Jets in the sky and nukes fuelled in their silos. But whatever happened, the world lost."

"Will there be other units out there who were put in bunkers?" Leclerc wondered.

"Yes, how were we overlooked?" Tse asked.

"Blind luck," Deeks muttered.

"Not necessarily," Wakely said. "Or not totally. We were under a block of stuff, remember? The brake lathes."

"Right," Sharpcot said. "What if the Accruers set up that block before they started looking for underground bunkers?"

"I guess we equate power with infallibility," Leclerc mused. "But they aren't mutual."

"What do you mean?" Deeks wondered.

"Being strong doesn't make you smart," Virago said.

"The Accruers are obviously smart," Deeks remarked.

"They are clearly *advanced*," Leclerc admitted. "But I've been considering the variance in block structure. Some are arranged

257

logically, according to the rules of packing problems, employing a mathematical optimization of space. But not all. Some are assembled with less, uh, *discipline.*"

"Right?" Deeks said. "Like if we all had a task to do we'd do it with our own style."

"What are we saying?" Tse asked. "That the Accruers have personalities? Which might make them fallible?"

Leclerc nodded. "I've catalogued seven different arrangement patterns. I call them: 'packing optimized,' 'intended upright,' 'chroma-grouped,' 'affect-aesthetic' . . ."

"We look forward to your whitepaper on the subject," Deeks interrupted. "But the sarge was talking."

They all looked to Sharpcot, who pressed an arm across her stomach. "I've failed you. In so many ways. Not finding a place where we can rest. Bronski and Loko."

"Bronski did that," Wakely stated.

"If I had been more careful with him. Seen the signs. He intended to shoot *me.* Loko was collateral to Bronski's strife with *me.*"

"Strife caused by you flawlessly performing your duty as section commander," Wakely insisted.

"There are ways to handle things," she stated. "Which I didn't use. I was preoccupied with finding . . . Lana. And he triggered me in a way I can't explain." She thought abruptly about Dwight, Lana's father, and like the lights coming on in a darkened room, she saw how features of his behaviour matched Bronski's. Resistance, defiance, contempt. Her expression might've changed at the recognition, and she fought to suppress it, continued speaking, "So I think it's time I stepped down. Stopped ordering you about. Let's just be a bunch of survivors trying to make it. Peers. I won't tell you what to do anymore. How about this: you tell me what to do."

"I won't accept it," Wakely said. "You've got us this far."

"Yeah, we order you to stay in charge," Deeks called.

"Where next, Sarge?" Tse asked. "Where next?"

"I don't know," Sharpcot answered. "It doesn't matter."

"It matters," Leclerc said.

"Come on, Sarge," Deeks said. "Tell us."

But Sharpcot turned away.

They continued south because no one could fault the logic of migrating birds. The disciplined arrangement of fireteam pairs travelling in file dissolved into a more amorphous and variable cluster, and while it bothered Sharpcot, she didn't assert herself. There was talk of shedding armour, helmets, even rifles and ammo, to improve their capacity to carry food they encountered, jars of baby artichoke hearts in oil, cans of sweety drop Peruvian peppers, bags of dried matsutake mushrooms, and she was relieved that Wakely refused to yield, explaining that animals continued to pose a threat, and 20 days outside the bunker was not enough time to safely conclude they wouldn't encounter other people, possibly in desperate straits and ready to fight. Wakely made one concession: grenades. These were heavy and of questionable utility in the maze's confines, and they buried them all, except for a couple of C8 smokes, potentially useful for concealment or signalling.

So they moved along in an organic group of people in CADPAT with rucks and rifles, walking between driveway salt bags and window cleaning spray bottles (full and not), the day warming and the September sun bright.

The wild variety of products began to lose its novelty, and they passed without comment through vistas of prodigious things — cookie cutters, flame throwers, kaleidoscopes, loofas — accepting them with numb disregard. They passed yet another block of fabric, assumed it was more of some article of clothing — clothing stacks tended to be among the largest, a mile of crewneck sweaters, two klicks of sweatpants — when Leclerc paused to pull one and unfurled a red hammer and sickle flag of the Soviet Union. The section began an exploration of the

259

block's composition, drawing flags of every kind: national, provincial and state, municipal, auto brands, terrorist groups, racing checkerboards, sports teams, road work warnings, beach conditions, retail savings events, sandwich shops, jolly rogers, mining companies, diving markers, computer brands, heraldic banners, and many Union Jacks, French Tricolours, Brazil's gold and green, German Bundesflagges, Japanese Hinomarus, Canadian Maple Leaf flags, and, exceeding all others in quantity by a large margin, American flags.

"Of course," Virago said cynically. "Americans are obsessed. It's got a hundred names: The Red, White, and Blue. Old Glory. Stars and Stripes. The Star-Spangled Banner. They pledge alliance to it — to *fabric*. There is a code in law with a bunch of strict rules about handling it. There are boxes in public libraries to collect flags for 'proper' disposal. It's the focus of their national anthem. It's not even allowed to *touch* anything."

"It's a sign of respect and pride," Sharpcot said.

"Or profound insecurity," Virago laughed.

Sharpcot bit her tongue, reminding herself she'd rescinded her command.

"Oh, I love this!" Virago said, pulling out a tangle of intermingled flags that included the Stars and Stripes, an Iranian flag, a tattered Nazi swastika, a gay pride rainbow flag, and a Dunkin' Donuts "America Runs on Dunkin" banner.

"That's enough, Private," Sharpcot snapped.

Virago lowered her head and let the flags fall.

"Sorry," Sharpcot said. "Habit. Carry on."

They left the corridor littered with flags and continued past stacks of stove elements, electric motor brushes, and then a colossal block of hydroelectric dam turbines, giant cylinders stacked two or three high. Water housings encased many of them, but others had been lifted free, and the travellers could see and touch the alloy turbine blades against which massive volumes of water had once pushed, powering civilization. They went on for kilometres, the adjacent passage boggy from water that had escaped the housings, and they trudged through mud while on the left other products were arrayed: train semaphore signals, fondue pots, citizens band radios, jukeboxes, tatami, and diamond engagement rings, the latter a diminutive block 40 or so metres on each dimension. It stopped the section dead, a wall of shining gold, dazzling where sunlight shot through diamonds, millions of diamonds, refracting, splitting into lancing rainbows of such intensity they had to shade their eyes from the glare and hurry to the next intersection. Leclerc gripped her head and complained of an instant migraine, and directed Tse to her ruck to find headache pills, and they stood looking back into the radiance of the corridor they'd just left. Virago stepped close to study the corner where the rings were piled to the sky, and Wakely saw in her expression a look of disgust.

"Want one?" Wakely asked, and plucked a ring from the wall. He buffed it against his shirt and held it out.

"You'll have to do better if you're proposing," she replied with a scowl. "A cynic like me who knows about a bullshit 'tradition' created by the diamond industry? Two-month salary guideline advertised like it's a law of physics. A greedy fabrication to fleece dumb dudes and their entitled fiancées. Not to mention many of those will be blood diamonds. 'Oh honey, I celebrate our love by wearing a rock impoverished kids died to mine!'"

"Huh. And I thought you'd feel strongly about it," he replied with a smirk. He kissed the ring, tossed it into the dirt, and for good measure ground it under his boot heel like a cigarette butt.

They crossed a stream that cut through the turbines on the right and cheerleading pom-poms on the left. Next past carrom boards, yerba mate gourds of metal, glass, ceramic, and glass, and then a mostly black stack of remote controls for TVs, VCRs, disc players, satellite, and cable boxes. The turbines ended and the next block was neckties, a mass that would've been impressively large if it hadn't come after the turbines. They passed along it for 60 metres before they came to church bells, the bronze and verdigris wall irregular where the lips of larger bells curved out.

"See that?" Leclerc noted as she paused to look. "A good example of the 'packing optimized' style. The space left by the waists of the big bells is filled with smaller ones."

Among the iconic bells of European design with wide openings and deep waists were many of Asian construction, which Leclerc called bonshos and zhongs, ornamented with bosses, knobs, inscriptions, and raised bands, with wider shoulders that curved, without flaring to their mouths.

They gazed as they walked, looking for the celebrity bells the block must contain: the Liberty Bell, the bells of St. Paul's or Big Ben or the Tsar Bell, the biggest in the world, which Leclerc told them had never rung, and sat on a pedestal near the Kremlin. The bells from carillons in Amsterdam and Oslo and Gainesville, Florida.

They looked in wonder how every gap had been cunningly packed with hand bells and prayer bells and schoolyard bells and ship's bells and fire bells and dinner bells and cowbells and Christmas ornament bells and dime-sized novelty bells. Most were tarnished, but sometimes a new specimen, shiny and bronze, glowed among the weathered green. While there was temptation to touch them, to strike them, to make them sound again, as much as they could in their packed state, the soldiers by tacit agreement passed in solemn quiet, leaving only the prairie wind and the creak of crickets.

12

Over the following days and weeks, Sharpcot catalogued a change in her own mood, one that reflected the section's temper, from curiosity and hope that they would reach an end to all this and find clues about humanity's fate, to despair, resignation, and weariness, with a focus on everyday survival, of discovering the next block of tinned meat or jarred fruit or dry beans, along with concern for other dwindling supplies: toothpaste, soap, toilet paper, shaving cream, razors, menstrual products. The only item they had in excess was deodorant.

Thoughts of Lana generated such dark, paralyzing feelings that Sharpcot avoided them, which she recognized as a harmful policy, but one she adopted for reasons of practicality. She couldn't function when those feelings intruded, and she reserved them for sentry time, while the others slept and night cloaked the world.

They bivouacked when they could in wooded glens boxed in by the walls of junk, once in a coulee beside a creek, another time on a bench of land below an outcrop to shelter from rain.

While their curiosity slackened, the blocks among which they travelled became no less diverse, from mundane structures of anonymous parts — an L-shaped bracket used in some common construction, a colossal battlement of rusting rebar — to diverse curiosities: antique malt mixers in chrome and turquoise, followed immediately by a staggering collection of reclining Buddhas, millions of small ones from the size of a finger, to a handspan, to the length of a person and larger, all of these clustered and packed around those of increasing scale, five metres, 10, 20, and ultimately grouped around 40 or so of titanic dimension, the largest, which Leclerc called Win Sein Taw Ya, 180 metres long and 30 metres high, made from cement, wearing a robe painted red and gold, with rubber eyelashes each a metre long and as thick as a finger. Openings in the structure allowed entry, and the section briefly explored the tile-floored rooms and hallways within.

The Buddhas lay all in parallel, on pedestals, in the same posture, reclined on their right side, some with head resting on a pillow or a flattened hand, still others with a bent elbow and head propped. They had sculpted faces, all with a serene expression, many with eyes shut. They were of weathered stone, granite, marble, cast bronze, iron, wood, and were painted and not, plated in gold, some ornamented with gemstones. They'd been transported from China, Thailand, Myanmar, Japan, Malaysia, Indonesia, Vietnam, Sri Lanka, Laos.

"Does that make you feel calm?" Virago asked Deeks as they passed the glossy white face of a Buddha, one made feminine by blue shading around its eyes and lips painted red.

"Freaking me out, actually," Deeks replied, then shouted at the statue. "Apparently you haven't heard the news!"

An hour later they passed one of the super stacks, 120 metres high, made of offshore oil platforms, all of similar design, ballasted pontoons resting on the prairie, with legs rising to decks crowded with superstructures featuring cranes and towers and radio masts and helicopter pads. They stepped warily past pontoons painted grey, black, yellow, orange, red, rusting, barnacled, stinking of fish and bilgewater and crude. The platforms cast cold shadows on ground salty and polluted, and the travellers could've wandered among the legs if they chose, but after discussing the possibility of climbing one — remembrance of Loko further dampening the mood — as it was understood that these were self-sustaining, that they had generators and heating systems and sheltered accommodations, it was reasoned that the Accruers would have, as they always did, removed any useful collateral, fuel and food and bedding and equipment, and sent them to their respective blocks.

"What's happened to fuel," Tse wondered, "and other liquids? What did the Accruers do with all the world's motor oil, transmission fluid. The gasoline?"

"Maybe there's a pond somewhere. Or a lake. Or an ocean," Virago suggested.

"Yeah, ponds of synthetic liquids. Like grape Fanta," Deeks said.

"Not just that, what about manufactured gases? Where'd they put stuff like, I don't know, anesthetic?" Wakely queried.

"Desflurane," Leclerc said.

"What's that, Wiki?" Deeks asked.

"A fluorinated methyl ethyl ether."

"Uh. You're putting me to sleep," Deeks joked, and Leclerc narrowed her eyes, then laughed.

The nights grew colder, and they had to wear layers and bundle up, and while it was on each person's mind that they could warm each other by sleeping closer, an insularity gripped the section, and they grew remote, and in the days staggered along in something resembling a death-march.

One night while huddled each under their own blanket in front of a sporadic campfire, a cold drizzle came and went from a sky that was opaque but for the ghost of a quarter moon, and Sharpcot leaned in to Wakely to confide that she was reconsidering their route south.

"South we end up in Kansas. We need to go either southeast, to the Gulf, or southwest, to reach northern California."

"What's your preference? Hurricanes or earthquakes?" Wakely asked.

"I know it's not rational, and politics are dead, but I don't relish living in the U.S. south. I'm more of a California dreamer."

"Life on the Pacific. Nice. We can fish. And the land is rich, and we can grow food year-round."

"Damn, Dorian," Sharpcot laughed. "You going to be a farmer?"

"If we're going to survive, yes. I have to admit it has appeal. We had a little garden in Shilo, Daisy and me. Well, she did. Tomatoes and cucumbers. And I gotta say, any time I ate that stuff it felt like a scam. Like we were cheating the system. Food straight from the ground. You grow it yourself, you eat it. And you use seeds from the food to grow *more* food. No wonder Monsanto tried to shut that down. It's the perfect anti-capitalism machine."

"You sound almost excited about it, Farmer Dory."

"Going west is the best idea all day, Sergeant. See? You should be in charge."

When dawn broke grey but rainless they looked down a passageway that ran between blocks of motorized foot spas on the left and on the right, phone booths, iconic red, blue, or white British boxes as well as glass and aluminum North American types, along with arrays of diverse international booths, turquoise from Korea, green and yellow from Budapest, some framed in wood, others with slick, modern designs, some unusual, like an antique one with a flared, latticed base in painted green steel, "Rikstelefon" on the white sign above a pair of doors, and topped with an ornate red dome. This was the route they thought they'd take today, but instead turned 90 degrees and set out on a new vector, westward, phone booths on the left, and on the right empty racks for gum and candy, the kind found near store checkouts, display plates fixed below or above where the product once rested showing familiar names and brands: Chiclets, Clorets, Certs, Dentyne, Trident, Rolaids, Wrigley's, Beeman's, Mentos, Mars, Snickers, Extra, Excel, Orbit, Ice, along with ones in Chinese, Thai, Japanese, Korean, Cyrillic, Arabic. In steel, acrylic, wood, nine storeys, half a kilometre of them, and they were weary of all this, of phone booths containing phones that connect to nothing and gum and candy racks devoid of gum and candy.

That night they camped in heavy rain at an intersection of tuning forks and phone pagers and ottomans and merry-go-rounds. They were drawn to a classic antique carousel that made up the block's corner. It was populated with horses, plus a lion, a tiger, a pig, a giant rabbit, a huge cat, a miniature giraffe. They hesitated in the rain, recognizing that the carousels provided shelter, but wary of their fragility, rickety old rides made from painted and re-painted wood, incapable of supporting the tremendous mass of the carousels above. Only that mysterious repulsive energy prevented them from collapsing under their own weight.

"I'm not sure I'm ready to trust that weird force," Deeks said.

"But we already trust it, every day," Leclerc explained. "These stacks would collapse on us without it."

That logic and the rain drove them under. They built a fire in the dirt between carousels, and spread their bedrolls on the wooden decking among creatures of wood and plaster.

Around midnight Wakely took watch from Deeks, and though weary she lingered, sitting with him on the seat of an elaborate carriage meant for riders who didn't want to ride the pistoning animals. The carousel's corner position provided a view down each of the four passageways, or at least it had during daylight. In the dark there was nothing to see, and they sat quietly listening to the rain, and he thought she'd fallen asleep, but she abruptly shivered and moved against him. At first he stiffened, sat rigid while her forehead pressed his shoulder, and she turned her head so her cheek moved against him, then her arm came up and crossed his chest and she gripped him fiercely. He reluctantly brought up his right arm and ran it across her back and held her. He felt hot tears soak through his shirt.

Then her face was against his stubbled chin and he turned down and her mouth met his with small kisses. She kissed and kissed him with growing urgency but he did not open his mouth to her. His mind and heart full of Daisy, the last woman he had kissed, really kissed, and he did not want to give that up. Not yet.

Eventually she stopped and lowered her face and held him and he had the smell of her hair in his nose, and it was not a good smell, and he feared she thought he rejected her because all of them needed a bath, but that wasn't the reason. The reason was Daisy and the end of the world.

After a time she slipped away and he sat there abruptly cold as rain lashed down.

The sun shone weakly through a gauze of cloud, and the day failed to warm beyond the mid-teens Celsius. Flocks of birds flew over, heading south, a reminder of impending winter. It was good travelling weather, and they humped along steadily, mostly silent, occasionally remarking on what they passed, stopping to examine a curiosity: a block of tongue depressors, a block of black twist ties, a block of cymbals. Everywhere they went, products were succumbing to nature, accumulating growths of mosses and lichens, grasses rising around block bases, tendrils of vines climbing their sides. Food spoiling in bags, plastic wrap, growing mouldy. Tarnish and rust setting in.

Wakely tried to catch Deeks's eye when they first emerged from the carousels, while they'd breakfasted on tinned lamb and pickled Brussels sprouts and collected their kits and rifles, but she avoided his gaze. Virago gave him a glance that suggested the previous night's incident had been discussed and analyzed. He looked away, and when he met her eye again she looked doleful, and he wondered if it was because she had only sprouts to eat, or something more.

They moved out in a file with Sharpcot at the head and Wakely trailing.

Later in the morning as they crossed an intersection bounded by push mowers, Chinese food takeout cartons, ski hill snow cannons, and rosary beads — wood, stone, crystal, strung together — Tse paused. He took off his helmet and pulled down one of the rosaries, unfurled it, and running his fingers along it performed the Apostles Creed, Our Father, some Hail Marys, and finally muttered, "Glory be to the Father, to the Son, and to the Holy Spirit, as it was, is now, and ever shall be, world without end. Amen." He looped it and pushed it back into the wall. Then he reached into his sleeve cuff and unwrapped his own rosary from his wrist and coiled it in his palm and kissed the cross, before he cleared a gap in the wall with his fingertips and inserted it there.

Sharpcot watched quietly. She wasn't a fan of the Roman Catholic Church, for various reasons, not the least of which was her mother's devastating tenure in a residential school, but witnessing Tse's abandonment of his faith chilled her.

"World without end," Wakely muttered to her.

Tse straightened, turned, and said, "Whoa. What are those?" as he stared down the southbound passage.

The rest looked to a tangle of grey and silver structures, angular, sharp-edged, a half mile away. Wakely got out his binoculars, looked, passed them to Sharpcot, who glanced before handing them to Tse.

"Wow, okay," Tse said. "Can we look?"

"I don't think it'll provide anything useful, but okay," Sharpcot replied.

They passed between the Chinese takeout containers — red, pink, black, plain brown, many white with red pagodas, words "Enjoy," "Thank You," nested in columns nine storeys tall, the air scented with spoiled food and soy sauce and sesame oil, and push mowers on the right, most oriented to parallel the alley, left wheel out, so the wall produced an aspect of discs in white and black and red and orange and yellow and green that stretched on for 700 metres before the group reached the end and a tremendous block made of all the fighter jets in the world.

Tse blew out a breath and moved back and forth along the passageway, taking it in.

They lay densely packed, with their noses, tail fins, wings, or afterburners constituting the block's limit. They were oriented every which way, wheels on the ground or the craft below, some inverted, or sideways with belly or canopy out, tail-down, nose-down. They presented a range of muted colours: solid green, grey, desert or jungle camo, blue, black, silver, with red stars or old or new USAF badges or Royal Air Force roundels or Australian kangaroos or Swedish triple-crowns or Iranian red, white, and green roundels. Fuselages decorated with wing and fighter group insignia: dragons, snakes, horses, cats, clovers, grim reapers, as well as stencilled pilot names: Capt Zoë Cornbroom, Lt Col Ralph "Koalabear" Arnovsky, a few with two or three names. The scent of kerosene saturated the air, and jet fuel lay puddled around the landing gear, leading Wakely to speculate that the tanks hadn't been drained.

"If we could dislodge one we could fly it to the coast," Tse joked. "Get there in a couple of hours."

"Right. Who would fly it?" Deeks demanded.

"Che Yat," Leclerc said.

"Who's that?" Virago asked.

"Me," Tse replied.

"I thought your name was Owen."

"His real name is Che Yat," Leclerc declared.

Sharpcot raised her eyebrows and traded glances with Deeks.

Tse moved along the passage, gazing with a wonder they hadn't seen him express before.

"F-16 Viper right there, pretty iconic. But right beside it is a rare old bird: an F3D Skyknight. We got an F-15 Eagle there, and a Saab Gripen, and—" and attention halted his words and he jogged down the alley where he stopped and stood with a hand over his mouth as he stared. The others moved between jets and push mowers (the north wall showing the fronts of the mowers — Ozito, Craftsman, Scotts, Remington, Eckman,

American, Great States) until they reached Tse and the jet he was looking at.

"What is it," Deeks asked. "What's special?"

"It's old," Wakely said. "But in good shape."

"It's a Heinkel He 162 Volksjäger," Tse said plainly, as if everyone recognized its significance.

"What's that?" Leclerc said.

"Bless me. Something Wiki doesn't know," Deeks remarked.

"One of the first jet fighters," Tse said. "A Luftwaffe jet. Nicknamed the Salamander."

Nestled among the larger, more angular aircraft stood a small green jet resting on its tail so they were viewing its top profile. It had stubby wings, each painted with an iron cross, and a single cylindrical jet engine attached to the fuselage abaft the cockpit bubble, cowling painted red. A swastika adorned the faces of the two vertical stabilizers.

"They've got one in the Aviation and Space Museum in Ottawa," Tse said. "But this one isn't it."

"How old?" Deeks asked.

"From the end of the war. These were last made in 1945." He began to move along the aisle, naming other aircraft as he went, "F-14 Tomcat, Sukhoi Su-27. That's a Mikoyan-Gurevich MiG-21. Mirage, Voodoo, Starfighter, F-86 Sabre, Phantom II, Harrier, Dassault Rafale . . ." He stopped again and nodded to a sleek jet two levels up. "And right there's your Lockheed Martin F-35 Lightning II." He studied it for a moment before he concluded, "The STOVL B-variant. Pretty much the most sophisticated fighter ever built. And a piece of junk."

"A 100-million-dollar-plus piece of junk," Virago added, then when Tse looked at her and was about to protest, she added, "Canadian dollars."

"That's about right," Tse conceded.

"All right," Sharpcot said, "Enough of the boys' show. Let's get moving." On the north side of the passage the lawnmowers ended, to be followed by a relatively small block that turned out to be polygraph machines, and then hooded salon hair dryers. The fighter craft went on for another 600 metres, and the subsequent block was citalopram — probably a half billion prescription bottles, clear, yellow, orange, blue, with prescription labels, and branded variously Denyl, Seropram, Zetalo, Humorup, Akarin, Oropram, Recital, Cilate, Ciprapine, Citox, Zylotex, Celexa.

"How anti-depressing," Deeks said.

"Just what we need," Virago said. "After all those patriarchal jets."

They moved along the wall, 70 metres long, looking at the prescription labels, dates, dosages, instructions, repeats. The trick was not to read the names, those of patients and their psychiatrists, the people these bottles represented. As they neared the end of the wall Deeks slowed and stopped and gazed up in deep thought. Then she swung her kit around and extracted a prescription bottle, held it up to the stack.

"Oh," Virago murmured. "Are you also losing your religion?"

"Are you kidding?" She rattled the few pills remaining in the battle. "I'm low and this is the best thing I've seen all day." She scanned through bottles looking to match her dose, consolidated pills into three bottles. "Now if we can locate the tampon tower, I'm all set. That and toothpaste and hand cream. And books. Where are the goddamn books? I'd hollow out a cave and spend the rest of my days there."

They trod on, through the day, through the maze. Late in the afternoon they encountered chain dog collars, pronged, choke, multi-row, Cuban linked, in silver and yellow and rose gold and pewter and black steel.

"Where are the dogs?" Virago asked as she pulled one of the chains and coiled it through her fingers.

Across from the collars, a stack of pouches that contained freeze-dried, no-refrigeration chicken chunks. Virago groaned, but like everyone else packed her ruck with all she could carry.

Three days later they encountered a river, much wider than the Assiniboine or Red, maybe two kilometres across, and they stood on the bank in the mid-afternoon sun watching light rippling on the water.

"Let's go downriver some, see if we can find something we can use to cross," Sharpcot said.

The local blocks (fax machines; phony "hoverboard" self-balancing scooters — some yet held a charge, but proved ineffective on the rough ground; reusable mustard squeeze bottles, Betamax videocassettes) ran only to the top of a shallow decline that ended at the water, leaving the bank clear for travel. They went about three kilometres past various useless items before they encountered a block of what looked from a distance like enormous timbers, but which turned out to be amusement park flume ride boats, simulated logs made from moulded fibreglass, with bumper wheels on sides and base, each numbered, with park names like Blackpool Pleasure Beach and Canobie Lake and Centreville and Knott's Berry Farm embossed or painted on prows or sterns.

As hard as they tried, they couldn't dislodge any of the boats from the base of the stack, and after some discussion Tse, Deeks, Virago, and Wakely climbed to the top, an easy ascent with ample handholds. They needed three boats, as each could accommodate two passengers and gear. The boats were built heavy for stability, and that combined with their bulky shapes and wheeled undercarriages, which tended to catch on the boats below, made for hard work, further complicated by the need to labour while standing in the seats of neighbouring logs, shoving and straining against those perched on the block's edge. When finally they freed one it fell the nine stories to earth and shattered.

"Oh yeah," Deeks said. "On this ride I hear that first drop is a doozy." She leaned over the edge and shouted, "Hey, Sarge, now what?"

273

Leclerc, who had been exploring the surrounding blocks while the others worked, reported to Sharpcot that the next one south was made of orthopaedic body pillows.

"Decorated with bishoujo and bishonen," she explained.

Sharpcot sighed, was about to ask what that meant, then said, "Show me."

They took a short jaunt past the log boats and she saw that each long pillow was adorned with colourful anime/manga characters, pretty, big-eyed girls and boys.

She called up to Wakely, and the team manoeuvred along the tops of the boats to the block's pillow side, where Sharpcot and Leclerc set to work building a wide, deep mattress below the boats. When it was done, the group up top strained and pushed on a boat until it fell free and landed on the pad with a whump and a scattering of polyester filling and urethane foam and settled more or less intact. While the group moved to the next boat, Sharpcot and Leclerc rushed to build another cushion below it. That boat and a third one were each successfully dislodged and dropped.

Winded and sweating from the effort, Wakely and the others rested, lounging in the boats, studying the view, the river running north and south and shimmering in the sunshine, riverbanks sloped and erratic against the regimented blocks mounted above the banks.

"What river is this?" Virago wondered. "The Mississippi?"

"It's not the Mississippi. That starts further east, in Minnesota," Wakely said. "Maybe the Missouri?"

"Oh, it's definitely the misery," Deeks stated.

"Well it meets up with the Mississippi," Virago said. "We're in the Mississippi drainage basin."

"Okay geography keener," Deeks quipped. "So where the hell are we?"

"South Dakota."

"We could ride this river to, what, Louisiana? The Gulf of Mexico?" Deeks exclaimed. "Beaches, crawfish and gumbo, and all without walking another goddamn step?"

"It would take three or four months," Virago said. "With the speed of the river, following every bend and turn. Not including stops for food and sleep. And these log boats aren't built for comfort."

"Not for three months, anyway. Bad enough on a three-minute ride," Wakely pointed out as he arched his back against the unpadded seat. "And who knows how they handle. They're built to run in a shallow, narrow channel, with a flat bottom." He was feeling vaguely guilty he and Sharpcot had unilaterally decided on California. Why couldn't they ride this flume to the Gulf?

"You soldiers ever planning on coming down?" Sharpcot shouted from below.

Once on the ground, Wakely picked up one of the body pillows and said, "Right, dakimakura. Daisy used one of these when I went on deployments." He didn't add that hers featured the front and back of a *Rising of the Shield Hero* character on it, a scantily clad blond waif that aroused complex feelings when he saw her lying with a leg thrown over it.

They inspected the boats, and Wakely volunteered to take one for a quick float to ensure its river worthiness, but it occurred to him that he had no way to control it. Somewhere in this kingdom of paraphernalia were blocks of oars, paddles, sculls, and blades, and any would aid in navigation, but with none in reach, they had to improvise. Clusters of short, bushy trees populated the bank, and from one of them Wakely cut a branch. He trimmed away twigs to form a handle and made a few paddling motions with it.

"You look like a moron. With a branch," Deeks said, and everyone looked at her.

"Private Deeks," Sharpcot barked in her old sergeant's voice, which she hadn't used since Bronski.

"Sorry. I'm sorry," she said, blushing.

"Right," Wakely said quickly, to defuse the awkwardness. "Let's haul one of these down to the bank."

They chose the smallest of the three, a rustic boat with deep brown "bark" and the words "Thorpe Park" on its prow. They tried to push it, but the rubber wheels were too small to ride the rough earth, and it was too heavy to lift.

"It's a goddamn log," Deeks exclaimed. "Let's roll it like a log."

So they rolled it and got it to the water. Launching it also proved challenging, and they had to get out of their boots and stand barefoot in the icy water as they wrangled it into the river. Its high sides, designed for step-down entry from the deck of an amusement ride station, made boarding a chore, and finally sitting in the seat with his makeshift paddle, Wakely had to agree with Deeks's assessment: he looked like a moron holding a branch, in a log flume boat, on the Missouri River. It took effort from everyone to clear the shallows and get it out into the current. He was immediately in trouble. While less tippy than he'd expected, it had no keel, so paddling only turned it in circles, while its mass created more momentum than the branch could counteract. After a few concerted strokes, the branch snapped. He threw it away and peeled off most of his clothes before scrambling over the side, gasping when he hit the cold water. He kicked furiously, managed to nudge the boat close enough that the section, which had paced along beside him, could splash out into the water and take hold and haul it up.

"That's not going to work," Wakely said, panting, self-conscious in his underwear. He pulled on his pants over his wet legs. "Branch is useless. The current is too strong, and the boat weighs a ton."

"We could just drift until we ground somewhere," Tse said. "I saw from the top of the stack that the river takes a hard turn about two clicks downstream."

"Lash the boats together to keep us from drifting apart," Sharpcot said.

"Nothing will keep us from drifting apart," Deeks muttered.

"Let's do it. We dine on the west bank," Wakely said.

They rolled the other boats to the water and floated them to where the first was grounded, and lashed them together with 550 cord, tightly, hull-to-hull, which also aided with their stability. They were on the river within the hour, drifting lazily southward, and Sharpcot thought maybe they should just do this, ride the river to the Gulf, to the sea, make for Mexico's east coast, proceed to Cancun to live out their days.

They passed blocks on both banks assembled from items difficult to discern at the distance, but one clearly of mirrored dance balls, countless tiny mirrors reflecting landscape and sky, sending back a million suns, and another of water towers, all of the same "ball and tee" design, with a slender stalk topped by a round tank, decorated in different colours, and painted with names: Plymouth, Mt. Orab, Sandwich, Gonzales, Boonville, Pensacola Beach, Cal Expo, and huddled among them a yellow one with a smiley face. They saw debris on the river, but only natural materials: leaves, branches, the carcass of a deer. After an hour and a half, they hit the bend Tse had seen, and the boats drifted into a bay where the current slowed and the water shallowed. Wakely, Tse, and Virago climbed out and swam against the raft until they reached a sandy bottom. They stood and began shoving the boat assembly towards the beach.

"What's that noise?" Sharpcot wondered as she sat up in the boat's seat.

It sounded like mechanical crickets, a hundred thousand of them, and it came from the block of off-white plastic objects that shadowed the beach. The chirps came from random locations on the wall, producing a constant, muttering din.

The swimmers got the raft to shore and unloaded it and considered letting it drift away but decided to pull it up on the bank in case they reached an impasse here and needed to relocate downstream.

"Or if we decide to go to Mardi Gras," Deeks said. "In New *Oh*'leans."

Wakely met Sharpcot's eye, feeling doubt about walking to California. Couldn't they float downstream in their raft, maybe find something better for the journey in the blocks they passed? But he knew the intractable determination in her look, and he collected his ruck from the boat and began to dry off and dress, surprised when Virago came in her wet sports bra and leggings to towel off beside him, shivering and her skin, from what he could see between the tapestry of tattoos, blue with cold.

"Thanks for being my wind block," she murmured self-consciously. "Now hold my towel up and look away."

Sharpcot lifted rifles and helmets from the boats, feeling far from certain about California, and she admitted to herself she was following an instinct, foolishly coloured by political prejudice. But she also felt agriculture would be more viable in California, mindful of all the fruit and vegetables that state produced. While the Accruers had apparently wiped out the crops on prairie land where they'd assembled the maze, in non-block areas they'd left cultivated flora, like orchards of apple and pear, stands of raspberries, grape vines. The travellers occasionally encountered in zones protected from block construction individual crop specimens: cornstalks, canola, flax, soybeans.

Crossing the mountains worried her. They'd likely be free of blocks, as they'd already encountered an occasional steep-sloped hill or drumlin that was surrounded, but not covered by, the maze. In fact, it appeared by the rarity of these and the consistent flatness of the landscape that some land grading had been conducted before the blocks were set, making the topography artificially flat. It was logical that when the hills and foothills and mountains exceeded whatever tolerance had been established to flatten them, the blocks would end. They already knew that trees and other plants above a certain size had, in general, been spared where they could, with the blocks shaped to avoid them. What would happen when they encountered big forests, something that would certainly happen before they reached the Rocky Mountain foothills? Would they just be forests? Cleared of their garbage, fences, cabins, roads, trail markings?

What drew her, despite the barrier of mountains they had to cross, was the hilly terrain of California, incapable of accommodating blocks, probably rich with ready-to-harvest crops. She would have to explain that to the others. If anyone asked.

"Smoke detectors," Virago remarked when she and Wakely returned from the wall. "We are hearing low-battery warnings from all over the block."

"Probably a bad idea to build a fire here," Leclerc said.

"Why?" Deeks wondered, then, "Oh, right," when she imagined their campsmoke drifting into the wall.

They went upstream, bivouacked at the foot of a monument made from plastic tabs of various colours, and all of approximately the same size and shape, all branded "Hot Wheels."

"Track connectors," Tse reported after studying one. He thought for a moment, then said, "When I was about eight, I got a track set for Christmas — 'Criss Cross Crash.' — I couldn't finish building it because the box was short one of these. I prayed — literally prayed — for one. And now this." He gazed at the tower.

"Nice fucking work, God!" Deeks shouted, and Tse frowned and looked at her. "Too soon?" she asked, and he nodded.

They built a big fire using wood from the riverbank, and Tse and Leclerc ventured into the blocks to search for useful provisions.

"Find sour cream and onion chips," Deeks called after them. "And tequila!" When they were gone, she muttered as she sat

279

on a flat rock by the fire, "They'll be back with nothing but smiles on their faces."

Wakely, who was transcribing their latest finds into his notebook, looked up and asked, "What's that?"

"Uh," she replied, looking at Virago.

"Come on," Wakely said. "What?"

"What what?" Virago answered. She was still shivering from cold, and she leaned towards the fire with her hands raised.

"What's going on?"

Deeks sat up and sighed, "They're fucking."

It was not what Wakely had expected. He tried to maintain a neutral expression, but his eyes shifted and met Deeks's, the reception chilly. He glanced at Virago, who looked away, across the river.

Recognizing that her response demanded a reply, he said, "Ah." Then: "Does Sergeant Sharpcot know?"

"Know what?" Sharpcot asked from behind him. She'd been down at the river, collecting wood, and Wakely hadn't heard her over the crackle of the fire.

"Leclerc and Tse. I believe they're. Fraternizing."

"I thought everyone knew that," she replied, dropping an armful of branches beside the fire and sitting on the rock next to Deeks.

"Apparently everyone in the world knew," Deeks replied. "Except the perceptive Master Corporal."

"So one-sixth of the world's population was in the dark," Virago said.

"Half of the men," Deeks added.

"Really all of the men, considering that the other half is actually involved in the, uh, intrigue," Virago pointed out.

"Intrigue, also known as 'gossip,'" Wakely complained, his face hot under the gaze of 75 percent of the world's women. "I'm getting more wood." He rose and headed for a copse of cottonwoods on the riverbank.

Leclerc and Tse returned an hour later bearing Christmas-branded tins of powdered hot chocolate and sachets of noodle soup. The back of Tse's jacket matted with grass.

They ate noodles and drank hot chocolate until they were sick of both. At the moment of sunset a moon almost full climbed fat and orange above the blocks on the river's east bank and as it rose it cooled to an icy blue. Fatigued by the labour of the flume boats and swimming in the icy water, Wakely found himself nodding off, and retired first.

He woke in the night to see the moon floating at zenith, casting a cold light. He found his arm had escaped from beneath his ranger blanket and lay stretched out on cold soil. But his hand was warm because the person beside him was clutching it tightly under their own blanket. He couldn't see who: their face lay hidden in the blanket's folds. He could see beyond the silhouetted form that Corporal Tse stood sentry, illuminated by firelight, smoking a cigarette. Which explained why he still had some left — he smoked them only at night, while alone on watch.

Wakely shut his eyes, planning in a moment to lift his head to determine the identity of the hand-holder, but sleep swept over him, and he awoke in the morning with Sharpcot shaking his shoulder.

"Slept late, buddy," she said, and he lifted his head to see everyone on their feet and kitting up for travel.

They pushed west, went hard for several days at Sharpcot's urging, which she tried to frame as suggestion or guidance rather than command.

The pace took a toll, resulting in fatigue, blisters, aches. One afternoon Leclerc leapt across a stream and landed hard on the far bank and went down in the grass. Tse rushed to where she lay, gripping a foot and moaning, and he loosed

281

her boot and tenderly removed it. He gathered her ankle in his hands as Sharpcot squatted beside them.

"Is it bad?" she asked, trying to keep impatience from her voice. "Are you all right?"

"It's fine," Leclerc replied, then yowled as Tse gave her ankle a tentative flex.

"We could ice it if these damn chests held anything," Deeks said, indicating the block of foam ice chests that towered above them. She punched a fist through one and a quantity of fishy water leaked out.

"Think you can walk?" Sharpcot asked.

"If you order me to," Leclerc replied.

"I'm obviously not going to do that. I'm not in command, remember? Better rest it. Let's quit for the day, get an early start tomorrow."

The soldiers dropped their gear, squirmed out of jackets and vests. Sharpcot set her ruck against the wall opposite, constructed from curling irons, and sat with her back against it and took off her boots.

"I'll scout a bit. Anyone want to join me?" Wakely asked.

Deeks and Virago both volunteered, and Sharpcot watched them go with a hint of irritation she refused to acknowledge. Instead, she closed her eyes and visualized their destination: the west coast, the Pacific ocean. She'd once fantasized about quitting the army and moving to Vancouver, with Lana. But Dwight would never allow it, and what would she do if not command an army section? Not to mention the cost of living there. Well, that housing bubble finally burst.

The ache about Lana was wide and deep and had so thoroughly saturated her that she almost found comfort in it. A familiar presence. The hard, deep longing to see her, to talk with her, to even know whether or not she lived — all of this dwarfed her shock and horror about the apparent end of human civilization. Which itself was too big to manage.

She'd lost track of the exact date, and that alarmed her. First week in October? Wakely would know.

The landscape was becoming restless. They encountered areas where a hill rose among the blocks that surrounded it, too steep to populate. Each day the sun inched south. Winter presented a hard deadline that would make the mountains untenable. She thought about California forests: sequoia and giant redwoods. There would be animals to hunt and berries to collect, streams hopping with salmon. Competition from bears and wolves and cougars. Not just competition: predators. She found herself gripping the stock of her rifle.

She pictured a log cabin in a green forest. Smoke curling from the chimney. But who is inside? There's a room for Tse and Leclerc, another for Wakely and — who? Virago or Deeks, or maybe both of them in some kind of post-civilization poly-amorous arrangement. Endless bickering.

Dorian Wakely. Her 2IC. Her friend. Her brother. She couldn't imagine herself and Wakely in that room together.

Of course, any entanglement with Virago and/or Deeks would be obstructed by his romantic intransigence, that persistent faithfulness to Daisy. The grief that for some reason everyone elevated above their own. They'd all lost everyone. Or had they? It was a plague of uncertainty. Wakely got to hold Daisy as she passed, to witness her last breath. What was this surreal nightmare to that sureness? She envied him for it.

It was madness to worry about sleeping arrangements in their hypothetical California cabin. Between here and there stood mountains, literal mountains, snowcapped, and each day colder, the snow deeper. It would soon enough coat the foothills, and roll east to bury all of this.

"Oh god, what's that stink?" Virago cried.

They had just emerged from an aisle between cashmere

cardigans, where Deeks had grabbed one, made in Italy, heather grey with drop-shoulder seams, and on the other side spray cans of footwear waterproofer.

"How many of these do I own?" Virago wondered, pulling one down.

"One for every pair of boots," Deeks said. "The salesperson talks you into it. You use it once, the day you get the boots home."

They'd rounded a corner that put on their left a wall of thigh toners with pastel pink, baby blue, yellow, and orange foam rubber protectors, and the cardigans on the right, when a miasma of excrement drifted towards them.

"Do we want to know?" Wakely asked, squinting down the passage.

Holding their noses they advanced along it until they spotted a mesa of plastic bags, green, black, brown, white, striped, polka-dotted, each knotted shut, each containing lumpy matter.

"Dog shit," Deeks groaned as she looked down the passage at the wall retreating half a kilometre into the west.

"Tell me about it," Virago said, holding her nose. "I took care of my aunt's bichon frisé and it was four, five bags per day with that dog."

"Sure it wasn't a shih tzu?" Deeks asked.

"Do we have to keep standing here?"

"Hold steady, privates. I just need to write this down," Wakely said, fumbling to get out his notebook, opening it, and writing with slow deliberation while saying, "dog . . . shit . . . bags."

Deeks, breathing through the cuff of her jacket, whacked him on the arm and she and Virago jogged up the next passageway, and he followed.

"You soldiers need to toughen up," he laughed when he caught them beyond that corona of stink. "We dug in downwind from towns in Kandahar Province that smelled worse than that."

They continued past cardigans right and realtor signs left, stacked vertically, faces turned outward, showing familiar company names: Re/Max, Coldwell Banker, Prudential, Century 21, Sutton, Sotheby's, and then many others, companies they'd never heard of, independents, from other countries, in other languages, Se Vende, A Vendre, À Venda, Tekoop, Na prodaju, In vendita, Binebenta, Ar Werth; in Cyrillic, Greek, Thai, Korean, Chinese, Arabic, Aramaic, Zapotec, yet names and phone numbers always in Latin script, some with a Sold or equivalent sticker pasted across. Many included photos of the realtors themselves, all of a species: head cocked, arms crossed with chest out, some leaning tentatively forward, the women in blouses or power suits, flaunting jewellery — diamond earrings, pearl necklaces — hairdos, highlights, bangs, bobcut, or long sweeping coifs, faces makeup-caked; the men in dark suits, with tie or open-collared, and all of these people grinning, earnest, trust me, I want your money, but trust me.

"Look at these smug fuckers," Deeks growled. "Think they're goddamn celebrities."

They reached a corner of garden hose reels, without hoses, and similarly vacant server racks, used in data centres, tens of millions of them, devoid of their web servers and cloud servers and database servers, the associated disk arrays, switches, and UPSs, for Google, Apple, Facebook, Twitter, Microsoft, Amazon, IBM, Oracle, all the big companies with their giant server farms, along with every ISP and web host, plus every office server room and server closet on Earth.

Sharpcot woke at sunrise a few days later and lifting on one elbow was slammed by panic at what she saw: the blankets of the others dusted with snow. She got up and pulled on her boots and stepped around the sleeping bodies, whacked each to wake them.

"Who had watch?" she demanded as the sleepers roused.

"Me," Deeks admitted. "I got in bed to keep warm. I fell asleep. Is this what we're on guard for? Rogue weather?"

"That's not for you to question, Private," Sharpcot snapped.

"Didn't you resign? Back at the lighthouses?"

Sharpcot prepared to challenge the insubordination but recognized she had in fact resigned. It just didn't take.

"We can't get complacent," Wakely said as he shook snow from his blanket. "Jesus it's cold."

He looked at the backhoes that walled them on one side, cabs and shovels powdered with snow, and forming the opposite wall, whistles — coach whistles, lifeguard whistles, nautical whistles, rape whistles — all of the same basic shape, a circular sound chamber, flat mouthpiece.

"Fine," Deeks replied. "I fucked up. What do you want from me?"

"Not to fuck up," Virago suggested.

The snow melted within an hour and the day warmed, but the winter sign spurred them westward. Whenever they encountered trees they collected and carried firewood. The terrain grew more varied, with occasional hills standing like islands among a sea of blocks.

At some point they would enter Montana or Wyoming, hard to know how far south they'd travelled on their trek across South Dakota, always skewing to the left when they encountered a T-intersection, making their heading west-southwest, and they passed through landscapes of flat-screen televisions and woks and glass fever thermometers and hazmat suits and house slippers and bags of pretzel sticks — which they broke open and ate, stowed additional packs — and ceramic egg cups decorated with flowers and polka dots and chickens and Paris, some shaped like sheep, fish, flamingoes, giraffe heads, Homer Simpson.

They travelled along a passage between reel-to-reel tape machines — TEAC, Sony, Ballfinger, Akai, Pioneer, Korting, Marantz, Studer, Cadenza, Ferrograph, Webcor, Dynaco, Brenell, Telefunken, both vintage and rebirth, all minus their reels and tapes, which lay collected elsewhere — and some kind of two-piece cooking pot with a shallow base and a cone-shaped lid with a hole in the top, mostly earthenware, but also in ceramic, glass, and cast iron. "Tajines," Leclerc explained. "From Morocco and Algiers." As they closed on the next intersection Deeks stopped to sniff the air, noting something floral, and Sharpcot also halted and declared, "Chanel Number Five."

"God yes," Deeks said. "My mom wears that."

"Mine too," Sharpcot sighed, and their eyes met briefly before Sharpcot lowered hers. Deeks put a hand on the sergeant's arm and Sharpcot covered Deeks's hand with her own before they let go and continued on, crossed the intersection and passed along yellow, brown, and black train cars, new and derelict, each fitted with an enormous turbine on one end — rotary snowploughs — and on the opposite side of the aisle, engineered cork flooring tiles. Sharpcot slowed as the perfume scent thickened into a blend of other perfumes, producing an increasingly powerful and nauseating atmosphere.

"Uhhh, folks?" Tse called from the tail of the group.

Everyone turned and saw Tse gazing down the passage behind them at something that his large form eclipsed. Sharpcot sidestepped to look, and what she saw quickened her pulse: a large dog was standing in the passageway a hundred metres away, regarding them in a posture that was not altogether friendly. Pitbull terrier, with a thick, powerful body and a massive skull.

Leclerc stepped behind Tse, whispered, "I hate dogs. And those are the worst."

Sharpcot and Wakely traded glances, and Wakely moved towards the dog, snugging rifle to shoulder and studying it through the scope. He thumbed off the safety and set the crosshairs on the dog's face.

The canine lifted its head to watch a trio of swallows dart overhead from among the railcars.

"You see that, El?" Wakely asked.

"Three Section," Sharpcot called. "Anyone not wearing armour, put it on now. Helmets too. I need full fighting order. Come on, people."

"It's a dog," Deeks stated. "Oh wait, you think it's carrying?"

"It's wearing a chain collar," Wakely told her.

"Didn't we pass a block of those a few weeks back?"

"Looks well-fed, too," Sharpcot added.

Deeks looked back at the dog. "That must mean . . . oh shit. Full battle rattle!"

Wakely watched the dog while Sharpcot turned her attention the opposite way and rapidly surveyed the passage. Leclerc and Deeks dropped rucks and pulled out flak vests and shed their combat jackets and vests and drew on their armour.

Deeks pulled her TAC vest and jacket back on, settled her helmet in place, and stepped beside Virago. She slapped her chest. "Thought I'd never have to wear flak again. Not like you, keener."

"I keep mine on because we're in America," Virago muttered.

"Let's move," Sharpcot said. "Corporal Tse, I want the machine gun up front. Private Deeks, take the rear and watch that dog." Deeks fell to the back of the column and adopted a side-stepping walk that allowed her to observe the dog, which stood panting, watching them move away.

As they approached the next intersection the smell of perfume grew suffocatingly strong, and they saw where the train cars ended a new block: perfume bottles in cut glass, round and square and of all manner of other shapes: hearts, diamonds, ovals, cylinders, printed with names and embellishments, and many filled at least partially with coloured liquids: pink, red, blue, gold, refracting polychromatic light into the corridor. The wind came from the southeast, pushing much of the scent away, but it was overpowering nevertheless, like the perfume aisle of a department store but an order of magnitude stronger.

"Makes you lightheaded," Sharpcot muttered to Wakely as they paused at the next crossroads.

"T-intersection past this one," Wakely noted, looking through his scope. "Looks like an area of multi-block towers at the end. Narrow stacks of crap. I see columns of blue glitter pens and — I don't know what else. Rubber worms?"

"I miss dog shit," Virago said, suppressing a gag.

"Can we go back and around?" Leclerc asked with her face mashed into her sleeve.

"I don't know if that thing will let us," Deeks said, maintaining her vigilance of the dog, which now sat scratching itself. "And hey, I thought the army was supposed to be a scent-free workplace!"

"We could go left up here," Wakely said to Sharpcot, nodding ahead. Small machines, barrels with a belt-driven motor, comprised the southwest corner. "I don't like this corridor."

"Guys," Deeks called. "Guys, guys?" She'd lifted her rifle when the dog rose and started to trot towards them. "His ears went up and he got to his feet and here he comes and okay what do I do?"

The dog closed, 100 metres, 75 metres. Deeks felt blindly along her rifle's grip, had to tilt it to locate the safety. She flicked it to single-fire mode, remembered to draw back the cocking handle, and when she pulled the stock to her shoulder saw the dog at 50 metres and still closing.

"Jack, I got a rotten feeling," Sharpcot said. "Let's get everyone down."

"You heard your sergeant! Everyone on the ground," Wakely called, dropping to his belly in the knee-deep grass, the others following suit.

"What about this dog?" Deeks cried as she continued to stand, tracking the advancing dog. "I don't want to shoot someone's pet today!"

"Scare it off!" Virago called back.

289

"Wait!" Sharpcot called, but too late. Deeks fired a round well above the dog's head. The shot's vast echo hadn't yet faded when an explosion of automatic gunfire opened up from the opposite direction, and the air came alive with bullets and then fragments blasted from the surrounding rail cars and cork tile.

"What are you waiting for, soldiers?" Sharpcot shouted. "Return fire!"

13

For Wakely, everything fell to a rhythm of reflex. By feel he set his C7's fire control selector to full-auto, cycled the cocking handle, set his eye to the scope. He rose slightly and peered through grass down the corridor, and counted five, maybe six muzzle flashes among the small pillars of stuff, most of the attackers shooting indiscriminately.

Debris filled the air from fire hitting the block walls, mostly cork, which was mercifully light when it came down, but he could see fragments of wood and metal coming off the train cars on the corridor's far side where Virago and Leclerc lay. To his right, Tse stretched out on his belly against the foot of the cork tile. He opened the machine gun's feed tray and pulled the belt from the ammo box and was trying to find the receiver by touch while keeping his head low.

On his right and slightly forward of their position lay Sharpcot, who was also struggling to fire her weapon. He shouted to her but above the din of the incoming fire and destruction from the walls he couldn't hear his own voice. To his right he could see Virago, also prone. She pulled her weapon's trigger but nothing happened.

"Addy!" he called. He tried a second time and she turned. He tapped his weapon's fire selector, and she looked at her own, shook her head in disbelief, and nodded.

When he turned back to his scope he saw that one of their attackers, emboldened by the apparent lack of a response from the soldiers, had stepped out from behind a pillar and stood boldly in the middle of the aisle, spraddle-legged, firing on full-auto as he swept the corridor. He was white, mid-fifties with a grizzled beard, wearing civilian camouflage, pants and coat, a baseball cap turned askew. His face grim as he fired.

Bullets struck the ground ahead of Wakely, spraying him with dirt. He thumbed the fire control to single-shot mode, set the shooter's forehead in his crosshairs, and fired once. The man's throat burst open and he flew backwards, gun still firing, flinging rounds into the sky.

He wondered if his scope had gone out of alignment, was making a mental a note to calibrate it later, when he recognized that he'd just killed a person. He felt himself subsiding into rumination, when he was roused by Tse opening up with the Minimi, the rapid clatter of rounds leaping away, a fountain of hot shell casings washing against his arm and helmet and flank as the pillars down the corridor erupted with hits. Virago also began firing, long discharges on full-auto. He rolled towards her.

"Shorter bursts. And move after you shoot," he shouted into her ear. "Or they'll find you by your muzzle flash! Tell Cheree!" Then he gave her a shove and she rolled away, fired a brief volley, rolled again towards the aisle's far side where Leclerc was firing single rounds.

Wakely dug his toes into the earth and propelled himself towards Sharpcot, slapped the back of her calf.

She turned and said something inaudible over bursts from the machine gun.

"Say again!" he shouted.

"Throw smoke!"

He cursed himself for not thinking of it, reached under his body and tore a smoke grenade from its pouch, pulled the pin, and tossed it as far as he could from his prone position. It landed in the cross passageway ahead and spewed a jet of red smoke, but it lay with its nozzle pointing north, and wind from the south carried most of the smoke up the passageway.

Sharpcot tried her rifle again, hammered it in frustration. Wakely rolled left, felt the whisper of the C9 rounds pass nearby, fired a burst, rolled back and threw himself forward so he was beside her.

"Check the bolt carrier," he shouted, reaching for the rifle. She knocked his hand away.

"I got it," she shouted back, working on the rifle: she drew back the handle, locked it, fished fingers into the receiver and pulled out a dead grasshopper, which she showed him before flicking it away. She pushed on the bolt catch and the handle snapped in place, tapped the plunger, and fired a quick blast. She rolled right.

"They've got cover in those pillars. We're ducks out here," he cried.

"And liberal with ammo. They're well equipped. But undisciplined."

They each fired and rolled, careful to go neither too far right, which would put them in front of Virago and Leclerc, or left, ahead of Tse.

"Can you see Abby?" Sharpcot called.

He turned back to look, shook his head.

"We need a plan. We'll go dry before they do," she cried as she switched magazines, fired and rolled.

"How many?" he called when he reached her again.

"Five or six. Only one down as far as I can tell."

"At least we know we're not the last people on Earth," he yelled.

"Yeah. Too bad it's these assholes," she remarked, and fired.

Someone, a woman, wearing black and holding a civilian assault rifle, stepped from among the pillars, very briefly, and ducked into the righthand passage, getting behind the perfume bottles. Wakely followed her and fired a round into the corner, hoping to hit her through the glass. A small cascade of bottles poured into the alley.

"Wait a second," Sharpcot cried. "I've got a better idea. The bottles. Go for the bottles!"

Wakely shifted aim, started firing short bursts into the wall, and Sharpcot did the same. Brief landslides of bottles erupted around the location of the hit, but that alien attractive force maintained the block's overall integrity. Sharpcot seized Wakely's arm.

"Tse!" she cried.

Wakely pushed himself backwards and rolled left. As he lifted his head to speak a bullet creased the side of his helmet, sending it askew and forcing his head down.

Tse stopped firing and seized Wakely's shoulder.

"You okay, boss?" he said when Wakely's head came up.

Wakely blinked, ears ringing. He spent a moment trying to recall something important he needed to say. He glanced forward and saw rounds from Sharpcot's rifle exploding along the face of perfume bottles. "Right. Uh. Corporal, see what you can do to take out the end of that bottle block!"

Tse nodded, tracked the C9 sideways and up, aiming into the west end of the block above the attackers, pouring rounds into it. The machine gun cut a deep trough, sending a flow of bottles into the passageway in front of the attackers. He swept the fire around, seeking the key, the keystone that held it all together, but the block held, seemed to shed only brief waves of glass, until abruptly a cataract flowed into the corridor in front of them, obstructing the enemy's fire. Tse paused to retrieve a new ammo box from his ruck and set to feeding the belt into the tray. Sharpcot glanced at the block's far end, which now looked like something from Dr. Seuss, a massive cliff perched atop a heavily eroded undercut, dripping bottles that smashed against the pile below. They could hear indiscriminate shouting among their adversaries. The wind had subsided and smoke from the grenade abruptly clouded the passageway.

Sharpcot rose to her knees, called, "Virago, Leclerc, status?"

"I'm almost out," Virago said, dropping her rifle's magazine and pulling another from beneath her abdomen.

"I'm still good," Leclerc said. "Firing singles."

Sharpcot turned and was just seeing and apprehending that Deeks was down, also on her belly behind them, but facing the opposite way, a furry mound of something indiscriminate not far past her, when a rifle round slammed her sideways and onto her back in the grass.

Wakely saw through a rift in the smoke that a man with a red beard and wearing camouflage had lifted over the drift of glass in the passage to pop off a round. The man ducked before Wakely could get a clear shot, but he fired anyway, clipped the top of the bottles to shower the attacker with glass.

He moved to where Sharpcot lay on her back, gasping for breath.

"El!" he called. "El, you all right?" He saw the tear in her TAC vest and armour, the dimple in the steel plate.

A voice floated down the passage, a woman's shout: "Righteous, go around and get to their right flank!"

"I'm okay," Sharpcot cried, shoving him away. "Tell Tse to get on that block!"

Wakely didn't have to tell him. Tse rose to his feet and lifted the C9 and opened up, confident he knew where to concentrate fire. The gun thundered as he excavated a deep hollow in the most precarious part of the structure, undercutting the crown of glass above. A swift river of bottles began to flow outwards, and as the smoke grenade sputtered out Wakely saw through the thinning vapour the man who'd shot Sharpcot rise from cover, looking at the brink of glass towering above as Tse's Minimi devoured its base. Terror on his scratched and bloodied face evident through the scope. It was a clean shot, but Wakely saved the bullet. As the river turned into a cataract, the man stumbled to get away.

In the next instant the massive end of the block collapsed with an extraordinary crash, the flow spreading outwards with a sustained roar. An avalanche of bottles, a tsunami. The soldiers rose to their feet, wary of the north end that towered over them, which despite the dissolution of the opposite end maintained its integrity, as they watched the block's entire west end deluge outward, filling the passageway ahead to a depth of 10 metres, while a scree of bottles inundated the smaller stacks among which the attackers had concealed themselves. It filled the spaces between, burying everyone and everything.

After gunfire and that cataclysmic crash, a rich quiet, punctuated by the occasional creak of glass from settling bottles, propagated over the landscape. Then a wave of perfume swept in and set everyone to coughing and retching.

"Stay sharp!" Sharpcot shouted, wiping her eyes, wet from smoke and evaporating alcohol. "This might not be done." She staggered to the corner and swept the passageways.

"Abby, Abby!" she heard, and turned to see Virago move to where Deeks lay, face down and still. Sharpcot already knew it, had absorbed but not apprehended in the instant before she'd taken that round to her breastplate Deeks's unnatural posture on the ground, oriented towards the dog.

She approached Leclerc and Tse, who were each standing, weary, filthy with dirt and soot, looking stunned at Virago and Wakely kneeling on each side of Deeks.

She steered Leclerc to one intersection corner, directed Tse to the other. "Anyone comes down either passage, shoot them," she instructed.

She came softly to the others, as if fearful of disturbing them. Her eyes met Wakely's and he gave a brief shake of his head. She kneeled by Deeks's shoulder, glancing at the bloodied dog which lay a few paces back, lips drawn taut in a mortal grin.

Deeks had been stuck from behind by multiple rounds. Armour had protected her back, but she'd taken a bullet to her shoulder, two more to her right thigh. One had severed her femoral artery. The grass around her legs saturated with blood.

"She stayed on her feet to handle the dog as it moved in on us," Wakely said.

Virago tried to speak but her first utterance became a sob. She slid Deeks's helmet off and pushed a hand into her friend's hair.

"What's happening?" Leclerc called from the corner. "How is Abby?"

Wakely went to her, and Sharpcot watched him speak quietly, and saw Leclerc nodding, her face grim. He spoke more and she nodded and stepped over the litter of shell casings and slumped at Deeks's side while Wakely took her position at the corner. He glanced across the aisle at Tse, who stood upright, covering the south passage with the C9.

"Rock tumblers," Tse said.

"What?"

Tse nodded at the opposite corner.

"Yeah," Wakely replied, glancing at the stack of machines, then back up the north passageway. "Goddamn rock tumblers."

Sharpcot went back. She walked east down the passage the way they'd come, past Deeks with Virago and Leclerc keeping vigil over her body, past the dead dog, then she jogged between snowplough cars and cork tile, thinking about their arrival and progress coming west, how long ago, 10, 15 minutes? Deeks still alive, quipping and laughing.

She reached the next intersection and looked back at their diminished group, men at the corners, women on the ground. Seeing them there, this sad tableau, so small among the towers, backdropped by a mountain of glass washed up against the opposite wall, made her recognize their vulnerability. This might not be done. She backed against the corner and made a quick survey north and south along the passage, then stepped into it and sprinted north between plough cars and tajines. It was a long way to the next intersection, and she kept up the pace, exertion batting away desolation, and when she reached the next intersection she was panting, lungs burning, but the air mercifully clear of perfume. She leaned against a train car and gazed at the new towers: a collection of fine strips of white paper stacked on the right, and tent trailers — pop-up campers — all of them cranked shut, on the left.

When she'd caught her breath and checked both passages she went to the opposite corner, vigilant for movement, and ran her hand along the wall and dislodged one of the slips of paper. It fluttered to the ground. She picked it up and studied it: rounded at one end with a small fold at the other, perfectly iconic — the backing for an adhesive bandage. She regarded the stack that towered over her, wondering when she'd finally be numbed to civilization's excess.

She had her breath back, ran west along the passage, parallel to the one where the others waited, keeping her eyes up to watch the distance, safety off, full-auto. If there were more they'd come this way, or possibly the passageway south of the section, but instinct told her they'd come north because of the way the glass had coursed.

She didn't see what tripped her, but she was abruptly down in the grass, winded. Checked the forward distance; it remained clear. She was alone. And she was crying. More than crying — bawling. On her belly, rifle trapped beneath her. She lifted herself and dislodged it, moved it to her side, in ready reach. Keeping her wits while she lost herself in despair. She cried for Lana, for her mother and sisters, for the world. She cried for Deeks, and she cried for Loko and Bronski. A thought flitted past as she wept: this was the first time in many months she was alone, actually alone. She cried tears of relief, at the brief release from her position of authority. But that made her think of poor Deeks, how she'd failed to protect her.

She cried hard and loud with her cheek against the earth.

Someone was watching her. She snapped her head up and seized the rifle before she spied a duo of prairie dogs as they vanished into their hole. She sat up and glanced back and noted another hole, the one that had tripped her. She flexed her ankle, which felt fine, but her knee ached from striking the ground. She wouldn't know if it was a problem until she walked on it. A few metres away, from a third hole, a dog popped up and regarded her.

"Hey," she said quietly, and it ducked to escape, then changed its mind, decided she wasn't a threat, stood watching.

"El," a voice shouted, scaring it down, and she scrambled for her rifle, but it was Wakely, pacing down the aisle from the west, rifle up, swinging behind and ahead as he approached.

"I fell," she called, digging into her vest for tissues to clean up the mess of her tears, her runny nose.

"Can you walk?" he asked as he arrived, squatting beside her.

"It's not serious. I used it as an opportunity for an . . . emotional reset."

He nodded, glanced west, muttered, "There may be more."

"Yes. Two more down that hole there."

"Not what I meant."

"Obviously. My sense is they'll come at us this way."

"My thought too," he replied. He stood and put out a hand and she took it and got to her feet, tested the banged knee.

"It's good," she said, but it wasn't quite.

They went west, Sharpcot a step behind so he wouldn't see her limp. When they reached the next corner — intact end of the perfume bottles on the left, tent trailers continuing ahead — he said, "We need to investigate. But not with that knee."

"I'm fine," she said, but knew that while he hadn't seen her limp, he'd heard it. A good soldier uses every sense.

"Get Virago and send her up here. I'd like it if you could move everyone to this position, as it's only three approaches to cover. Though I know we need to do something about Abby."

299

He dropped his eyes as he said name, and Sharpcot touched his arm. "Not your fault, Jack."

"Yeah. Not yours either."

She opened her mouth to reply, but he stopped her with a raised hand. "Go get Addy."

She moved away, imagined his eyes on her as she tried to minimize her limp, but when she turned he was looking away, covering the west corridor.

Wakely and Virago advanced between perfume bottles and tent trailers, Wakely always in front, which he didn't realize until she mentioned it.

"Aren't we supposed to cover each other?"

He considered for a moment. He was shielding her. As he failed to shield Deeks.

She stepped past him to the wall opposite while he covered her. They continued along the passage, leapfrogging, until they neared the northwest corner of the perfume block. While the southwest section had been devastated by the attack, you couldn't tell it from here, as a substantial portion of the block stood intact. Beyond it they saw stainless steel magazine racks. The sun emerged from a cloud, illuminating the perfume block from within, bending and refracting through vessels filled with polychromatic fluids, producing a monument of light and colour. He nodded her forward, but as she neared the intersection he darted forward and put a hand on her arm to stop her.

He whispered, "We crawl from here."

She looked at the wall's terminus and whispered back, "Right. Because our motion might be visible through the glass."

She followed him in a bear crawl to the junction. When they were close he put up a hand to halt her and switched to leopard crawl with his rifle braced across his arms. She watched him reach the corner, heart racing, wanting to grab his boot and pull him back, to cover him with her body. But she sat on her knees, rifle raised, finger on the trigger.

He flashed a look around the corner, drew back, then got to his knees and leaned into the passage. Keeping his rifle raised he stood and stepped in, turning his head and nodding for her to follow.

They faced a mountain of broken bottles, the scent of perfume surging. The avalanche had flowed to within 20 metres of the crossroads and rose swiftly to a height of 15 metres. The wave had washed up against the magazine rack block, which ran about 30 metres wide and was followed by the mini stacks in which the attackers had concealed themselves, each a metre or two in width, pillars in a sea of glass.

Wakely squatted and looked at the grass, trod flat by footsteps. By their bias he decided people had walked into the corridor from the north, as he and Virago had, but probably hadn't come out of it.

He rose and they crept forward, hearing the occasional clink and chime as glass continued to settle. He reached the foot of the slope and stepped onto this glacier of glass. Guerlain, Gucci, Opium, Eternity. Bottles crunched under his boots, Burberry, Shalimar, Terre d'Hermès, Juicy Couture. Bottles shifted and he flailed one arm to keep balance. He continued to climb, sending down landslides, Beautiful Belle, Aromatics Elixir, Mermaid Moon, Pleasure Gardenia.

"Where are you going?" she asked.

He signalled for silence, waved her to cover the intersection. He stepped higher, Amongst the Waves, Juliette Has a Gun, Moonlight in Heaven, Tin House Forbidden Affair.

Survivalists. That had been his first thought when they opened fire, confirmed by the garb and stance and attitude of the man he'd shot in the throat. Preppers. Doomsday cultists. Well, they turned out to be right. Doomsday came.

He continued to climb, but his mind ran unbidden from the man he'd shot to the boy he'd shot. On patrol in the Arghandab

Valley. They'd risen from a wadi and startled him, kneeling in front of an artillery shell with a strand of orange wire trailing from the nosecone. The sight of that toxic orange wire branded forever in Wakely's brain. The kid moved his hand and Wakely shot him through the chest. That was all. Shot the kid, who fell, lay gasping as the rest of the patrol surged into the clearing to check for other insurgents, everyone scared, jumpy, the kid dying, medic kneeling at his side, and Wakely just stood there and watched.

"Good job, man," someone said, slapping his shoulder. Corporal Shanks. "Got him before he tripped it."

Good job.

He earned the Medal of Bravery and a permanent stain on his conscience. He'd relived it every day for the last seven years. Kid reaches for detonator, Wakely pulls trigger, kid dies. Every day.

The glass shifted and he dropped to a crouch to keep from falling, steadied himself with his hands. Most bottles intact, but some chipped or broken, and he was glad for his gloves. From now on they would smell of — he picked up the cubic black bottle under his right hand and studied the label — Eau de Gaga. He shifted focus to the glass below and then shifted it again, drove his perspective deeper, into the flow, where he spied an outline refracted through prisms of cut glass, transmitted through the coloured fluids: a sprawled body, arms out, legs splayed, head askew. Dead survivalist. Like an ancient hominid frozen in ice.

He resumed his climb until he reached the end of the magazine racks, grabbed one to pull himself up the slope of bottles, eyed the passageway that ran west away from the perfume. Bottles had surged deep into it, 40 or 50 metres out, racks on the right, and pillars of stuff running along the left, grey O-rings, then dollhouse armoires, then, what, artist palettes? Paint-stained and in a stack two metres wide. Everything beyond that distance indistinct. The passage ran for 200 metres, ended at a wall of flat plastic in white, blue, red, green. But also at the far end, in the passageway, scattered objects. He looked at them through his rifle scope: crates, boxes, bags, equipment. A woman. Slouched against one of the pillars. She was wearing black, and a rifle lay on the ground beside her. At the distance he couldn't make out much more than that, other than the fact that she did not move, because if she had he would've shot her.

Virago watched him skid and slip down the glass hill and when he reached her he said, "We're going this way." They proceeded between magazine racks and pop-up campers, Starcraft, Palomino, Jayco, Coachmen, Clipper, Fleetwood, Rockwood, Forest River, Flagstaff, Coleman, Keystone, Thor, SylvanSport, while he told her what he'd seen, and what to expect.

When they reached the end of the magazine racks — RVs continued beyond them — they entered the passageway with care and he noted the grass here had been flattened by much activity.

He looked at the new block, pulled out a lid, Rubbermaid stamped in the plastic.

"Aw. I've been looking for that," Virago whispered. "Too bad I threw out the container."

"Pretty much," he replied.

"It's a joke Abby would've made," Virago said, frowning. Before she could be overcome he tugged at her arm and they continued until they arrived at the west end of the passage he'd scoped. Despite his warning, Virago gasped when she saw the woman. What Wakely hadn't seen through his scope was the blood. She'd been shot in the abdomen. Her eyes open, staring vacantly through him as he kneeled and took off a glove and checked her carotid. No pulse. Skin cold. He was startled to see she was wearing eyeshadow and mascara. Jolted too seeing a new face, after their weeks underground and months travelling, the first person, first new face, he'd seen since. She might've been 30. Why did they have to attack? Their groups could've merged, helped each other. Survived together.

He looked at the rifle beside her, some kind of Barrett AR-15 derivative, then lifted his eyes to study the stack against which the woman lay slumped: Garfield, the comic book cat, figurines, all identical. He pulled one out, found it to be a tree ornament, the iconic cat tangled in Christmas lights. The tower to the left made from uluit, flat blades with bone handles. An Inuit tool.

He regarded the objects scattered about, went to a carton, found it crammed with food tins. "Are you at the point where you'll eat salmon, Private?" he asked, holding up a can.

"I don't know, wild or farmed?" she asked, then added soberly: "Kidding."

They scouted among the nearby stacks, each made from some small and rare and minimally produced product: collectible toys, tchotchkes, jewellery, dollar-store junk, machine parts, money clips identical to a type Wakely once got in a Christmas cracker. They found wrappers and empty tins, the remains of a campfire, a small cookpot, utensils. They found boxes of ammunition. And in an aisle with nothing else, a bundle of cloth, which when unwrapped revealed a single dark turd that unleashed a stink the perfume could not repel.

"What the hell," Wakely murmured as he rolled it tightly and tossed it.

"A diaper?" Virago wondered.

They returned to find the others digging a grave, already deep in the soft earth. Wakely and Virago took over, briefed the others while they worked, describing the extent of the bottles' spread, the dead survivalist, the provisions, ammunition. Wakely thought Virago might mention the diaper, but she didn't. But neither did he.

Late in the afternoon, they laid Abby to rest.

They stood silently around the hole, and Sharpcot cleared her throat, but nothing came. At last she said, "Abby," then could say nothing else for a moment, trying to manage the emotion. She tried again: "Abigail. Private Abigail Ophelia Deeks."

Hearing her friend's full name, which she didn't know, broke Virago. She bent and sobbed, and it set off everyone else. It granted permission to cry, and they cried, the five of them, for a long time. Touching hands, holding each other. When finally it subsided, there seemed to be nothing more to say, no words that could surpass what those minutes of anguish had expressed. And still they stood, looking down at her on the floor of the hole, before Wakely squatted and took off a glove and gathered a handful of dirt and tossed it onto her breast. Then he stalked away and the others began to fill the hole.

He returned after a few minutes and pitched in, and for the final minutes asked to work alone. The others stepped back and let him finish.

They divided her gear and provisions and left her rifle and ruck with what was left — clothing, brush, comb, toothbrush, on the soft mound of earth as a kind of headstone.

Wakely and Virago led them back to the alley with the dead woman and supplies, and they rummaged through the packs, collected tinned salmon, cartons of Kraft Dinner, bags of prawn crackers, jars of pickled herring, and cans of something with a Chinese label, which Tse translated uncertainly as shredded radish.

They found books, which aided their morale, until they turned out to be Christian bibles. All of them bibles. The ammunition for the AR-15 was standard NATO 5.56mm rounds, and with it they reloaded their depleted magazines. There was more than they could carry, and for their safety, and as she had with Deeks's C7, Sharpcot pulled the AR-15's firing pin, rendering it useless.

They found knives, can openers, candles, matches, flashlights, batteries, tarps, a saw, a hatchet, wire cutters, lengths of rope, duct tape, sewing supplies, a knife sharpener, a folding shovel, as well as water filters and purification tablets. There was also a compact fishing rod with line, hooks, and lures, and a Primus stove and gas cylinder. Compact nesting anodized aluminum pots, foldable cutlery, tin cups. Seeds too: squash, sunflowers, onions, spinach, tomatoes, cucumber, peas, and beans. A *Rand McNally Road Atlas*. Sharpcot fanned through it, stopped on South Dakota, ran a finger along the Missouri River to a spot where it bent in a way that matched her memory of their crossing in the log flume boats, then traced a path that went west-southwest. Somewhat arbitrarily tapped a spot, and decided it represented their location. When she looked up from the atlas, Wakely stood before her holding the folding shovel, its blade extended. He nodded to the dead woman propped against the Garfield ornaments.

"We buried her friends in glass," he said. "Should we finish?"

"I hope they would've done the same for us," she replied, and he and Tse dug a hole, not as deep as Abby's, but sufficient. Rigour mortis prevented the woman from lying flat, so they put her on her side. Wakely handed the shovel to Virago, who at first refused to accept it. He lay it at her feet and walked away, and she reluctantly picked it up and worked with Tse and Leclerc to cover the woman.

They returned to the passage with the tent trailers, headed west, checking every passage before crossing it.

They hit a wall of coins, mostly American quarters, but also coins of similar dimension, the Canadian and Bahamas quarter, Australian shilling, British shilling, Israeli 5 new sheqalim, and Euro 50-cent piece, the latter thicker than the rest. The wall was 80 metres wide, and the coins were lined up in perfect columns to maximize density.

"It smells like money," Leclerc said.

"It is money," Tse said.

"Except it's worth nothing," Wakely said. "We can't buy a goddamn thing with it."

"It's metal," Sharpcot pointed out. "And that has value."

No one answered. They went south to get around it, travelled into evening, pushed on until dark, making distance from the location of the attack. Gutted by grief. Leaving Abby behind.

They made a fireless camp, to avoid illuminating their position, and Tse took first watch, but at first no one could sleep. They talked about Abby until exhaustion carried each away. Wakely relieved Tse, stayed on through Virago's shift, letting her sleep. A fox visited, its eyes twin gemstones in the flashlight's beam. When he spoke a greeting, it loped away.

He sat watching the sky bloated with stars and thought night would never end. He'd had other certainties destroyed recently. It would not surprise him. But after a time the sky bloomed, and the sun rose, and the day began.

The days and nights warmed and they saw no more snow, but they heeded the warning and daily covered as much ground as they could while avoiding excessive fatigue or injury. They discussed weather and climate, considered how the blocks that now populated the centre of the continent reflected sunlight or held or released heat differently than the grasses and crops they now obscured. Sharpcot wondered about the sudden cease of carbon emissions from fossil fuel burning, though as Virago pointed out, feedback loops like the melting of permafrost and loss of arctic ice would likely continue to warm the climate for the foreseeable future.

"Before it settles down to where it should be," she added. "Before we fucked it up."

"You sound almost glad civilization ended," Wakely muttered to her as they travelled.

"I'm glad for the planet," she replied simply. "It's free of a brief, harmful parasite."

Wakely stopped walking momentarily when she said that, then hurried to catch up, realizing she wasn't wrong. From any perspective but our own — unmilked cows aside — our removal was a good thing. Maybe that was the Accruers' goal. Collect our mess.

It was hard to fathom areas of the planet without the maze, as day after day they passed variable objects: jars of turmeric, ornate lacquered Japanese table cabinets, kitchen colanders, jumbo slow-rising squishy toy hamburgers, Earthbound Farms–branded clamshells full of rotting organic baby arugula, wet floral foam bricks used for flower arranging, found mostly in green but also in other colours, and eye-testing refractors (Leclerc: "Phoropters." Which she clarified by quoting the optometrist, "Which is better, one, or two . . . one . . . or two?") before they passed along the north face of a block of blue jeans, which stretched 10 kilometres along its north wall and an unknown distance south. They each sized and collected a few pairs, but Sharpcot wouldn't let anyone wear them, not yet. To Wakely it seemed irrational — jeans were as good as any camouflage against this landscape of stuff.

The terrain underwent subtle changes, became increasingly variable, and after a few days they came to a region of bare hills that rose higher than the blocks assembled around them. Sparse yellow grasses matted their tops, and the section climbed the highest to take a survey, scanning the landscape to plot a route. Morning haze limited visibility, but some distance to the south stood a series of massive objects like gigantic flowers. They were dish antennae, radio telescopes, the largest one white and a hundred metres in diameter, with a scalloped edge and superstructure built on the rim to suspend the receiver above the collecting surface, others built from meshes of rusting steel atop various types of articulating platforms to aim them at the heavens, still others in the range of 40 to 70 metres with circular brick bases, windowed buildings, set intact, and then more junior dishes of 20 to 30 metres, the kind used in astronomical large arrays. And smaller still, from military installations or TV broadcasters for satellite uplinking, all standing waist-deep in a nine-storey block made from hundreds of millions of smaller antennae, from residential rooftops, designed to drink in television satellite signals.

They passed Wakely's binoculars around, each scanning, trying to discern objects that made up the surrounding blocks, mostly guessing because of the distance and the haze. Free weights? Airport x-ray machines? Wheelchairs?

They lunched on the hilltop on rice noodles they'd found earlier that day. As the afternoon cleared, Sharpcot squinted into the deep distance, then with growing astonishment climbed to her feet and requested the binoculars.

That spire she had spotted from the lighthouses, the needle of glass, stood 20 kilometres distant, distinct in the clearing day, and now apparently surrounded by other towers of inferior height, arranged as the lighthouses were, by size, with the tallest, the one she'd originally seen, standing nearest to them, at the southeast corner, then on each side and behind it, the next tallest, and on down, in a descending sweep, into the northwest and beyond the horizon. The tallest was a stepped spire, and it was flanked on both shoulders by structures about 200 metres shorter — on the left, a building with a twisted body and a curve at its top that met a vertical right angle, and on its right, a tower constructed from a grey steel mesh with a fat pod at mid-height and a smaller one two-thirds up. The other buildings, only nominally shorter, stood clustered around and beyond these three, each with its own unique features, one of them with a gigantic clock face and topped by a mast. They couldn't make out the shorter structures behind those on the outside, but they could see lined towards the north and west a long line of other buildings declining into the distance. Sharpcot scanned them with the binoculars, saying nothing. She handed the glasses to Wakely, who saw standing a few buildings to the right another tower with observation pods, a landmark from Toronto. He continued to study the structures for something recognizable, and about 10 buildings to the left he made out the iconic deco shape of the Empire State Building. He sighed and dropped the binoculars and passed them to Leclerc, who named buildings: "Burj Khalifa, Tokyo Skytree, Shanghai Tower, Canton Tower, Makkah Royal Clock Tower, CN Tower . . ."

Sharpcot stood for a long time, unmoving, looking at that block formed by all the buildings of humankind stretching into the west and north in diminishing height, dropping rapidly from the mega- and supertall city showpieces designed to express wealth and power and architectural mastery, to more quotidian structures, office towers, apartment and condo buildings, running away into the far distance, smaller and smaller, until they disappeared from view. What else constituted this block? Would it reach nine-storey apartment buildings? Eight, down to four, then houses of three and two storeys, maybe stacked atop one another to reach the standard block height, bungalows stacked nine-high. And then what? Tiny cottages, shacks, garden sheds? Dwight's house, where Lana stayed when she wasn't with Sharpcot, her mother's house in Thunder Bay, two storeys, grey brick with tattered awnings shading the windows.

It was one thing to be in the maze, seeing the products of humankind up close, like aisles in a warehouse. But to see this, the recognizable structures assembled here so competently, according to the simple rules of the maze, and the way this implied all buildings laid out here in a superblock that covered thousands of square kilometres of land. The Burj Khalifa. The CN Tower. The Empire State Building. In South Dakota.

"It really is over," Sharpcot whispered. She'd said it to herself a thousand times on this journey, and while it was always true, each utterance made it more real. And never to see Lana again, or her mother and sister and nephews or her friends. The darkness began to fall over her and she stopped it by turning to the section and saying, "What do you say?"

"To what, Sarge?" Virago asked.

"Heading over for a look."

"A look *at* them, or a look *from* them," Wakely asked.

310

"Depends on what we find when we get there. And if we can get to a high vantage, it'll help us plan our route."

They descended into the maze on the west side of the hill, empty egg cartons on the south damping the sound of their footsteps. On their opposite flank, ancient teletype machines in grey and tan and black, keyboards like teeth. Sharpcot stopped a number of times and the section followed suit while she glanced around and listened.

"What is it?" Wakely asked after the third time.

"I don't know. Nothing. Except after that firefight nothing feels the same. This all got to seem safe. But it's no longer safe."

They adopted a route of alternating westward and northward corridors, passing among items they barely had time to identify — enormous grilles of some type (building air intakes?), vinyl binders, plastic dresser handles, wooden coat hangers, outdoor ice merchandisers ("Don't forget the ice!"), power supplies in aluminum cases with heatsink fins along one face. They encountered wool sweaters, sheep's wool: traditional, ribbed, cable, bouclé knits; in various neck types and styles; white, black, grey, solid and multi-colour; in every size imaginable, from infant to giant, and in under 20 minutes of sorting they had each selected one, recognizing their value as temperatures dropped.

And then golf carts.

Tse stopped them just as they were reaching the end of these to suggest they extract one for transport.

"What's the range of a golf cart?" Sharpcot asked. "Is it worth it?"

"Full charge maybe 50 klicks," Tse said.

"Fifty would help," Sharpcot said. "Even half that would be great. Let's do it."

They chose a cart oriented with its nose to the outside, the one above set perpendicular and resting on the carts on either side of the one they selected. With considerable effort, they managed to drag it out, cracking its canopy.

The key needed to start it lay in a block elsewhere, likely the one at the Forks in Winnipeg.

"I can probably hotwire it," Leclerc said. "How hard can it be?"

"They anti-theft these things the way they do with cars," Tse said. "Maybe the high-end ones, but this guy's pretty modest."

He used his entrenching tool to bash the dashboard open and Leclerc went at the key switch, tore out the leads and experimentally touched them together in different sequences until the LED battery gauge lit up, showing a three-quarter charge. She tapped the pedal and the cart jumped forward and crashed lightly into the wall opposite, made from garden arches in wood, stone, brick, steel, trellises with filigree accents, rounded, peaked, flat-topped, black, white, orange, faux rusted, wood-stained. She twisted the leads together.

"Ready to roll," she said.

A multi-point turn would have been required to orient the cart in the narrow alley, so instead they lifted it and pivoted it to face north, loaded their gear. There was seating for four, two up front and two on the back, facing backwards.

"Jack, I want you and Virago and Leclerc in the back, cover the rear and sides. Tse, you're up front with me. Knock out that windshield so you can set the Minimi. Let's go."

Tse kicked out the plastic windshield and squeezed into the front seat, set the machine gun tripod on the cart's petite hood, while Wakely, Virago, and Leclerc crammed onto the rear-facing bench, Virago in the middle, pressed tight between each. Sharpcot tapped the pedal and the cart moved, groaning under the weight, gradually reaching its maximum speed.

"How fast are these things?" she asked Tse over the motor's laboured whine.

"I think they max out at 25 kilometres per hour. I don't know if we'll reach that. But quicker than walking."

312

"Too bad we haven't found the Ferraris," she mused. "Yet."

She kept her attention forward, the narrowness of the passage accentuating their speed. She had to keep from trying to identify objects that comprised the blocks — fluorescent vests, aquariums, ping pong tables, vacuum tubes? Bumps made the frame quake and sent everyone scrambling for handholds.

They met a T-intersection at a wall of automatic teller machines, went left and ran past them for a long while before they reached another corner and headed north. She zigged west and north, starting to fear that she'd miscalculated and they'd gone too far west when they made a northward turn and the tops of the towers appeared above a block of what looked like small shrines with murtis, all of Ganesh, the Hindu elephant god. She spied the tip of the Burj Khalifa first, and then after a moment a golden crescent on the mast of the Makkah Clock Tower and then the top of Shanghai Tower, light from the setting sun reflecting from its glass and lighting up the passageway with panels of sunshine.

In the back, Wakely sat with his rifle across his knees and his notebook on his thigh. He jotted down things he could definitively identify. The three of them glanced to their flanks each time they crossed a passageway, and sometimes they saw trees in brilliant fall colours, and once, buffalo grazing on the grass of a passage.

"We can always eat those," Wakely remarked.

"Sure. If absolutely necessary," Virago said.

"Something not processed. I feel like I'm getting scurvy or something. How would I know if I have scurvy?" He directed this question at Leclerc.

"Hair and teeth falling out," Leclerc replied.

Wakely tapped his teeth with the pencil. "So far so good," he said.

Sharpcot glanced up occasionally to watch more of the towers slide into view. They had to jig west around a block of industrial centrifuges. They reached a northbound passage with the Burj Khalifa visible in its entirety. She turned the cart and they sped up an alley sided on the right by paper lampshades and glass tube fuses on the left, as the height of the tower and its neighbours dominated the sky above. They crossed an intersection to pass a smaller block of erhu — Chinese violins — on the right and ice cube trays on the left.

The full height of the Burj came into view, its tri-lobed base sat partially encased in a glass and steel structure, with one of the lobes forming the southeast corner of the block, leaving a wide expanse of space between each of the lobes. Sharpcot steered into the grassy open and headed for a curving entrance sheltered by an awning of stainless steel and fronted by a number of thick bollards in polished black marble. To the right of the entrance stood a wide black monolith, also of black marble, on which was engraved Armani Hotel Dubai, the name repeated in Arabic script below. Sharpcot slowed and glanced at Tse, who was leaning forward with his eyes turned up to take in as much of the tower as he could, but the top was obscured by the stepped columns that formed the structure. The ground on which they drove was the usual grassy prairie they'd been walking along for the last three months. But it ended at the concrete curb that sloped in the middle to put the lip flush with the ground, presumably where it had met the driveway and offered accessibility for luggage carts, wheelchairs, strollers.

She stopped before the glass entrance doors. At first no one moved. The silence of the world was more palpable here, at the plaza before this most cosmopolitan of structures, the world's tallest building, product of peak human culture and engineering and finance. What was the bustle like at this entrance, valets racing to attend to Lamborghinis and Land Rovers, limousines drawing up to release their wealthy guests briefly into Dubai's staggering heat before they promenaded

314

through the entrance into a civilized, air-conditioned chill? This structure relocated intact by an act of incomprehensible aptitude and now standing here on dry, cold prairie as night fell on an autumn evening.

Sharpcot stepped out and stayed close to the cart, glancing about with her gun levelled. She shivered but not from cold — she felt desperately nervous. Standing beneath the tallest tower on Earth. She looked at the glass around the entrance and saw her reflection and the reflection of the golf cart with its beleaguered occupants. Saw Wakely dutifully step out to provide cover, with Leclerc and Virago following. Saw the wall behind them, ice cube trays mostly in white and blue and a few in more exotic tones, red and orange and green.

She cast her eyes up, studying the lower parts of the hotel and tower, looking for the smallest mark or mar, a cracked window pane, a bent or missing spar, but except for dust and water stains on the glass from the prairie weather, all appeared perfectly intact. It engulfed her in a wave of hopelessness, if one considered the Accruers as adversary, which she very much did. If they could move this building, they were by all human standards ridiculously advanced and infallible. If her soldiers by some circumstance encountered them — and irrationally she thought they must be lodging here, in this prime structure, enjoying the luxuries of those they had conquered — there'd be no contest. Which seemed obvious, considering all the Accruers had done to the world, having defeated with apparently no effort — she thought of the warships and warplanes they'd discovered gently ensconced in their respective blocks — even the mighty and paranoid Americans, what were five weary, heartbroken soldiers?

"Boss?" Wakely said, and she knew it was his second attempt to get her attention.

"Yeah," she replied. "Let's go in."

She stepped up the curb and approached the front door, her reflection coming up to meet her. The handle she reached

315

for was comprised of four peaked arches, split across the pair of doors. She expected it to be locked, but it wasn't. The door opened smoothly. She went through and walked purposefully into the centre of the lobby, the section falling in behind. The space was empty but had clearly been populated by furniture and art. There were steel posts in a dark brown hue that arched overhead and met above and beyond them a hallway on which were signs that read Armani Residences Dubai on the left and Armani Hotel Dubai on the right. It was all dark wood and marble. There was something drab about the space, and then she realized it was designed to benefit from accent lighting. There was no light except what came from the doors behind them and the high windows above. The hallway before them dark. Silence oppressive.

She moved boldly down the hallway, the collective thump of army boots echoing. They reached the elevators, one of which stood open. Sharpcot got out a flashlight and shined it around inside.

"Fancy," she said. "Let's find the stairs."

"You want to do this now, Sarge?" Wakely asked. "Climb to the top?"

"Not the top, but let's get out of this lobby. We'll go up a few levels and spend the night on or close to one of the terraces, keep a lookout."

They went through various doors and open areas that had once contained opulent furnishings but were now vacant. Tse said it looked like the place was for rent.

They passed through corridors and lobbies, all of them empty and frosted with dust, came to the residential lobby and an art display made up of cymbals on long posts set in shallow pools filled with murky water, some with green slime coating the once-pristine tiles. Sharpcot wondered if they had been full during transport, if this was Dubai water.

No one spoke as they checked doors, searching for a staircase. They found one but it took them only a few floors up. They found themselves on a level with hotel rooms when Leclerc suddenly needed a bathroom.

Tse kicked in one of the room doors and she went inside and the section waited in the hallway. They looked at each other when they heard a toilet flush. She came out smiling shyly.

"It was a real toilet! I'd forgotten how amazing it is to use a real toilet."

"What, I want to go now," Virago said.

Leclerc held her back from going into the room. "There was only one flush. The reservoir is empty."

"Then I won't flush. I don't care, I just want to go without pissing on my boots."

"Why don't we bust open a bunch of rooms," Wakely suggested. "Everyone can have their own toilet, plus one flush." He went to the next door in the corridor and with a few kicks broke it in and flagged Virago inside. Then he went to the next door and did the same, while Tse kicked in another. Soon there were five busted doors and five flushed toilets.

"If only there was toilet paper," Sharpcot said when she came out. "And running water."

"God, if the showers worked," Leclerc said.

"You tried it, didn't you?" Tse asked.

"Well, it's reasonable. If there's water in the fountains, there's water in the pipes. And that would mean a considerable volume of water in floors above us. It was worth a shot. I got only a handful of water, but there was something nostalgic and satisfying about it coming out of the tap. Turn a valve, get water. Remember that?"

They spent time exploring different levels, took in the view from windows, could see from the southeast corner the way they'd come and to the west, the direction they had yet to travel.

The place was opulent, featuring unfettered use of premium wood and steel and glass and marble, but without furniture, without people, it felt like a mausoleum.

While many of the floors took in a generous amount of

natural light — only the staircases and some hallways required flashlights — the setting of the sun made navigation and investigation more challenging, and when they reached a lobby on the 43rd floor they halted for the night. The level held residences, and then they discovered a spa area that included a small pool full of saltwater, fresh and clear compared to the ground floor fountains, plus doors to an outdoor terrace that faced northwest and on which there were a couple of smaller pools. It offered a northwest view, which consisted of the 43rd level of the buildings that filled the block behind the Burj, standing uncomfortably close. They looked up but could still not view the Burj's spire due to the building's tiered design. They went inside to the residences and bashed in a few doors and found spacious luxury apartments with divots in the carpet where furniture once stood, high-end dishwashers and built-in fridges — empty, and they didn't even smell, so thorough had been their evacuation — cooktops and ovens, marble countertops. Cupboards bare.

But they'd come for the view, already comprehensive at this height. After some study Sharpcot spotted through binoculars the hilltop where they'd seen the towers, and made out what was probably the tallest standing portion of the perfume block. She panned to the dish antenna block, saw outcrops further south that were similarly oversized structures of indeterminate material. From here the configuration of the maze, which they'd glimpsed briefly with the drone, was apparent: corridors rigidly aligned in a north-south and east-west grid, and planned with exquisite care to ensure that each block fit together while maintaining four-way intersections wherever possible.

Leclerc posited that the Accruers' dedication to maintaining this arrangement explained the apparent randomness of the blocks; they placed blocks not to group related items together — say, iron cookpots with iron woks and iron flying pans — but to accommodate an algorithm to sustain the pattern.

Sharpcot looked around the apartment, registering what was here and what wasn't, trying to understand the method of the Accruers. She began to move through the place, a large two-bedroom, probably worth millions not for just its address and view, but the fineness of the finishing — wood cabinetry and accents, exotic timber floors and skirting, and floor-to-ceiling panoramic windows. It had three bathrooms — a powder room, a smaller washroom, and an ensuite with two sinks, an oval tub, a toilet, and a bidet. She stood in the doorway looking at the fixtures. These had been left in the building because they were part of its structure. As were the light dimmers, outlets, faucets, and appliances such as dishwasher and cooktop. But there was no toaster, not on the countertop or in a cupboard — if there had been one, it was removed and now constituted the toaster "quarry" they'd encountered in Manitoba.

To put it plainly, fixed items — things that were screwed, glued, or bolted in place — were considered part of the primary object. Now she understood the relatively small scale of the toilet block they'd encountered atop the bunker: it represented uninstalled units only, from store showrooms and warehouses and landfill. The rest remained installed in their respective buildings, within the Burj Khalifa and all those that swept away to the north and west of it. Anything moveable — small appliances and dishes and cutlery and foodstuffs and furniture and clothing and books and knickknacks and electronics — everything you'd box up and take away when you move — all that had been collected and distributed to its corresponding block. For all its logistical complexity, the intent was devastatingly simple.

She saw something on the bathroom mirror, stepped with her boots on the tile floor and approached, squinting in the dying light which barely lit this room through its open doorway. She found her flashlight and lit it, saw a lipstick mouthprint on the glass, where someone had kissed it. A playful gesture, maybe a lover's farewell? The lipstick from a tube that lay in a nine-storey block they'd passed weeks ago near the Canada-U.S. border.

"Boss?" Wakely asked, breaking her reverie.

She clicked off the flashlight and turned.

"What is it, Jack?"

"Wondering if you're hungry. And if you want to take a dip in the pool."

In the morning, they climbed. Walking had made them strong, but not for this. Climbing stairs taxed an alternative set of muscles, already sapped by the previous day's 43-storey ascent. They'd slept hard and deep after bathing in the pool, leaving the water considerably dirtier than they found it, then each taking an apartment and rolling out their pads, waking at dawn with the first sunlight filling the rooms long before it touched the blocks below. They'd breakfasted, then found a stairwell that would take them up.

"My skin's all creaky from that salt pool," Virago said, flexing her arms.

"I rinsed in my room's shower," Leclerc said. "I got about two minutes of cold water from the pipes. I was right, they stored water in tanks to sustain water pressure."

They reached another lobby and fitness area on the 76th floor, found another swimming pool, this one with apertures at water level to allow swimmers to pass freely inside and outside. The building tapered in a stepped pattern as it rose, with diminishing floorspace as they climbed. They rested briefly, taking in the view, before they resumed their ascent. They reached the next lobby on the 122nd floor and explored a restaurant, At.mosphere, its large kitchen area, serving stations, glass partitions separating dining areas from walkways, artistic light fixtures, elegant, curved bar, and built-in couches before which tables once stood. The paths of servers worn into the dark carpet.

Sharpcot went to the glass and looked out. The day was perfectly clear and the horizon lay 75 kilometres away, and it was possible to make out from this height a variance in the flatness of the landscape. To the distant south, high, bare hills.

They climbed a staircase from the restaurant level that followed the curve of the glass, went up a few levels before they had to resort to internal staircases.

They reached the official observation deck at level 154, spilled onto a terrace domed by the vast sky and buffeted by a frigid wind. They stood eye-to-eye with the tops of many of the towers, which filled an arc from west to north. The Shanghai Tower entirely obstructed their view north.

"Most of the other towers are just masts at this point, to make them taller," Virago noted. "Cheating."

Leclerc wondered how when winter arrived the building would perform, considering it had been built for the high ambient temperatures of the desert, then mentioned in passing that it shouldn't even be able to stand.

"What do you mean?" Virago asked.

"Who's even to say the ground here is suitable to sustain a building like this. Let alone all the ones around it. Every one of these structures has some kind of specialized foundation catered to the ground in which they were constructed. Did the foundations come with them, or are these things sitting flush against the Earth?"

"So what are you really saying?" Tse wanted to know.

"Something is holding these buildings up. Keeping them from toppling like dominoes. Probably the force that maintains the integrity of blocks. But stronger."

They looked at each other uneasily.

"You want to keep going up?" Wakely asked Sharpcot.

"No point climbing Everest and missing the summit."

They went inside and passed through the observation area, noted at the glass a number of stainless steel consoles on pedestals, which they concluded were digital telescopes of some kind, useless without power. They busted through a fire door into a stairwell and went up a few more storeys, entered a mechanical room with no windows, and went back down a couple of floors until they reached a floor with a small office and windows. The extra height contributed little to the view, so they returned to the public observation level, from where they took up a position looking southwest, the narrow top of the Tokyo Skytree and beyond it the mast and crescent rising from the Makkah Clock Tower followed by the Shanghai World Financial Centre, topped by a trapezoidal aperture that made it look like an enormous can opener, partially obscuring the full westward view.

Wakely and Sharpcot went outside and scanned the landscape, Wakely taking notes and making tiny sketches of the route and identifiable block contents nearby in his notebook, until they remembered the road atlas they'd found among prepper's supplies. They used it to try to orient their location. A green cluster of hills 60 kilometres to the south may have been the Black Hills. If they decided to go that way, they could discover a cliff face on which the presidents of Mount Rushmore either remained, or had been sliced clean and carted off by the Accruers.

As they scanned the landscape, they identified larger objects: a big block of helicopters lay about four kilometres west-southwest of their location; another block made up of combine harvesters, further to the south; farm silos, a lot of them, a long way off to the southwest and covering a vast area. The occasional superblock rising above the lower ones. One on the horizon might be Ferris wheels — arranged with the largest to the south and smaller ones as the block progressed northward. The London Eye. Las Vegas's High Roller. Another block far to the southeast might've been power plant cooling towers. Wakely wondered again, as they had at the ships, where the world's nuclear reactors lay, and in what state. Had they been safely shut down, or brutally severed from their cooling pipes and control systems, conveyed to a spot where even now they were melting down, spewing radioactivity into the environment? He should probably check the dosimeter's batteries.

Virago, Leclerc, and Tse meanwhile walked the perimeter, taking in the view of the world's tallest buildings at close range.

The CN Tower from Toronto, iconic, was mostly obscured by the mildly corkscrewed bulk of Shanghai Tower, and they could make out just behind it what Leclerc said was One World Trade Centre, built on the site of the Twin Towers. Next to it, the bridged Petronas Towers pair from Kuala Lumpur, and behind them, the black stepped block of the Willis Tower from Chicago. There were skyscrapers halted in mid-construction to the northwest, cranes still in place, one with a load of girders suspended from its cable, which spun idly in the wind. The view that progressed beyond was a nauseating slope of progressively shorter buildings stretching away to the horizon. Tse pointed out the Empire State Building nestled among the skyscrapers and spires, half as tall as the structure in which they stood.

"This is so fucked up," Virago said.

"Totally fucked up," Leclerc said.

"Fucked up," Tse added.

They remained silent for a long time, looking at the buildings. Virago took slow, mindful breaths, trying to keep her mind from wandering back to her friend, her sister, Abigail Deeks, poor Abby, lying cold and dead in a grave down there on the prairie. A local grief against the enormous sorrow of lost civilization. The end of everything she knew. Looking out at the glittering structures, she let herself pretend she inhabited a futuristic city of supertall buildings that stood shoulder-to-shoulder. They were full of people, tens of thousands, busy at their desks on this autumn afternoon, or some at home sleeping or reading or caring for children, playing with their cats, others working out in gyms, or shopping in boutiques, dining in restaurants. Like in a film, a science fiction film of the future, utopian Earth. But thinking about films reminded her there were no more films, there would never be films again, that the films made were all that humanity would ever make, and they were still out there, in film cans, on DVDs and Blu-ray discs and VHS and Betamax cassettes, on laser discs, on hard disks, stored on laptops and phones and the entertainment centres of commercial aircraft to be watched in-flight.

All the actors, crew, composers, producers, directors of those films — gone? Why were the people gone? Where had the people gone? It was the first question they'd asked when they became aware of the situation. They were always here, up ahead, and they would soon find them, if they travelled to Shilo, if they travelled to Winnipeg, they would find them all, waiting. The lost billions.

And she suddenly imagined a block made of bodies. Of all the bodies of humankind stacked naked like cordwood. A rotting mass. Like a holocaust horror, human bodies like trash, row-upon-row. The people she'd known, she'd loved, who'd loved her, siblings and friends and boyfriends and acquaintances and hook-ups and random people in movie theatres and malls and passing in the street and dancing in clubs and swimming in lakes and cheering at music festivals and sitting row-upon-row in classroom lectures, taking notes, listening, learning. And those who'd given her life, her parents, her grandparents. And she could not resist the inevitable thought that intruded, that she could not force back, could not refuse to conceptualize, to visualize, no matter how hard she tried: how big was that block? Nine storeys tall, and how much on each dimension? Realizing it had been her fear all along, every step she took every day, whenever a new intersection appeared, terrified that this would be it, the block of the dead. All the blocks were built from what humans had made, and weren't we all made by humans? Knowing she wasn't alone in this fear, that it ran through everyone's mind — where were the people? I hope we find the people. And oh god I hope we do not find the people.

"Adonia?" Leclerc asked, touching her elbow.

Virago turned her tear-stained face to Leclerc and tried to speak, but instead fell into Leclerc's arms and bawled, slowly collapsing, sliding down, her rifle clattering to the wood planking as she fell to her knees and Leclerc gripped her and cried. Tse standing helpless before the two clutching women as they cried for everything lost.

Virago felt other arms around her and lifted her face and saw Wakely there pulling her and Leclerc tightly against him, and Sharpcot was there too gripping them, and Tse moved in, towering above them all, circling the group in his powerful arms.

The clutch lasted an indeterminate amount of time, and was broken when a squall of wind tore across the terrace and the whole building quaked, changing sorrow into panic, and the circle broke and everyone stepped back suddenly ashamed of the rawness of their grief and possibly relieved to face the less vulnerable feeling of fear.

"Let's get out of here," Sharpcot said, and they collected their things and made for the staircase.

14

They emerged into the residential lobby with the cymbal art and pools of rancid water, made their way to the hotel lobby and were about to push through the doors when Wakely called a halt and ordered everyone down.

"What's up, Jack?" Sharpcot asked from a squat.

He nodded outside. "Golf cart is gone."

Sharpcot looked through the glass and suffered a cold slam of fear.

"Goddamn it. Let's get closer to the wall."

They backed to a position further from the doors and everyone looked around both inside the lobby and through the glass to the plaza.

"Someone is fucking with us," Sharpcot muttered.

"Or maybe just took the cart," Leclerc said.

"It means we are not alone. Some preppers got away."

"Might be a whole other group," Tse suggested.

"How likely that we see no one for months and encounter two different groups within 40 clicks of one another?" Sharpcot hissed. "They followed us here."

"Probably right," Wakely said. "But now what? You want me to go outside and scout around?"

"No," she said quickly.

"So we spend the rest of our lives here?" he asked.

"You're out of line, Jack," she snapped.

"Sorry, Sarge. You're right. But we need to do something. Up to a higher floor and scout? If they've set up an ambush we could spot it from above."

They went up to one of the low terraces of the hotel, first had everyone scope the windows of the neighbouring buildings — while Tokyo Sky Tree on the west was fairly easy, its mesh steel construction offering few concealed positions, Shanghai Tower on the north was problematic in that thousands of clear windows populated its spiral body for hundreds of metres above them. However, light pouring through its lower section around the inner core aided spotting, and after a few minutes the section moved on to the railing and scanned the intersection in all directions.

"Looks clear," Wakely said.

"So who took our cart? And where did they go?" Sharpcot wondered.

"Won't get far on the charge that was left," Tse said.

"Tall grass here," Wakely said. "We can probably track them."

"Do we want to? Or steer clear?" Sharpcot wondered.

"We should figure out who we're dealing with. Better we find them than they find us."

"Which they did already," Sharpcot reminded him. "And now they're trying to lure us in."

They returned to ground level and emerged warily from the lobby, alert and twitchy. After checking every angle and nook, they stood looking at the flattened grass where the cart had stood. Sharpcot could see the subtle bias of the grass where the tires had passed and the blades had sprung back, leaving a faint path to this spot and a more pronounced footprint where the cart had rested overnight. The path resumed towards the west, fresher, its departure recent, and they followed it past the base of the Sky Tree, then the massive Makkah Clock Tower, Shanghai World Financial Centre, the silver-glassed

International Commerce Centre. Like a narrow city street sided on the left by a nine-storey building — made from ice cube trays — facing a wall of the tallest structures ever built, declining in height, disappearing into the forever.

They followed the cart's trail into the next southbound passage. Sharpcot was glad to escape the buildings and their rich sniping positions. Ice cube trays ended, facing handheld electronic testers, likely telephone line test sets. They went south until the next intersection — polarized glasses of the type they hand out at 3D films, across from specimen jars on the left, all containing formaldehyde (strong scent) and human fetuses at various stages of gestation. Not a huge block, but startling and macabre. The cart's imprint went west here, now parallel to the buildings but with the block of phone testers between. The next intersection with curling stones on the right and handheld nets — for fishing, bug, and butterfly catching — on the left. They grabbed a few to supplement the fishing rod they'd acquired from the preppers' stash.

As they walked Tse asked Wakely if observations from the tower had revealed a favourable western route, and what of interest they'd spotted.

"Buildings went on as far as we could see to the west, which makes sense if these are all the buildings in the world," Wakely said. "So there's no going north anytime soon. Not through a passage." He imagined them travelling building-to-building, stepping from an apartment balcony onto the terrace of a neighbouring condo. "Which is fine," he continued. "We're heading west and slightly south in the hopes we can stay south of the Rockies but north of the Uinta Mountains, get to the top of Utah, and make our way along the salt flats."

"You think the maze will run out at some point?"

"We've already seen that hilltops are clear, and they don't build where there are trees. When the prairies end we'll run into forests and foothills and mountains. Pretty sure it's just going to be land returned to its natural state."

"And are there blocks past the mountains? Or is everything in the prairies?"

Leclerc, who had been listening, said, "If they filled the prairies at this density, there's nothing left."

Tse thought about this. "So if we went to the Australian outback or to Germany or the Sahara, it would be empty? Everything is here?"

"In theory," Leclerc said.

"And nothing past the mountains? On the coast?"

"Trees and ocean," Leclerc said.

"Hmm," Tse replied. "Sounds kinda nice."

"It'll be hard," Leclerc said. "We have to build shelters, hunt, trap, fish, collect berries."

"We got a cache of seeds from the dead preppers," Wakely stated.

"And then repopulate," Leclerc said.

Tse didn't say anything to that, and neither did Wakely. They were approaching another intersection and had to tighten up, cover one another as they checked the north-south passageway before crossing it. Stethoscopes on the right, T-squares on the left. And soon, another intersection, laundry and dishwasher soap pods, the block melting from rainfall and a soapy residue in the earth of the surrounding passages stinking of lavender joy, wildflower and waterfall, spring meadow, ocean mist. Dollhouses opposite: small and big, plastic and wood, ancient and modern, Little Tikes and Fisher-Price, handbuilt, manufactured, some turned outward showing astonishing facades with verandahs and gingerbread scrollwork, belvederes, mansard roofs, turned spandrels, corbels, all empty of dolls and furniture, those items to be found in blocks elsewhere, the tiny side tables and canopied cribs and ironing boards and tea service sets and armoires, hadn't they already seen dollhouse armoires? Each in their own block somewhere in the middle of the continent.

A wind shot in from the north and cut at them every time they crossed a passage. Wakely mentioned that from their observations in the tower they expected helicopters to appear a block or two further south, and Tse stopped and put a hand on Wakely's shoulder.

"Helicopters? For sure?" he asked.

"Pretty sure."

"What's the hold up?" Sharpcot asked, turning back and approaching.

"Sergeant, you know I can probably fly a helicopter."

"No," Sharpcot replied. "I did not know that. And what do you mean 'probably'?"

"My Aunt Solina in Hong Kong flies. In the early 90s she was a pilot in the Royal Hong Kong Auxiliary Force. Now she owns a company that trains pilots for tour companies. I spent a summer two years ago with her and she would take me flying. She let me fly."

"That doesn't sound like probably," Sharpcot stated.

"I mean fly a lot. I have almost 100 hours in a Bell Global-Ranger," he said.

"Okay, that's not nothing. Go on."

"If we find one with fuel we could take weeks off our travel."

"Plus we could survey for stuff we need," Wakely said. "Rather than happening across things. We need to find something new to eat."

"Sounds ambitious," Sharpcot said. "But I like the idea of taking a big hop west. That cold wind is a warning. Which way, Jack?"

He squatted to study the grass. "South here." They scoped the passage clear and headed down it.

They crossed two intersections and passed between vegetable spiralizers and darts of varying sizes, from pub darts to lawn darts, the passage obstructed by a block they'd spotted from the tower, very big, and now they saw why: office dividers and partitions for cubicles. They moved west again, along a nine-storey wall of soft grey and beige and black panels in steel frames, the industrial-grade fabric absorbing sound and muffling their footsteps, while on the right they passed a surprisingly large block of wired earbuds mostly in black and white and grey, with other colours thrown in, rose gold, yellow, blue, red, green; Apple, Sony, Samsung, Panasonic, Skullcandy, Shure, Sennheiser, JBL, Bose, and dozens of lesser brands. They ended at a block of braided poufs — overstuffed foot rests.

Tse walked in a daze, nervous at the prospect of the helicopters, imagining himself at the controls with no one to guide him, without stern instruction from Aunt Solina, who demanded precision and discipline, reminding him that every pilot-error crash came as a result of a brief deviation from attention and protocol. He reviewed what he knew, visualized the controls and their operation, tried to predict the state of the block, fearful that once they climbed it they would not be able to free one. What make and model, how old, what condition, how much fuel, and after all that, would he be able to fly it?

He abruptly found himself thrown forward, came down hard on his C9, the impact broken by his armour, but winding him nevertheless. He turned to look and saw Sharpcot on the ground beside him, hand still on his back. He was about ask what was happening when she silenced him and nodded ahead. The nose of the golf cart projected from the passageway where the office partitions ended, about three hundred metres away. He rolled off the gun and unfolded the bipod and centred the cart in the sight.

Sharpcot glanced back to make sure the rest of the section lay flat. Wakely crawled up beside her and put his eye to his scope, "Looks like a girl. Wearing a . . . well it looks like a hijab. She's holding something."

Sharpcot was looking through her own scope. "Another kid. Little one. A toddler."

"Jesus Christ," Wakely said. He rolled to the passage's right side, closer to the wall of poufs, still sighting down his rifle, to try to get a view beyond the cart. "Clear past it. But we can't see what's in the cross passage. Could be a trap."

"Clearly it's a trap," Sharpcot replied.

"Moving up." He made a low dash a dozen metres forward and dropped.

Sharpcot told Virago and Leclerc to cover the eastern approach, protect their rear. They were 60 metres past the previous intersection.

Sharpcot watched Wakely make quick sprints up the passage, drop, rise again. She was about to call out when he rose to his feet and went on in a crouched position, alert with his rifle covering the cart, skimming along the pouf wall. He glanced back once and continued towards the cart. The poufs ended and he sighted up the new righthand alley before crossing it. The new block: prosthetic arms. He wondered vaguely how these had been acquired from their owners. Then thought back to hearing aids, contacts lenses, wedding rings, and wondered the same of those. Poor thoughts to entertain while springing a trap.

He got to within 50 metres of the cart, dropped to one knee and with the rifle at his shoulder, its barrel trained a few metres to the right of the cart, called out, "Hey."

The girl sat looking at him but did not reply. But the toddler sat up to gaze over the dashboard, lifted a hand and waggled it in an awkward wave.

"Who's down the passage. Behind you?" he asked in a friendly tone.

"Nobody," the girl replied. She had dark eyes and an olive complexion. The toddler she clutched was black, with curly hair and wide, wild eyes.

"Are those cheese graters?"

The girl glanced at the wall behind her.

"I guess they are," she replied.

He kept his eyes fixed on her, trying to read her expression, while in his peripheral noted the approach of the rest of the section. He eyed the tops of the blocks to ensure they were clear, then stepping sideways arrived at the corner of the arms.

He looked at the girl, and her eyes shifted to the passage into which he was about to step. She seemed about to speak when he was swatted across his helmet by a prosthetic arm. He managed to block a second blow with his rifle, knocking the arm to the ground, but then his attacker — also a girl, older than the first, curled under him and drove forward. He briefly apprehended in her fist an enormous hunting knife before she jabbed it into his chest. The blade glanced off his armour plate, bending the girl's wrist so she cried out, but she didn't yield, instead came up with it, slicing towards his face. He drew his chin back and at the same time swung his rifle around and caught her against the hip. She let out a gasp and dropped the knife and stepped back with one hand raised, the other rubbing her side.

He stood looking at her. She was tall, Latine, wore a pair of thick-rimmed glasses, and the look on her face was not rage, but confusion. She was about the age of the Afghan boy with the artillery shell. It was not an insignificant observation as he stood there with his rifle trained at her chest.

"Hello," he stated, trying to steady his voice. "I'm Dorian."

Sharpcot arrived, along with the rest of the section. They spilled into the crossroads, checking each approach. Tse told the girl to get out of the cart.

"How many are you?" Sharpcot demanded as she bent to retrieve the knife.

"As you see," the tall girl replied.

"What's your name?"

The girl turned her head away.

"I'm Elsie," Sharpcot said.

"Tried that," Wakely said. "Nicely, you know. First names."

"I'm Sergeant Elisabeth Sharpcot, Three Section of Two Platoon of Bravo Company of the Second Battalion of the Princess Patricia's Canadian Light Infantry."

"You're Canadian?" the girl asked.

Wakely turned his shoulder to show the muted Canada flag patch.

"Why is that funny?" Sharpcot asked.

The girl shrugged. The little one started crying and Sharpcot turned to see that Virago had taken the child from the first girl to allow Leclerc to frisk her. The girl stood patiently while Leclerc cautiously patted her down.

Sharpcot handed Wakely her rifle and pivoted the older girl to the wall and frisked her. "Why didn't you use this?" she asked the girl, holding up a Glock she pulled from the girl's waistband.

"No bullets."

Sharpcot handed the pistol to Wakely who dropped the magazine while Sharpcot continued to frisk, came up with a small switchblade, a bag of M&Ms which when she squeezed found contained only one candy, a compass, a beaded necklace. She handed all but the switchblade back to the girl.

"Yolanda," the girl said quietly.

"What?" Sharpcot asked.

"My name is Yolanda."

"Elsie."

"So you said."

Sharpcot thought for a moment, then handed the switchblade back to the girl. "Just don't kill us."

"What about the big knife?" Yolanda asked.

"Don't push it."

Sharpcot went to the others. The toddler was still crying, and Leclerc had a handful of items she'd found on the other girl: hair clips, some smooth stones, a pocketknife.

"Can you, uh, do you know what to do with this?" Virago asked, holding out the kid to Sharpcot.

"Just put him down. He's old enough to stand."

Virago set the child tentatively on the ground and the crying diminished to a blubber. Sharpcot kneeled in front of the kid. "Hi. I'm Elsie. What's your name?" she asked.

The child looked to the other girl, then to Yolanda, who had come over with Wakely. Yolanda nodded encouragingly and the kid spat out his name: "Ike."

"Ike? Hey, Ike," Sharpcot said. "Are you hungry?" The boy wore a dirty hoodie, with a blue rubber star attached to one of the hood strings, on which he chewed. He nodded emphatically, and Sharpcot regarded the girls and saw the same was true for them.

"When did you last eat?" she asked the girl in the hijab, who was in her mid-teens. She looked to Yolanda.

"Three days?" Yolanda said. "What do you say, Nasim?"

"More like four," Nasim said.

"We have food we can share. I'm Elsie. That there's Dorian. Adonia, Cheree, and Che Yat."

"Call me Owen, if that's easier."

"Che Yat," Ike said, pointing at Tse.

"Are you the captain?" Nasim asked.

"Not quite. Sergeant," Sharpcot replied, pulling off her ruck and going through it.

"But you're in charge?" Yolanda asked, scrutinizing the other soldiers. "Nice."

Wakely threw off his pack and squatted beside Sharpcot. "Come on," she said, inviting Nasim and Yolanda to kneel with them in the grass. Yolanda stepped towards the cart and was reaching for a small backpack in the seat when Tse intercepted her, grabbed the pack. He looked at Sharpcot who said, "Let her bring it." Tse handed it over and Yolanda sat beside Sharpcot and the others came and sat in a circle. Yolanda set the backpack on the ground and rifled through it, extracting a sketchpad of scribbles and drawings, crayons and markers, a couple of Hot Wheels, a round tin containing a card game. She pulled out a box of breath mints, and a flattened prawn chip bag. Sharpcot put a hand on the girl's arm, turned to her own pack and got out her own bag of the same brand of prawn chips, which they'd found among the prepper supplies.

"Yeah, those are disgusting," Yolanda said. "Also: you killed our parents."

Sharpcot blinked a couple of times and looked at each of the girls. Nasim was staring at a spot on the ground, but Yolanda boldly met her eye.

"Look, if they hadn't ambushed us . . ." Wakely started to say, but Sharpcot cut him off with a raised hand.

"So you were with them," Sharpcot said. "And you followed us." She waited for Yolanda and Nasim to nod before she continued. "I'm sorry all that happened. They took us by surprise and we did what we had to do. We defended ourselves. We would've been happy to join with your group if they'd approached us peacefully."

"They would never do that," Yolanda said. "They said you're government. Can't be trusted."

"We're just people. And we lost someone in that fight too. Our friend, Abigail Deeks. Abby."

"We're sorry for that," Nasim said.

Everyone was silent a moment, and when Yolanda tried to speak again she instead began to cry. Sharpcot patted her arm awkwardly, and when she looked she saw Nasim was also crying, but in a measured, controlled way, arms clamped to her sides and head lowered, silently quaking as tears fell in her lap. Ike sat gnawing the plastic star, looking from one girl to the other. When Sharpcot glanced across the circle she saw Virago wipe her eye. No one moved, as if waiting for a dangerous beast to pass, fearful they would rouse its ire.

Ike broke the spell by struggling to his feet and reeling towards Sharpcot. He squatted and put a hand on her boot and said, "Hungry."

"You're hungry, little one?" Sharpcot asked kindly, drawing her ruck close and digging around until she came up with a bag of pretzel sticks. She tore it open, and handed him one, which he jammed in his mouth. "Careful," she said as he chewed while fishing his hand in the bag for more. Yolanda sat up and went

336

into her pack and pulled out a sippy cup and handed it to Ike, who drank and ate pretzels. Yolanda leaned in and took a few for herself. Virago came up with more bags, handed them to Nasim and Yolanda. They tore them open and ate.

"These are incredible," Yolanda said as she chewed. "Oh my god I hope we're not pigs."

"Don't worry about it," Virago said.

"So we are? We are pigs?" Yolanda laughed. "Oh well."

The soldiers opened their kits and produced other items: beef sticks, a last can of lobster meat, noodles — which Wakely boiled for them on the Primus stove — as well as raspberries and blueberries, which though past their prime were appreciated.

"Fresh fruit," Nasim said wistfully, watching Ike pluck berries from Virago's hand. She sat in the grass very straight, with her legs turned to the side, and met no one's eye. She might be 15, not much younger than Yolanda, who when asked said she was almost 17.

"What have you been eating? I mean with your . . . group?" Sharpcot asked.

"We ran out of most of the shelter supplies about three weeks ago," Yolanda explained, slurping noodles from a tin cup. "So stuff we find in the grid."

"You were in a bunker," Leclerc said. "Like us. When they came."

"They? You mean the aliens? The Hoarder Horde?" Yolanda said.

"We call them the Accruers," Virago said.

"Your name's better," Yolanda replied. "Hoarder Horde sounds like a bad 70s band. Gentle Christian came up with it."

"Who?"

"Our 'dad,'" she said, with air quotes.

"His name was 'Gentle Christian'?" Wakely asked.

"It's what he called himself," Nasim said. "His made-up name."

337

Wakely thought about the bearded man he'd shot in the throat. Gentle Christian blasting away at them with an AR-15.

"Oh, and my name's 'Blessed'?" Yolanda said. "Blessed Christian. Pleased to meet you."

"They wouldn't let us use our real names," Nasim said. "But that didn't stop us, behind their backs. I was 'Cherished.' Ikemba here was 'Noble.'"

The boy looked up at the sound of his names. Real and imposed.

"And then there was Gabriel," Yolanda said.

"Who was that?" Sharpcot asked.

"The dog. He was named after an angel. But us kids gave him the nickname 'Bub' and the grownups didn't figure out why. For Beelzebub. Because he was a devil."

"What do you mean they wouldn't let you use your real names?" Sharpcot asked. "Would they hurt you?"

Nasim and Yolanda looked at each other. Nasim shrugged.

"Those weren't Christians," Tse muttered. "That's not Christian."

"And your mother?" Sharpcot asked, then added air quotes.

"Oh, that would be Chaste," Yolanda laughed. "Chaste Christian. Which explains their reliance on international adoption to create a 'family.'" She added quotes for the last word.

"So who all were they?" Sharpcot asked. "In your group."

"Other than the three of us," Yolanda explained, "Gentle and Chaste Christian, Gentle's brother, Righteous, his wife Purity, as well as her sister Modesty and her husband Beneficent."

Sharpcot watched Nasim as Yolanda listed the family, her eyes narrowing and head sagging, and then a shudder when she reached the last name, Beneficent.

"Not so beneficent," Sharpcot said.

"No," Nasim said. "No, no. But. Well, he is dead now, isn't he."

Wakely wondered if this was the man who'd popped off a shot that hit Sharpcot's armour before they saw him buried by perfume bottles. Beneficent Christian.

Sharpcot had to resist the urge to keep moving, to set off, and drag the kids along if they wanted to come, leave them behind if they didn't.

The kids' previous nights of fearful, fitful sleep had taken a toll, and after eating they begged for rest. When Sharpcot agreed they pulled from a large backpack stashed in the rear of the cart a trio of high-tech sleeping bags. Yolanda saw Sharpcot's curiosity about the pack and offered it for inspection.

While they slept, Sharpcot knelt a distance away and unpacked it. She discovered for each child: sweats, tops, leggings, rain gear, warm but light coats. Good mittens and toques. They were better-equipped for cold than the soldiers. She regretted that they hadn't discovered the survivalists' primary cache, now buried beneath perfume.

She spread on the ground a small button-up shirt for Ikemba, certain it would not fit him for long. But Nasim was petite, which meant Ike could transition to some of her wardrobe when the time came. She sat back at the thought, breathless at the abruptness of the new situation. Planning a future.

She gazed at the sleeping kids. Nasim was snoring lightly, until she turned onto her side and sighed. Yolanda muttered, then cried out, "Déjame en paz!" Ike kept opening his eyes and gazing about before shutting them.

"I guess they're coming with us?" Wakely asked softly, crouching beside her. He examined the clothing, lifted one of the coats.

"It's up to them."

"They won't survive alone."

"That Yolanda almost took you out with a plastic arm and a hunting knife."

Wakely fingered the hole in his TAC vest where the knife had punched through to his armour. "True. And they did a hell of a job tracking us," Wakely admitted. "They came all that way behind us, right to the Burj, on foot, and we didn't know it."

"They might even be an asset," Sharpcot said. "Though we need to recognize and honour their trauma. What they've been through: adoption, then the end of the world, followed by the violent deaths of their nutty, adoptive family. However abusive they were. Buried in perfume. That's trauma."

"Killed by us," Wakely added. "How's that going to sit?"

"We saved them. But yeah, the psyche isn't logical. They will need patience. While we race to the coast, before we freeze to death."

They saw Tse rise from the camp and approach, pause at a distance. Sharpcot waved him over.

"Any idea when we can move out?" he asked quietly, glancing at the kids.

"I guess when they wake up. And decide if they're coming along," Sharpcot replied.

"Do they have a choice?" he asked.

"I won't compel them," Sharpcot said. "But remember, they came looking for us. Lured us here. They'll come."

"Did they explain why they did all that?" Tse asked. "I mean followed us, and took the cart, and made us find them?"

"There's a psychology there," Wakely said. "If you think about it. They wanted us to find them."

"Yeah. Adoption is the only method they know," Sharpcot said. She looked to the kids. Yolanda was sitting up, glancing sleepily round. "Let's make them feel wanted. It's important they feel wanted. We're their family now." She rose and headed to the camp, steeling herself for a negotiation with only one practical outcome.

"We are eight again," Virago said as Wakely caught up to her when she slowed to let the others pass.

"Then why do I feel 80?" Wakely replied as they plodded west, then turned to meet her eye. "But you're right. Party of eight. So who do you think little Ike represents?" He nodded ahead to where the toddler rode in a stroller, pushed by Yolanda. "Sometimes Loko, sometimes Bronski."

His concern about Ike impeding their pace was allayed when Nasim tugged from the back of the cart a collapsed jogging stroller. Unfolding it revealed three big wheels with pneumatic tires, good on grass and rough terrain, though he thought the tires needed inflation, impossible without a pump. How could it be that the only way to fill tires with Schrader valves was with a specialized instrument? So absent encountering a block of bicycle pumps, the tires would go flat. Another deadline to spur them on. As it was, pushing the stroller proved laborious, and they took turns. As he watched, Leclerc leaned in to Yolanda and offered to push, and the tall girl yielded with gratitude, scurried to catch up with Sharpcot at the front of the column.

"That Yolanda," Wakely said. "I think she's taken to the sarge. The girl's a firecracker: smart and confident and funny. A lot like our Abigail."

Virago didn't reply, and he glanced at her, watched her walk with head lowered. He was about to say something else, change the topic, when Virago looked at him and said quietly, "Can I tell you something about Abby? A few days before. Before the battle. She . . . propositioned me."

"For what?" he asked too quickly.

"I mean she, she made a pass at me? Pass. That sounds frivolous. She requested the comfort of my companionship. I mean beyond friendship."

Wakely walked silently, digesting this information, thinking about the rainy night on the carousel.

"Yeah, me too," he admitted.

Virago nodded. "She told me."

"I didn't know."

"What?"

"That she was . . ."

"Queer? Bi? Not something you brag about in the army."

"Right," he replied. "And you said . . . ?"

"That I'd think about it. That it wasn't . . . a way I thought I could go. But under the circumstances, maybe . . ."

He looked at the walls: on the left, automatic dishwasher cutlery baskets, and on the right, outdoor fountains made from stacked bowls, resembling stone, but made from fibreglass, each with a power cord dangling from its base. Then he said without much thought, "You know when we find a place to settle, it might be good to have . . ." He cleared his throat. "Companionship."

She sidestepped and pressed herself briefly against him before moving away. They walked on.

They came across the helicopters mid-afternoon under an overcast sky, in a massive block, after passing between windshield squeegees and elliptical machines. Rattan outdoor furniture made from resin wicker formed the wall across the aisle. Tse and Wakely stood at the corner formed from chopper noses and bubble canopies. Tse had sprinted the last hundred metres, and Wakely had jogged to keep up.

"Thank goodness they're set upright," Tse said, breathless.

The machines stretched away to the south and west, presenting a kaleidoscope of colour and design: navy blue with SkyForce10 and the NBC peacock; red Blackcomb Helicopters; deep blue with yellow top Australian Defence Force training; U.S. Army in desert camouflage; silver and yellow U.S. Air Force rescue with "Hopalong" in red on the nose; others in colourful TV news livery, or muted navy grey, or solid forest green with Belgian roundels, red and white with Red Cross, orange air ambulance branded "Orng." Classic *M*A*S*H* bubble-shelled Bell 47G "Whirlybird," twin-engine load-lifting Sikorsky Skycrane, and then a black one with "Uber" painted on its flank. Walls of Sea Kings, Seasprites, Seahawks, Black Hawks, Little Birds, Cobras, Apache gunship with 30mm chaingun and Hellfire rocket racks. Some carried enormous steerable spotlamps and camera pods. They saw an Indian Air Force Chinook, and nestled between its twin rotors a petite two-seater Aerokopter Sanka. Bridged above both, an enormous Russian Mi-26 Halo troop carrier. Tse naming them off.

Some of the machines were shiny and polished, others grimy, soot-streaked; still others were busted, rusted, burned-out, derelict. The skids and wheels were set back from the passage boundary to accommodate rotors, which stretched above their heads in a dense network of spars.

"This is a hell of a thing," Wakely said, gazing upward.

"If we can get one going," Tse said, and had to pause to govern his nerves. "And we can make some distance. We'll be set."

"True enough. You ready?"

"Sure," he said, and they both set their weapons down, shucked rucks and jackets.

Virago arrived then, panting, hands on knees. "I'm coming too," she stated, and threw off her gear.

A grey two-seater with open sides, Schweizer 300C by the name printed on its side, formed the block's cornerstone, and Tse put one foot into the cockpit opening and gripped the top of the bubble and put his other boot onto the edge of the seat and pulled himself up until he stood on the roof, gripping the skids of the helicopter above it. Virago followed, then Wakely. They made rapid progress, with struts, fins, rotor blades, and weapon hardpoints serving as hand- and footholds. Before the climb, Wakely had sighted up the corner, counted 11 machines, wedged together so skids sat not on the rotors of the machine below, but atop fuselages, with the rotors of the chopper below set to allow the top helicopter to rest between the blades, and therefore maximize density. They scrambled over the bodies of Airbus and Eurocopter and AgustaWestland and Qingdao Haili, sea rescue and heli-ski and firefighting and police.

Virago glanced down and saw Sharpcot arrive in the passage below with Leclerc and the kids, Ike in his stroller pushed by

Sharpcot, all of them watching their ascent. She felt queasy, but dismissed the feeling and continued to climb. She looked to her right and saw Wakely slightly below, trying to find a handhold on a red and gold machine with "Grand Canyon" painted on the side, and she pointed to a vent into which he jammed a gloved hand to draw himself up. Tse was far above, climbing too hastily, taking risks. Within minutes he reached the top helicopter, perched on the corner, painted red and white.

"Hey! This guy's a Bell JetRanger 206," he called down. "Actually, the LongRanger variant."

"Is that good?" Wakely called up.

"It's fucking great. Uh, sir. Master Jack. I mean it's an older model, but should handle like the GlobalRanger."

Tse stood on the flexing rotor of the helicopter below, hand cupped against the glass of the LongRanger, studying its interior. He tested the door but found it locked, shimmied back a couple of steps and stretched his fingertips to the rear passenger door.

"Dammit, Corporal, take it easy," Wakely called from below.

The door swung abruptly open and Tse grappled with it as his boots came off the blade. Wakely and Virago saw his feet kick in the air. He still had the door in his grip, but it wasn't designed to take that weight and it creaked as his feet flailed for the blade below. Wakely calculated that if Tse fell he'd hit him and take him down too, but didn't consider moving, just tightened his grip on a yellow and red rescue chopper, thinking a good hold might at least slow the corporal's fall, when Tse swung back and managed to seize a seatbelt that had flopped out of the door. For agonizing seconds they watched him haul his bulk into the helicopter's cabin.

"How do I restart my heart?" Virago gasped, looking across at Wakely. He reached out and she did too and they gripped hands for a moment before resuming their climb. When they got to the top they found a red and white chopper perched at the block's corner, nose out, tail boom overlapping with the tail of the copter behind, which faced the opposite way. They worked their way along the landing skid past the passenger door, opened it, and slipped into the passenger cabin, where they found three forward-facing chairs across from two rear-facing. Beyond them, up front, Tse, ensconced in the pilot's chair, grinning triumphantly.

"How the hell you get up there?" Virago asked. A pillar between the rear-facing seats blocked access to the front.

"Unlocked the pilot's door from back there." He hooked a thumb over his shoulder. "Got out through that door, in through this one."

"Well done," Wakely said, both admiring and fearing his determination to make this work.

"I can absolutely fly this," he declared, fanning his hands over the controls.

"You got power? Fuel?" Wakely asked as he leaned over the seatback and into the cockpit.

"I won't know until I power up, but I'm scared to, if the battery is low. Turbine engine. Tricky. We get only one crack at a start."

"No point if there's no juice. Give it a flick and then turn it right off."

Tse looked up and studied the overhead panel, then put a finger on the battery switch.

"Here goes," he said, and flicked it.

The panel came to life, several lights coming on: ENG OUT, TRANS OIL PRESS, ROTOR LOW RPM, and some of the gauges jumped. A low fan noise began, which gave Wakely a thrill. It was like witnessing the awakening of some ancient technology. Tse's synesthesia interpreted the fizz of the fans as a bluish glow as he ran his eyes rapidly over the panel before he switched off and the noise ceased and all settled to silence

"We have power," Tse said. "And if the gauges are true, fuel."

"Yeah, but it looked like only half," Wakely said. "Less than half. Might not be worth it."

Tse didn't answer, but he slumped a little in the chair.

"If this helicopter has fuel, so will others," Virago said.

"Likely," Wakely replied. "But how do we get it?"

"There are ways," she said.

After he heard her idea, Wakely looked out the right window at the adjacent machine, a tiny yellow two-seater with an expansive bubble. It sat atop a burnt-out chopper, just a shell: no rotor, glass gone, charred and rusting. It might be a UH-1 Huey, ubiquitous in the Vietnam War. He squinted to see the machine beyond the yellow one, and though larger it still looked compact, at least backdropped by the third one along, a monstrous multi-bladed U.S. Marines transport in desert camouflage.

"Think we can take out that little guy?" Tse wondered, pointing to the yellow one.

Wakely opened the right passenger door into the space behind the small chopper's cabin. He glanced down, planted a foot on the rotor hub of the machine below, and put a hand on the tail of the yellow machine, jiggled to test its weight. The whole machine responded, shifting on its skids. He leaned back inside. "Thing weighs nothing: five, maybe 600 pounds. Gimme a hand."

He ducked under the little helicopter's tail, mindful of his footing — if he fell, he'd plummet into the gap between machines below, with no escape. Virago and Tse each emerged, looking into the variegated depths below with the same thought.

"What do you want to do?" Virago asked.

"One second."

He stooped back under the tail and squeezed past Tse, set his boots on the LongRanger's skid, and eased forward until he stood at its nose, hand gripping a pitot tube. He peered across the passageway to the stacked and enmeshed elliptical machines forming the adjacent block, then peered into the canyon below, saw Sharpcot and Leclerc and the three kids settling in at the intersection.

"Hey, Sarge!" he shouted, and she looked up.

"What do you got, Jack?" she called up.

"A candidate copter. It's well-placed. Corporal feels confident. There's juice in the battery and fuel in the tanks. We're just clearing space up here, and stuff will be coming down."

"What kind of stuff?"

He worried about the potential deflection created by all those protruding rotor blades. "Just — you better move. Up that way, a good distance."

Sharpcot ushered Leclerc and the kids a hundred metres north, between sectionals and squeegees.

Wakely returned to where Virago and Tse waited.

"Before we toss it, might be something useful here," Virago said, and they bent to study the yellow chopper's engine, which lay exposed behind the passenger compartment, and she searched among the pipes and cable harnesses and found what she wanted, a length of clear PVC tubing snaking between a reservoir inside the shell and a filter assembly mounted on the engine. She and Wakely gripped it and together yanked out the tube. She studied and pocketed it.

"Ready?" Wakely asked.

They pushed against the fuselage, and without much effort, the machine budged. In a few seconds the skids were grinding across the shell of the helicopter below. It went over.

On the ground, up the passageway, Sharpcot watched the yellow helicopter emerge from the top of the block and pitch forward. In a breath it flipped over, tail smashing against the top of the elliptical stack, one rotor plunging into the mass of them, binding there, and making the fuselage swing down, slamming into the wall, shattering the bubble. The machine hung up for a moment before it resumed its descent, bashing and bouncing between the walls, crashing against helicopters, tearing down ellipticals, which fell along with it, until it struck earth heavily on its nose, ellipticals raining down.

347

"More to come!" Wakely called, and in a few minutes a second helicopter, black and grey and bigger than the first, tumbled down in similar fashion, pulling elliptical machines and pieces of other helicopters with it, this one landing hard on its skids and sending up a cloud of dust.

Yolanda whooped. "You guys are next level!" she cried, while Ike hopped and laughed at the spectacle.

Up top, Tse studied the blue helicopter that stood tail-to-tail with the LongRanger. He stooped under the Ranger's tail and put his hands against the blue machine's fin and began to push, and Virago and Wakely joined in. As the helicopter began to pivot, Wakely wondered how that alien repulsive force contributed to their ability to move it, for this was not a small machine like the others. They got the tail boom out as far as they could without risking a fall. Tse looked at the space cleared around the LongRanger's tail rotor, and didn't look completely satisfied, but it would have to do. Then the three of them picked their way across the open space they had created, surveying it. Wakely looked north to regard that tremendous wall of tall buildings maybe 10 klicks away, the highest at the right with the Burj Khalifa and its brethren, descending endlessly westward in a tremendous arc.

"Uh, should we have grabbed fuel from those machines we threw over?" Virago wondered.

"No good," Tse replied. "Piston engines. Avgas. We need jet fuel, for the turbine. Could draw it from that one. That one too."

"What do you think of the space here. Enough?" Wakely asked.

"It's good. I'd only want to shift the blades of those choppers out of the way. I mean there's probably enough clearance, but ..."

"Up to you, boss," Wakely told him. He and Virago spotted each other for safe places to step as they turned or pinned aside rotors of neighbouring helicopters to ensure clearance. After they adjusted the blades of a sleek helicopter painted white

348

and gold, Virago peered through its side window. She tried the door, found it unlocked.

"God, look at it in here," she exclaimed, and they stood in the doorway, regarding the luxurious interior, its polished wood surfaces and enormous, modular chairs. A console stood at the compartment's centre, and Virago climbed inside and opened it.

"I expect champagne's in a block elsewhere," Wakely commented.

"Hope we find it by New Year's Eve," she said, lifting out its plastic liner. "But this is what I'm looking for."

They went to the chopper's filler cap and pulled it, and Virago ran the PVC tube into the tank.

"Let me," Wakely said. "But you watch." He pinched the clear tube where it started to arc downward. "Warn me when it gets to here."

He put his mouth on the tube and sucked. After a moment Virago cried, "It's there!" He released the tube and dropped the end into the reservoir, which he'd set well below the fuselage, at the skid. A steady stream of jet fuel came up from the tank and flowed into the bucket, straw-coloured and pungent.

"Ah. Smells like the airport. Smells like . . . civilization," Virago said.

"Tastes like it too," Wakely said, and spat into the gap below, wiped his mouth. "I guess vapour comes up ahead of the liquid." Virago held his gaze for a moment, and it spurred in her an unbidden thought: that if he kissed her right now she'd taste jet fuel.

He looked down at the progress of liquid through the tube. The reservoir was full before the tank ran dry, and he raised the hose to stop the flow, then withdrew it from the spigot and shook it out. He and Virago each took an end, and, awkwardly, cautiously, carried it between them across the backs of helicopters, set it down on a flat spot of the machine below the LongRanger. They could determine no easy way to fill the spigot from the container without spilling, until Virago suggested they prop it on the shelf where the fuselage's curve met the engine compartment, and use the tube to siphon from the bucket and into the tank. Virago volunteered to suck on the tube this time, but Wakely refused.

"I already got the taste in my mouth," he said. He siphoned it out and ran fuel down into the LongRanger's tank until it overflowed, capped it, and set aside the liner and tube in case they needed it again.

Tse was back inside the cabin, studying the controls. Wakely knocked and Tse cracked the door and he and Virago clustered at the opening. "Fuelled and ready," Virago told him. "How's it going?"

"Well. Normally there'd be a manual here." Tse tapped a cubby above the dashboard. "Or at the very least a checklist. But as you know those are in their respective helicopter manual and checklist stacks."

"Is it tricky?" Wakely asked.

Tse looked pained and replied. "It's the turbine. Requires a specific and careful procedure to keep from toasting the engine. I've done it a few times in the Global. I'm not sure how it's different in this model. But we have a bigger issue."

"What's that?" Virago asked.

"We get one shot. I can't go for a trial flight and then land somewhere to pick everyone up. There's nowhere to land."

"What about back here, on this spot?" Wakely asked.

"Too tight. Plus this chopper has been set exactly on top of the ones below it. Even an inch to the left or right and it might not be flat and stable."

Virago said, "It means we've got to get everyone up here and inside before you take off."

"Yeah. Can we even get those kids up here?"

"We'll find a way," Virago said.

Wakely asked, "Corporal, are you confident you can do this? You can fly this thing?"

"Yessir," he replied immediately.

"And what's the range? With full tanks?" Wakely asked.

Tse hesitated, said, "Maybe six hundred clicks? Depending on conditions. Air pressure, and you'd expect a headwind if we're flying west."

Wakely leaned back and put his hand to his chin, surprised, as he was every time, to find scruff. They needed to find the shaving cream block, though he was probably too shaggy for the razor. "Six hundred kilometres. That's a hell of a boost."

"And then land on a block."

"Right. Or find a spot without blocks," Wakely said.

"If there's no block it's for a reason — too hard to build, like a hilltop. But that's a difficult landing zone," Tse mused.

"Unless we're past it. The maze," Virago suggested. "Like Cheree says, it can't be infinite."

Wakely looked past the LongRanger's nose at the ellipticals across the passageway, the wall's top where tossed helicopters had excavated a rift. "It's a gamble, for sure." He looked at Virago.

"Which might kill us."

"Like every day," Tse reminded her.

"Anyway, it's up to the sarge," Wakely said. "She'll want to go. I'll take what she decides, and so will you."

"So much for autonomy," Virago sighed.

"You're in the army now," Wakely said.

As the afternoon wore on with Wakely and Tse and Virago up top preparing the chopper, Sharpcot recognized they would travel no more today, especially if this mad goal of flying out was realized, so with the help of Leclerc and the girls she arranged a camp between the rattan sectionals and squeegees. They built a fire, and Leclerc and Yolanda hauled a couple of sectionals out of the wall and set them up around the firepit, creating a homey camp. "Hygge," Leclerc declared when she stepped back and regarded it, the pair of sectionals — arrayed with sleeping pads and ranger blankets (original cushions in a block somewhere) — bracketing the fire.

After that Leclerc entertained Ike on one of the couches, demonstrating that a Lego racing car she found in the pocket of his hoodie could be remade into something else, his panic when she disassembled it changing to wonder when she rebuilt it as a boat. She formed the ranger blanket into a stormy sea, which tossed the boat about.

From the couch opposite Sharpcot watched them, with an abstract thought of how valuable it would be to carry a sack of Lego on their journey, forming it into whatever they needed: boat, wagon, ladder, shelter. Where was the Lego block?

The girls sat on either side of her and asked questions about how she came to command the section, what it was like in the army, specifically as a woman of colour. Sharpcot was honest: "Brutal," she said. "Just being a woman in charge of men is bad enough. What was it like living in — where was it again? — Bowmanville?"

"Bowman. North Dakota," Nasim said. "Though we lived outside town. About 12 miles out."

"You want to know what it's like?" Yolanda said as she crossed her arms and leaned forward. "Whenever we went into Bowman, we had to pass one of those 'welcome to this shitty town' signs. Well this one had a 'statue' beside it, of a cowboy riding a rocket on top of a vintage fire engine."

"It's an awful place," Nasim said. "And I'm from Afghanistan."

This struck Yolanda as funny, and she doubled over, laughing.

"How were they about your faith?" Sharpcot asked Nasim, who looked away and shook her head. "The Christian family. Would they let you practice?"

"Ha!" Yolanda cried. "Ten minutes after they were dead she put her hijab back on. Inshallah."

"That's not how you use that word," Nasim reproved her.

352

"I know!" Yolanda replied, pushing her face into her hands. "I will figure it out."

"Inshallah," Sharpcot said, and though Nasim didn't look at her, she saw her smile. "I've been to your country," Sharpcot added, and now Nasim did meet her eye.

"As a soldier?"

"A decade ago. Myself and Jack. Dorian. It's where we met."

She watched Nasim process this information. Then she asked, "Where?"

"Kandahar Province. Where are you from?"

"Herat."

"I never got there. I heard it was lovely."

"It is," Nasim replied, and Sharpcot saw the girl's frown, her confused expression. At the tense: *is* versus *was*. Sharpcot realized that the Christians may not have reached the same conclusions about the world's state as she and the section had. And she suffered panic at the thought. That the kids might be stranded where she and the section were in the first days after the bunker: believing they were surrounded by a local phenomenon, with the whole world alive and active beyond the maze.

"What," she asked cautiously, "did the Christian family think about all this?" She waved to take in the stacks.

"Oh, you know," Yolanda replied. "The Rapture. Except Gentle managed to fudge it. He said the sinners were all harpazoed and sent to hell, and we were left to repopulate. Beneficent Christian was eager to get that part going." Those last words spoken with disdain.

"Yolanda took a bad slap from Chaste for saying all this seemed like the Tribulation part," Nasim said, and Yolanda touched her cheek in recollection of the stroke.

They sat quietly, and Sharpcot leaned forward and threw a log onto the fire.

"I grew up in Coyame," Yolanda said.

"Yes?" Sharpcot asked.

353

"You've probably never heard of it," Yolanda added. "A town in northeastern Chihuahua. Pretty small. About half the size of Bowman."

"When were you were adopted?"

"Three years ago." After a long pause she said, "And Ikemba. He's from Africa. Nigeria."

Ike, gnawing on his rubber star, looked up.

"How old is he?" Sharpcot asked. "How old are you, Ike?"

Ike looked at Yolanda, then Leclerc, and held up a spread hand.

"No, silly," Nasim said. "This much." She held up three fingers, and Leclerc took Ike's hand and gently folded his thumb and pinky to mimic the gesture.

"There's news," Leclerc said, sitting up and looking past Sharpcot.

Sharpcot turned and watched Tse, Virago, and Wakely approach.

"Mom and Dad are fighting," Yolanda said, nodding down the passage. Across the fire, Tse and Leclerc, who'd been leaning into each other and whispering, turned to see Sharpcot and Wakely a hundred metres down the corridor. They saw Wakely put his hand to his forehead while Sharpcot spoke passionately with her palms raised.

"I didn't expect this," Virago said from where she stood by the fire, warming her hands. "Jack wants to fly, but Elsie's not keen."

Sharpcot was not keen. She said, with her hands up in a stalled shrug, "Even the best outcome, it saves us 12 days of walking."

"Twelve days? Twelve days is huge," Wakely replied. "Remember the snow. And it doesn't just save us time, it saves us fatigue. We've got those kids with us now, do you think they can do 50 klicks a day? Pushing that stroller?"

Sharpcot lowered her hands, and Wakely pressed on. "It also protects us from injury. We've been lucky so far, El. Only blisters, minor strains and pulls. What if one of us suffers a bad sprain, a broken leg? Going by chopper represents a dozen days we're not on the ground potentially hurting ourselves."

"Jack, that helicopter has been sitting there for two months, unmaintained. And who knows its state after the Accruers hauled it here with the rest."

"In the Burj. Remember the water? In the fountains, in the pools. I don't know how they did it, but they moved everything, completely intact. Giant building, half a million tons of steel and glass, 12,000 kilometres. Why wouldn't the same be true for a little helicopter?"

"Well, there's Tse. His lack of experience."

"He's confident he can fly it. The guy has a hundred hours."

"Almost a hundred," she corrected. "That's what he told me."

"He says you need less than half that to get your licence."

She looked at the ground and thought. "You're sure this isn't a bunch of boys wanting to play with toys?"

"You said it yourself: get to the coast before winter pins us down. At our pace, we won't make it."

She turned and walked away and came back. She glanced to the top of the helicopter block where the LongRanger stood at the corner, clear of its neighbours. The sun, which had recently emerged from cloud, flooded the cabin with light.

"It's just a feeling, you know?" she said, pressing a fist to her sternum.

"I know," he replied gently, mimicking the gesture. "I got it too."

"You do?"

"Of course. It's a scary prospect. A gamble. With a big payoff."

She wanted to agree. She wondered if the helicopters they'd thrown over to make room, watching them crash in the passageway, the wreckage she could see from here, had biased her against the plan. Imagining all of them inside one of those smashed machines. She sighed. Sighed again, then gave a small nod. "Okay. Okay. If the weather's good, we go tomorrow. At dawn."

"Right. Once we get everyone to the top of that stack," he replied. And she looked again, nine storeys up, at the chopper poised there.

A dawn liftoff proved ambitious, because they first had to get everyone and everything they wanted to bring to the top. That meant not just the people, but rucks, rifles, and the stroller, which being large and robust with pneumatic tires made it ponderous and awkward to lift into anything higher than the trunk of a car, let alone a helicopter cabin 28 metres up. Tse did it, with the thing folded and strapped to his back and Virago climbing alongside. He reached the top sweating and breathless, fell forward, and when Virago voiced concern that exhaustion would hamper his ability to fly, he leapt to his feet to demonstrate his fitness, swung the stroller around, and tossed it inside the chopper.

Sharpcot expected the girls to be reticent to climb, but Nasim ascended with skill reminiscent of Loko, clambering up the helicopters like walking across a room. Yolanda was less enthusiastic, begged to climb alongside Sharpcot, who had to swallow her fear and embrace the task with false confidence. In the end, Yolanda proved helpful, scrambling around Sharpcot when her boot jammed between the pipes of a chopper's turbine, freeing her foot and allowing them to resume the ascent.

Tse made the climb three times: once with the stroller, the second alongside Leclerc, who initially refused to do it, and required firm coaching. She finally agreed when he fashioned a harness from paracord and a carabiner (red pressed steel, which Wakely located in his vest pocket) that he clipped above her, and past which she would slowly climb. Then she would pause,

356

holding on desperately, while Tse removed the clip and reattached it above her for the next rise. He made the third ascent with Ike tucked into his emptied ruck, straps secured and just his head sticking out, wide-eyed and exclaiming all the way up.

Virago greeted them at the top, went behind and uncinched the straps and lifted the toddler into her arms. He wanted down, to walk around and explore, but the chasms between packed helicopters and the precipice made that impossible, and she ushered him into the passenger compartment, where Yolanda received him. Sharpcot sat up front in the cockpit, while Wakely helped the kids stow loose items, rifles, and rucks. There was a problem with inadequate seating, unless someone held Ike in their lap, but Yolanda had a better idea.

"If we set up the stroller on the floor here, sideways, and weigh the wheels down with the packs and guns, Ike can sit in it. Safer than a lap."

"Smart," Wakely said, and they unfolded the stroller and buckled Ike in.

"Everything okay?" Sharpcot asked as she peered over the seats.

Virago and Wakely went together to check on Tse, found him seated on the rotor blade of the helicopter below them, drinking water and sweating.

"You good?" she asked.

"Great, actually." He wiped his brow, the sides of his face. "It's been weeks since I had a proper workout."

"How are you feeling about . . . ?" Wakely glanced at the helicopter.

"Great. Winds calm, excellent visibility. It's now or never."

"That's not what we're asking," Virago said.

"Me? I'm great. Seriously. I'm at my best after working out. Brings focus."

Wakely leaned in and gripped Tse's forearm. "Good thing, buddy. Time to fly."

357

Tse got up, took a breath, steady and ready, and walked up the side of the chopper and climbed into the pilot's chair. He grinned at Sharpcot in the seat beside him and belted himself in.

Virago got in back, and before he boarded, Wakely took in the scene around him, the blue sky, the landscape of helicopters. He glanced along the flank of the LongRanger illuminated by the morning sun, then climbed inside.

Virago squeezed past the stroller into the lefthand seat, propped her boots on weapons and packs. She looked across at Nasim, who sat facing her in the chair opposite, eyes shut, her lips moving, possibly in prayer. Virago turned and watched Wakely climb in and regard the cramped compartment. He met her eye with likely the same thought: too heavy? But they'd shed anything they didn't need long ago.

Wakely buckled in and nodded at Yolanda in the facing seat.

"Trays stowed and in their upright position?" Leclerc said from beside him, her short legs bracketing the stroller. She clutched her helmet in her lap.

"Why do you get the crappy middle seat?" he asked her. "You should sit here so you can look out the window."

"I'd rather not," she replied. "I appreciate a cushion between my body and the airframe." She pulled on her helmet.

I'm the cushion, he thought as he bent forward and dug through the rucks on the floor, found his and came up with his own helmet, which he passed to Yolanda. "In case it gets bumpy," he said, and she put it on. With her thick-rimmed glasses she looked like a Latin-American revolutionary. Virago found her own helmet and passed it to Nasim, who turned it over in her hands before putting it over her hijab.

After a moment, Leclerc took hers off and offered it across to Ike, who chewed on his rubber star and looked at it.

"Too big," Virago said. "More likely to hurt him."

Leclerc set it back on her head, cinched the strap.

358

"This might help," Yolanda said, and reached over to raise the hood of his hoodie. "Better than nothing."

"First helicopter ride?" Wakely asked, glancing around the cabin. He answered their nods with a forced smile and, "It's going to be fun." He remembered his first ride, in a big, twin-rotor Chinook. He'd just shot the boy with the artillery shell, and as a gift for his heroism was spared the drive back to Kandahar in a light armoured vehicle along a bomb-plagued highway. He cleared his throat and called, "Ready back here."

"Good work. Need a minute," Sharpcot replied as she looked through the canopy at the wall of ellipticals, observing the rift created when they'd toppled the two smaller choppers. In her lap she clutched Wakely's binoculars and the road atlas, open to South Dakota, with a line drawn in pencil running west-southwest off the page. It continued on the Wyoming map, running southwest below Yellowstone, intercepted a spur of the Rocky Mountains (which they would circumnavigate if they made it that far), and then into northern Utah, with Great Salt Lake as their ultimate target, but that was purely theoretical, the direction they would walk once they put down. They had to do all their talking now, agreed on a few simple hand gestures, as the absence of audio headsets would impede in-flight talk, and there'd be nothing to mitigate the noise of the engine and rotors. "It's going to get loud," he added as he conjured in his mind a block of aviation headsets, branded Peltor, David Clark, Bose, Lightspeed, Sigtronics, Faro.

He leaned forward, scrounging his memory as he jotted on a notepad a checklist for starting the turbine. He'd done it a dozen times on the GlobalRanger, with his aunt strictly monitoring each step. She had drilled into him the ease with which a turbine engine could be destroyed through an improper start. And with the battery where it was, they had one shot. He reviewed the list one last time and clipped it to the instrument panel.

It was clear and calm, 13 degrees Celsius, excellent flying conditions, at least where they stood at the moment. He'd kill for TAFs or METARs for here and along their route. Without the impressive aviation infrastructure that had developed over the last century, they were like early aviators. No weather, no directional beacons, no control towers with the reassuring voices of ATC to assist and guide them. No GPS. Not even a good map. The road atlas provided little useful detail, highlighting the locations of dismantled towns, stripped highways. They'd have to rely for reference on sparsely documented natural landmarks: forests, rivers, lakes. They'd use that in concert with the magnetic compass, which currently showed a grossly inaccurate heading of 120 degrees, skewed by the steel of the chopper block, the steel of the elliptical block, and who knew what else. For now, he used the orientation of the passages between blocks, always aligned to the cardinal points, to conclude they were facing due east. He set the gyrocompass to 90 degrees.

He looked at Sharpcot, and pushed his sunglasses up his nose.

"Ready when you are, Cap'n," she said, and saluted him.

He let out a long breath, lifted his hand to the overhead panel, and said, "Battery on." He flicked the switch. The soft whirr they'd heard earlier commenced, telltales lit up along the top of the instrument panel, and needles jumped and quivered. He tried the TOT LT TEST button and the warning light came on, as it should, switched on the fuel and closed the guard. Noted fuel pressure, and that the fuel gauge showed past full. He adjusted the collective, ensured the throttle was closed, and took a big breath before he put his thumb on the starter button, and here he locked his eyes on the Turbine Outlet Temperature gauge as the starter kicked and the rotors began to turn, lazily, rocking the copter on its skids. Tse suddenly remembered they were balanced precariously on the back of another helicopter perched above a nine-storey canyon. He had to disregard this concern as he tweaked the throttle while watching the Gas Producer RPM indicator, bringing it to 60 percent before he released the starter button. He opened the throttle to bring the Gas Producer to 70 percent, the helicopter quaking heavily now and the noise building. Panic struck when he heard from behind him a new whine he couldn't identify, until he realized it was little Ike in the passenger compartment, wailing. He switched the generator on, knew there was a runup test he should do, as well as a whole procedure for checking the hydraulic system, but the vibration was becoming violent and the machine started tiptoeing towards the abyss between the blocks. There were additional steps he could safely disregard — radios and navigation lights — and he went right to the throttle, cranked it to full power.

When he brought the collective up, the machine began to slump to the left, and he couldn't determine why, thought it was a mechanical failure, until he recognized he hadn't anticipated unbalanced lift: on the left, the rotor downwash fell into open air, while on the right there was ground effect as the draft hit the top of the block. He rocked the cyclic to the right, breathing into panic as he gently raised the collective. The helicopter seemed to crane upwards and abruptly lifted. They were airborne. The machine began to pivot clockwise until he pushed the left pedal and tweaked the cyclic, conscious of the tail rotor and the helicopter behind. He maintained a gradual but steady rise and slowed to a hover, which he maintained with considerable effort, 10 metres above the block. Off the skids and clear of the engine's roar bouncing off neighbouring helicopters, the hover felt almost peaceful, at least to Sharpcot. There was still the thunder of the turbine and throb of rotors, a smell of engine exhaust, and Tse struggled with a hundred minor adjustments of collective, cyclic, and pedals to remain steady, but they were flying. He imagined Aunt Solina's solemn nod, which for her was the peak of praise.

Sharpcot reached out with her forearm, shoved it inexplicably before his eyes, and he was about to cry out when she ran her sleeve across his brow, wiping away the sweat that risked raining into his eyes and blinding him.

He hazarded a glance and saw her smiling. She nodded upwards, and he increased their altitude while pivoting slowly, granting them a view through the bubble, which was open from above their heads to below the pedals. The block of towers and buildings loomed surprisingly large and close, the tops of the Burj and its neighbours high above. When they were 50 metres above the block and facing due west according to the grid of passages below, he tuned the gyrocompass, and saw that the magnetic compass, now clear of helicopters and ellipticals, showed a more or less accurate reading.

He pointed them to the west-southwest, nudged the cyclic forward and compensated with corresponding collective. By the uncalibrated altimeter they were around 3,500 feet above sea level, 260 feet AGL. Give or take. As he accelerated, he maintained a sustained watch of the gauges — Rotor Power Turbine, Torque Percent, Airspeed, engine and transmission oil pressure and temperatures. Everything looked good. His armpits and back were drenched.

The helicopter block went on for some time before it ended and they found themselves over the circular tops of some kind of large metal canisters they couldn't identify. It was the same with the next block, black and silver and rust-coloured beams set in east-west or north-south orientation.

Sharpcot had fantasized they would spot essential items and swoop in to pick them up, like plucking products off super-market shelves, oatmeal, coffee, sugar, cookies. Just after takeoff she'd glimpsed through the binoculars a million million jars of pickles, in a stack immediately west of the outdoor sectionals. The last pickles in the world, left behind, stirring a craving that would never be sated. And now their speed and height made identification of anything but major objects challenging. They saw stretch limos and terminal port grain elevators — assembled conglomerations of concrete cylinders — but the rest became an indiscernible blur of multicoloured and multitextured materials.

Tse had warned her they'd need to travel high enough and fast enough to allow for autorotation. "If the engine fails, the rotor can spin freely, slowing our descent, like a parachute. But you need altitude and speed to accomplish it."

Suddenly, below them, trees in autumn bloom, orange and yellow, and a river cutting between blocks, then trees again, more blocks. A winding cut through the forest that may have accommodated a road. She tried to find corresponding landmarks on the map, couldn't. She grew conscious of the burn of fuel, the urgency of going west, and she signalled him to go, go, take them up to the safest and most efficient speed and altitude, cover the maximum distance.

They flew on, past other forested zones, hills and rocky outcrops, but mostly blocks, blocks of stuff. They saw to the south a superblock, taller than the others, and Sharpcot directed Tse to fly close enough to identify it. They saw massive slabs of concrete, stunned to recognize them as hydroelectric dams, some of them taller than their current altitude. As they neared the northwest corner, Sharpcot jabbed a thumb upward and Tse climbed to exceed the dam height, and slowed, offering a perspective. All of them arch dams, curved and nested together like seashells. The tallest of them, at the west end of the block, stood a thousand feet tall. Plucked from whatever canyon it had once occupied. Sharpcot wondered about that event: the moment the Accruers pulled that dam, abruptly releasing the reservoir it held back. Were there people downstream, or had they already been . . . Here her mind seized, remembering they still didn't know the fate of the people. Removed? Collected? Exterminated?

She waved her hand forward and Tse pushed the cyclic and resumed their west-southwest progress.

Blocks of stuff large and small slid beneath the helicopter, the maze of passageways that separated them a nauseating lattice that Sharpcot could imagine with too much fidelity navigating step-by-step, day by day with the section and these kids. She visualized the swift passage of the chopper consuming hundreds of thousands of steps. Superblocks marched past in the distance, massive structures too far off to identify. With Wakely's binoculars she saw one that might be oil refineries, another, gothic cathedrals. They passed close to one of shipyard gantries in yellow and red and blue and orange.

After an hour of smooth flying, she noted two changes: a plane of dark cloud had edged over the horizon, shading the maze in the west, and the landscape began to rise and transform. She watched the altimeter increase as Tse maintained ground height, and across the land the blocks became increasingly interrupted by knolls and mesas and bluffs. Far to the south she watched an area of forested hills slip past.

Tse pointed to something up ahead — Sharpcot looked, scanning the landscape, and saw nothing of note but the endless arrangement of blocks, but when she looked at Tse he nodded ahead and called over the noise of the turbine, "Snow."

She looked at the sky and saw to the southwest and piercing through the band of dark clouds a beam of sunlight, made substantial by the swirl of snowflakes it illuminated. Like a column of sun in a dusty room. She cast a nervous glance at Tse, and he returned it.

In the rear cabin, Yolanda watched Wakely nod in and out of sleep. His gloved hands clutching and unclutching. She saw the first flakes of snow whip past the window, looked around the cabin to see if anyone else had noticed. Her eyes met Virago's and she saw the woman's mouth pressed into a frown. Yolanda stretched out a foot and tapped Wakely's knee with her boot. He woke with a start and a panic. Disoriented and shocked to find himself in a helicopter, though not in Kandahar Province. He looked at Yolanda, who nodded out the window just as a flurry of snowflakes swarmed past and a gust shook the helicopter, causing a sudden descent that made everyone's guts drop and sent them scrambling for handholds. Ike flailed his arms, laughing. The chopper stabilized but the snow outside thickened. Sharpcot grabbed her seat whenever a gust hit. She trusted Tse — his flying had been better than she'd expected, especially considering conditions — but the weather was degrading.

"Take us lower!" she shouted, jabbing a thumb downward.

Tse resisted. He understood the impulse to reduce height, to mitigate the distance to ground, but any lower and they'd wander into the "dead man's curve," altitude and speed that made autorotation impossible. But lower meant warmer, and possibly a reduction in snow. Flakes blistered past the perspex, which was beginning to fog around the edges. Sharpcot pressed forward against the seatbelt restraint, peering through binoculars at the blocks below, but she couldn't make out any with a flat, even top. He leaned and shouted into her ear, "Defogger!"

She searched the dashboard with its quivering gauges, scanned the console between the seats and its useless radios and GPS, found nothing. She looked at Tse, who didn't dare release the controls. He nodded upward and she directed her attention to the overhead panel, found one labelled DEFOG BLOWER, and switched it on.

"There's one beside it that says 'Pitot Heat.' Should I turn that on too?" she cried into his ear.

He gave a sharp nod, frightened he hadn't thought of that, suddenly unable to trust the instruments because the tubes might be plugged with snow and ice.

Sharpcot also saw a switch ANTI COL LT — anti-collision lights — flicked them on, but the strobes illuminated the snowflakes around the craft like uniform bursts of lightning, briefly obliterating visibility, and she cut them off. No fear of aircraft collision.

"Engine anti-icing," he shouted, pointing with the hand that clutched the cyclic to a panel on the console pedestal. Sharpcot located a switch labelled ENG ANTI ICING and toggled it on.

Tse recognized this moment as a pivotal one, where a decision would determine an outcome of either success or disaster. They might punch through the squall in a few minutes, or it could worsen and force them violently down. They'd made good progress, but not the distance they'd hoped to cover. Most of the blocks they'd encountered in their months of travels produced uneven, unstable tops. He thought about the few suitable ones they'd met: jersey barriers, washing machines, cans of peas, those kitchen countertops Loko had climbed, a few others. Or oil platforms, all of which included an actual helicopter landing pad. He considered the buildings, with flat tops, but they'd moved far south of those. They could turn back and escape the storm, outrun it. But that meant erasing their progress, perhaps setting them even further back.

He suffered a panic of indecision. If they had time and quiet, he and Sharpcot could discuss it, weigh pros and cons. Meanwhile he fought to keep the craft stable, making rapid, exhausting adjustments to cyclic, collective, pedals. He sweated despite a chill in the cabin. He was immensely thirsty. The blowers seemed unable to impede the fog creeping in from the margins of the bubble. They passed over a river that threaded through blocks, saw snow accumulated on the trees lining its banks.

Without a decision, he flew on, waiting for Sharpcot to intervene, but she didn't.

Then, for an instant, a shot of sunshine burned through a rift in the clouds, lancing through the snow and striking a block a kilometre ahead. The shiny objects that comprised it formed a beacon of light. Sharpcot raised the binoculars, wincing at the scintillation, looked past it, and saw a clear area beyond. She tried to make out why, expecting the usual suspects: a forest, a lake, a rocky hill, but saw none of that. She panned left, saw a block of darker material, but again, past it: nothing. The block to the right, objects of modest size, in muted hues, also backed by nothing discernible. Could this be it? The edge of the maze?

Its western border? It had to end somewhere. As Leclerc had reasoned, all of human creation wouldn't fill the prairies, and the prairies were ending.

"Past the blocks," she called into his ear.

"What?"

She fanned her hands forward. "Just keep going!"

The sunlight faded. Tse leaned forward, squinting through the snowflakes rushing at them and splitting around the windscreen. Then he saw it too, a ruler-straight boundary that ran north and south as far as he could see, separating the variegated tiles of the maze from an expanse of vacant land beyond.

The engine coughed, socking Sharpcot with panic. It lasted an instant before reengaging.

"What was that?" she cried.

"Turbine is sucking snow," he yelled back. Engine icing too, he thought. Why had he neglected that switch? He began a descent, hoping to enter warmer air.

The turbine hacked again, and this time the loss of power was palpable as the helicopter dropped a few metres before trembling and surging upward as the engine reignited.

Sharpcot pushed herself back and gripped the chair's rim. She tried to relax her shoulders, which were raised in a rigid shrug, as if trying to keep the craft aloft. The chopper laboured into a headwind and their progress towards that borderline felt interminable. She could see through the bubble past the pedals the block below them, all jagged and sharp steel. It looked like bear traps, ten million bear traps, but was likely something more quotidian, a component used in construction or shipbuilding or other manufacturing. It made no difference — they couldn't land there. Descent gave an illusion that the boundary was retreating, even as they approached it.

Sharpcot turned her head and shouted into the rear compartment: "Brace for hard landing!"

Wakely heard the panic in Sharpcot's voice, and Sharpcot only panicked when it was justified.

"Grab onto something, and bend forward, like this," he shouted, assuming the position he'd seen on laminated cards found in airline seat pockets. Involuntarily imagining a nine-storey block of those cards. Everyone complied, even Ike, mimicking the others.

From his bent vantage Wakely glanced out the side window and saw through thick snow nothing but blocks. And then, to the west, and without fanfare, their terminus. On the right, maze, on the left, barren earth and scrub stretching beyond sight. The helicopter descended rapidly as it charged into the west wind, and he felt the force of it against the airframe, buffeting them. The torrent of snow rushing over the edge of the block below revealed the contour of airflow as it struck the wall and soared upwards, resisting the descending craft.

In the cockpit, Tse tried to assess the complications presented by wind and blocks. Through the lower bubble past his feet he watched snow fling itself up and over the wall. He forced himself to breathe, trying to temper his prodigious grip on the cyclic, knowing that without a lighter touch he wouldn't be able to finesse the chopper through the rapidly changing conditions. The machine hesitated in its descent while the updraft buoyed it upward. The ground appeared close, but achievable only by negotiating the gale that harried their flight path. He suffered a moment of doubt — the conditions were beyond him, beyond even an expert pilot.

He picked a spot, focused on it. Just put the machine there, right there, 50 metres away. Snowflakes poured around the canopy. He thought of the turbine, sucking them in. He imagined ice accumulating around the bellmouth, choking it. They hung, suspended over the wall's face in a moment of fragile equilibrium as rotors fought against wind and gravity. Behind them stretched the maze, and ahead, land, foothills, mountains, the sea.

He glanced at Sharpcot, found she'd been watching him, her expression calm. She tipped her head forward, an invitation: let's land. He nodded, set his attention ahead. He released the collective and they fell. He threw the stick forward and the helicopter swooped. The wind and blade downdraft danced elaborately, and he stopped trying to analyze their interaction, surrendered to instinct. It was all he had. The machine charged into the gale, falling towards earth, and when they were two metres above the ground, he jerked the stick back just enough to halt their descent. The wind began to carry them backwards, towards the wall, but in a moment they would be down, and he focused on lowering the collective while watching between his feet the approaching ground. A bench of stone slid into view, he couldn't tell how high, but putting the right skid on it might spill them sideways. A glance right showed it flatter there, a good spot, and he swung the stick and pushed the right pedal. The craft slid sideways and yawed, which brought the left side of the fuselage against the gale, windcocking them hard to the right. Tse jammed the left pedal, but it was too late, the wind had them, swivelling them fully broadside, its force shoving them towards the maze. For an instant they accelerated sideways, until the rotors struck the wall and dug in, flinging consoles of some kind out of the block and hurling them far and wide. As the rotors came apart, Tse rammed the right pedal to the floor, transmitting to the tail rotor a final command, and it pivoted them clockwise, turning the nose towards the wall. The cockpit's right side crashed into the consoles. Tse saw the sound as an amorphous sphere of violet light.

Sharpcot heard wind, a pelt of rain. The roar of the turbine abruptly silenced. She slumped against the seat harness, dazed, limbs slack, listening, until she smelled an electrical burn. She tried to turn to Tse, but before she could, the door flew open and an icy wind accompanied by a cloud of wet snowflakes flooded the cabin.

Wakely was climbing into the cockpit, and she couldn't figure out why.

"There's no room for you," she said, pushing him away.

He defied the shove, leaned in and worked at her harness, released the buckles, then yanked her out of the chair. Something got hung up, an arm behind the seatbelt, and she felt powerless to do anything but look at it, trapped there. Wakely reached in and freed it, then pulled her roughly as he stepped backwards through the door. She came out of the cockpit falling, but Wakely had her, propped her up. She looked into his eyes and saw fire reflected in them. It didn't make sense. He set her down, released her, said, "You all right," a statement, then pushed past her, went back into the cockpit. She glanced around, dazed, the inside of her thigh bruised from hitting the stick when Wakely pulled her free. She took off her helmet and looked into the sky, wondered what was fluttering about, filling the air: cottonwood seeds, moths, confetti? Then the wind struck her, almost bowling her over, and she felt the cold. The rear door stood open, and Virago and Leclerc worked frantically to excavate their meagre possessions, kits and weapons, from the floor of the cabin, casting them onto the ground. She watched the girls, Nasim and . . . she couldn't remember the other's name, the taller one. Yolanda. Watched them dart forward and grab the things, carry them away. The stroller with Ike buckled in stood a short distance away, and he watched it all. Their eyes met, and the boy looked as dazed as she felt. A moment later, a gust of wind came up, and she watched helplessly as it caught the stroller and threw it onto its side. She ran to him, righted it, and kneeled in front of him. She expected him to cry but he didn't, and then she considered that he might be in shock.

One of the devices thrown clear by the rotors lay nearby, and she leaned closer to regard it: a vintage oscilloscope, from the 50s or 60s, faced with knobs and a round screen etched with reference guides. Its side was dished in, by the rotors or from glancing off a nearby outcrop. Gobs of wet snow collecting on the case.

370

A feeling that she had neglected something unsettled her, and she thought it had to do with Lana, maybe forgot to pack pads for her before she went to her father's, who never remembered to stock them. She heard a shriek and turned and saw Leclerc and Virago pressed into the helicopter's front door and the teenaged girls standing off, watching helplessly. Fire sputtered along the top of the machine, around the rotor. She could not decide if this was good or bad. Maybe good because of the cold. A gust of wind rammed her, and she caught the stroller before it went over again. The fire blossomed.

Wakely kneeled in the co-pilot's seat, reaching through the wreckage of the cockpit, trying to release Tse's seatbelt. "That was some excellent flying, Corporal. I can't imagine a better landing considering the circumstances." He continued to talk while he worked, though Tse, eyes shut, did not respond.

He sensed motion above and watched a thread of fire transit the overhead switch console like the tendril of a sea creature. He wondered idly about the location of the helicopter's fuel tanks. The reek of burning insulation filled his nostrils, and he held his breath as he worked. The pilot's side of the cockpit had taken the brunt of the impact. It had snapped the instrument pedestal inward, clamping Tse's lower body into his chair. The cabin was cluttered with bent steel and shattered polycarbonate, along with a smashed oscilloscope that had fallen through the broken canopy.

Wakely worked methodically, rejecting the thought that he should check for a pulse, as it would waste time he could spend freeing the man. He finally got the belt off and bunched Tse's coat in his fists and pulled. Tse's upper body flexed, but his lower half remained obstinately pinned. Tse's helmet came off as he came forward, and Wakely saw the trauma in the light of the fire, a bloody gash from temple to ear.

Someone grabbed the back of Wakely's jacket and pulled. He maintained his grip on Tse, trying to use the combined force to free him.

"Let him go, Jack!" a voice screamed. He expected Sharpcot, but it was Virago. He couldn't wait, he had to take a breath, and the air that filled his mouth and lungs was hot and toxic, and he coughed percussively, loosening his grip on Tse, which launched him backwards as Virago continued to haul. They both went down hard, and he got back up to return to the cockpit. Virago, still down, seized the cuff of his pants and cried, "No!"

He shook her hand free, and as he stepped towards the door a nimbus of flame flared inside the cockpit and engulfed Tse's body. Wakely staggered backwards as Virago continued to pull him. A curtain of fire swept through the cabin and a wall of heat slammed them.

Leclerc stood nearby, her fist at her mouth as she watched the conflagration, and Virago caught her sleeve and pulled. She resisted for an instant, but the heat was tremendous, and she yielded, and they fled together.

They reached Sharpcot and the kids, who had removed to a safe distance. They watched it burn. After a minute, the fire reached the fuel tanks and they blew, scattering debris around them. They felt the heat and the shockwave and saw the snow in the intervening space turn briefly to rain. A hot wind struck them. The chopper continued to burn, along with the face of the block behind it, fire bolstered by wind.

Sharpcot clenched her helmet, feeling the heat against her face and the icy wind at her back, watching the blaze. Corporal Che Yat Tse. That impossible landing. Despite his inexperience and the conditions, he'd managed to not just get them down, but deliberately — it had to be deliberate, and that made him a hero — perform a manoeuvre that saved everyone but himself. Taking the full impact on the pilot's side. Leclerc's face buried in Virago's chest as they held each other. She looked at Wakely, who stood watching the fire, fists opening and closing, when he abruptly doubled forward to cough violently, an extended bout of hacking from which he couldn't seem to recover. She moved to him, hammered his back, she thought too hard because he fell to his knees. She squatted beside him as at last the fit ended and he laboured for breath. He tugged off a glove and wiped the back of a hand across his nose and mouth and it came away smudged black. Virago and Leclerc squatted beside him and Virago said, "What's wrong? Dorian, what's wrong?"

He worked to answer but the breath wouldn't come and he coughed more and at last was able to inhale, but then coughed again, a percussive, hacking bark.

"He inhaled smoke," Leclerc said, wiping her eyes. "He's having trouble breathing."

Wakely tried to speak, but couldn't, nodded, cheeks wet with tears.

"What can we do?" Sharpcot asked.

"Treatment would be oxygen. Through a ventilator. But—"

"I'll be okay," Wakely grunted, his voice hoarse and fragile. He sat back and looked at them each, his breath a soggy wheeze.

"Carbon monoxide and hydrogen cyanide poisoning are risk factors," Leclerc said. "And thermal damage to the mucous membranes. Sir, did you inhale hot smoke?"

He shook his head and shuddered and Virago leaned in and put her arms around him.

"We've got to get out of this wind," Sharpcot said, glancing around. The fire had diminished to the point that it provided no more heat. She looked warily at the wall of blocks, felt the first sense of relief at finally having escaped that maze, but resigned herself to the recognition that it would provide shelter.

"Can you walk?" she asked Wakely.

He nodded, but she knew he'd do that, even if it was barely true.

"Where can we go?" Virago asked. She was pressed against Wakely, almost on top of him, gripping him in her arms.

"Back into the maze. Find a north-south passage. That'll block the wind." Sharpcot swung her ruck onto her back, picked up her rifle. "Let's go."

15

Virago stepped out of the maze from between blocks, the right one enormous and composed of the inner lid seals from jars and bottles, billions of them, foil, foam, paper; blank, patterned, printed with manufacturer logos, "sealed for your protection," "sealed for freshness," "Safety Seal™"; some with a plastic semi-circle "Lift'n'Peel™" tab; from dime-sized to dinnerplate; all of them round, or originally round, many torn. They had sealed shut bottles of medicine, vitamins, peanut butter, mayonnaise, vegetable oil, condiments, juice, sauce, soup, snacks, instant coffee, bodybuilding formula, pet treats, toothpaste, body lotion, makeup, plant food, motor oil, engine coolant, and all manner of products. Peeled and tossed, forgotten. Yet here they were.

"Induction seals," Leclerc said when she thumbed out a few and spread them on her palm. "Blame the Chicago Tylenol poisoner." Virago didn't know what that meant and was too weary to ask.

The left block was all six-sided dice, most of a standard size, in white, with black dots, but others minuscule or gigantic, and in every colour, with different finishes: smooth, bronzed, woodgrain, translucent. They were made from plastic, glass, wood, foam, ceramic, metal. As she passed along the wall, she reached up to stroke the face of a fuzzy pink one. She encountered one the size of a desk and made from concrete, with crudely painted dots, five of them on the exposed face. While most showed dots, other symbols decorated some: numerals, letters, lightning bolts, musical notes, anchors, currency symbols, letters, hearts, skulls, stars, planets, emoji, cartoon characters, expletives. Congratulations, you rolled a "fuck."

Virago collected a few of each, a sampling of lid seals, a bunch of dice, and put them in her pocket to show Wakely. The snow had ceased and melted on the ground, but stepping outside the maze she saw in a copse a hundred metres away that snow yet clung to scrub and trees. She set out towards it. The squall had passed, and while cloud still occluded the overhead sky, to the west — the vast, unobscured-by-blocks west — the cloud had lifted, and from below its hem she saw the setting sun, light casting upwards to brush the clouds, illuminating them from beneath with ochre light. The air didn't feel cold, maybe because of the sun, but night would fall soon and they needed firewood.

As she approached the thicket, the expansiveness beyond the maze immense and unnerving, she cast a rightward glance towards the crash site, several blocks north, beyond the lid seals and a wall of metal sockets, the type you affix to ratchets and wrenches, chrome and molybdenum and brushed steel, from pin-sized to the width of milk jugs. The helicopter was a charred ruin against the foot of the oscilloscopes, a filigree of smoke aglow with sunlight hanging above it. A crematorium for their friend, their brother, Che Yat.

She looked ahead again, banishing it from her sight as she tried to be mindful. Here, free of the maze, now among trees, the air cold and fresh. Picking up deadfall. Feeling the bark's texture against her palms.

Dread at the fringes of her mind, encroaching. Abby gone, now Tse. And Wakely hurt. The picture of him when they'd got him into a sheltered passageway, curled on his side, panting, labouring to catch his breath after the brief walk. Wracked by coughs.

The feeling that intruded wasn't fear or sorrow — it was anger. At his empty heroics. Trying to save Tse, when he couldn't. Futility.

She ducked from under a low branch and watched the sun's crown as it narrowed to a splinter above the hills, then vanished. Cold swept in. She could run away. Without her kit, with nothing. Back into the maze, or set out on her own into a world unpopulated. A thing she'd often wanted to do while civilization existed.

From far off, beyond the whisper of wind, a long, desperate howl. Wolves. It sent a shock through her limbs and made her heart race. A reminder of the world's wildness. The peace left her, and cold and terror replaced it. She pulled the logs and sticks against her breast and dashed back into the maze.

In the alley behind the oscilloscopes, Wakely lay atop a pair of stacked sleeping pads — one was Tse's, rescued from the floor of the chopper along with the rest of his things: kit, C9 machine gun, ammo boxes — covered in a blanket, within a sheltered hollow built from stacked oscilloscopes. A fire burned at the open end of the enclosure, near enough to warm him, but with enough distance to keep the smoke away. Millions of workout tights formed the east wall of the passage, a fabric block that smelled faintly of sweat.

Sharpcot sat with her back to an oscilloscope, watching him, exhausted from the day's events, her neck stiff from the crash. She felt lightheaded, fearing other injuries, until she realized she'd been trying to influence Wakely's tormented breathing with her own deep and measured respiration.

She recalled a childhood memory: kneeling on the planks of her grandfather's verandah, watching his old dog Shebah, a big, kind-hearted husky, draw her last breaths.

She looked across the passageway at Leclerc, who sat hunched with arms folded across her chest, staring vacantly. The girls had taken Ike for a walk, on foot, left the stroller behind in the hopes of tiring him out. He'd grown agitated, then inconsolable, while they built the oscilloscope shelter, and when Wakely folded on the pad and fell into a rough slumber the boy urged him to get up, "Get up!" His voice growing louder with each call, as he bent his knees and threw his arms skyward like a preacher.

Virago returned with an armful of wood and tossed it on the pile.

"I heard wolves," she said.

"Next time take your rifle," Sharpcot replied.

Virago looked at Leclerc, was about to speak, just touched her shoulder and sat beside her. She looked at Wakely, saw that his lips were chapped and peeling as he laboured for breath.

The kids returned, Yolanda carrying Ike, who was asleep. Virago got up and they arranged a nest for him from blankets.

"What did you see?" Sharpcot asked the girls as they settled around the fire. Nasim was shivering, leaned towards the flames.

"Thumbtacks. Miso soup packs. Then a huge block of these." Yolanda pulled out a stack of buff-coloured cards, elongated, covered in rows of numbers, with many small square holes. She handed one to Sharpcot.

"I don't know," she said as she held it to the light. "Looks familiar though."

"Can I see?" Leclerc asked, abruptly present. Sharpcot passed her the card. "Yes. Computer punch card."

"What's that?" Nasim asked.

"It's how they used to store digital information," Leclerc replied, sitting up. "Before tape, disks, solid-state memory. You'd need 200 million of these to match the memory in a low-end phone."

"Well, we found a thousand phones worth," Yolanda said. "Over that way. Across from these." She opened her hand to show them a small white power brick.

"Apple iPhone 5-Watt USB adaptor," Leclerc stated.

"I know. That block went on forever. Like 500 feet, both directions."

"Billions of chargers, and nothing to plug them in to," Virago said. "I'd kill to hear music right now. Even one song."

Sharpcot thought to ask her what song, but couldn't answer that question herself. A final song. A question too monumental to answer. "Greensleeves"? "What a Wonderful World"? "Respect"? "Stairway to Heaven"? "Hey Jude"? "Stayin' Alive"? "Uptown Funk"? "No One Is Lost"?

She set a pot of water to boil for miso soup, and they sat silently looking at the fire, listening to Wakely's wheezing.

They ate soup from tin cups. It was hot and salty and good, and when Sharpcot looked at Wakely he was leaning on an elbow watching them.

"Smells good," he croaked, trying and failing to suppress a cough.

"I'll get you some," Virago said, concealing the relief she felt at seeing him conscious and alert. They had no clean cups so she added some to her own from the pot at the edge of the fire. She kneeled before him and lifted a spoonful and said, "I hope you don't mind my germs."

"Don't mind," he replied, and sipped from the spoon, swallowed, and gripped his throat. "Maybe let it cool."

"Don't worry about germs," Leclerc said. "Cold and flu viruses are dead by now, with no one left to carry them."

"Do you always find the bright side?" Yolanda asked her.

"It's just a fact," Leclerc said.

Virago helped prop Wakely against the oscilloscope wall, padding his blanket behind him. She blew on a spoonful of soup to cool it.

Wakely suffered a coughing fit, bent sideways with Virago's hand on his shoulder as he pulled aside the sleeping pad, she couldn't determine why, until he spat a gob of black mucus onto the earth. She couldn't tell in the low light if it was soot, blood, or both. She gave him water and he drank, tried to get him to eat more soup, but he wanted lie down.

"Not flat," he said, and she and Sharpcot arranged clothing from their rucks into a ramp. He fell into restless slumber punctuated by coughs and groans. Virago watched his shifting eyelids, wondered what he was dreaming.

Maintaining a good fire required fuel, and Virago volunteered to collect more.

"Rifle. And someone to help," Sharpcot ordered.

Yolanda volunteered but asked first for the return of her hunting knife. Sharpcot dug around in her ruck and handed it to the girl, and she stowed it in a sheath on her belt.

Looking at the pair of them, Sharpcot said she pitied any beast or man they encountered.

They set off into the dark with a flashlight, used it only sporadically to conserve the battery. Nighttime always provided a clear reminder of civilization's demise, but it was intensified when they stepped outside the maze and were no longer surrounded by products. A stiff wind greeted them as they treaded towards the trees.

"You said you heard wolves?" Yolanda asked.

"Far off."

"Still, let's keep the flashlight on. More or less."

"I vote more," Virago replied, and illuminated their path.

They arrived at the copse and collected as much as they could carry, had turned back to the dark wall of the maze when Yolanda exclaimed, "What's that?"

A crown of light rose above the blocks some distance to the southeast. It reminded Virago of the light a sports field or stadium casts into a summer sky, like the baseball diamond behind her high school during night games.

"It must be people," Virago stated.

"That's a lot of light. They have some tech."

"Maybe medical stuff."

They hurried back, fear of wolves forgotten.

Sharpcot thought it wiser to wait until morning to investigate. "But what if they have medicine? Oxygen?" Virago insisted. "You're sure it wasn't something else? The moon?" Sharpcot asked.

Virago and Yolanda answered simultaneously: "Definitely not the moon." "You should see, it's like a small city."

Sharpcot considered for only a minute before she told them to go. "Take Cheree."

The three of them set off along an eastbound passage, Virago worried they'd be unable to locate it from within the maze, but while crossing the fifth intersection they saw a corona of light in the sky, some distance to the south. They headed towards it, glancing at items revealed in the flashlight's beam: 16mm film projectors, duck decoys, triangular wooden frames used to rack billiard balls, as well as useful items they collected: thermoses, blunt-nosed pliers, purple shotgun shells, tins of mandarin oranges in light syrup. The luminescence grew as they approached, and Virago turned off the flashlight. The white light glanced down the passageway, illuminating a wall of kitchen hutches on the right, the glare from their glass doors forcing Virago to tip her head and block it with her helmet's brim. They moved cautiously, pausing frequently and squatting to survey the passage. Virago glanced through her rifle's scope and fouled night vision in one eye, and she didn't do it again. The scale of the light suggested many congregated people. In preparation for an encounter, Virago and Leclerc walked with their rifles lowered but ready, and they put Yolanda behind them. She complained, but Virago hushed her, then tilted her head, listening for voices.

They passed a block of mouldering toaster waffles, formerly frozen, the smell bad. They continued to approach, shading their eyes as the source came into view.

Nasim glanced up in alarm, her eyes on the intersection 20 metres below the camp, and Sharpcot turned and saw bluish light flickering in the passage. She grabbed her rifle and they both rose and moved cautiously towards the crossroads, saw the light propagate along sliver cylinders — vertical autoclaves — that constituted the south wall of the passage.

"That you, Princess Pats?" Sharpcot called before peering around the corner to watch the approach of a multitude of clustered lights, blinding after the dim firelight.

"It's us," Virago replied, and they arrived in a sphere of light, each of them clutching a bouquet of glowing lanterns. They were LED landscaping lamps, each on a stalk with a spike, topped by a capped globe with an embedded solar panel.

Wakely watched them file into the camp like a holy procession, conveying the last light of civilization. They staked them around the camp, and a cool, bluish radiance spread out on the ground and illuminated the walls.

"Good score," he croaked when Virago sat near him.

"We hoped it was something else," Virago confessed as she sat, but didn't elaborate.

"These are great," he reassured her. "Charge in the daytime, and they'll burn half the night."

She wanted to tell him about their arrival at the block, millions of devices that captured sunlight all day, only to liberate it throughout the night. He'd like that evocation. She wanted to describe that titanic cube of brilliance. Wanted to explain her feelings, disappointment at the discovery, and even confess her irrational notion that illumination had to mean medical care. As she prepared to speak, she realized she'd never wanted to share feelings and ideas of that kind — foolish ones, illogical ones — with anyone before. With him it felt okay. It felt safe.

But before she could talk he began to cough, doubling sideways. He spit dark phlegm into a cup.

"I'm so sorry," he said as she took the cup, and she tried to tell him it was all right. But was too scared to speak. She went

382

around the corner and dumped it in the earth, returned and rinsed it with water from her canteen, and when she kneeled beside him to talk she saw he'd closed his eyes, the light tinting his lips blue, and she feared it wasn't just the light.

They spread their plunder, shotgun shells, pliers, a couple of thermoses. Sharpcot immediately set a pot to boil, to fill them for ready access to hot water. They opened tins of oranges, feasted on them, the little wedges, the sweet syrup.

"We found these dollhouse tables on the way back," Yolanda said, holding out a palm to show a couple of round white disks with legs.

"Not tables," Sharpcot said.

"What then?"

"You don't eat pizza?" Virago asked the girl.

"Sure. We'd eat at the one shitty pizzeria in Bowman. With this racist waiter who always got into lame debates about us with Gentle."

"Right," Sharpcot said. "But these. I don't know what you call them."

"Pizza savers," Leclerc said.

Sharpcot set one of the tables upright in her hand. "Goes in the middle of the pizza, keeps the box lid from squishing the toppings."

"Well there were a fuck-load of them," Yolanda replied.

"I'd kill even for that crappy Bowman pizza right now," Nasim sighed.

Wakely spent two days in fitful slumber, coughing, his sputum, though prodigious, becoming clearer and less bloody. But short walks leaning on Sharpcot or Virago winded him, forcing him back to the sleeping pad.

The days warmed, and the others explored, venturing far, encountering curiosities: money counting machines, burr coffee grinders, sea sponges, disposable nipple covers, jars of Ninja

Squirrel hot sauce, faux wood Venetian blind wands, dry farfalle pasta, multicoloured pipe cleaners. They collected what was useful: a couple of sponges, one jar of hot sauce, as much pasta as they could carry.

"So no nipple covers?" Yolanda wondered as they moved past the small block made of beige, brown, and black discs in satin, silicone, cotton, and polyester.

"We'll need them when our bras start failing," Virago said. "And we have a formal event to attend." She tugged at a strap through her T-shirt. "Do we even need to keep wearing these?"

"Speak for yourself, sister," Leclerc said. "I need support."

"So take yours off," Yolanda said to Virago. "Maybe it'll revive Jack."

Virago felt her face go hot, and Yolanda laughed, while Nasim scowled.

"Come on, Nas," Yolanda said. "Nothing's proper anymore."

Leclerc was stricken in that moment by a surge of grief, and she sat heavily on the ground and bawled while the others kneeled around her, respecting her aversion to physical contact she didn't herself initiate, quietly letting it run its course. When she recovered Yolanda handed her a nipple cover.

"Save Kleenex," she said, and Leclerc blew her nose into it, and that set off a wave of hilarity, and they laughed until they cried.

"We need more pipe cleaners," Leclerc said suddenly, but wouldn't say why, and they hurried back a few blocks and collected handfuls.

When they neared the camp Leclerc dashed ahead and kneeled in front of Ike and pulled out the pipe cleaners and together they made things: a cat, a giraffe, an airplane, pairs of enormous glasses for everyone.

Wakely woke in afternoon sunshine, his vision rimmed in a pinkish glow, and looked across the fire at Sharpcot holding Ike and reading a board book. He reached up and pulled off a pair of pink glasses formed from pipe cleaners. He slipped them back on, and said, "Hey."

Ike and Sharpcot looked up from the book, and Ike laughed so hard he fell out of Sharpcot's lap.

Wakely woke to a cold, clear dawn. He felt marginally better, his throat and lungs yet raw. As he surveyed the sleepers in the nascent light, a cough threatened to erupt, and he invoked mindful calm to suppress it. When he lifted his cup to drink his lip broke a skin of ice.

Sharpcot woke and he told her it was time to go.

"We're not leaving you," she stated.

"I know that," he laughed, suppressing a cough. "I'm coming."

"It's a bad idea."

"Staying here is a bad idea. Winter here is a bad idea."

Leclerc suggested ibuprofen might help him.

"But it isn't my head."

"The problem is inflammation in your lungs and throat," Leclerc explained. "Ibuprofen is a non-steroidal anti-inflammatory. It won't cure you, but it will help you breathe."

She went to her ruck and got out a bottle and handed it to him.

He shook it, and it sounded only a quarter full. "What about your migraines?"

"They've been less frequent. And this is more important," she replied.

"And Tylenol?" Sharpcot asked. "I have some for menstrual cramps. I can't take ibu because it wrecks my stomach. But I remember once when Lana was really sick the doctor gave her both."

"It's not an NSAID, but it will help with the pain."

They crushed the tablets and dissolved them in warm water because he couldn't bear to swallow them whole. Sharpcot ordered rest while they broke camp, and as he lay wheezing he thought only a miracle would get him moving. Willing the drugs to deliver one. Sharpcot wouldn't leave him behind. He'd either manage the walking, or it would kill him. Either way, it meant these people, his friends, his family, would be on their way.

There was too much to carry, and they parsed the goods by utility. Nutritionally dense foods took priority, as well as much of what they had collected from the survivalists: tools, knives, a saw, a hatchet, the fishing rod, camping cookware, seeds. From their own supplies, warm clothing, blankets, rain ponchos, which could be arranged into shelters.

Distributing Tse's possessions proved to be difficult for everyone, especially Leclerc. His XXL clothing was useful, but not much else.

"What about the Minimi?" Virago wondered, nodding at Tse's machine gun propped against the oscilloscopes.

"One of you want to carry it?" Sharpcot asked the teenaged girls.

"No thank you," Yolanda said quickly, palms raised. Nasim bent her head, shaking it.

"We'll teach you to use the rifles. The machine gun is less useful for hunting. But we'll take the ammo. Same rounds as the C7. They use disintegrating links." She drew a belt end from the ammunition box and pushed a bullet free from the link. She held it up and said, "That'll fit your rifle."

Yolanda said, "You kick ass, Sarge."

They paused at the helicopter wreck, its burned-out skeleton, to pay respects to Corporal Tse. Sharpcot didn't know what to say, until Leclerc handed her a tiny Holy Bible. She'd found it in his ruck, one page bookmarked with a maple key. Sharpcot surveyed the onionskin, picked out a section from Matthew 6, and read, "Therefore I tell you, do not worry about your life, what you will eat or drink; or about your body, what you will wear. Is not life more than food, and the body more than clothes?

Look at the birds of the air; they do not sow or reap or store away in barns, and yet your heavenly Father feeds them. Are you not much more valuable than they? Can any one of you by worrying add a single hour to your life?"

She lifted her face, and everyone seemed to be waiting for her to make sense of the words. Other than, "don't fuss, God will make it okay," she had no answer. What significance had the page held for Che Yat? Or was the maple key randomly lodged there? And if so, what did that mean?

They left his discarded possessions at the foot of the wreck, the machine gun, disabled; personal items: a small photo album of his parents; his dead phone; a notebook in which he'd been practicing Chinese logograms; the Bible.

Then they moved out of the shadow of the wall to where the sunshine warmed them.

"Take point," Sharpcot said to Wakely. "Set a pace you can manage."

They travelled due south, parallel to the wall. Earlier, Sharpcot and Wakely had conferred over the road atlas and estimated their position. Reasoning that roads were placed to negotiate the easiest route over land, they proposed locating Interstate 90, its stripped roadbed, which ran west. Before it hit higher elevations, they'd take Interstate 25 south, then state highways that would keep them on a more or less straight trajectory to Interstate 80. That would lead them through Salt Lake City, the Great Salt Lake Desert — 80 kilometres, good it wasn't summertime — through Reno, the Sierra Nevadas (Sharpcot's greatest concern), Sacramento, and finally on to San Francisco. Then down the coast to Santa Cruz, why not settle in Monterey?

"I hear it's suddenly affordable," Virago said.

For now, they moved parallel to the maze, for its potential to offer practical resources, food or tools. They could always hope to find a block of vehicles of some kind. ATVs. Segways.

"I'd settle for a gas-guzzling Hummer," Virago confessed.

Wakely's kit and other items had been distributed among the group, everything but his rifle, which he insisted on carrying. There might be wolves, bears, cougars, or worse: humans.

They halted frequently, the stops called by Sharpcot when she saw Wakely flagging, and though he insisted he was fine, he would lie down and wheeze, close his eyes and then startle out of sleep with coughs. Then he would be up again and insisting they move.

They kept to the sunshine beyond the maze's shadow, for warmth and to charge the garden lanterns, which they'd fastened to their kits. Sharpcot sent Virago, Leclerc, or the girls into corridors in the maze as they passed, where they'd go in and hook right and sprint through the alley that paralleled their path and emerge from the next passageway to describe the composition of the blocks they encountered. They discovered electric fans, church pews, gyroscopes, bird cages, pinball machines, flyswatters, coffee tampers, and shields made from natural materials — animal hide, turtle shells — along with the usual assortment of unknown gewgaws, unidentifiable machine parts, and building supplies. Wakely taking it all down in his notebook. Also, food: tins of pumpkin pie filling, tins of sliced beets, pouches of chocolate-covered almonds.

They stopped for a long lunch during which Wakely drifted into a fitful sleep. They ate exclusively from the local foods they'd found, which they'd over-collected. It made for a weird, nauseating lunch. Yolanda, who could stand neither pumpkin nor beets, forced herself to eat some of each, chased them with a handful almonds, and promptly threw up behind a shrub. Ike couldn't stomach the sweetened pumpkin filling, but surprised everyone by gorging on beets.

"That's going to make a pretty mess," Nasim mumbled.

"At least he's done with diapers," Yolanda said, her eyes rimmed by tears from vomiting. "Which became necessary the moment we ran out of diapers."

The talk of excretion made Ike need to go, and Nasim took him off beyond a small rise.

When Virago and Leclerc went to explore the local blocks, Yolanda rose to join them, but sat again, nauseated. Sharpcot gave her miso soup, which she'd prepared that morning in a thermos. The girl sipped it, colour returning to her cheeks. Nasim and Ike returned, the boy restless and bored. Yolanda told him to find a stick, and he hunted around and brought her several. She selected one, got out the hunting knife, and began to whittle. "What making?" Ike asked, but Yolanda hushed him and demanded patience.

Wakely woke with a coughing fit, but it seemed to Sharpcot brief and less intense. Wasn't it? He sat up and looked around, his face grey and filmed with sweat.

"What are we eating?" he asked.

"Beets," Sharpcot replied.

"For god's sake," he moaned.

"Or pumpkin pie. Well, the filling."

"This is a special hell."

Sharpcot held out the sack of chocolate almonds and he smiled weakly, took a few.

They went on in the afternoon, and as they travelled, the landscape to the west began to rise into scrub-covered hills, and at one point a ridge pushed close to the maze, and the party had to follow its contour, moving into a narrow gap between the hill's foot and a block comprised of sewer grates.

They passed spice jars of paprika, scenting the air, followed by hydraulic car jacks, honey wands, and then a block of the same basic figurine in ceramic and wood and pewter and plastic: a man in robes, gazing downwards, sometimes holding a staff,. sometimes reaching out, or with a raised palm, or a hand on his breast. His expression amazed.

"It's Joseph," Yolanda laughed, holding one up. "From Christmas nativity scenes. See? He's looking at the baby Jesus." Then she added in a fool's tone, "Yo, I don't think that's my kid."

"Chastity would beat you so hard for that, Yol," Nasim muttered.

They overnighted in a glade beside a stream, where they built a fire on the bank and slept to the purl of water over flat stones. The night cold and moonless and the stars almost too sharp to look at. Sharpcot slept well with the river's burble drowning out the rasp and gurgle of Wakely's breathing. And once during the night Virago awoke to see his face so pale in the starlight. She watched for a while, then in fear leaned in close to listen. If anything his breathing sounded clearer, and she took his hand gently, and fell asleep clutching it.

Sharpcot tried to locate in the atlas the roads that once occupied the bare roadbeds they crossed, but couldn't find a definitive match, casting doubt on their conjectured position. She knew that sooner or later they would have to cross Interstate 90, which she hoped would be identifiable as such. The terrain became increasingly variable, with rocky, scrubby hills to the west, and on the east, areas where the maze had to negotiate rises and descents, while the block height obstinately followed the land's contour.

Wakely drove himself hard, wouldn't stop until he staggered, sometimes fell, and even then they had to urge him to rest. He refused any more of the pills, claimed they didn't work, though Sharpcot suspected he meant to conserve them. Doubt plagued her as she tried to find a balance between time lost resting and the pace gained by those rests. Would two or three more days of convalescence pay off? She didn't know, and Wakely wouldn't relent. "Winter," he would remind her whenever she broached the topic. They'd decided it would take 60 days to reach the coast. Symbolically, that would put them there on the first calendar day of winter. But anything could happen with the weather, especially through the higher altitudes, the mountain passes.

They walked in a line on the hardpacked earth, the girls in good hiking boots, Sharpcot silently thanking their survivalist custodians for splurging on premium gear. Everyone took turns pushing the stroller, sometimes portaging it, dodging through scrub, over hillocks, through scree and gravel. The sun weak beyond a veil of cirrus.

Sharpcot decided earlier that day to increase their distance from the maze boundary, when she realized someone or something could surprise them from one of the apertures, but they continuously drifted closer, as if craving civilization's trappings. Their curiosity about the blocks drawing them in. Sharpcot the one to notice, to call out, let's take it away from the wall, keep our distance. As she herself tried to resist the pull.

They ran past furniture casters, shower heads, pool skimmers, designer makeup bags, garage door opener remotes, and elongated steel tanks, painted maroon.

"Unfair, and frankly ironic," Leclerc declared as they passed them.

"Why?" Virago asked.

"That colour means they're filled with acetylene."

"Why is that unfair?"

"Because for welding they get paired with oxygen bottles. The master corporal doesn't need acetylene."

Virago looked ahead to Wakely, staggering along. Tears of rage filled her eyes, blurring the landscape. Acetylene when he needed oxygen. Goddamn it. Why?

They passed Hanukkah menorahs, many ornate, ancient, others clean and modern, all in gold and silver and pewter and steel, big and small. There was a brass one 30 feet high embedded in the wall. These were followed by aluminum street lamps, stacked vertically, end-on-end, three high to reach block height, packed together like asparagus, with the booms on which lights were mounted all oriented to the left. The group maintained their distance, viewing from far off the stalks, with their million million glass globes, shining in sunlight. They passed it for two kilometres, and when it ended they encountered a strange block of various large, delicate objects that glittered strangely.

It brought Wakely to a stop, and Leclerc drew up beside him, and they stared at it, a hundred metres away, not a large collection, not after the street lamps. The way its diverse surfaces reflected sunlight made it appear, in some inexplicable way, auspicious.

Leclerc begin to walk towards the wall as if spellbound, and Wakely followed, tried to keep up, but she moved at a strong pace, with a curious air of purpose, something that had been lacking since the crash and Tse's death.

She reached the foot of the wall and gazed up. Wakely approached, taking in the view, the intricacy and dazzle, perceiving iconic shapes in its composition.

"Is it . . . ?" Wakely asked when he arrived, sweating and panting. He knew what it was, but couldn't finish the question, because the implications devastated him.

"Spacecraft," Leclerc said. "Satellites." The glint of sunlight on solar panels, gold foil, antennae, parabolic dishes, lenses, attitude thrusters.

A wave of fatigue gripped him, and he stumbled, and Leclerc moved to catch him, threw her arm around his waist. He laboured for breath, leaned away from her, knowing her aversion to touch, but she held on, keeping him upright. He'd never appreciated how short she was until she stood against him. Her intelligence enlarged her in his mind. And yet after all these months, in the bunker, through the maze, he didn't know her at all.

She spotted something high up and let go, forgetting him as she stepped back for a better view. He caught a spar on the satellite at eye level, steadying himself.

"That boxy one up there with the multitude of protuberances," she explained. "That's a global positioning satellite. No wonder we couldn't get a GPS fix."

Wakely gazed up, asked, "You don't think they're from a facility somewhere, warehoused, freshly built? Waiting to get launched?"

She moved closer, reached up to touch a strut that supported an expansive panel of deep, reflective black, etched with hairline patterns, one of the object's twin solar panels. "This one isn't new. It's been up there, in orbit. The metal is pitted. Abraded."

"By what?"

"Micrometeorite collisions. Space debris. Junk in orbit travelling at 28,000 kilometres per hour. Moving at that speed even a fleck of paint will inflict damage."

Wakely panted, looking up at the block. "It must've been retrieved from orbit. You know, for repair."

"They're all like that," Leclerc said, moving her hands to the next object, a large cylinder with its body shrouded in the borosilicate of solar panels. It seemed antiquated, more distressed. She bent, tracing with fingertips, studying its exposed side, and found an aluminum plate affixed to the base. On it, a hammer and sickle. CCCP. "This is Soviet," she said.

"Russian."

"Soviet," she said, pointing to the label.

"From a museum."

She was about to protest, to tell him satellites came down one way, in burning fragments, but she turned and saw his stricken expression, watched him labour for breath.

He released the spar, steadied himself, and began to pace laterally along the block. It wasn't huge — the standard nine stories, around 100 metres on its western face. It had a surreal quality, exotic, alien. All of these devices, built for space, in cleanrooms, by technicians in hooded suits. They were simultaneously delicate — to conserve weight for transport, and because they would live in microgravity — and hardy, to withstand the high Gs of launch, then the hard vacuum, radiation, and enormous temperature gradients of space. Some shelled in solar panels, others with deployed arrays, spread wide and intermingled.

Seized from the sky and returned to this quotidian Earth.

Sharpcot impatiently watched the pair lingering at the wall's foot, was about to call for a resumption of travel when she saw Wakely back away from it and stop, head raised, scrutinizing.

Virago set out to meet him, but hesitated, struck by his sudden fragility, where previously, even in illness, he'd been determined, resilient, immutable.

"What are you looking for, Jack?" she called.

"Something I spotted from back there," he replied without turning.

She came forward and halted just behind him and heard the caustic rasp of his breath. They mustn't travel further — this thought came to her forcefully — they must stop until he recovers. She walked past him, cut to the right to check the next block for anything useful, but it was nothing but spirit levels, in wood and steel and plastic. When she turned she saw him step to the wall, examining a tetartoidal satellite at eye level. He reached out, gripped a beam, she thought at first to dislodge it, break it free, but at the same moment he jammed a boot into the gap between the satellite and the boxy one below it, and he hauled himself up. Climbing.

She surged forward, saw Sharpcot by the kids also start towards him.

"Jack!" Sharpcot exclaimed.

Wakely planted his other foot into a recess as he tugged himself higher. With determination he got above the two bottom satellites and was on to the next before Virago arrived below, arms upraised as if to prop him up, or catch him if he fell. Sharpcot broke into a run, calling for his attention, her voice frayed with alarm.

Virago grabbed the same beam Wakely had used, put in a boot, and drew herself up. She moved to his left, finding ample handholds, reminding her of the helicopter climb. He paused for breath, fogging the glass of the solar panel in front of him, and in a few expert motions she reached him.

"Jack. Dorian. Come on down now. You're going to fall."

He didn't look at her, resumed the plodding climb, panting and wheezing, face drenched with sweat. She followed beside him, and when she didn't need her right arm she pressed it to his back, supporting him. They were three metres above the ground, then four.

Sharpcot had reached the wall's base and called in an official tone, "Master Corporal Wakely, would you mind explaining what you are doing?" He ignored her and continued his ascent. "Jack, I *order* you to stop climbing and come down."

Wakely persevered, and Virago continued to shadow him. He was slowing, each pull more laboured than the last. He rubbed a brow against his shoulder to keep the sweat from running into his eyes. Virago looked down and didn't like their height. A fall would break limbs, or worse.

She thought exhaustion would convince him to stop, to retreat, but he doubled down on his efforts, working with such resolution that his face flushed and cords stood out on his neck. She kept pace with him, then moved laterally so she was pressing against him from behind, propping him up, keeping him aloft. At one point he sagged against her, would have fallen had she not received the weight of his body.

"Come on now, Dorian," she whispered into his ear. "Please." Trying to mask the fact that she was crying. He was trying to kill himself. When he was high enough, he would let go. She would not allow it to happen. Her own limbs ached, but she forced her body against his, holding him there. He climbed higher and she moved with him.

"Here," he croaked suddenly, pausing. They were 20 metres up, and had reached the top of a barrel-shaped satellite. Just above it lay a small craft crowned by a vast white dish, easily 12 feet in diameter, the antenna's rim flush with the wall's perimeter, leaving a recessed area, a shelf. With gasps and grunts, Wakely hauled his body into this alcove and fell against the craft's V-shaped legs, panting and coughing. Instrument clusters branched left and right, mingling with the panels and peripherals of the satellites packed around it. Virago climbed into the nook beside him, waved down to the others. Sharpcot stood glaring upwards, hands on hips.

Wakely kneeled, each cough wracking him with agony, and she put her hands on his back and implored him to lie down, to rest, but he reached for the satellite, gripped a spar, and yanked himself upright, intent on examining the craft.

Its body was an octahedron shrouded in black fabric, with cutouts for vents on the left and right. The object of Wakely's fascination, however, was mounted on the centre face: a golden disc a foot in diameter, on which there were curious engravings. Wakely gripped one of the spars and his head fell against the craft's hull, the blanket, with his cheek against the disc.

Virago sat back, watching him. His coughs had ceased, but only because he was too weak. He sweated profusely, face colourless but calm. Eyes closed, lids tinted blue. It felt warm in the nook, despite an icy wind that imposed from the west. She thought the warmth was due to exertion, but that wasn't it. The craft itself the apparent source of heat. There was something alive about it, functional. It was powered up. There was no hum or vibration to suggest it, just the heat, and a sense of alertness.

"What is happening up there?" Sharpcot called.

Virago leaned out. "Resting," she called. "Just . . . resting."

Sharpcot was about to demand further information, but Virago drew back into the cavity. She moved beside Wakely, studied the disc. It had a circle engraved at the upper left, what looked like an exploding star with long lines at the bottom left, some zigzags and rectangles on the right side. She looked out at the land, the kids seated on a low outcrop, Ike pushing the stroller around in a flat area. She spotted just south of their position something that looked like a wide path, a trough in the earth a foot deep. It emerged from beneath the maze and traversed the landscape as far as she could see, into the distant mountains. The interstate.

When she turned back Wakely hadn't moved, but his eyes were open, examining the disc.

"Jack, what is this thing? What kind of satellite?"

"Not satellite," he gasped. "Probe. Space probe."

"Like the kind that went to Mars?"

"Yes. And no. Not a lander. *Voyager*."

"So it voyages?"

"It's named *Voyager*. Not sure which one; there were two. Are two."

He brought up a hand and traced the disc with his fingers. He muttered something she couldn't hear.

"Pardon?"

"They want to erase us," he whispered.

"Who?"

"The Accruers."

"Erase us? What does that mean?"

He finally turned and she looked into his eyes. They were deep brown, almost black. She hadn't noticed that before, wondered if they had darkened. Could the smoke have done that?

"My grandparents, my mom's parents. They're, uh, what do you call them? Snowbirds. Have this condo in Florida. One year when I was 12 they brought me a poster from Cape Canaveral, a NASA poster. Of the *Voyager* spacecraft. You know, a painting of one of them passing Jupiter, a schematic, facts and figures, launched in 1977, the most distant manmade objects, and still travelling away from Earth."

He wheezed for a time, and he gazed out at the world, expansive beyond the maze, and she thought that was all he had to say, but it wasn't. He turned back to the craft against which he rested.

"It's just a thing. A thing I would google every few years. Where are you now, *Voyager 1* and *2*? Always further from Earth, and still broadcasting. Last time I checked they were 20 billion kilometres out, and still going, still functioning. But here, right here, is one of them." He patted its hull. "And the other is probably in this same block."

"Maybe it's just a model, from a museum," Virago said quietly.

He ran a palm over the disc, felt its abraded surface, relentlessly pinged by the solar wind and microscopic particles. He shook his head. But it was more than that. This craft felt old, well-travelled. There was something worn about it, a kind of structural exhaustion. It had been out there, like nothing else, ever.

He suffered a deep hacking fit, doubled over, face pressed to his knee, barking and gasping. He wiped his mouth and the back of his hand showed a bloody streak. He looked up, dazed and dizzy, his eyes drifting over Virago and then back at *Voyager*, a look of surprise passing over his features, as if seeing it for the first time. He reached up and touched the disc.

"What have you seen, old friend?" he muttered.

"What is that round thing?" Virago asked. She didn't care but had to keep him talking. She kneeled and shifted closer, traced a finger over the engraved surface.

"There's a record inside," he said. "For the aliens."

"What does that mean?"

"A gold record. With information encoded on it. If the craft ever encountered another intelligent species, out there, they could play the record and find out about us. About Earth. Humans. Pictures, voices, music."

"And what's all this?" she asked, indicating the engraved surface.

"Instructions on how to play it. How to build a record player and find out who we are."

"I guess the Accruers never bothered," she whispered.

A single nut at the cover's centre held it in place. She reached up and closed its sprocketed head between her fingers and gave it an experimental turn, and to her surprise, it moved without much effort. Maybe 40 billion kilometres of travel had loosened it. In a few turns the nut came off and she was holding the recessed cover, with the record inside its shell, in her hands. She set the cover down and lifted out the record.

"It's heavy," she said. "Is it solid gold?"

"Copper. Plated in gold," Wakely said.

She clasped the rim between her palms and regarded the label, which read, in curved lettering, "THE SOUNDS OF EARTH." And below that, in smaller text: "Side 1. NASA. UNITED STATES OF AMERICA. PLANET EARTH." Something was hand-etched into the takeout grooves, and she tilted it to the light and read the words aloud: "To the makers of music — all worlds, all times."

When she looked at Wakely, he had a hand out. He looked gravely ill, but he stretched for it, grunting, and she placed it in his hand. She wanted to say something as his fingertips closed clumsily over the grooved face, but she remained mute, watching.

He examined it briefly, turned it over in his hands, then in one swift move, flung the disk away, so it frisbeed into the open air. It fell 20 metres and struck the ground on its rim and rolled a few metres, wobbling on the flattened edge, before it flopped over in the dry scrub.

"We are conquered," Wakely said to Virago's astonished gaze. He drew his knees up and pushed his face against them and let out a long sigh, and lay motionless, quaking, barely breathing.

Virago sat up, suddenly alert, as if an announcement had been made, and she better pay attention. Nothing seemed to be different, yet everything was. She became acutely aware of everything around her, the wheeze of Wakely's breath, the shudder of his jacket collar in the wind, the way the sheath of the satellite on which she kneeled yielded under her weight. There was a smell to these craft that she couldn't identify. The smell of space.

When she looked out of the alcove she saw the land, the sky, the brush. The wind had come a long way to reach her, and it had a long way to go after it passed. The kids had moved off to a series of boulders, among which the teens were playing tag with Ike. None of them showed any joy at the game; they played because they had to. She looked up to the white ceiling of *Voyager*'s high gain antenna curving upwards to a sky that was azure beyond the dish's stark rim.

She heard a noise from below and when she looked she saw Sharpcot climbing to meet them. She watched the sergeant's cautious ascent, reaching gingerly for hand- and footholds, but also her strength, her mastery of an activity she didn't relish. A woman climbing a wall of satellites and space probes. She watched until Sharpcot arrived, put out a hand to pull her into the alcove.

Sharpcot's attention landed on Wakely, who did not acknowledge her arrival.

"Hey, Jack?" she said softly, rested a hand on his arm. He shifted away from her.

"He just needs rest," Virago said.

Sharpcot turned to Virago with a look of annoyance. She was about to speak, but didn't, appeared to be governing her emotion in a way Virago realized she always did, but in this instance her control had slipped. Which frightened her.

"We have to get him down," Sharpcot said. "Jack, can you climb? Dorian?"

They took shifts sitting with him in the alcove while the others camped below at the mouth of the passageway between satellites and spirit levels. Sharpcot didn't sleep that night, sat awake beside him, listening to his fitful breaths. Wind rumpled the barrier made from raincoats they'd stretched over the opening, and yet the nook felt curiously warm, even in the depths of night. Leclerc explained a possible source of heat: the probe's radioisotope thermoelectric generator, which contained capsules of decaying plutonium-238.

Virago saw light coming up on the face of the satellite over which she was climbing, and by the time she reached the shelf,

400

the overcast sky had taken on a grey cast. She pulled herself into the cavity and tied open the curtain to let in the nascent light. She and Sharpcot spoke quietly of the prospects for the coming days and how they would manage the camp while Wakely convalesced.

"We can wait a week, no more," Sharpcot whispered.

"A week should be enough. He'll get better. He's strong," Virago replied.

They sat in silence for a few minutes. When Sharpcot checked on Wakely, she discovered he'd stopped breathing. There was no apparent violence in the transition; he was alive, and then he wasn't.

The two women sat looking at each other in the half-light, both of them thinking of CPR, and artificial resuscitation, but neither moved, knowing it was hopeless. Their friend was gone. Sharpcot put a hand on his shoulder and took it away again. Virago wept hard, but silently, as if afraid to disturb him.

The day came on as if nothing had changed.

They left him there, against the hull of a craft that was expected to spend eternity crossing the heavens, and they packed up, and went west, leaving all that was left of Dorian Wakely, and all that was left of civilization, behind.

Epilogue

It was New Year's Day, and Sharpcot saw the ocean.

The Pacific was a distant and unending plate of blue that appeared abruptly when they topped a rise. They'd been smelling it since yesterday, and here it was.

They descended along the bed of a two-lane highway. The sky and the sea were the same blue, but the sea showed whitecaps crawling towards the coast. They passed through the place where a small town and been, evidenced by the patterns of remediated earth that once underpinned streets and houses and storefronts and offices, and here was the outline of a gas station, and they kept on until they reached a path they followed down to the beach.

Yolanda pulled off her boots and raced down to the water and stepped into the surf.

"Come on, Ike!" she cried, and Nasim lifted him out of the stroller. She bent to remove his shoes but before she could the boy raced away down the sand and splashed into the water, shrieking as waves soaked his feet.

Virago and Sharpcot stood close together, arms linked, taking in the ocean and the sand, the rocky outcrop to the south, sunlight scattered on water. Virago turned and watched Leclerc make her way down the sand, a hand on her brow, looking nauseated.

"Tabarnak, how long do I have to put up with this?" she moaned.

"You're almost out of it," Sharpcot reassured her. "Second trimester is always better."

They'd come through mountains and desert, through vineyards and forests, rain and snow. They'd shot deer and elk and repelled a pack of wolves, killing two. Nasim proved to be a natural sharpshooter. A patience and stillness in her body before she squeezed off each shot. They'd fished for salmon and trout, once caught a white sturgeon longer than their rifles. They'd eaten frog legs, and once, snails. "Escargot," they said over and over, dreaming of butter and garlic.

They were weary, but elated.

"We made it," Virago said.

"I really thought we'd find someone," Sharpcot replied. "I really thought we'd find the people."

"We still might."

"Yeah," Sharpcot replied. "We'll keep looking, anyway."

A wave turned at the foot of the beach and rolled in and when it retreated it left a brief mirror in which the sky was reflected, before the water subsided and the sheen faded. But in a moment it was replaced by another wave, and then another.

Acknowledgements

Firstly, I want to express huge and expansive gratitude to my partner and best friend, Lex Dyer. Your love and support provided the foundation on which this book was written.

Much love to family: our kids El and Calen, as well as my West Coast support team: Susan and Bob; Justin, Saleena, Zach, and Zahra. To my siblings Amber, John, Nat, and Neal — love you guys. And big love to the pets: Spencer, Myzie, and Leo.

Thank you to Alexia (Lex) Dyer, Neal Panhuyzen, and Alan Tomassini for reading drafts and providing valuable feedback. Special appreciation goes to OCdt Helen Hawes, MMM, CD, who offered insights concerning the Canadian Forces (although I take full responsibility for any errors). And warm recognition goes to Kathryn Kuitenbrouwer, for recommending Helen as a reader, and for friendship and advice.

It is always a joy to work with ECW Press, and I appreciate the attention of the many people behind this book: friend and editor Michael Holmes, copy editor Jen Albert, Digital and Art Director Jessica Albert, Managing and Development Editor Shannon Parr, Publicist Emily Varsava, cover designer Michel Vrana, Production Coordinator Victoria Cozza, Senior Editor Jen Knoch, and publishers Jack David and David Caron.

I would also like to acknowledge the cafés where this book was written. I appreciate these spaces and the kind staff who indulge us laptop jockeys when we spend too much time occupying valuable table space:

Toronto

Bodega Henriette
Dineen Outpost
The Flying Pony
Elvy and Flo (miss you!)
Lazy Daisy's Cafe
The Only Cafe
Tango Palace Coffee Company
Te Aro/Pilot Coffee Roasters
Pâtisserie La Cigogne
 (Danforth)
Zav Coffee Shop & Gallery
The Black Pony
The Sidekick
Riverdale Perk (when they
 had WiFi)
Prologue Cafe
The Rooster Coffee House
 (Broadview)
Red Rocket Coffee
The Common Bloor
Balzacs Coffee Roasters
 (Distillery District)
SUPERNOVA Coffee
Poured Coffee
Merchants of Green Coffee
Dark Horse Espresso
 (Queen East)
The Schmooz
Son of a Bean
Mofer Coffee Danforth
Morning Parade Coffee Bar
Boxcar Social Riverside
The Bandit Coffee Group

North Vancouver

Blenz Coffee
Caffe Artigiano
Roastmastirs
Bean Around the
 World Coffees

BH Panhuyzen has previously published three works of literary fiction: a collection of short stories and two novels, along with stories in literary and speculative fiction journals. He wrote for the Just for Laughs Festival and has penned and performed his own stand-up comedy. A passionate, blundering musician (piano/guitar/drums/uke), he lives in Toronto with partner Lex, kids El and Calen, plus Leo (dog) and Myzie (cat), while writing in the morning and spending afternoons as an independent FileMaker Pro developer. He has taken the Giving What We Can Pledge, and donates 10% of all income to effective altruism charities.

brianpanhuyzen.com